REVENGE IS
WICKED SWEET...

BOOKS BY

C.M. STUNICH

ROMANCE NOVELS

HARD ROCK ROOTS SERIES
Real Ugly
Get Bent
Tough Luck
Bad Day
Born Wrong
Hard Rock Roots Box Set (1-5)
Dead Serious
Doll Face
Heart Broke
Get Hitched
Screw Up

TASTING NEVER SERIES
Tasting Never
Finding Never
Keeping Never
Tasting, Finding, Keeping
Never Can Tell
Never Let Go
Never Did Say
Never Could Stop

ROCK-HARD BEAUTIFUL
Groupie
Roadie
Moxie

THE BAD NANNY TRILOGY
Bad Nanny
Good Boyfriend
Great Husband

TRIPLE M SERIES
Losing Me, Finding You
Loving Me, Trusting You
Needing Me, Wanting You
Craving Me, Desiring You

A DUET
Paint Me Beautiful
Color Me Pretty

FIVE FORGOTTEN SOULS
Beautiful Survivors
Alluring Outcasts

MAFIA QUEEN
Lure
Lavish
Luxe

DEATH BY DAYBREAK MC
I Was Born Ruined
I Am Dressed in Sin

STAND-ALONE NOVELS
Baby Girl
All for 1
Blizzards and Bastards
Fuck Valentine's Day
Broken Pasts
Crushing Summer
Taboo Unchained
Taming Her Boss
Kicked

BAD BOYS MC TRILOGY
Raw and Dirty
Risky and Wild
Savage and Racy

HERS TO KEEP TRILOGY
Biker Rockstar Billionaire CEO Alpha
Biker Rockstar Billionaire CEO Dom
Biker Rockstar Billionaire CEO Boss

RICH BOYS OF BURBERRY PREP
Filthy Rich Boys
Bad, Bad BlueBloods
The Envy of Idols
In the Arms of the Elite

STAND-ALONE
Football Dick
Stepbrother Inked
Glacier

BOOKS BY

C.M. STUNICH

Fantasy Novels

THE SEVEN MATES OF ZARA WOLF

Pack Ebon Red
Pack Violet Shadow
Pack Obsidian Gold
Pack Ivory Emerald
Pack Amber Ash
Pack Azure Frost
Pack Crimson Dusk

ACADEMY OF SPIRITS AND SHADOWS

Spirited
Haunted
Shadowed

TEN CATS PARANORMAL SOCIETY

Possessed

TRUST NO EVIL

See No Devils
Hear No Demons
Speak No Curses

THE SEVEN WICKED SERIES

Seven Wicked Creatures
Six Wicked Beasts
Five Wicked Monsters
Four Wicked Fiends

THE WICKED WIZARDS OF OZ

Very Bad Wizards

HOWLING HOLIDAYS

Werewolf Kisses

OTHER FANTASY NOVELS

Gray and Graves
Indigo & Iris
She Lies Twisted
Hell Inc.
DeadBorn
Chryer's Crest
Stiltz

SIRENS OF A SINFUL SEA TRILOGY

Under the Wild Waves

(With Tate James)

HIJINKS HAREM

Elements of Mischief
Elements of Ruin
Elements of Desire

THE WILD HUNT MOTORCYCLE CLUB

Dark Glitter

FOXFIRE BURNING

The Nine
Tail Game

OTHER

And Today I Die

ROYAL
LAKESIDE LODGE

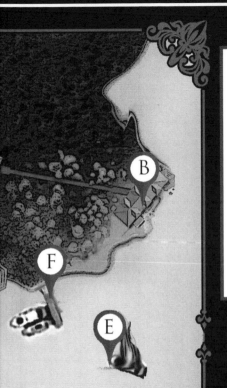

MAP KEY

A. MAIN HOUSE
B. BEACH HOUSE
C. PARKING LOT
D. GAZEBO
E. BOAT FIRE
F. DOCK

BURBERRY
PREPARATORY ACADEMY
EST 1883

POINTE
AND GUESTHOUSE

BAD, BAD BLUE BLOODS

C.M. STUNICH
INTERNATIONAL BESTSELLING AUTHOR

this book is dedicated to friendship
as rare as diamonds and twice as precious
to my true friends: you know who you are

Author's

Note

Possible Spoilers

Bad, Bad Bluebloods is a reverse harem, high school bully romance, and the sequel to *Filthy Rich Boys*. What does that mean exactly? It means our female main character, Marnye Reed, will end up with at least three love interests by the end of the series. It also means that for a good portion of this book, the love interests and the main character are at each other's throats. This book in no way condones revenge plots, nor does it romanticize them. If the love interests in this story want to win the main character over, they'll have to change their ways, accept her revenge, and embrace her forgiveness.

Karma is a bitch, especially when it comes in the form of Marnye Reed.

Any kissing/sexual scenes featuring Marnye are consensual. This book might be about high school students, but it is not what I would consider young adult. The characters are brutal, the emotions real, the f-word in prolific use. There's some underage drinking, sexual situations, mentions of past suicide attempts, and other adult scenarios.

None of the main characters is under the age of sixteen. This series will have a happy ending in the fourth and final book.

RICH BOYS OF BURBERRY PREP

SERIES READING
ORDER

FILTHY RICH BOYS

BAD, BAD BLUEBLOODS

THE ENVY OF IDOLS

IN THE ARMS OF THE ELITE

PROLOGUE

There are flames dancing across the water.

How that happened, I have no idea. I clutch my fingers to my chest, heart pounding. *I almost lost my ability to make music with the harp ... forever.* This thing with the Idol girls is so much more than just a nasty case of bullying. Everything to do with the Infinity Club is so much darker and more involved than I first thought.

Tristan grits his teeth, his hands curled into fists at his sides. The way he looks at Harper du Pont is terrifying. If I were her, I would leave. Now. But she doesn't. Instead, she flicks that blue gaze of hers to the right, checking to make sure her cronies are in tow before she launches another attack.

"Whatever you're thinking about doing right now," Tristan says, his voice as smooth as silk, "don't." His tone hardens on that last syllable, a perfect match to the rage in his face. *They saved me,* I think, glancing from Tristan to Zayd's bloody lip to Creed with his arm around Miranda. Zack is standing on the opposite side of the boat, behind Harper and her new friends.

"If you do this," Harper says, taking a step forward, her short brown hair billowing in the breeze. It makes me feel good to see it cut like that. *Don't dish it if you can't take it.* I take a step back and bump into Zayd. He puts an arm around me, and all these strange feelings flood over me. My mind changes with each beat of my heart. *Please don't touch me; touch me more; get away from me; kiss me until I see stars.* "Then you're giving up control of the school. You're Plebs, all of you."

Abigail Fanning and Valentina Pitt flank Harper as she steps forward, the chair they'd tied me to dividing the space between us. I try to look past them to see Zack, and I notice that he's bleeding, too, but much worse than Zayd.

"If you think we'll fold that easy," Creed begins as bored as always, but when I glance over at him, his blue eyes meet mine, and a strange spark passes between us. He's shaking, too, but he tries to hide it as he pushes a lock of white-blond hair from his face. "Then you clearly haven't been paying attention. We'll destroy you."

Harper's mouth is so wicked when it curves up in a smirk, and the reflection of the flames in her eyes mirrors the hate in her heart. Most of the Inner Circle is standing with her, her new girlfriends, and the three boys she's handpicked to take Tristan's, Zayd's, and Creed's spots as Idols.

"So you'll break up the greatest collection of Bluebloods in the history of Burberry Prep for some commoner? We're the future rulers of the *world*. People live and die based on the decisions our families make. Tristan, I'm your *fiancée*." Harper takes another step forward, and then pauses as the ladder on her right creaks and sways.

Windsor York, the screw in the cogs of this machine, appears, his mouth twisted in a wry little smirk.

"Well, bloody hell," he curses, pulling himself over the edge and then standing up. He brushes his palms down the front of his white second-year uniform. His hazel eyes glitter as he takes in Harper, the chair, me. "Looks like I'm a bit late to the party."

He walks over to stand in front of Zayd, reaching out a hand for me. The flames catch on his red hair, bathing it in orange light. I reach out to touch him, but Zayd pulls me back. Windsor raises an eyebrow and sighs.

"Yeah, way late, asshole," Zayd snaps, but I elbow him and step away from his embrace, wrapping my arms around myself and keeping my own space. I need to stand on my own; I can't trust anyone. Not anymore. "If we hadn't gotten here when we did ..." His voice trails off, but he has to know that Windsor's on my side. He has been since moment one.

Turning, the prince gives Harper's group a skeptical sort of look.

"I disabled the motor on your friends' boat," he says, his English accent crisp and charming. "I don't imagine they'll be showing up tonight." Harper's face, already colored red-orange by the fire, looks like a ripe tomato now. She's furious. "And I'm not late." He rolls his eyes and flashes me a wink and a smile. I almost smile back. Almost. I'm too confused right now. "I saw Zack on his way up here, with these idiots trailing behind." He gestures with his thumb in the direction of the Idol boys, and Tristan growls at him. Almost quite literally. "My time was better spent elsewhere.

Oh." Windsor snaps his fingers and then reaches down to pull up the edge of his shirt.

There's a tattoo there, an infinity tattoo.

Everyone goes silent as Windsor drops his shirt and sighs.

"I've been resisting the Club for a long, long time, but Marnye needs someone on the inside to watch her back, so … here I am!" He raises his arms up in the air for emphasis, and then drops them by his sides. "Oh, and I'm an awful, dirty fucking wanker. I don't have a trust fund, or parents breathing down my neck that control my purse strings: I have *nine billion* in personal assets to play with." Windsor pauses, crossing one arm over his chest and resting the elbow of the other in his palm. "Well, *twelve* billion in US dollars, I suppose."

"Do you think I'm threatened by you?" Harper chokes out with a laugh. "Some tenth-string prince from a country nobody even knows about?"

"England?" Windsor asks, his voice colored with wry humor. "You do understand where the pilgrims came from, right?"

Harper turns from him to Tristan, clearly realizing that there's no making headway with Windsor York. He just does what he wants, the rest of the world be damned.

"Last chance, Tristan," she says, and when I see him unleash a whiplike smirk, I know he's not going back.

"You're going to wish you'd never met me," Tristan says, his voice like steel. He watches as Zack moves around behind the pack of Bluebloods to stand beside me. There's blood running down the side of his face, and I decide that as soon as

4

we get out of here, he's going to a doctor. His dark eyes catch on mine, and I shiver. If he hadn't taken on Greg and John for me …

"Consider that goal accomplished," Harper screeches, tearing the ring from her finger and throwing it at Tristan. He catches it, perfectly, one-handed. My heart skips several beats as he turns to me, silver eyes flashing.

"Let's go. I've got one of Dad's yachts." He moves over to stand in front of me, reaches down, and cups the side of my face. Zayd, Creed, and Zack all stiffen up. Windsor chuckles, this light, airy sound that echoes across the lake. Tristan reaches up to cup the side of my face, runs his thumb along my lower lip, and then sneers at Windsor. While he's turned away, I pull back, putting distance between myself and the guys.

Miranda meets my eyes, and there's this interesting dichotomy in hers: half fear, half envy.

She moves toward me, away from Creed's arms, and his jaw tightens as Miranda puts her lips near my ear.

"Which one?" she whispers, flicking her gaze at the five boys on the boat. Harper and her cronies are leaving, slowly, but there's venom on both sides. Next year … there's going to be a war.

Before I get a chance to answer her, Tristan gets up in Windsor's face.

"You, go home to England and fuck off; we don't need you here."

"And who, precisely, is *we*?" Windsor asks, leveling his hazel eyes on me. They reflect back the dancing flames as he smiles and cocks a single dark brow. Tristan looks between the two of us and scowls, standing up tall and straightening out his wool coat. "As far as I can see it, Marnye very much needs me."

"How so?" Tristan snaps, lifting his chin. Despite the inner fighting amongst the Idol boys for the throne … I think Tristan Vanderbilt still holds the crown. He's a powerful enemy, and a potential ally. But can I trust him?

Doubtful.

"Because," Windsor says, blinking innocently and holding a hand out to indicate me, "we're dating."

Zayd curses under his breath, Creed sneers, and Zack frowns.

Tristan says nothing, looking down at me with storm-gray eyes. And then he turns, walks away, and pauses at the edge of the boat. Harper du Pont is standing there waiting. She meets Tristan's eyes first and then flicks her gaze over to mine.

"Enjoy the summer, Marnye. It's going to be your last." She turns, disappears down the ladder, and soon we hear the sound of a boat engine being started.

"Did she just threaten my life?" I wonder aloud, but nobody says anything. School is out, summer has started, and in the morning, we're all going home. I'll go back to Cruz Bay and my Dad while the boys go … wherever it is that they go.

For now, it's all on hold.

Come September, all gloves are off.

"Come on, Marnye, I've got a boat, too," Miranda says, taking my hand and leading me away from the boys. I don't look at any of them as I walk away, past Tristan, and down the ladder.

Second year at Burberry Preparatory Academy was tough.

Third year's going to be a nightmare.

CHAPTER

1

The last person I expect to see on my doorstep is Zack Brooks.

My mouth drops open in surprise, and I slam the door closed on him. He reaches up with his palm and stops it in its tracks, pushing his way inside as I back up against the counter in shock. His brown eyes are dark with anger, and they're narrowed on me.

"Zack," I start, my heart pounding in my chest. I haven't seen him since that fateful day at the lodge. We haven't even texted. Well, maybe he texted me, but I blocked him months ago.

"Marnye." He exhales, standing over me in a letterman jacket and jeans. His dark hair is longer than when I last saw it, and the way it falls over his forehead makes my hands tremble. "You won't talk to me. I had no choice but to come here."

Bad, Bad Blue Bloods

"No choice but to fight your way into my house?" I ask, realizing as we stand there that the Train Car is far too small for his large body. He takes over the space with his presence, filling it so completely that I find it hard to breathe. "Maybe you could've taken the hint? I don't *want* to talk to you."

I look away, and my heart stutters a little. That's a lie. I do want to talk to him; I'm just not going to.

"Too bad. I want to talk to you. I have a right to explain without … *them* stirring up drama." He takes a step toward me, but I keep my face turned away. I'm not going to look at him, not right now. The last few months have been okay, filled with sunshine, day trips to the beach, and my tenth and eleventh rereads of the Harry Potter books. This is the last thing I need, a bump in the road to destroy my last peaceful week of summer. "Don't think I didn't hear about what happened on the last day of—"

"Please don't," I choke out. That's the last thing I want to think about right now, about the paint dripping down the sides of my face, my split lip, and the look on Zayd's face … *"The only prize … was that trophy. We did it for fun."* Tristan's words slice through me, and I push away from the counter, heading down the hall toward my room.

Zack follows me, and I end up trapped on my bed with his huge body filling my doorway.

My hands curl into fists. I added his name to my revenge list. Why shouldn't I? He tried to break me in middle school, and for what? A bet. A bet to get into that stupid fucking Club.

The Infinity Club is going down, I think, and I drop my hand to my right hip. There's a tattoo artist that some of my classmates bribed during my time at Lower Banks in order to get illegal ink. I'm taking a thousand dollars out of the money I won and heading down there tomorrow to get a tattoo of my own.

What I don't need is Zack Brooks, standing in my room and staring at me with those umber depths.

"You have to at least hear me out," he says as I sit down on the edge of my bed.

I've spent all summer writing horrible things about him in my notebook, but it was all venting. I don't know how to make him hurt the way he made me hurt. Looking up, all I see is apology and sorrow in his eyes. Not like Creed. Or Zayd. Or Tristan. They definitely were *not* sorry.

My fingers dig into the bedspread; it's the only way to keep them from reaching for the necklace that hangs over my chest. I tried to sell it—twice—but I couldn't do it. Selling it felt like I was letting him win. I don't need or want Tristan Vanderbilt's money. I'm giving it back the first day of school.

"Haven't you done enough damage?" I whisper, and we both freeze at the sound of the front door opening.

"Honey, it's just me." Dad's voice echoes in the small space just before I hear his footsteps. He pauses in the hall that connects the second passenger car, which holds our bedrooms, to the first train car which has the living room, kitchen, and bathroom. "Zack, long time no see. Would you like to stay for dinner?"

"Can't. Plans with my mom." Zack leans his shoulder against the wall, his relentless gaze pinning me to the bed. I feel like I couldn't stand up if I tried.

10

"Well, if you have time on Friday, it's Marnye's birthday," Dad starts, and I cringe. "Since it's just me and her, it might be nice to have a friend to tag along?" He sounds earnest enough, but I wonder if Dad knows his words cut me to the core. I *had* friends. For a while, I had a lot. I had Miranda and Andrew, Zack and Lizzie, and … the Idols.

For a while there, I really and truly believed I had them.

Of course, those friendships slipped through my fingers like sand, and Dad had to see … well, more than a dad should ever see. He saw me kissing Creed in a towel, making out with Zayd on my bed, and letting Tristan grope me in the library. And my panties …

Humiliation washes over me in wave, but I've had an entire summer to learn how to channel it into anger. My eyes flick over to my leather bookbag, resting on the edge of my desk. I've taped my revenge list into a notebook and filled it with ideas. Ideas, and rules. Because if you can't trust yourself, then you're doomed to fail.

"Friday …" Zack starts, and then sighs as he tucks his hands into his pockets. "I'll be here."

"Great! We leave at eight sharp, no later. It's tradition to have pancakes at the Railroad Station on Marnye's birthday." Dad slips back outside, letting the door slam behind him. I can hear him wheeling the grill into place.

"I don't expect you to forgive me, but I wanted to at least come and tell you that I'd planned on having a conversation with you that night."

"Sure you did," I say, debating the chances of me getting up and down the hall before Zack cuts me off. "Look, you're a little bit off my radar right now, so why don't you just leave and we can pretend we've never met each other?"

"At least unblock Lizzie and talk to her," he says, but there's no way. Even if I were inclined to speak to Lizzie again, she's too tangled up with Tristan. "Give her a chance to apologize. She's been sick over the whole thing, and not just about our bet. She's furious with the Burberry Bluebloods. Hell, she basically pit Coventry Prep Elite against them this summer. The Hamptons … turned into a social bloodbath."

My interest is piqued at that, but to get more information, I'll have to either talk to Lizzie or Zack. Neither of whom is someone I want in my life right now. The majority of my anger is focused on the Idol boys. I have to go back to that school, with those people, and I need to do more than just stay on the defensive. If I want to have a successful career at Burberry Prep, I need to show the others that I won't be pushed around, not anymore.

"I don't care," I whisper, and Zack grunts, pushing up from the wall and taking a step toward me. The space is so small, it basically puts us toe-to-toe.

"You do care. Because Tristan Vanderbilt is in love with Lizzie Walton, and she put him through the wringer this summer. All I'm saying is that you've got an ally there, if you want her."

"What good does that do me when she's in a completely different school?" I snap, feeling that anger overtake me again. That's going to be the hardest part, holding it back and channeling it appropriately. "It's just me against the world at Burberry Prep; I've already accepted that."

"I wouldn't say that," Zack tells me, his eyes like hot

coals as they rake over my body. After a moment, he turns and heads back down the hall, pausing just before he slips out the front door. "See you on Friday."

"Don't count on it," I whisper, and then I stand up and grab my notebook from my bag. The cover is just one, giant red infinity symbol with a slash through it. The Infinity Club. Their parents might have unlimited resources, as Lizzie said they might control the world, but this is the junior version.

It's never too early to learn humility.

The next day, I slip out of the house after dad leaves for work, and walk six blocks to a tattoo parlor called Shade's Dungeon. The guy who runs it is a creep, but he's also the only person in town that I know of who'll tattoo an almost-sixteen year old girl, actually do a good job, use a clean needle, *and* avoid infection.

"You actually showed up," he says when I walk inside, wiping down the chair with a strong antiseptic. "You got the money?" I take out the wad of cash I got from the ATM and hand it over. He counts it—twice—and then tucks it in his back pocket. "Take a seat, and let's get this over with."

13

I pause, my hand still resting on the door. It's not too late for me to turn around and walk away. Part of me wonders if I should, if I should give up this stupid revenge plot and just leave Burberry Prep. Grenadine Heights is a good school, and I'd still get into a great university after graduation …

But no. No.

The Idols … they need to know that their money doesn't make them gods. They have no right to play with peoples' lives the way they played with mine. My eyes close suddenly and tears come, but I've fought them off a number of times throughout the summer. What's one more?

"Look, kid, if you're not gonna get the ink—"

My eyes flick open.

"I'm getting it." I move over to the leather seat and sit down as the tattoo artist rolls his eyes at me and curses inappropriately under his breath, something about *fucking idiot kids* or whatnot. I ignore him. This is important to me, a physical manifestation of all the pain I suffered on that day, that *year.*

Tristan, Zayd, and Creed played on my vulnerabilities and offered me the one thing I wanted most: friendship.

My throat closes again, and my hands tremble, but I roll up my tank top to expose my stomach and then push down the waistband on my leggings. The tattoo artist—I think his name is something old-fashioned like Sybil—holds up a design.

"How does this look?"

There's an infinity symbol on the piece of paper, one with a horizontal slash through it, just like I saw on Derrick Barr when he was booted from the Club.

"That's perfect," I say, waiting as Sybil transfers the design to my skin and then picks up the tattoo machine.

"You ready?" he asks me, sounding bored. I suck in a breath and nod. The needle touches my skin, pain rockets through me, and I grit my teeth. This is nothing compared to how I felt that last day, with paint running down my shirt and between my breasts, my ribs and face aching, my heart shattered.

I had a chipped tooth, and a broken rib. The day after I got home, I went to the doctor and found out about the latter. I'd told Dad that I'd fallen down the stairs; he hadn't believed me. But then, we hadn't talked much about what happened, not about the video of me with the boys, the panties, any of it. Instead of being upset about it, I feel like Charlie's been in an exceptional mood for weeks. He hasn't had a single drink that I know of either.

"Done." Sybil steps back and then grabs a mirror, handing it over to me. "Take a look."

I do, and it's perfect, a solid black mark on my skin, a permanent reminder.

'Marnye, you forgive too easily,' Dad says, smiling down at me.

Maybe before, but not now. Not anymore.

"It's perfect," I say, staring at the design in the mirror. He cleans me up, bandages it, and off I go.

Before school starts next week, I have a couple of errands I need to run.

They're imperative.

Grenadine Heights is the place to go for designer clothes, top-notch salons, and preppy assholes flashing me looks. Only, this time they're looking at me like maybe they should be scared.

At the risk of getting a mark on my first day back, I've worn my new second-year Burberry Prep uniform to go shopping in downtown Grenadine Heights. The skirt is solid white, as opposed to first-year red. The black shoes and white blouse are the same, but the tie is red and there's a single red and a single black stripe on each elbow of the jacket, a perfect match to the red and black Burberry Prep crest on the pocket, complete with pair of griffins. I've even got on the thigh-high socks with the matching stripe at the top.

Every student at GHHS knows where Burberry Prep is and who goes to it. Their football team kicks Burberry's ass every year, but it doesn't matter: everyone on the GHHS side gazes across the field and knows the grass is greener on the other side.

So when I walk into the salon with my head held high, wearing my Burberry uniform, the women in there treat me like I have money.

It's kind of … sad, actually. According to my dad, my mother once saved up for a haircut and dye job here for months, and then when she walked in, she was treated like less than dirt. He said she came home crying.

I guess I picked this place for a reason.

"I have an appointment," I tell the girl at the front. She's clearly part-time, a student herself if the GHHS pin she's got on her shirt is any indication. She looks at me … like I'm a god. I tell myself that's a good thing, that I must be projecting self-confidence, but I don't like it, using my uniform to intimidate people. That makes me feel like … them.

I force myself to put on a huge smile.

The girl flushes and then checks me in, showing me to a chair right in the front. When the stylist comes over and sees my roots, the pretty but imperfect haircut Miranda gave me, and the fading rose gold dye, she cringes.

"I want this," I tell her, pointing at my own head, "just … elevated." *Rose gold realness,* is what I want to say, but nobody here would appreciate that. *But they will, when they see it.* At least, I think they will. As far as I could tell, not all of the emotions I shared with the Idol boys were fake. I remember Zayd bobbing in moonlight, his wet hair stuck to his face, eyes shining. No. No, it might've been a bet but it wasn't all fake. Somehow, that makes the whole situation seem even worse.

The stylist gets to work, and two hours later, I'm staring at a different person in the mirror. The color is that perfect mix of dusty pink and glimmering gold, and the cut has gone from passable to edgy. I make myself smile.

"It looks great." The stylist seems to sigh with relief as I stand up and head over to the register to pay, leaving a generous tip. My eyes meet the receptionist's as she passes me a bag with some shampoo and conditioner I picked out. She's too young to have been here when Jennifer was treated so poorly. Same with the stylist. Even if I were interested in exacting revenge for my absentee mother, there's no justice to be had here.

I turn around to leave just as the door opens and two blond teens step instead the salon.

My heart stops beating.

"Miranda," I choke out, her blue eyes widening as they meet mine.

"Marnye, please open the door!" I can see Miranda standing outside the academy's car, trying to pull it open with the handle. The other Bluebloods hang back as the amphitheater empties out into the courtyard. Miranda whirls around when Creed tries to touch her shoulder, and throws him off. I think she's defending me. Maybe. But I don't open the door until Charlie appears. Jennifer ... she hangs back and says nothing.

"What are you doing here?" Miranda asks me, her eyes flicking from my uniform to my hair. Creed is completely frozen behind her, his bored princely look stuck on his face like a mask. There's a tension in his shoulders that I don't miss, a tightness in his jaw. I don't look at him; I can't. My hands curl into fists at my sides.

"I ..." Words fail me as Miranda and I stare at each other. Did she betray me, too? Did she know what was coming? "I'm sorry." The words fall out before I can stop them. I really am sorry, sorry that I made that bet with Creed, sorry that I let her down the same way the Idols let me down. I move to rush past her when Creed grabs my arm.

"You can't be serious?" he asks me, his voice like ice. I shove his hand off, and our eyes lock together. A spark passes between us, sending my still heart into a beating frenzy. My mouth tightens and my eyes narrow. "You can't possibly expect to survive a week back at Burberry Prep."

"Get your hand off of me," I snarl as Miranda steps close and pushes her brother back.

"Leave her alone, Creed," she says, her voice threaded with steel. "Marnye," Miranda starts, turning back to look at me, but I'm already turning away and heading out the salon door. I run almost two blocks before I slow down, panting and shaking. *How am I going to do this?* I wonder as I stand up and lean against the brick wall of a deli. It smells like freshly baked bread out here. *If I can barely look at them, how am I going to walk in there, purse-first, and tear down the system?* For a second there, it's hard to breathe.

"You can't possibly expect to survive a week back at Burberry Prep."

I've heard that before, and I proved them wrong, all of them.

I can do it again.

Several deep breaths later, and I'm ready to finish up my checklist for the day: new clothes, assorted supplies, and a few other random beauty stops. The best sort of revenge lifts you up, instead of putting others down. So … maybe I don't need all this superficial stuff, but it'll make me feel better. I want to get dressed up, and I want to waltz into that school with my head held high, my new hair and makeup a shield against their stares.

Pushing off from the wall, I take off down the street, and I finish my plans.

The morning of my sixteenth birthday, I wake up to fresh coffee and a package neatly wrapped in brown butcher paper. Dad's even added a pink ribbon to the top. He grins at me as I sit down on the couch with my mug, finishing a gulp of milky, sugary goodness before I set the cup aside to open the gift.

"You didn't have to get me anything," I say, feeling guilty that I haven't told him about the money I won. I should just give it all to Dad; he deserves it. Instead, I'm keeping it in case of emergency. And how sad is that, that I expect emergencies during my second year of high school? This should be my time to study, to make music, to make *friends.* Instead, I'm just … trying to upset the ancient social hierarchy of classism?

I've kinda got my work cut out for me.

"Yeah, well," Dad starts, running his fingers through his

shaggy brown hair. He nods his chin in the direction of the package, and I start to unwrap it. His voice is so soft, surprisingly gentle. *"Your dad got some news last night."* Zack told me that the day Dad got drunk during Parents' Week. And yet, I still don't know what it is. "I hope you like it, honey."

I'd like it best if it was a jar of blue blood and tears from the Idols.

"I'm sure I will," I tell him as I get the ribbon and paper off, opening the box to find mounds of tissue paper. Inside, a blue velvet box is nestled, and when I crack it open, I find Grandma June's antique bracelet. For as long as I can remember, I've been obsessed with this thing. It's always hung on Dad's side of the bed, and I can remember countless times that I've walked in and found him, head bent over, fingers rubbing the little copper charms. There are four of them: a tiny steam train, a loaf of bread, a dress, and a baby. But one charm was always missing, right in the center: all that remains is a tiny ring where it used to hang. Now, that ring has something else dangling from it: Dad's wedding band.

"What …?" I start, holding the bracelet up. It's clearly been polished to a shine, the dull patina gone, the copper gleaming as I hold it up to the light. "Why are you giving me this?" My eyes drift to Dad's, but he's completely unreadable. He tucks his hands in the pockets of his jeans and forces a smile.

"You should have a piece of our family history with you. It'll give you strength." My mouth opens, but no words come out. How am I supposed to respond to that? "Are you sure you want to go back to that awful school?"

A groan escapes me, and I look away, clutching the bracelet in my palm.

"The academy will set me up for the best possible future —" I start, but Dad cuts me off, coming over to kneel beside me. He puts his hand on my knee, and I turn back to look at him.

"Don't go back to that school for boys, Marnye," he says, voice rough. He almost sounds like he's pleading with me, and my heart hurts. "Just don't do it. And … don't go back because you think you have something to prove."

"I …" How can I really respond to that? Is that what I'm doing? Going back to prove myself? To exact revenge? Or is it really because I want the best academic career possible? I can't even answer that question for myself, so how can I tell Dad what's going on inside me?

"You could move in with your mother, and go to Grenadine Heights High—"

My turn to cut him off.

"Move in with *Jennifer*?" I choke out, pulling away and pushing my body into the worn couch cushions, as if putting distance between me and Charlie will erase his suggestion from the air. "I barely know her."

"Marnye," Dad says, uncurling my palm and taking the bracelet. He puts it on my wrist as I sit there, staring at him like he's grown a second head. "I'm not saying your mother hasn't made mistakes in the past, but she's really trying here. She wants to get to know you."

"The feeling is not mutual," I reply, pulling my arm to my

chest and playing with the bracelet. "I'm not giving up my scholarship because of some bullying."

"That was more than just bullying, Marnye. Those boys —" My eyes close and Dad stops talking, like he can see how pained just the mention of that day makes me. "Look, you're a smart girl, always have been. You're more driven than I ever was, smarter, too. If you want to go back there, I won't question it, but know that you have other options." Dad sighs and rises to his feet, pausing at a knock on the door. "That should be Zack," he says, and my eyes go wide.

I rise from the couch, but I'm not fast enough to get past before Zack Brooks steps into the trailer, dressed in a tight black tee that pulls across his muscles, dark denim jeans, and brown boots. He stares at me from those dark brown eyes of his, gaze flickering over my black leggings, tight black tank, and total lack of bra, before he returns his attention to my face.

"Happy birthday," he says, but it's hard to take him seriously when he made it his mission to see that I would never have another birthday again.

"Excuse me." I push past the two men, being careful not to even brush against Zack, and get dressed in one of my new outfits from yesterday. May as well test it out on him before heading back to that den of wolves.

If Dad notices that I'm wearing a new pink jumpsuit and black wedges, he doesn't say anything. If he asks, I'll … well, I won't lie about it. But he doesn't. Zack takes me in carefully, my new hairdo, the bit of makeup I managed to put on with a YouTube tutorial, and my eyelash extensions. Didn't even know that was a thing until I Googled it.

"You look beautiful," Zack says, holding out a package wrapped in opalescent paper. It's very pretty, but I'm loath to take it. Dad is watching though, and I don't want him to know anything about the Zack situation. It'd just stress him out on top of everything else, and I can tell he's already pushed to the limit. He looks thinner, paler, and he sleeps a lot more than usual. I'm honestly worried about him, but he seems to like Zack; they're sort of buddies now. I may as well let Dad keep that relationship. "Just something small. You can open it later, if you want."

"Later is good," I tell him, putting the package on the stove. Zack nods and steps back, leaving room for Charlie and me to step out of the train car. The sky is gray, but the rain hasn't started yet. Zack has his orange McLaren, but it's only a two-seater, so we take Dad's Ford instead.

Charlie does his best to make conversation on the drive, but it's not easy, not with the tangible tension between me and Zack.

When we get to the Railroad Station restaurant—this funky little twenty-four hour diner that's been here forever—Dad excuses himself to the restroom, and I'm left alone with Zack.

"You're crashing my daddy-daughter time," I whisper, and his narrowed eyes soften slightly.

"You want me to leave?" he asks, and I nod.

A long silence follows.

"Only you're not going to because your wants and needs are more important than mine," I whisper, and Zack stiffens up, like I've slapped him.

"Marnye, I want to help," he says, but I'm already shaking my head.

"You've helped enough, Zack." I look him straight in the face, and memories flicker across my vision: the bathroom door opening, Zack pulling me into his arms, putting his fingers down my throat. He saved me, but he also pushed me to that point for a bet. How can I ever forgive that? One time, he cornered me outside my math classroom and told me he knew all about my mother, how she didn't love me enough, how she doted on her other daughter in way she'd never dote on me. My mouth flattens into a thin line. "I don't know what you're seeking from me, but if it's forgiveness, I'm not ready yet."

Zack's mouth tightens, and he looks away for a moment before rising to his feet. I glance back at him, my arms crossed over my chest, and I wait. I don't actually expect him to leave. He pushes in the chair, tosses down a wad of cash on the table, and then holds up his hand when I try to give it back.

"Enjoy breakfast with your dad on me," he says, moving away from the table towards the door. But he stops when he's behind me, leaning over and putting his cheek so close to mine that I can feel his stubble. His right hand curves over my shoulder and squeezes, sending a swarm of butterflies winging through me. "But … whether you want to deal with me or not, I'm going to destroy those preppy academy pricks for you."

"Hypocrite," I mumble, because it's the only thing I can think to say. Zack's hand tightens on my shoulder, and I suck in a sharp breath. "You're just as bad as they are—maybe worse. Don't pretend otherwise."

"I wouldn't dare." Zack presses a sudden kiss to my cheek and my body goes white-hot before my emotions freeze over, and I'm ice-cold on the inside. "Happy birthday, Marnye." He rises to his feet just as Dad is making his way back from the bathroom. Zack gives him a little wave and then slips out the door, leaving me to answer awkward questions.

"What happened to Zack?" Charlie asks, taking his seat and then pausing to look at the heaping pile of cash on the table. He whistles and reaches up to adjust his gray fedora. "I think he left a hundred on accident," he says, and I smile, but I don't think it was an accident at all.

But maybe what Zack doesn't get, and Tristan doesn't get, Creed, Zayd … money isn't that important to me. Now, only a truly privileged person will tell you it doesn't matter: it does. Food, clothing, shelter, security, medical care … Those things require money, but I don't worship the green. It doesn't impress me. It doesn't buy my friendship or my love.

My throat gets tight.

"Zack had a thing he forgot about," I say with a shrug, and while Dad raises an eyebrow, he doesn't say anything. When our orders come out, I glance at Zack's plate of pancakes, his empty chair, and I think about his statement: *I'm going to destroy those preppy academy pricks for you.*

Only … he's not. Because that's my job.

It's my job to destroy the Bluebloods of Burberry Prep. Those bad, bad Bluebloods.

CHAPTER

2

The end of the year prank that left me reeling, it did not go unnoticed by the staff. As Dad grabs some snacks for the drive back to Burberry Preparatory Academy, I head online and look at all the beginning of the year emails with information about classes, school policies ... and bullying.

Burberry Prep is now a zero tolerance campus. Students involved in bullying incidents will be subject to suspension or expulsion depending on the severity of the offense. Respect towards peers and staff is not just encouraged, it is mandatory. If you have any questions regarding this policy, please see Ms. Felton or Principal Collins during their office hours.

My lips feel suddenly dry, so I push my laptop aside and head over to the printer to grab my class schedule. The no electronics rule will go into effect as soon as I set foot on campus. No, before. Actually, the drivers of the academy-issued cars that travel between the visitors' lot and the school, they're the ones that take the phones.

"They may as well post my name right there on the front page for everyone to see," I grumble as I grab the page, give it a quick glance, and pull some lip balm out of the drawer on my side table. My bags are packed, my heart is in my throat, and I'm ready.

I'm ready.

I can do this.

My phone pings, and I turn it over to see a text from Miranda.

Can we talk sometime today?

My palms feel suddenly sweaty, and I tuck my phone into the front of my leather bookbag.

Miranda's been out of the country most of the summer, but this isn't the first text I've received from her. Actually, she's sent me several. I've replied, but barely. We clearly aren't friends again yet. I mean, if we ever will be again.

Grabbing my bookbag in one hand and my duffel in the other, I head out the door and pause when a white limo pulls across the gravel in front of our house. Dad is standing there watching like he's as confused as I am.

The driver parks and climbs out, tipping his hat to me. "Marnye Reed?"

"That's me," I mumble, thoroughly confused and hoping like crazy that none of the guys sent this car. If they did, I'm refusing to get in. But of course, what a stupid thought that is. Why on earth would they send a car to get me unless they wanted to crash it into the ocean?

"Hey." Andrew rolls down the window, and my eyes go wide as he waves at me, a half-smile on his face. He looks unsure, as tentative as I feel. "We're going the same way, so I thought …" The driver moves between us to open the back door, and Andrew climbs out, dressed in jeans and a t-shirt. I'm not in my uniform either. Instead, I've got on black leggings and a tank top for the drive. I planned on switching clothes in the visitors' bathroom like I did last year. "I thought you might want a ride." He tucks his hands into his pockets, the sun catching on his chestnut hair. His blue eyes take in the Train Car, my dad, and me with a flicker of something I can't quite recognize. Pity? It might be pity.

I sigh.

"Dad, this is Andrew Payson. Andrew, this is Charlie Reed." The two men shake hands, but I can see from my dad's face that he isn't sure about this. "He wasn't involved in the prank," I whisper, and both Charlie and Andrew stiffen slightly.

"I see." Dad studies Andrew carefully, like he isn't quite sure he believes me. I don't blame him. There were dozens of boys in academy uniforms brandishing my underwear in the crowd. Andrew just wasn't one of the many. "You're offering Marnye a ride?"

"I was on my way through," he says, glancing from my dad to me. "I know Kathleen Cabot offered to send a car, and you refused, but I thought maybe we could talk?"

My revenge list is burning a hole in my pocket. It still has Andrew's name on it. There's a reason for that. I hope it's the reason he came to talk to me about.

"I was hoping to spend some time with my dad," I start, but Charlie's already smiling and waving me away.

"It's okay, honey, you go with your friend. I was actually

29

concerned that the Ford might not make it there anyway." He takes one of my bags from the dusty driveway and passes it over to the limo's driver, pulling the duffel from my hand before giving me a huge hug. "We'll see each other again soon, I promise," he tells me, and I know he means Parents' Week. Mm. Like that wasn't a disaster last year. I *still* don't know what set Charlie off. I'm starting to wonder if I ever will. "I want you to have friends," he tells me, kissing my cheek and stepping back.

"I love you," I tell him, and he smiles back at me.

"I love you, too, honey." *And you're the only person that does,* I think, trying not to let that hollow feeling in my chest take over. Since I made the list, I've been determined, almost desperate to get back to Burberry Prep and kick some ass. Standing here right now, saying goodbye to my father, it doesn't feel quite so simple as that.

With one last wave, I head over to the limo and slide into the cool, air conditioned back. The seats are sumptuous brown leather, and there's a TV, a mini-fridge, and some bedding stuffed in the corner. Andrew lets me have the larger bench seat, the one that's perpendicular to his.

The driver shuts the door, and we start off, making a slow circle of the Cruz Bay Trailer Park before we're back on the main street again. Andrew is the first one to break the silence.

"I would've texted you sooner, but my parents put me on a full summer ban from texting, phone calls, and social media." He pauses and sighs, looking toward the tinted back window. "They found out about …" There's a long pause, but Andrew doesn't need to fill in the words. I know what he's going to say. "They know I was dating a guy."

We just stare at each other, and my cheeks go pink. I feel awful about what I did to Miranda and Andrew, but … I'm not entirely sure I was the only one who made mistakes. I'm willing to hear him out, but for now, his name is still on my list. Miranda … I don't think I could retaliate against her if I wanted to. Besides, unlike every other Blueblood at Burberry Prep, she is *not* a member of the infamous Infinity Club.

"Are you in trouble?" I ask, trying to wrap my mind around the concept. What sort of parent would punish their kid for being gay? It's beyond my scope of understanding. My dad might be dirt poor, but he loves me no matter what. Something as inconsequential as sexual preference could never take that away from me.

"I'm …" Andrew sighs and slumps back into the seat, closing his eyes. I remember meeting him last year, the things he said. *'I'm not quite that lucky, and I'm definitely not that gay—unfortunately. Between you and me, most of the girls here are already engaged.'* Mm. Poor Andrew. He was already in hiding. "I'm engaged."

"You're … what?!" I choke out, and start coughing so badly that Andrew ends up grabbing me a cold can of soda from the fridge. I crack the top and take a huge drink as he grimaces.

"My parents chose a fiancée for me. I either marry her, or I'm cut off and disowned." He stares at me across the limo like this is the most normal, average thing ever, parents threatening to disown their kids.

"I'm …" I take a deep breath and set my drink aside. "I'm really sorry."

Andrew shrugs his shoulders, but I can see it's weighing heavily on him.

"Is it so bad, being …" He trails off, and his eyes widen slightly, like he thinks he might've pissed me off.

"Being poor?" I ask, and he shrugs again. Maybe he's thinking of following his heart and telling his parents to kiss his ass? Maybe not. But with his education from Burberry Prep, he could go to any college, get a good job … and then he could make his own fortune. "Depends." Our eyes meet and something passes between us, a flicker of nervous energy. "Did you drug me?"

Andrew's mouth opens, and then snaps closed. He looks away sharply.

When I was making the list, I almost crossed his name out. I did. But then I started thinking about the day my hair was cut. It was hard to remember exactly what happened because every time I try to access those memories, I think about Tristan having sex with Kiara Xiao over the sink in the girls' bathroom.

"We had breakfast together that morning," I say, exhaling and closing my eyes. I don't *really* want to know the answer to this question. When I open them again, Andrew's staring at me. "And I don't think Miranda did it."

"Would you believe I'm sorry about it?" he whispers, and I can feel it, that anger inside of me, like lines of fire ants crawling through my veins, biting me, spurring me to action. "If it makes it any better, I stayed around to make sure they only messed with your hair …"

"As opposed to what?" I snap, my voice coming out in a

growl. This is good practice for me, confronting Andrew. Compared to the Idol boys, he's a kitten. "I'd been growing my hair out my whole life. I *liked* my hair." I reach a hand up to touch the short locks on my head. "I've embraced the change, but that doesn't make it right." I'm panting now, my heart thundering wildly in my chest. "Was it for a bet?"

"What do you think?" he asks me, and we stare at each other again. "You know how the Infinity Club works now." My mouth purses, and I look away for a moment, staring out at the yellow-brown grass on the side of the road. It's been a hot, hot summer.

"Who was it?" I whisper, wondering if any of the guys were in on this one.

"Becky, Harper, Abigail, and Valentina," Andrew says, and then sighs, like it feels good to get that off of his chest. "The other girls call them the fucked-up foursome behind their backs." I look back at him, slumped in a white tee and expensive jeans. He looks defeated. There's no sense of victory or justice in this.

"Did you know about …" I can't even force my lips to form the words. *Did you know about the beating I got backstage? How about the video? The paint? The panties? Anything at all?* Because if he did …

"Miranda and I knew nothing," he says, sighing again. "I'm not in the Inner Circle anymore."

My mouth pops open, and my eyes go wide.

"How do you even know that? Do the Idols send out secret emails or something?"

"When you're no longer a Blueblood, you know it." Andrew sits up straight and looks me dead in the eye, reaching up to run his palm over his hair. I hate to stereotype, but no wonder he smells so good, like coconuts and sunshine; I should've known he was gay. All those vibes I was getting off of him, all those appreciative looks ... they were bestie vibes, not boyfriend vibes. "I knew about the, uh, to make you fall in love, the ..."

"The bet." I say it for him, thinking about that awful, awful trophy. "Go on."

"Just that. It's why I wanted to take you to the winter formal, why I encouraged you away from them." He leans forward and puts his face in his hands. Taking revenge on Andrew would be like kicking a sad puppy. I can't do it. Because no matter what, I am *not* like them. I don't want to be like them. I used to think becoming my mother was the worst possible fate, but now I've decided that becoming like the Idols is a fate worse than death.

I'll take my revenge, but I have rules.

I pull out the notebook from my bag and open to the first page, penning a new line on the bottom.

Marnye's Rules for Revenge
1. *No physical violence*
2. *No friendly fire*
3. *No innocent bystanders*
4. *No sexism, racism, homophobia et al*
5. *Let them hang themselves with their own rope*
6. ***Know when enough is enough***

Andrew lifts his head to look at me, blue eyes dark with

regret and frustration.

"What else?" I ask, swallowing a lump. "Is there anything else you did? Because this is your last chance to be honest."

"What are you going to do?" Andrew asks as I flip the page to the back cover where I've taped in my revenge list. I spin it around for him to look at, and he raises his eyebrows. He notices his own name and lifts his face, meeting my eyes. "Be careful with them, Marnye. If you think last year was bad, then rest assured they'll amp it up this time. They'll be gunning for you."

"Answer the question." I keep my pen poised above the page, and Andrew exhales sharply.

"Nothing else. And Miranda—" I hold up my hand. Miranda and I need to talk. But I don't want any information second-hand; it all has to come from the source. "Nothing else. I'm so sorry, Marnye."

"I'm sorry, too," I say, feeling this wave of relief rush over me. I never wanted to hurt Andrew. "Look: grant me one small favor, and we'll call it even?" He nods, and I uncap my red Sharpie. I have five of them in my bag, just for this sort of occasion. As Andrew watches, I make an adjustment.

Revenge On *The Bluebloods of Burberry Prep*
A list by ~~Miranda Cabot~~ Marnye Reed

*The Idols (guys): Tristan Vanderbilt (year ~~one~~ **two**), Zayd Kaiser (year ~~one~~ **two**), and Creed Cabot (year ~~one~~ **two**)*
*The Idols (girls): Harper du Pont (year ~~one~~ **two**), Becky Platter (year ~~one~~ **two**), ~~and Gena Whitley (year four)~~*
(graduated)

The Inner Circle: **~~Andrew Payson~~**, *Anna Kirkpatrick, Myron Talbot, Ebony Peterson, Gregory Van Horn, Abigail Fanning, John Hannibal, Valentina Pitt, Sai Patel, Mayleen Zhang, Jalen Donner ...* ~~*and, I guess, me!*~~
Plebs: everyone else~~, sorry. XOXO~~
Zack Brooks

The limo reeks like Sharpie for a moment as I pop the cap back on, tuck my notebook away, and look over at Andrew.

"So. You were in the Hamptons part of the summer, right?" Andrew raises his eyebrows, but nods. "I hear shit went down. Tell me about it."

His forlorn facial expression evolves into a grin, and for a second there, I see a glimmer of the real Andrew hidden underneath the shell.

"Oh wait until you hear this T," he starts, and he fills me in on everything that happened over the last few months.

It's ... interesting, to say the least.

I may have more to work with than I thought.

36

Andrew and I take turns changing into our uniforms, using the back of the limo and its tinted windows for privacy, and then we slide into the backseat of the shiny black Cadillac with the academy's logo on the side. My heart is racing, palms sweaty. I feel like I might choke.

If I walk in there nervous, they'll know. They're predators, all of them; they'll smell my fear.

"Is any part of you still into them?" Andrew asks as we drive down the winding gravel road. I give him a look of such horror that he quickly closes his mouth and glances away. When we arrive at the courtyard with its stag fountain, I find myself with an escort.

"Miss Reed," Ms. Felton says, smiling softly at me. There's so much pity in her eyes that I find it hard to hold her gaze. "Welcome back." She nods at Andrew and then stands there politely until he gets the hint and leaves. Standing behind her coiffed form is a tall man in a suit that makes me a little nervous. I eye him warily. "Have you spoken to Kathleen Cabot yet today?" I nod and shrug. She did call and offer me a limo for the drive to Burberry Prep. Well, most recently she offered me a limo. Yesterday, she offered to buy me a car. On the last day of school, she … apologized profusely for her son.

My jaw clenches slightly as I think about Creed Cabot, and his angelic white-blond hair, his piercing blue eyes, the lazy insouciant way he holds himself. Prince of Assholes, that can be his title while he competes with Tristan Vanderbilt for King of Dickheads. I don't think about Zayd.

"Well, this is Kyle Carlin." She gestures at the man, her outfit much the same as dozens of others I saw her wear last year. "Principal Collins, Mrs. Cabot, and myself conferred with your father over the last few weeks, and well, we felt it'd be nice if you had an escort on campus." She must see the expression on my face because she adds, "at least until you get back into the swing of things."

"An escort?" I ask, looking at Kyle's hulking frame and huge muscles with my eyelid quivering. That's sort of the last thing I need, some giant bodyguard trailing me. I may as well just announce my weakness to the whole school. What sort of high school life is that, having some random dude following me everywhere? "I'm not interested in an escort." Ms. Felton purses her lips and exchanges a look with Kyle. He's tall, dark-haired, and mean in the face. Very intimidating.

"I understand it's not ideal," Ms. Felton begins, and I shake my head.

"No. I don't want a bodyguard." There's no way in hell I can exact my revenge with someone tailing me all day. I lift my chin and meet Ms. Felton's eyes. I'm not sure if it's possible, but I think I grew a couple of inches over the summer; I feel taller. "Is this compulsory?" My voice stays calm, even as Ms. Felton is staring at me like I've lost my mind.

"It's not …" she begins, and I nod. No way. Sure, I bet the bodyguard would keep the Bluebloods away from me. But that's all he would do. I'd still have to see Tristan's gray gaze from across the room, hear Zayd's raucous laughter, listen to Creed entertaining his subjects in The Mess. "Well, if you change your mind, Kyle will be patrolling the campus. We're taking this bullying thing very seriously." I nod and start to move away when Ms. Felton puts a hand on my arm. "If you want to take your meals in your room, we've made those arrangements with the kitchen."

I give her a tight smile and pull away.

I can feel their eyes on me as I head up the steps, my white second-year skirt billowing in a breeze.

My feet move just fine until I hit the stained glass doors at the end of the outdoor corridor.

You can do this, I tell myself, breathing hard, pulse racing. *Your uniform is clean and pressed, you've got on a garter belt and the thigh-high socks you didn't bother with last year. Your hair is done, your makeup ... passable, extensions on your lashes, brows waxed.* My breath exhales, and I pull out a tube of bright red lipstick, smearing it across my mouth and then checking my teeth in a small compact mirror. I start to head in and then pause, smiling as I roll the waistband of my skirt.

"Here goes nothing."

I push inside the chapel building, and the hall goes silent. Dead silent. There are students everywhere, in every year of uniform, and they're all staring at me. The only sound is that of my shiny black dress shoes clacking across the stone floors as I hold my bookbag over one shoulder and march down the hall with my shoulders straightened, my chin up, my back ramrod straight.

My locker is in the same place as last year, the keys to my dorm tucked in my bag. I head straight for the chapel hall for morning announcements, wishing Miranda were here. I texted her back a simple but critical: *see me at lunch in The Mess,* but now I'm phone-less with no way to contact her. Patching things up with Andrew felt good. I want … I *need* the same thing with my best friend, the only one I've ever really had.

Instead, I turn the corner and run straight into an ambush.

Tristan Vanderbilt is even more terrifying than I remember.

He stands at the point of the Blueblood crowd behind him, arms crossed over his second-year uniform: white pants, white shirt, white jacket, and red tie. He looks good in it, too, which I hate him for. Those blade gray eyes of his narrow on me, and my throat tightens.

I can't do this, my brain shrieks, wanting to panic, to run. But my heart was forged in fire. I stay put.

"Well, well, well, the Working Girl showed back up for a second round." His voice is dark, shadowed with wicked intent, and his smile is terrifying. It's obvious he's enjoying this moment, reveling in it really. I expected that. What I didn't expect is the pain, the fury. The two emotions fill me to the brim, until I feel like I'm spilling over. My hands shake.

"I told you I'd be here," I say, reaching up to pull the necklace from inside my shirt. Triumph flares in Tristan's silver gaze, but I can't quite figure out why. Does he think I'm still pining for him? Does he want me to grovel and beg? Whatever the reason, even he can't hide the surprise on his face when I tear the necklace off and chuck it at him.

He catches it in his palm as Harper slices through the crowd, making a beeline for us.

"I don't want or need your money. You keep that. You need it more than I do." I stride forward and past them, heading down the hall, when I feel something hit the back of my head. Spinning around, the white pleats of my skirt fluttering, I see Harper. She's picked her way through the crowd and now stands triumphant at Tristan's side, eyes glittering.

That night on the way to winter formal, in the limo, I think she was legitimately upset. And Tristan treated her like garbage. That was *not* a part of the act. No matter how many times I go over it, I just don't think so. That's how I figured out the first part of my plan: use Tristan against his own people. I don't have to destroy Harper du Pont: he's going to do it for me.

"Physical violence might be fun for you, but it's not how I'm going to win this game." I stay where I am, locking eyes with Harper. She hasn't changed much over the summer, save a few lighter streaks in her brunette hair. She's still rich, popular, pretty. But she's desperate for approval from her peers. She'll be an easy target. "Enjoy your first day back. Today, I'm focused on settling in. Tomorrow, I'm focused on you."

"I'm not afraid of some working class loser," Harper snaps, but I'm already turning away and ignoring her. It's not worth my time to get into verbal scuffles. Besides, if the verbal scuffles escalate to physical ones, I'm screwed. They'll all gang up on me.

I head down the hall and turn another corner, slamming into something firm and hard and sweet smelling, like geranium and sage.

"Whoa, cool your jets." Zayd Kaiser puts his hands on my shoulders and steadies me, a grin working its way across his handsome face until he sees who it is that he's touching. He rears back from me like he's been burned, and I get at least some small satisfaction out of that. "You."

"Where's your trophy?" I ask, my voice like ice as his green eyes lock on mine. "Did you put it on a shelf in your dorm, so you can look at it and praise yourself for actually making me like you? What an incredible award to have won, being yourself around someone until they become vulnerable to you, and then breaking them."

"You had your warnings," Zayd scoffs, but I think I've caught him off-guard a little. There is no *way* that all of those moments we spent together were bullshit. No way. None. Months of being on the road have left Zayd with a fresh tan, some new tattoos, and a headful of silver-ash colored hair. The red he dyed it for the graduation gala is gone. Good. I didn't want to see it like that anyway.

Before that day, Zayd had easily been the nicest to me, the one with a lot less to answer for. Creed had stolen my essay and read it aloud; Tristan facilitated the purchase and burning of that book. But Zayd? He'd just been an all-around, general sort of asshole. That was easy enough to forgive.

But now? I'd chosen him, and he'd destroyed me. All for the sake of winning a stupid bet.

"What are you even doing here?" he asks, like he's exasperated with me. "Do you ever get enough?"

My eyes burn, but crying in front of these monsters is not an option. They'd probably film it, and make a new video. As it is, the one they already worked on, with me and the guys in compromising positions, had ended up on YouTube. Within two days it was gone, but that didn't stop it from racking up over ten thousand views first.

"Get out of my way," I snap, pushing past him. He moves, but only because he wants to, and I can feel his eyes on me as I head toward the chapel. Everyone moves out of my way, Plebs scattering as the Working Girl stomps up the center of the aisle and takes a seat in the frontmost pew. There's a visible bubble around me, an emptiness that I know isn't going to be filled.

It's fine. I expected it. I'm okay with it.

The talking and giggling soon starts up again, and I can very clearly hear remarks made intentionally for me. I ignore them. They'll get what's coming to them; it's just a matter of time. I exhale and glance up at the Gallery. There's a scattering of familiar faces up there: John Hannibal, Gregory Van Horn, Ebony Peterson. And Creed Cabot.

His blue gaze drops down to mine, eyes widening imperceptibly before he controls himself, fading back into the bored royalty routine. I don't look away and neither does he; it feels like a challenge, and I refuse to back down. *Day one, step one, remind the Idols that I'm not one of their groupies.* Creed holds my stare, his eyes narrowing the longer our confrontation continues.

All around us, people stop talking and turn to stare, watching the exchange with drool hanging from their mouths. Okay, so not really, but they might as well. They all look like wolves, smacking their lips in anticipation of a fresh kill.

That is, until the last of the students funnel in and the staff moves to close the chapel doors. An instant later, they burst open and a dull roar emanates from the back of the room, spreading toward the front like wildfire. Creed's head whips

43

around and his eyes widen. Since he's broken our stare down first, I turn and look.

My breath leaves me in such a rush that I feel lightheaded, my stomach twisting into knots as Zack freaking Brooks makes his way down the aisle, dressed in the white blazer, red tie, and white slacks of a Burberry Prep second year student. Holy. Shit.

He pauses next to the pew I'm sitting on, indicating the empty space on either side of me with an outstretched hand. He's got a letterman jacket over the top of his blazer, and it's in the red and black colors of Burberry Prep Academy.

"Do you mind if I sit here?" he asks, his eyes burning a hole straight through me. My teeth clench, and I want to scream in frustration. Instead, I glance back at the Gallery to find Tristan, Creed, and Zayd all watching me.

Hm.

They don't like Zack, none of them do. When they were wooing me, they pretended it was because of the bet he made with Lizzie. Clearly, they couldn't care less about me, so it's got to be something else. Based on their facial expressions, it's obvious they're not happy about Zack's presence here.

"Why not?" I whisper, but the room is now so quiet that my voice echoes in the chapel. Zack sits beside me, pressing his thigh against mine. Where our bodies touch, my skin burns, but I ignore that sensation. I'll admit it: last year, I was desperate for friendship, for companionship, for … romance. This year, I won't make the same mistakes. I won't give into the hot ache inside my chest when the guys are around, and I won't let the empty siren song of my loneliness drag me to the rocks. "Why are you here, and how did you get that jacket?" I shouldn't even bother asking, but my curiosity is killing me.

"Coach saw me play when Burberry went up against Coventry Prep." Zack shrugs his big shoulders, dark hair shaved into a crew cut. He looks straight ahead and keeps his palms flat on his thighs. He acts like he doesn't notice everyone staring at us. I call bullshit. "He got tired of losing to public schools, and convinced the admins to let me in." Zack glances over at me, eyes shadowed and unreadable. "I'm such a legend, I'm the only second-year on varsity." He grins and pinches the shoulder of his jacket, pausing as Miranda appears in front of me.

We stare at each other, and I swear, I've never been more of a nervous wreck.

Ms. Felton is already taking the stage behind her, so instead of talking, Miranda just flops down on my other side, being careful to keep her leg from touching mine. I have no idea what this means between us, but when I hazard one, last glance at the Bluebloods, I can see the tightness in Creed's face, and I wet my lips.

There's a list in my notebook with his name on it.

Creed Cabot's Weaknesses
1. *Miranda Cabot*
2. *Kathleen Cabot*
3. *Jealous of Tristan*
4. *Desperate to shed the 'new money' name*
5. *Bullied in public school*

Repairing my relationship with Miranda is paramount, not just for my own sake, but for … everything else, too. I need her on my side.

Principal Collins moves up to stand beside Ms. Felton, and clears her throat. The room is already quiet, save for the gossipy whispers of some of the students, but it falls into a deathly silence at the sound of her voice.

"Welcome back," she begins, her gray eyes scanning the crowd. When her gaze passes over me, there's a small flicker of sympathy and regret. I've been seeing it on the faces of every adult here, and I'm sick of it. My mouth flattens into a thin line as I flick my attention to Zack. His words suddenly make a lot more sense to me.

"It's just me against the world at Burberry Prep; I've already accepted that."

"I wouldn't say that."

I wonder how long Zack's been planning this.

"As I'm sure most of you are aware," Principal Collins continues, moving across the stage with slow, deliberate footsteps, "the way last year ended was an embarrassment to the Burberry Prep name, a smear on our traditions, and a horrific example of unchecked privilege." She pauses at the very edge of the platform, and I definitely don't miss it when she turns her attention briefly up to the Gallery and the gathered Bluebloods. I shift in my seat; I sense a possible ally in Mrs. Collins. I'll have to be careful to cultivate that relationship. "This year, we won't make the same mistakes again. Read up on the school handbook because you're responsible for being aware of all the changes to our academic policies. Those in violation will face suspension or expulsion, no exceptions."

She pauses, stares the crowd down once more, and then proceeds with the usual first day announcements.

But there's not an eye in that room that isn't on me.

Good.

Let them look.

There's going to be a lot to see.

CHAPTER

3

By the end of the first day, I'm exhausted, and my mind is spinning with possibilities, desperate for some way to right the wrong that was committed against me. I've already got a head start, my summer plans unfolding into glorious action. But not yet. Not quite yet.

I head for The Mess, taking a seat by the window at the table I used to share with Miranda. We have pretty different schedules this year it seems, so if she wants to find me, this is her chance. I'm not going to chase her, not if she isn't ready.

So I sit down, ignoring the stares and the whispers, the way the Idols' table goes silent as I pull out a journal (not my revenge one, a different one), lay it on the table, and leave it there while I check the menu. After I've placed my order, I hunch over and begin to write.

It takes all of two minutes for Tristan Vanderbilt to make

his way over to me.

"You're not allowed in here this year," he tells me, voice as smooth as silk. I can practically feel it trailing across my body, awakening every nerve ending in my skin. Goose bumps prickle my arms, but I ignore them. Lust is an emotion I can ignore if I have to. Screw Tristan Vanderbilt. "Did you hear me, Charity?" He leans over and puts his elbows on the table. I wonder at his lack of back-up, but take advantage of it by looking up and meeting his gray gaze. "I know you've been given permission to take your meals in your room. Get your ass up and go stuff your fat face in there."

His words sting me, like running through a field of nettles, little barbs embedding themselves into my skin. I brush the pain aside by slamming my notebook closed and flicking the lock on the side. Tristan takes note of the action, and then refocuses on me.

"Did you know they broke my ribs?" I ask, and he stares at me with an impassivity that's frightening. There's no sign of any normal, human emotion in there, just cold steel and ice.

"I don't know what you're talking about, and I don't care. Get up and go back to your room before I make you do it." I smile at him, but I'm not afraid, not at all.

"Harper, Becky, the other girls …" I trail off, gesturing in their direction with my hand. "Did you know they were going to take it that far?" Tristan narrows his eyes and scowls at me, but at least there's some humanity in the gesture; I'll take it.

"What are you even babbling about?" he snaps, but clearly I've touched a nerve because Tristan's already getting angry with me, and I've just started.

"When the girls cornered me backstage before my harp solo, did you know they were going to beat me so badly that I'd break my ribs and crack a tooth?" My eyes are locked on him, so when his widen imperceptibly, I catch it. He quickly schools himself, standing up straight and running his palm down the length of his red tie. But it was there, that little tell that gives me all the information I need: he didn't know. Tristan, the self-proclaimed King of the Academy, didn't know about the girls' plan.

The first seed of doubt has been sowed.

"This is your last warning: take your meal and go back to your room."

"Or what, Vanderbilt?" a disturbingly dark voice asks from behind him. Tristan and I turn to find Zack Brooks leaning against the wall with his eyes slitted, his mouth turned up in a crooked scowl. "You gonna beat her like your girlfriend did? Leave her covered in bruises and blood?"

Tristan's entire body is so stiff that I have to wonder if his muscles hurt, being held like that for so long. He just stares Zack down, and then finally, moves several steps closer. The two boys are toe-to-toe, and honestly, I'm content to watch. Maybe they'll beat each other up right here in front of everyone, and then start the year with a suspension on their records?

"You think you're so different," Tristan purrs, reaching up to run his long fingers through his raven-black hair. "You think because you're *sorry* that you're somehow better than us?" Zack's hands curl into fists by his sides.

"I never said I was better; I said I was on Marnye's side.

That's it." He flicks his gaze past Tristan's shoulder to meet mine. "I'm already an asshole. I'm already tainted. I won't let her sully herself to try to combat you. I'll take you down first."

Tristan turns, smirking and raising his brows at me.

"You? Take us down?" The laugh that spills from his throat tears my heart in half, but I let it happen, let myself bleed. He never cared about me, not when he was kissing me on the steamboat, not when he was giving me the necklace, not when he defended me in the vice principal's office. Every single second was fake … wasn't it? "Please. With what resources? That change I tossed in your piggy bank?"

"I'm going to make you sorry," I whisper, but not because I'm scared, but because my voice is husky with determination and menace both. Tristan simply laughs at me.

"You and what army?"

"This one," Miranda blurts, and I jump in my seat. I turn to look at her, my mouth dropping open as I realize she snuck in while I was preoccupied with the boys. Her bookbag is held over one shoulder, her blue eyes hard, mouth set in a thin line.

Creed is standing behind her, frozen in the doorway with his eyes jumping from me to Tristan to Zack, and finally over to Miranda. His mouth curls down in a frown.

"My family has more money than yours, Tristan," Miranda snaps, dropping her bag to her side as she waltzes into the room, just as much a Blueblood as the rest of them. Her eyes glitter with frustration. "And if I have to give Marnye every *cent* to bring you down, I will."

"Creed, put a leash on your bitch of a sister," Tristan

drawls, waving his hand absently. Creed's face tightens up, and I can see a muscle in his neck working as he tries to push back the rage. "If you don't, then she's out of the Inner Circle. I'm done with this crap."

"Leave it, Tristan," Creed hisses, taking a few steps forward. "Miranda is off-limits, period. I won't fight about this again." *Mm. Creed versus Tristan.* That's going to be a useful tool.

"Then kick me out," Miranda says, reaching under her shirt and pulling out a set of keys. I wonder what those are for and then remember the Gallery and the locked door. A special set of keys, just for the elite members of the school. She chucks them at Tristan's chest, and just like with the necklace, he manages to catch these, too. "Good riddance." She moves over to my table, stares Tristan dead in the face, and then hip bumps him out of the way while the Idol girls gasp and squeal like stuck pigs. Miranda grabs her menu, tosses her hair (or tries to anyway), and then looks across the table with a smile. "I have *soooo* much gossip to tell you," she begins, and then I know for certain that things are going to be okay between us.

We have a lot of work to do, hard conversations to be had, but this is our new beginning.

I focus on my menu as Andrew moves into the room and takes the third seat. Zack moves for the fourth, but my hand lashes out, and I curl my fingers around the back of the chair.

"I'm not ready," I tell him, and he nods. But then, of course, he takes up a table one over from us, watching and waiting.

"She's eating in The Mess," Zack says, lifting his eyes to

look up at Tristan, and then Creed. Zayd comes in a moment later with Becky clinging to his arm like a leech. My blood goes cold at the sight, and I whip out my journal again, scribbling furiously in it. My eyes lift from the page to find Tristan's gaze locked on me. He scowls and turns away, storming out of the dining hall and slamming the door behind him.

Zayd and Creed say nothing, moving past me to sit at the Bluebloods' table in the corner.

I glance at Zack, and he gives me a small, private little smile that Miranda notices, sucking in a deep breath.

"You have so much to tell me," she whispers, and I grin.

It's good to have her back … even if I don't trust her. Not yet anyway.

My room is much the same as it was last year with the exception of one thing: new locks on the door. Not that I think it'll stop the Bluebloods completely, but it should buy me some extra time.

Miranda takes a spot on the end of my bed, and this strenuous silence falls between us. I bite my lip and lean my back against the door, searching for the right words to say.

"There's so much I need to tell you," she starts, taking the words right out of my mouth. Her blue eyes flick up to mine, and I hate that her gaze reminds me so much of Creed. I don't want to think about Creed unless I'm thinking about how to destroy him. "First off: have you heard about Windsor York?"

My brows go up. The name isn't familiar, so I shake my head, pushing off from the door and moving over to the fridge in the kitchenette for a pair of sodas. I toss one to Miranda as she grins big.

"He's tenth in line for the throne, you know," she continues, popping the top on her can and taking a sip.

"The throne ... what throne?" I ask, and Miranda laughs.

"You really don't keep up on current events, do you?" she asks, cocking a brow. She flashes me a smile before continuing on. "The throne of England, silly, duh. You know, like Prince William and his wife, Kate?" I just stare at her. "Kate Middleton? Like, *everyone* is talking about her? Prince Harry and Meghan Markle? No?!" Miranda exhales and stands up, like this is too important to let go of. Personally, I think this is a stall tactic to keep us from discussing real issues. She waves her hand dismissively. "Windsor is, like, well, technically he's a *prince*. He's the queen's great-grandson" I just stare at her as she bites her lower lip. "He stole his parents' yacht and crashed into a dock, sent ten people to the hospital. He's just lucky he didn't kill anyone."

"What does this have to do with anything?" I ask, opening my own soda and taking a drink. The fizzy liquid coats my tongue as I look Miranda in the eyes and try to pretend like nothing happened between us. So much did. So, so much. But how do I even broach the subject? "Miranda, I'm—" I move to apologize again, but she cuts me off. Maybe she doesn't want to talk about it at all?

"He's been kicked out of so many schools all over Europe. They really want him to get his act together, so they're sending him overseas." She grins at me and then picks at the top of one of her socks. She's got on the super tall ones today, too. I wonder if she's still seeing that girl, Jessie Maker. Do I even have a right to ask? I figure I probably don't. "Specifically, they're sending him to America." She pauses for dramatic effect. "*California.*"

"So?" I ask again, and Miranda leaps to her feet.

"There are only three prep schools in California worthy of a prince: Coventry Prep, Beverly Hills Prep, and Burberry Prep. Marnye, I'm pretty sure he's coming here." I'm not entirely sure what this conversation has to do with anything, but I also don't want to spit on Miranda's goodwill, so I make myself smile.

"That's amazing," I tell her, my voice far too soft for such a normal conversation. She stops talking and her mouth purses into a thin line, eyes flicking to the side, like she can't quite bear to look at me full-on just yet. I try one last time. "Miranda, I …"

"Marnye," she blurts, lifting her gaze up to my face. "You know I tried to message you over the summer, right?" I nod, and hold back a sniffle. I'm not going to cry, and I'm not going to be wishy-washy. I'm going to kick some Blueblood ass is what I'm going to do. Just … not Miranda's. "But I understood when you didn't reply. We both needed time, and

Creed …" She trails off as my lips curl into a slight sneer. "What my brother did to you was unforgivable. I've barely spoken to him since. If it gives you any peace of mind, it's killing him inside." She smiles at me, but there's not a lot of joy in it; she doesn't like hurting her twin.

But that's exactly what I'm going to do.

"I'm going to make him suffer," I tell her, and she bites her lip for a moment before nodding.

"Yeah, I figured as much." Her smile gets a little bigger, a little wider. "I wouldn't expect anything less out of you. And besides," she pauses to reach into her shirt, pulling out the necklace that Tristan gave me, "if you did anything less, they would crucify you. Fight back, Marnye, and show them what I already know: you deserve to be here even more than they do."

She takes my hand and drops the necklace into my palm.

"What is this?" I choke out, and Miranda's smile gets even bigger.

"Tristan stashed this in his pocket, and then he and Harper and a full-on screaming match in the hall about it. *Everyone* saw, and I mean *everyone.*" She waves her hand dismissively. "Anyway, when he wasn't paying attention, Harper took it. She threw it in the trash, and *I* dug it out. Keep it. You might find a use for it later." Miranda leans in and gives me a kiss on the cheek before heading for the door. My hand curls around the necklace and squeezes it tight. "Meet me in the morning for breakfast, and watch your back. They're gunning for you, Marnye, and it's going to so much worse than last year."

CHAPTER

4

The most important items I packed in my duffel bag were cameras that I ordered online. They connect wirelessly to my phone, so I can watch the footage at any time. As I position them around my room, I feel a smirk working its way over my face. The best way to bring the Bluebloods down is to let them drown themselves. If they break into my room again, I'll have proof.

As soon as that's done, I get dressed in the crisp perfection of my academy uniform, put on some makeup, and fix my hair as best as I can. It doesn't look as nice as it did at the salon, but it's still edgy and pretty, just long to curl around my ears. Next, I collect my schedule, and head into the hall. I bump face to chest into Zack Brooks.

"What are you doing here?" I groan as I rub at my nose, looking up at him with a scowl. "We're not exactly friends."

"Only because you don't want to be," he says, eyes, face, and voice dark and unreadable as always. My attention goes straight to his mouth, remembering that one, fierce make-out session we had during our brief dating session, and the magical way his tongue traced my lower lip.

Shivers take over me, but I'm not interested in Zack or Creed or Tristan or Zayd. Not anymore. Screw them all. Zack's sins might be older than the other boys' transgressions, but honestly, they're almost worse. He made me want to take my life, him and Lizzie. I exhale. The only reason she's not on my list is because she doesn't go to this school, and I have no way of getting back at her. Zack is on it because I always have a connection to him because of his friendship with my dad. But now, at least, I've got him right here in front of me.

"Please move," I say, tucking my bookbag against my chest. Zack stares at me for a moment, and I can't help but notice that scent of his, sporty and cool and well-rounded. It gives me butterflies and that just pisses me off, too. "*Move.*"

"You don't have to be on my side, but I'm on yours," he says, but I'm done listening, so I brush past him and continue on down the hall and around the corner.

At breakfast, I pull out my journal and start writing furiously. There are so many things I need to say with messy cursive between those lines. The girls are in The Mess, but the boys are nowhere to be seen. They watch me as I eat, voices muted, hatred muffled.

With the extra security provided by the school, we're all going to have to be careful. It's why I'm not making my move until Friday, at the first party the year.

The door to The Mess opens, and Zack walks in, pausing briefly, eyes landing on me before he makes his way over to his own table. A few minutes later, Miranda and Andrew appear, taking up seats across from me.

"What are you planning on doing?" Miranda whispers as she leans in to look at me, white-blond hair swinging forward and brushing across the table. The color reminds me of Creed yet again, but I don't let my thoughts go there, so I smile instead.

"Whatever do you mean?" I ask grinning sheepishly. I close the journal with a smack, making sure to take extra care to secure the lock and slide it into my bookbag. Andrew watches me the whole time, one brow raised.

"Well," he begins looking from Miranda to me, "Miranda here thinks revenge is best served hot and steaming, but I think it's best served cold." Andrew gives me a slow, easy smile, and I can see how I thought he was flirting with me those few times. He's a genuinely open person, naturally friendly and charismatic. I guess my gay-dar just doesn't work properly. "But you *are* planning on doing something to the Bluebloods, aren't you?" He leans his forearms on the table, and his smile gets a little bigger. "Let me in on it, please. They already kicked me out …" Andrew exhales, like he's just remembered his own fate. When he looks back at me, it's with a slightly more serious expression. "I want to be a part of this."

"You know we're going to help you, whether you like or not," Miranda says, leaning back and tucking her hair behind her ear. "So you may as well tell us all about your genius plans now." She attempts a hair toss, but it fails miserably. I grin.

I'm not about to tell Andrew and Miranda anything, especially not the fact that I'm not putting my trust in anyone this year. I can barely trust myself. I decided I needed to make a stand, that I needed to make the Bluebloods pay, that I needed to pave a spot for myself at the school. But it's a slippery slope, and I don't want to end up like *them*. It took me a long time to find out who I am, and an even longer time to start to like the person that I'm becoming, so I can't let this ruin me. It's going to be a challenge. For now though, I'm going to keep any thoughts of revenge to myself.

"Oh, if I've got something planned … you'll see."

On Friday, I intend to show them, what, exactly I've got up my sleeve.

The first week of school comes to a close without any major events. There are too many staff members in the halls, and even though I turned down that bodyguard guy, Kyle or Keith or whatever, he's still around, acting like the Burberry prep campus cop. It doesn't stop the girls from saying things to me as they pass in the hall, but all I do is smile. I know what I've got planned.

The Idol boys seem to be going out of their way to steer clear of me. Whether that's because they're having a hard time facing up to what they did (doubtful) or because they hate me so much they're not sure if they can control themselves in my presence, I'm not sure. For whatever reason, I see very little of the three boys I started falling for last year.

Zack, however, is a different story. He sits next to me during the morning announcements and in every class we share. On Friday, as I'm getting ready for the party, he shows up at my door again.

I check the peephole and sigh, throwing the door open and moving back, so he can step inside the room. He's so freaking tall and wide, he takes up the whole space with his presence. My heart skips a few beats before I manage to get a hold of myself. It helps that Andrew's lounging on my bed, and Miranda's in the bathroom spinning her long hair into curls. My rose gold locks are twisted in gentle waves around my face, hair-sprayed to hell, and covered in glitter.

Zack looks me over with those dark eyes of his, taking me in from head to toe, his face entirely impassive. He rarely shows emotion. The face he has on now could be the same one he used when he was tormenting me at Lower Banks. Hell, it could be the same expression he wore when he cupped my face in his big hands and kissed me on the mouth. My first kiss. Our last kiss.

I cross my arms over my chest, fully aware that I'm wearing nothing but a robe with lingerie underneath. Don't get any ideas: the lingerie isn't for anyone but me. It makes *me* feel more confident.

"You look good, Reed," Zack says, wearing his letterman jacket with a tight black t-shirt, dark jeans, and shiny new sneakers. He looks like a million bucks. His outfit, as unassuming as it is, probably costs about the same. "Off to the party, I'm guessing?"

"What do you want, Zack?" I ask, looking at him and wondering if he's here out of guilt, worry, curiosity, all three? I don't need him to pay attention to me because he feels like he has to. And I didn't need him to transfer here out of some sick sense of duty. He can be as nice as he wants to me; it doesn't change anything. His name is still on my list.

"Let me be your backup," he says with a loose shrug of his massive shoulders. The movement makes the muscles in his chest shift, and my eyes catch on the fabric of his tee as it strains with the motion. Good god. No wonder the coach was okay with taking a second year onto the varsity team. Zack is bigger than every other guy at this school, including the fourth years. I bet he crushes dudes on the field. "The staff doesn't know about the party tonight. It's going to be rough."

I smile.

That's exactly what I was hoping for, I think, but I don't say anything. Miranda comes out of the bathroom and pauses, looking Zack over carefully. She hasn't made up her mind about him one way or another. And by that, I mean she hasn't decided if he should drown in an icy lake or burn up in a fiery explosion.

"What the hell do you want?" she demands, sauntering up to stand beside me. She's so regal, and daring. Her replacement in the Inner Circle is a girl called Ileana Taittinger, a first year who became an instant dislike for me when she told me I was too ugly to be a Working Girl on her second day of class. I've added her name to my list. Andrew's replacement has yet to be determined, but I'm sure whoever he is, he'll be another one for the books.

"Let me drive you to the party tonight. I won't hang too close, but at least let me help you make an entrance. You know those guys hate my guts, right? They'll fucking hate seeing us there together." I snort, glancing away toward where Andrew's waiting on the bed. He's still dressed in his uniform, and even though he hasn't said anything, there's this eagerness in him. I think he's excited to see Gary Jacobs at the party.

"Why *do* they hate you so much?" I ask, cocking my head to one side and studying Zack. "I mean, they warned me off of you before they even made their stupid bet. Clearly, that wasn't out of fondness for me. What is it about you that disturbs them so much?"

"My brother might be a cruel jerk, but he would never take it as far as you did. You almost killed Marnye. You're irredeemable, Zack. Get fucked." Miranda tosses her hair and smacks me in the face with it. I brush strands away from my glossed lips as she turns on her heel and storms back to the bathroom.

"So you think Creed's redeemable, huh?" Zack asks, reaching up to rub at his lower lip with his thumb. "You think that bet's the worst the Infinity Club's ever come up with? You're definitely drinking from the cup of naivety when it comes to your twin."

My brows go up as Miranda turns right around and marches back into the room, blue eyes narrowed to slits. Wow. She looks *just* like Creed when she does that. A shiver overtakes me, and I cross my arms like I'm hugging myself.

"What exactly does that mean?" she snaps, the words

flicking off her tongue like a whip. I cringe a bit, but Zack just stands there, staring at us both.

"If I could tell you, I would." I snort at that and he flicks his gaze over to me. "What? It's the truth. The day they told you what Lizzie and I did, I'd already come up with a plan. I was—"

"—going to tell me out of pity and guilt? That's not good enough for me, Zack." I exhale sharply and raise my chin defiantly. Our eyes meet, and a small thrill goes through me. He looks sorry, like really freaking sorry. There's a depth to his sorrow that makes my blood sing. Good. Good, let him be sorry for what he did. "If Lizzie hadn't changed the terms of the bet, what then? What would you have done?"

"Marnye," he starts, his dark voice cracking slightly. "I ..." Zack just stops talking, sighs, and then closes his eyes. When he opens them, that same old wall is back, crashing in front of his emotions and cutting them off at the source. He reaches up and rakes his fingers through his short, dark hair. "There's nothing I can say to make up for what I've done. Nothing. I'll go."

"Excellent," Miranda says, pushing him toward the door and opening it up. He lets himself be pushed into the hallway, and the last thing I see before she slams it shut is his face, a deep frown etched into his mouth, his eyes mournful. "What a total douche. I cannot even *believe* that I pushed you to date him."

"You think Creed is redeemable?" I ask, and Miranda freezes. She's turned away, so I can't see her face, but when she glances over her shoulder, I see that it's true. She really does. But, I mean, he's her brother, so what else can I expect?

"I mean, he's not as bad as Zack ..." she starts before turning to look at me. "He's been really supportive about my being gay, and he even banned the Bluebloods from making homophobic comments."

"He's a real winner," Andrew says with a roll of his eyes. He sits up and gives her a sharp look. "Don't make excuses for him. I'm not saying Zack's a good guy, but at least he's trying to apologize. Creed doesn't give a crap about how he hurt Marnye."

Miranda sighs, and nods her head.

I hate to come between her and her brother, but if she sticks with me, it's going to happen one way or another. I'm not even going to have to take her away from him. He'll do that all on his own. I close my eyes and remember rule number five on my list: *Let them hang themselves with their own rope.*

"I won't make excuses for him," she says, meeting my eyes. I nod and then grab my new dress off the chair in the corner.

"Let's get going: I want to make an entrance."

And so it begins ...

The favor I asked from Andrew was simple: let me borrow his car for the year. Technically, no student is allowed to keep a car without special permission. But they all do it anyway. Last year, they literally just tossed caution to the wind and parked in one of the staff lots. This year, with all the new security and scrutiny, they've all paid to have their cars delivered to a lot just off the campus property. Getting to it means sneaking through the woods in glittering party dresses and trailing perfume. I swear, there's so much cologne and body spray in this copse of trees, I feel like I might choke.

"I think every freaking student in the school is here," Miranda whispers as we walk across the wet grass in flats, our heels clutched in our hands, purses slung over our shoulders. I've embraced the Burberry Prep lifestyle: I'm wearing a dress that costs too much money for me to fathom, and I've got the heels that Creed bought me. All in all, including the jewelry I borrowed from Miranda, I'm wearing over *five thousand dollars* in clothing and accessories.

I almost gag at that thought.

Also, pretty sure I'm the most frugally dressed one there anyway.

"It's like a mass exodus," Andrew whispers, passing me his keys. I can see the bright glare of phone screens, and the sparkle of jewelry and dresses winking at me from various spots in the trees. If the staff doesn't know what we're all up to, I'd be surprised. Then again, how can they really bust every student in the academy? The hair on the back of my neck prickles, and I look around, expecting that Kyle guy to appear out of the shadows.

"It isn't *like* one," Miranda whispers, biting her lower lip, "it *is* one."

We hit the edge of the trees without encountering any of the Bluebloods, and I have to whistle at the shining red beauty of Andrew's car.

"Holy crap, Andrew," I whisper, running my hand over the hood. Telling someone you have a red Lamborghini, and actually seeing it in person? Two totally different things. Like, I'm not even into cars, but this one … hot as hell. "What does your family do again?"

He tucks his fingers in his pockets and shrugs his shoulders, crinkling his academy jacket.

"We manufacture vehicles," he says, and then grins at me. "Pretty much any car made in the USA or Italy has the Payson stamp on it somewhere." I smile back, but actually, I already knew the answer to that question. I studied every Blueblood on that list, their family, and their net worth. I know who's the richest of the rich, and who's just hanging on by a thread.

Raucous laughter rings across the lot, and I lift my head to find Zayd with his head thrown back. He's howling over something Greg's just said, his arm around Becky's waist. My blood boils hot as they all pile into a blue Jaguar F-type convertible, gravel churning as they take off out of the parking lot with no regard to anyone else. I cringe as Zayd just barely misses smashing the front of his car into Valentina's Porsche.

"Idiots," I mumble as I spot Zack's orange McLaren parked across the way. He's leaning against it, watching me. "Stalker," I add, flipping him off before I unlock the doors to the Lambo and move around to the driver's side. Before I climb in, I see Tristan and Creed standing next to a Bentley Bentayga, basically this super pretentious white SUV. As if they sense me looking their way, they both turn in unison, gray and blue eyes locked on mine.

I smirk at the Idols, twirl Andrew's keys around my fingers, and slide into the driver's seat.

"Creed got a car?" I ask as I shut the door and watch through the tinted window as Tristan takes off for his dad's Ferrari Spider, and Creed climbs into the Bentley. *I swear, every rich person gets a car for their sixteenth birthday.* "And did Tristan steal his dad's car or did he give it to him?"

"My dad offered us a choice: car or money in our trust. Creed chose the car; I chose the cash. Oh, and Tristan stole the Ferrari again," Miranda adds with a shrug. "He's been driving it all summer. His dad has so many cars, he probably didn't notice. Or care. William Vanderbilt doesn't exactly pay a lot of attention to his son." She checks her phone and then squeals so loudly in my ear that I jump. "Don't go anywhere yet!"

Miranda scrambles out of the back, crushing Andrew with

the front seat as she pushes past him. She's not two steps out of the vehicle before she's throwing her arms around a girl that I vaguely recognize as Jessie Maker, the same girl I saw her with last year. They hug so tight it looks like they might break each other's ribs, and then they pull back and just grin at each other.

Glancing back out the driver's side window, I see Creed sitting in his Bentley with the window rolled down, watching the pair of them. His hands are tight on the wheel, and I know he's as aware of Gregory Van Horn and John Hannibal watching her as I am. He turns away sharply and starts up the SUV, peeling out of there almost as fast as Zayd did.

"Is it okay if Jessie rides with us?" Miranda asks, cheeks pink, panting heavily as she peers into the car.

"It's fine with me," I say, and neither girl waits for Andrew before they push his seat forward and scramble into the back.

"Hey Marnye, I've heard a lot about you," Jessie says, her dark brown hair hanging shiny and straight around her thin shoulders. She has a genuinely nice smile, sparkling chestnut eyes, and a white dress that leaves little to the imagination.

"All good," Miranda assures me as I smile and shake hands with the new girl, starting up the Lambo's engine with a delicious purr. Like I said, not a car person but holy crap, the rumble of the engine through the black leather of the seat is almost enough to make me a convert.

Much more cautiously than the others, I back out of the space and take the same gravel road up and out of the lot, heading towards the location for the first party of the year: Ileana Taittinger's countryside mansion. It's about two hours north of Burberry Prep, up a winding coastal road that deviates around Santa Cruz, and ends in a gloriously long driveway topped with a fancy metal gate.

There are students—first years, based on their uniforms, and one third year—policing the gate, and opening it only after checking to see who's inside each car.

We are most definitely not invited.

"You still haven't told us how you plan on getting in there," Andrew says as we creep up the driveway, and I exhale sharply, glancing over at him with a sympathetic expression. He sees it and gets immediately suspicious. As he should.

"A favor is a favor," I tell him, and his face pales. We come to a stop just feet from the gate as one of the first year girls saunters over to us with her skirt billowing in the breeze, flashing a whole lot of lacy pink panty in the process. Hmm. I roll the window down and she leans her forearms on the door, her cloying perfume filling up the car and making me gag.

"Excuse you," she spits, and the vitriol in her voice makes me grit my teeth. This girl has *never* met me, and yet here she is, looking at me like I'm lower than pond scum. "No whores, hookers, or prostitutes allowed. Go turn your tricks in the city, Working Girl."

"Nice to meet you," I say, keeping my voice neutral, my face pleasant. I can feel the tension from Andrew, Miranda, and Jessie behind me. "My name is Marnye Reed, and I'll be attending this party, thank you very much." I continue to smile as the girl scowls at me, and a boy in a third year uniform approaches from the other side.

"No faggots," he says, shaking his head and sneering at Andrew through his partially rolled down window. "I don't care what Creed says. He's not coming into my little sister's party. Wouldn't want to get raped by a homo." The boy laughs, and the sound is rather like a donkey with a sore throat, grainy and snotty and ugly. I resist the urge to scream, my hands tightening around the wheel.

"Let's just go, Marnye," Andrew whispers, his voice and face dark. "We're not getting in here."

"Please open the gate," I repeat, and the girl laughs at me, moving away to stand next to the brick pillar on the left, tossing her hair *perfectly*, and then giggling at something one of the guys says. The other asshole, Ileana's older brother apparently, snorts and flips us off before sauntering back to the group. With a sigh, I put the Lambo in reverse and pretend like I'm leaving.

I'm not.

"Marnye ..." Andrew begins, just before I put the car back in drive, and slam my foot on the gas. With the squeal of tires and the stink of burnt rubber, we shoot forward and smash through the gate. It's not locked, so it opens easily, the metal flying back and smashing into the bricks. The kids gape at us as we roll across the lawn and park next to the dozens of other fancy cars already there.

I take note of Zayd's, Creed's, and Tristan's cars before I climb out and lock the doors, tucking the keys in my bra. Andrew's still gaping at me, and Miranda's grinning, just barely resisting the urge to hop up and down. Okay, so, maybe she jumps up and down a little. Jessie just raises her eyebrows and whistles in surprise.

"Okay, who are you, and what have you done with the Marnye Reed I know?" Miranda asks as the group from the gate storms across the yard towards me. I ignore them, toss my hair (poorly, I might add), and head for the front porch and the crowd of gawping students.

Zayd's right there in the thick of it, a beer in one hand, his mouth open, his green eyes tracking me as I make my way toward the front door.

"Hey!" the Taittinger guy shouts, pounding up the steps to cut me off. His ugly face is twisted in a sneer, and I'm pretty sure he's about ten seconds from putting his hands on me. The bitchy first year girl is right behind him, taking up on his left like a sentinel.

"You fucking bitch!" she snarls, and it's pretty disturbing to see such a hateful expression on her baby face. I look at them both with a *so what?* expression before glancing over at Andrew and smiling softly.

"I'm sorry about the car, but there doesn't even seem to be a scratch. Your family makes quality vehicles, I have to say." He stares at me for a second, blinking past the shock, and then grins.

"I guess we do."

"Shut your mouth, faggot," Taittinger sneers, stepping close to Andrew. He seems a bit tentative about hitting a girl, but I'm worried for Andrew.

"Back off of him, Craig!" Miranda shouts, just as much a Blueblood as she ever was. No, no, *more* of a Blueblood than she was before. She's practically regal in that cream colored dress of hers, like a princess. Or maybe even a queen. "If you touch him, I'll kill you."

"Yeah?" Craig sneers, shoving Andrew in the chest with a palm. Andrew stumbles back, nostrils flaring, but he holds his ground. Miranda is there in an instant, despite Jessie's attempts to pull her back. She throws herself at Craig Taittinger, and he raises a fist. I'm ready to step in if I'm wrong, but …

A pale hand clamps onto his wrist and jerks him back so hard that he stumbles, falling into a heap on the porch. A crowd's gathered around now, as Creed looks down at Ileana's brother with a face so full of darkness that I barely recognize him.

"Were you thinking about touching my sister?" he whispers, his voice like jagged sheets of ice, as sharp as glass and freezing cold. They can cut to bleed and poison the flesh with frostbite, all at once. "Are you fucking *kidding* me?" Creed puts his foot on Taittinger's throat, and the crowd gasps in shock. Me, I've got my phone recording and nobody knows it.

He's just protecting his sister, I think, but I banish the thought, remembering the impassive way he stared at me while I was humiliated, remembering my panties clutched in his hand. He threw them at me like he was tossing trash at a stray dog.

"Lay off, Cabot," the first year girl snaps, her hands curled into fists. "These idiots rushed the gate. Craig was just trying to help."

"By hitting my sister?" Creed Cabot says, his voice sending a chill down my spine. I remember the way he tore Derrick Barr up with words last year, and then proceeded to

73

flip him off the deck into the weeds. Scary. "And what did I say about homophobic garbage? I won't stand for it." He pushes his feet even harder into Craig's throat, and I feel this little twinge inside of me. I'm not a proponent of violence, but … Creed's message is a good one. Still, I keep recording. "Leave them alone."

"But the Working Girl—" the first year chick sputters, and Creed's eyes, normally half-lidded and lazy, snap up to her, sharp with rage. She retreats back a few steps and pinches her glossy red lips closed. A moment later, Tristan appears in the doorway with Ileana on his arm. She's giggling and flirting until she sees her brother on the ground.

"Craig!" She pushes away from Tristan and stumbles forward, knocking Creed out of the way in her frenzy. As he bumps into me, my hand sneaks into his pocket and fishes out his keys. They're in my own pocket before he realizes who he's just bumped into, turning to look at me. He's panting with rage, but he quickly closes his eyes, takes several deep breaths, and banishes the emotion. When he opens them back up, they're the same lazy, insouciant eyes I'm used to.

As he stares at me, I lean down and switch out my flats for the heels he bought me last year, the ones with the gold moon and silver star designs.

"What do you think you're doing here?" Tristan asks as Craig pushes up to his feet, choking and glaring at Creed. A good fourth of the crowd actually seems to be sympathetic towards him. Nice. *This should have been my seventh rule: Create a divide between the Plebs and the Bluebloods.* Craig Taittinger, as haughty and arrogant as he is, is still nothing but a Plebeian in the Burberry Prep social scene.

"Me?" I ask, sauntering up to Tristan and putting my hands on the front of his wool jacket. I trail them down, palms flat, as Tristan's blade gray gaze narrows. I know what I look like, dripping diamonds, wearing a tight, gold dress and heels. A whole summer of working out and preparing myself for this moment, and it shows. I'm still curvy, but my body is much tighter. He can see it, I know he can. *God, this is so weird,* I think as I curl my fingers around the edges of his pockets. As far as I can tell, there are no keys inside.

I'll have to look elsewhere.

"I'm here to party." I push Tristan back, and he stumbles. But only because he's not expecting the move. As Zayd watches us, still gaping, his eyes following me inside the door, I take off for the drink table and pour myself a beer. No way in hell I'm going to actually drink it, but when I see Harper du Pont glaring at me from across the crowd, I lift my cup in salute and pretend to take a chug. She sneers at me, but I just smile, waiting for Andrew, Miranda, and Jessie to catch up with me.

"What was *that* all about?" Miranda gasps, looking at me like she's never seen me before. "Was that part of your revenge plot?"

"It just happened," I say, which is true. It did. But there are certain ways to play this game, tips and tricks to set the Idols versus the Inner Circle, the Plebs versus the Bluebloods. When Harper's gaze is safely averted, I dump my beer in the sink and fill the cup with water. Next time she looks, I really do chug the entire cup in one go, getting a few stray cheers from some first years who don't quite know who I am yet.

"Well, that was scary," Miranda says, exhaling and running her hands down the front of her dress. "Jessie, drink? I know I could use one." Miranda starts mixing up two cocktails in red plastic cups while I peek out the back door and see, surprisingly, that the pool isn't in use. It's covered up with a tarp, but there's water pooled on the top along with heaps of dead leaves, weighing it down so that it sags into the pool water. As surreptitiously as I can, I refill my cup.

I look back at Andrew.

"What are you planning?" he asks me, and I shrug. I'm sort of playing things by ear. I mean, I have a list, but … this is much better, this new idea I'm cooking up. "What do you need from me?"

"Can you help me find Tristan's and Zayd's keys?" I ask, and he raises both brows before Zayd pops into the kitchen and interrupts us. It's awkward as hell when he pauses next to me and sighs, holding a beer bottle in his tattooed right hand. He clears his throat and tosses his chin in the direction of the living room.

"Beat it, Payson," he says, and Andrew frowns, but exchanges a quick look with me before heading in the direction of the staircase. I'm hoping he's off to find Tristan's keys. I turn my attention to Zayd. He returns my stare with a hard one of his own, his hand tightening even harder around the bottle. The motion makes his tattoos look like they're liable to slide right off his skin like stickers. "Marnye, come on, what are you doing here?"

"I'm partying," I say, tipping the drink to my lips and swallowing a huge mouthful. Zayd raises his pierced brow at me, teasing his right lip ring with his tongue. He's painfully beautiful, especially with that silver-gray hair of his. It's spiked up with gel, and as I watch, he reaches up to tease it with his fingers.

"Did you think last year was a joke? It was a warm-up session, Marnye. You shouldn't be here."

"So you keep saying," I retort, taking another sip of my water. Zayd frowns hard, and tips his beer back. *Irresistible* by Fall Out Boy and Demi Lovato comes on, and I smile. I don't know a lot of pop songs, but this is one of Miranda's favorites. She puts it on a lot when we're getting ready. "But what are you going to do about it? Is there a medal for destroying me a second time, something to hang up beside your trophy?"

Zayd just stares at and then chucks his beer into the sink. When he steps forward suddenly, I'm so surprised that I move back, my butt bumping into the counter. He puts a hand on either side of me, effectively penning me in. I can smell him now, that sweet tobacco and cloves scent that had me swooning last year. Then I remember that he brought a camera into my room to film us while we made out.

Piece of shit.

"You don't want to know what the Club will do to you if you don't leave," he threatens, using his rockstar purr of a voice. It gives me the chills all over, but I ignore the feeling and narrow my eyes. "What *I* will do to you if you don't leave." He puts a palm on my hip, but I shove his arm off, simultaneously diving into the back pocket of his jeans with one hand while I grab his face with the other.

You can do this, Marnye, you are so badass! I tell myself, but still … doesn't make this any easier. I kiss Zayd hard and fast, pushing my tongue between his lips at the same time I swipe his car keys. He groans and leans into me, putting his hand back on my hip and squeezing.

Oh my god, no. He tastes so damn good. My body melts into Zayd's even as my heart and soul remain hard as stone, unyielding and immovable. But those damn hormones … With a gasp, I shove away from Zayd, and stumble, spilling my water all over the floor. I ignore it, crushing the cup under my heels as I flee the room.

Fighting my way through the crowd, I somehow find my way over to Zack.

He takes one look at my face and curses.

"They're still getting to you," he growls at me as I stand there with my face flushed, feeling weirdly alien in my short dress and heels. I just look up at him, and I have no idea what to say. That it sucks to be crushing on the very same people you hate? That I know I'm an idiot, that I should be an emotionless badass in a catsuit, as tough and capable as my favorite urban fantasy character.

But I'm not.

"I … I need Tristan's car keys, and a serious distraction," I choke out, and Zack raises his dark brows at me. I cannot even *believe* I'm asking him for help, but there it is. He just stares at me for a moment, and then nods. Without a word, he pushes past me and then pauses when Andrew appears, breathless and holding out a jangling set of keys in his palm. "Thank you," I tell him, feeling a rush of adrenaline spike through me. I look to Zack, and he smiles with tight lips, pushing forward and finding John Hannibal in the crowd.

John turns to look at him, scowling slightly, and then Zack just hauls back and punches him right in the face.

"Fight!" someone screams, and the crowd surges toward that single point in the room, jostling me and Andrew in the process. I take his hand and push in the opposite direction, toward the back doors and the swimming pool. Once we're outside, I kick off my shoes and take off running, hauling Andrew along with me.

"Make sure nobody comes out here," I tell him, heading straight for Tristan's dad's Ferrari Spider. For some reason, I want to fuck with him first. Exhaling sharply, and holding strong to that red-hot thread of revenge inside of me, I climb into the driver's seat, start the vehicle and use it like a bumper car, slamming into the other students' rides indiscriminately. I don't go too hard or too fast, just enough to scrape, scratch, and ding as many as I can without making too much noise.

When I get to the edge of the pool, I climb out, put the car in neutral, and then move around behind to push it. Andrew starts to come toward me, but I shake my head, and he goes inside the house. At first, I can't figure out what he's up to, but then I hear the volume of the music crank up a few notches. A grin takes over my face as I step back and watch the eighteen *million* dollar car drive right over the edge, and into the swimming pool.

Believe me, this is an Olympic sized swimming pool, made of pure cash. It's huge, as long as the house is, with fountains and water slides, faux coves and caves and bits of aesthetically pleasing rock. There's plenty of room for a car. Or two. Or three.

I don't let myself enjoy the sight for too long, heading back for Creed's Bentley next. I do the same thing, scraping it along the other vehicles, and leaving it floating in the water with the windows rolled down. I'm not sure how long it'll take to sink (pretty sure it only takes a few minutes), but I don't care. Just seeing it partially submerged in water is enough.

Zayd's car is last, and by the time I'm letting that roll over the edge, both Andrew and Zack are standing on the back patio watching.

Zayd is not far behind.

"Holy … what the fuck?!" he screams as I stand there on the edge of the pool, barefoot and frowning. I don't smile as I pick up my shoes from the pavement and watch him stumble over to the edge of the water. The cars are very quickly disappearing beneath the surface. "Jesus Christ, are you fucking insane?!"

"You can't go around hurting people and expect to just get away with it," I tell him, glad that the kiss is already fading from my mind. I feel better now, more in control. I curl my hands into fists as Zayd drops to his knees next to the pool.

"My dad is going to flay me," he groans, putting his hands over his face.

"Babe?" Becky asks as she steps out the back door. She gasps and clamps a hand over her mouth as I flip open the top on my purse and dig around inside. "Oh my god. Oh my freaking god. Harper! Tristan!" Becky stumbles outside in her four inch stilettos and turns to look at me, face aghast with horror. "You psycho bitch," she snarls, blond curls billowing in the wind. I reach into my purse, grab the fancy scissors I bought from the salon, and then reach up and chop a huge hunk of her hair off at the scalp.

She screams and stumbles back toward the edge of the pool. It doesn't take much for me to reach over and push her in.

Miranda and Jessie appear just as the splash dissipates and Becky comes gasping to the surface, hauling herself over the edge. Zayd helps her up, but then just leaves her lying soggy and wet on the pavement as he turns to me. The edge of my lip quirks up in a half-smile, and I shrug one shoulder.

"I give as good as I get," I say, just as Tristan, Harper, Creed, and Ileana appear in the doorway. I wonder if she's going to be the next female Idol, taking Gena Whitley's place. At this point, I really don't care. I chuck the scissors in the pool, reach into my bra, and grab Andrew's keys. "Guys, you ready to go?"

Miranda makes a tiny squeaking sound and nods, grabbing Jessie by the arm and dragging her towards the Lambo. Andrew follows, and Zack pauses beside me, watching as I take in the Idols and their gaping faces. Even Tristan is wide-eyed, his face stricken. Actually, Creed seems the calmest. He turns to look at me, much like his sister did, like he's never seen me before.

"Do you have any idea what you've just done?" he asks, sounding as bored as he ever does. I meet his blue gaze, and ignore the little thrill that travels through me. I chalk it up to adrenaline. I'm practically dripping with it right now. "We report you and you're done. Permanently."

"Right," I say, pulling my journal out and cracking the

lock. As the party filters outside and the music stops, I scribble some things down inside before looking back up again. "Tell the administration how I somehow single-handedly got these three cars that you're not supposed to have, in the pool of a house we're not supposed to be at, surrounded by alcohol we're not supposed to be drinking, and see if that does the trick. Maybe I'll be expelled, maybe not. How satisfying would that win be for you?"

Several students lift up their phones and start recording, so I stop talking. I won't say anything else. I don't need to: Creed's face tells me everything I need to know. His shoulders stiffen, his jaw tightens, and his heavy-lidded eyes narrow to slits.

Without waiting another beat, I turn and head back to Andrew's car with Zack on my heels. Just before I climb in, I look at him, standing so close I can feel the heat of his body. He smells like citrus and musk, and my heart skips a few beats. I look up into his dark gaze.

"Thank you, but ... this doesn't change anything." He digs his hands into his pockets and shrugs his shoulders.

"I know. It's fine." He nods; I nod.

And then I climb in the Lamborghini and drive away.

When I get back to the academy, I change my clothes, wash the makeup from my face and the hairspray from my hair, and then I report the Bluebloods for drinking.

Oh, and their breathalyzers ... don't exactly zero out.

CHAPTER

5

My mind is focused on one thing above all else: college. That's why I'm here, suffering through this nightmare of a school. Burberry Prep will give me the best possible future, the greatest chance at a good life. So I've upped my game, and by the end of the second week, I've added a second language (Spanish) to my class roster, and tacked on a few extracurricular activities. I'm now part of the academy's book club, history club, and the model UN. The one place I am lacking in, however, is in sports.

Today, I'm going to make up for that.

Cheerleading tryouts are taking place in a special gymnasium once used to house the academy's gymnastics team. Since moving toward more academically focused endeavors, the school retired their gymnastics program and left the building more or less abandoned for close to a decade. This year, with the addition of Zack to the varsity football team, Burberry Prep is looking to dip its toes in the proverbial waters of sports.

This includes revamping the cheerleading team.

It's no longer going to be used as a sideline sport for football or basketball, but instead as a competition team, something to earn merits in its own right. For the first few football games of the season, the team remained unchanged from last year, but with Principal Collins putting pressure on the coach, she's having to open up the ranks.

Now, Burberry Prep is a snobby, academic-based school. Cheerleading is almost seen as a bit … basic. But while Harper and Becky have no interest in signing up, the rest of the Blueblood girls are not beyond the allure. So when I walk in with my gym bag over my shoulder, all eyes are on me.

Including Zack's.

He's standing in the center of a cluster of girls, smiling sweet as pie. The expression on his face puts a frown on mine, even as he separates himself from the team and they let out a collective groan. Ileana, in particular, is glaring daggers at me. Kiara, too. Maybe they're pissed that I single-handedly sent all three Idol boys, both remaining Idol girls, and half the Inner Circle to in-school suspension. It starts on Fridays right after class ends, and consists of school-related chores like stocking books in the library, dusting shelves, sweeping leaves, and scrubbing windows. From Friday evening until late Sunday, the in-school suspension students are locked down by staff members with brief nine hour breaks to sleep—and even then, they're checked on twice a night.

Basically, it's hell on earth.

"What are you doing in here?" I whisper as Zack comes up to stand beside me, towering over me like he always does. I know it's not on purpose, but it's intimidating. I refuse to let it get to me, and lift my chin in defiance, trying to make myself feel a little taller.

"Well, I *really* didn't expect you to be in here, so you can't claim I'm stalking you." He tucks his hands in his pockets and just stares at me. I can feel his gaze like a heated laser, searching across my face, seeking … something. It bugs me, but I also refuse to back down. "I'm a guest judge for tryouts." He shrugs his shoulders again, as if that makes it all better.

"*You* are a guest judge?" I ask, and I get a rare smirk from him, this sensual twisting of lips that makes me realize so very quickly why all those girls are swooning over there. Zack leans in close, putting his forearm on the wall above my head. He's all around me in that moment, hard muscles and musky smelling cologne. My lashes flutter, and I exhale past the hormones. Last year, they got me into trouble. This year, I won't let that happen again. "What makes you qualified to judge cheerleading?"

"Um, my sister Kelsey was the head of the Burberry Prep cheerleading team." Zack leans in a little closer, his letterman jacket falling open in the front, encompassing me. It'd be so easy for him to scoop me up and bundle me inside of it. That is, if I didn't hate his guts. "Also, my mom went through a spell where she was tired of being more than a boring ass trophy wife; she coached for like three seasons."

"I see …" I exhale, and blink a few times to clear away the cobwebs. I'd really like him to move away from me, but I feel like I can't say it. I don't want him to know how his presence is affecting me. "So … you'll make sure I get on the team then?"

Zack's brows go up, and a dark chuckle reverberates through him. I swear, I can feel it vibrating the air molecules between us.

"Are you asking me for help in your revenge plot?" He pauses for a second and shakes his head. "Not that you've needed much help thus far. Sinking the cars, that was brilliant. And Becky is *still* crying over her hair."

"Get me on the team," I tell him, staying firm. When he reaches out to touch a stray strand of rose gold hair, that's when I call it quits, ducking underneath his arm and putting my back to the room. Zack watches me and sighs, dropping his hand to his side.

"Done." The smirk disappears from his mouth and he frowns at me again. My mind conjures up an image of him dumping a garbage can full of used feminine products on my desk, and I almost throw up. I started my period earlier than most of the other girls, and I was mercilessly destroyed for it. Just one of the many, many things he did to me. I'll never forget that. "That is, I can fix my vote, and I can probably convince Amy to give you some good marks." The way he smiles when he says that tells me he thinks very highly of himself with the ladies. But then the frown's back as quick as the smile came. "Other than that, you're on your own. Do you know anything at all about cheerleading?"

My turn to vaguely shrug my shoulders.

"I was busy this summer," I tell him cryptically, turning and heading into the center of the gym. I push right through the crowd of girls, ignoring the whispered insults, and then lean down to sign the form on the table. The coach blinks at me in surprise and raises her eyebrows, but she doesn't say anything, just hands me a number, and tells me to get in line.

Zack takes his place behind the table as Coach Hannah explains how tryouts are going to work. The only girls who are here are the ones who were on the team before, plus a few first years like Ileana. That's it.

I'm the only outlier.

The only hated one.

"You're going to wish you'd never trashed my brother *or* my pool," Ileana whispers as she takes up my right side, and Kiara stands on my left.

"Did you really think Tristan was into you?" Kiara asks, scowling in my direction. Her dark hair is slicked back into a tight bun, making her face seem even more severe. It takes every ounce of effort I have not to imagine her bent over that counter in the bathroom. "He never liked you. He's on his way to being one of the most powerful men in the world. Did you really think some commoner trash like you would satisfy him?"

I ignore her as the coach speaks quietly with her assistant for a moment. My eyes meet Zack's from across the room. His gaze is so dark, so unreadable. It makes me want to pry it open and see what's going on inside. My original plan had been to destroy his football career. But I'm still not sure how to go about doing that without injuring him, and I refuse to hurt anyone physically. I nibble on my bottom lip as Kiara leans in close to me, frustrated with my lack of response to her taunts.

Once upon a time, the Marnye Reed I used to be would've felt those barbs deep down in her soul. She would've bled on the inside, cried on the out, and gone home to curl into a ball on her bed. Not anymore. Not ever again.

"How many times did you spread your whore legs for him before he dumped you like the useless slut you are?" Anger flares sharp and hot inside of me, but I ignore it. Kiara elbows me as hard as she can in the side, and I grunt, but before I can retaliate, Coach is turning back to face us.

Damn it!

Exhaling against the pain in my ribs, I listen to her instructions and toss my bag aside. I'm already dressed in my PE sweats and tank top, a sports bra, and sneakers. *I can do this.* I spent all summer working out, swimming, running. I'm in the best shape of my life.

We start with a warm up that I'm totally self-conscious about thanks to Zack. I can feel his eyes watching my every movement, tracing the beads of sweat on my forehead, the moisture sticking my shirt to my body. He leans forward, eyes heavy lidded but nowhere near as lazy as Creed. Instead, he looks … interested. My heart thunders as I struggle to keep up with the assistant coach and her quick, strong movements.

By the time it's over, I feel like I might pass out. The pain in my ribs is killing me, and I'm pretty sure if I had a knife, I'd stab both Kiara and Ileana. One is dark-haired, fair-skinned, and slender while the other is pale-haired, tan-skinned, and curvy. I hate them both equally. They flank me as I drink from my water bottle, and I make sure to stay out of their reach. Their eyes, however, follow me around the room, and when I step away from my water, I'm pretty sure they mess with it.

Sigh.

Since it's Friday, they both have their phones and they make no attempts to hide the fact that they're using them.

I'm assuming it's to text the Idols, because we're just getting ready to line up to learn the dance when the gym doors open, and Tristan walks in with Harper at his side. She's spitting mad, but nowhere near the level that Becky's at. The way she glares at me ... looks might not be able to kill, but I can feel the hatred on my skin like the searing heat of a scorching sun. My flesh feels like it's liable to peel off under her gaze.

She's got her long, blond hair tucked up in a bun, but it's impossible to miss the naked patch on the left side of her scalp. Harper might not know it, but she's next. I don't know how or when, but it's totally happening.

Zayd follows in behind Becky, his jaw so tight it looks like he might crack his teeth. His tattoos are bright and colorful, tracing their way up his muscular arms and disappearing briefly under the thin sleeve of his black wife beater. He's got on baggy jeans with zippers stitched across them, and Doc Martens. Basically, he's the opposite of Tristan with his freshly pressed white academy slacks, flawless jacket, and super straight tie.

Creed is somewhere in the middle, the top two buttons of his shirt undone, a pair of jeans and Barker Blacks paired with it. They might not technically be doing in-school suspension anymore, but they're also not allowed off-campus until after *Halloween.* If they're caught breaking that rule, it's an automatic expulsion.

I smile.

I've really fucked their party schedule up.

The Idols take a seat on the bleachers, a cadre of Bluebloods behind them. I recognize the usual suspects: Myron Talbot, Ebony Peterson, Gregory Van Horn, John Hannibal, Valentina Pitt, Sai Patel, and Jalen Donner.

The remaining girls: Anna, Abigail, and Mayleen are all here trying out for the team.

Looks like they have yet to find a replacement for Andrew, and I already know Ileana is Miranda's replacement. Great. So … the party's all here then?

It's impossible not to feel their eyes on me as I take my place in the center of the group. There's a visible amount of extra space around me, like I'm some sort of leper. I ignore it and focus on the dance moves instead. Well … the dance moves … and Zack's eyes.

There's something about his dark gaze that draws me in, focuses me. At first, it bothers me so much that I stumble and mess up the steps. Laughter bubbles up from the bleachers, but I ignore it. My attention becomes laser focused on the way Zack's watching me, his lips parting slightly, his lids getting heavier and heavier. At one point, he even runs his tongue across his lower lip, catches himself doing it, and curses. Amy Plumber, a fourth year seated next to him, jumps a whole foot in her seat, and I feel a grin split my lips.

We go over the dance several times before coach calls for another break. After this, we'll come out in groups of three and perform it in a row. Scores will be passed out, and after, members will be chosen for the team. I have to get on it. I have to invade their spaces. By lifting myself up, I put them down. And that's their own problem. My success should have nothing to do with them, but it pisses the Bluebloods off. Infuriates them. When I succeed, they feel like they've failed. If that's how they want to live their lives, I'm okay with that.

During the next water break, the entire crew heads over to worship at the Idols' feet, leaving me alone with the bottles, duffel bags, and an entire span of time where nobody is looking.

Kiara's orange bag, and Ileana's black one are right next to me. Bending down, I move my own bag, so that it looks like I'm digging through it. Instead, I search through theirs. Kiara's is empty save for her clothes and some condoms. But in Ileana's ... there's a half-empty bottle of ex-lax.

I *knew* she was up to something over here.

That bitch.

A shadow moves over me, and I jump, but it's just Zack.

"Do it, quick," he tells me, using his huge body to block me from the view of the Idols. While I've got a chance, I quickly dump Ileana's water into my own duffel bag, hoping the moisture resistant material will hide what I've done. It's worth the sacrifice. I pour the remainder of my own water into her bottle, and let fate take its course. If she hasn't messed with my water, she'll be fine.

If she has, she's screwed, and it's her own damn fault.

Zack moves out of the way just as I place Ileana's bottle back, and she appears on his left side.

I sit down and change out of my sneakers, grabbing a pair of socks that've managed to escape the water fiasco, and pretend like this is what I was doing all along. Ileana chugs her water and wipes her arm across her mouth as I stand up.

She moves toward us, a horrid smirk twisting her pretty features into something ugly.

She doesn't get a single word out before Zack is inserting himself between us and moving me behind him. I don't need his help, and frown, but he does it anyway.

"What? Are you her pet now, too?" Ileana asks, tossing her long, blond ponytail. "She spread her legs for you nice and good?"

"You should shut your mouth," Zack whispers, his voice so dark and cruel that I shiver. *"You should kill yourself, Marnye. Nobody would care. In fact, we'd have a party celebrate."* My mind shuts that down quick, locks the bad memory away, and tosses the key. That's the last thing I need to be thinking about right now. "And keep it closed before you say something that really pisses me off."

"What, you gonna hit me or something?" Ileana asks, stepping forward and getting in Zack's face. I move around to stand beside him and catch a glimpse of the darkness that skirts across his expression. It's ominous and chilly, and I realize then that the side of himself he turned on me is still very much there, crouching inside of him like a demon waiting in the shadows.

"No, but you'll wish I had, when I'm done with you." He looks her up and down, and then grins. Only it's not like a grin I've ever seen from him, not even when he was making my life a living hell at LBMS. No, this is glee in the maliciousness, something he never displayed to me before. "Why don't you tell everyone why you have those bruises on your inner arms? What sort of naughty things did you get into this summer? Because those are most definitely needle marks."

"I had tests done," Ileana blurts, but her face is reddening, and I can't tell if she's just embarrassed or if Zack is telling the truth.

"What kind of tests?" Zack presses, stepping even closer and putting his hands on her upper arms. Ileana shivers, but when she scowls, it's as nasty an expression as it ever was. "Surely, that'd be an easy question to answer … if you were actually telling the truth. What was it, really? Meth? Heroin? Careful, Ileana, your trailer park is showing." Her eyes widen, and I can see Zack's struck a nerve. He's good at that, though, and I get no pleasure out of watching him destroy someone else with his special talent. No, it hits too close to home. As awful as Ileana is, I can't watch this anymore. "Did you know her parents got cut off from their fortune once, just like I did? They ended up in a trailer park, high on drugs and out of their—"

"Zack." Just that one word from my mouth, harsh and final. *Rule #6: Know when enough is enough.* "Go back to the judges' table."

He stares at me for a moment, and then moves around Ileana.

I reach for her water bottle, but she jerks it out of my hand and spits on me. Literally. Spits right into my palm.

"Keep your grubby whore hands to yourself. The last thing I want is to get chlamydia."

"No, you're more likely to catch that from Tristan," I blurt into the silence. This tension settles over the room as Coach walks back inside with a duffel bag bursting with pom poms.

93

She sets it aside as I turn and meet Tristan's gray gaze from across the room. He's stoic and unmoving, looking at me like I'm a fly that needs to be pinned to a board and left to squirm.

I stare right back.

Ileana tips her water bottle to her lips and drinks deeply. She makes a weird face, and I wonder if the ex-lax has a taste. Unfortunately for her, she doesn't seem to make the connection.

Coach assigns her, me, and Kiara (go figure) into a group for the official tryout portion. Ileana doesn't make it through two minutes before she grabs her stomach and flashes me a look of terror. I don't stop dancing as she runs off toward the restrooms.

I'm not sure when she comes back, but when she does, I've already been measured for my uniform.

On my way out of the gym, I meet the stare of every Blueblood in that room—paying special attention to the three Idol guys—and then I flip them off and head outside into the starlight.

CHAPTER

6

By the time Parents' Week rolls around again, the Idols have made their decision: they've welcomed Ileana Taittinger into their ranks, promoted Kiara Xiao into the Inner Circle to take Miranda's place, and reluctantly chosen a fourth year named Ben Thresher to replace Andrew.

Their circle of arrogance, assholery, and privilege is once again complete.

The bullying has amped up again, too. We're back to condoms in my locker, stickers on my door, bags of dog shit on my welcome mat. But it's difficult for them to hit back at me where it counts, not with the heightened security on campus. They're going to have to try harder if they want to match me blow for blow.

"Something doesn't feel right," I tell Miranda on Sunday, staring at my phone and hating the butterflies in my stomach. Dad is coming back to the academy. This freaking academy where I was humiliated beyond belief. I hate that he had to see me like that; it kills me inside. Plus … if I said I wasn't still ashamed that he got drunk last time he was here, that would be a lie.

I'm nervous.

I'm terrified.

If the Idols wanted to find my weak spot, well, Charlie is it. Charlie is my beating heart, and if they do a damn thing to hurt him, I swear I'll kill them all. Closing my eyes, I exhale and then open them to find Miranda staring at me.

"Doesn't feel right, how?" she asks, lounging in a baggy pink sweater that looks worn and comfy but which I'm pretty sure is cashmere and costs like two hundred bucks. "Classes? Parents' Week? Cheerleading?" She grins at that last one. Miranda is beyond thrilled that I'm on the team with her girlfriend, Jessie. Well, I think they're dating anyway. Miranda's been pretty wishy-washy about it.

"The Bluebloods are too subdued," I say, sitting down on the end of my bed with a sigh. "I'm throwing everything I have at them, and they're just … sitting there. It's creepy, and it's making me nervous, and I'm starting to think they're planning something big." Miranda puts her phone down and pinches her lips tight.

"I'm not going to say you're wrong …" she starts, and then grimaces. "I mean, there's a good chance you're dead-on with your assessment. They've been quiet, but when they hit you, it's going to hurt." I nod. Pretty much what I expected. Actually, I expected worse. It's a strange form of psychological terror knowing they're holding back on me.

"How's Creed been doing?" I ask, trying to sound super casual. In reality, I want to hear that he's suffering, that he felt he made a mistake, that he—

"Dating that awful Valentina girl," Miranda spits, practically choking on the words. She tucks some blond hair behind her ear. "He stole her from John Hannibal, but only because it was a game. He doesn't like her."

"That doesn't seem to matter much around here," I murmur, touching a finger to the ice-blue dress in my closet, the one Creed sent me for the graduation gala, the dance where I definitely did not choose him. Thinking about it now, I wonder if I made a mistake, if I should've refused to pick between the boys and— Groaning, I lean my forehead against the door of the wardrobe. Really? I'm concerned about Creed's and Tristan's feelings *now*, after everything? How they felt when I walked in that room holding Zayd's hand is freaking irrelevant.

I slam the wardrobe closed and turn around.

"Is she the prettiest? Does she have the most money? Is her family name old and well-established? Can her parents' company get something from your parents' company, or vice versa? Because those all seem to be more important reasons than *love* or even *like* when it comes to marrying for the super-rich."

"Probably something to do with the stupid Club," Miranda scoffs, flicking her finger across her phone screen. Pretty sure she's on Tinder, scoping out girls. Now that we're both cool with her coming out, she's been obsessing over girls the way I obsessed over the Idol boys last year. I wonder if I was that sappy and hormone ridden? Yep, yep, I definitely was. "My dad actually wants me to join it. My mom says no way." She glances up and lets a soft smile fall across her lips. "You know, she's excited to see you tomorrow."

I grimace and turn away. I will *never* forget Kathleen Cabot's face on that awful day, the way she looked at her son, like he was the scum of the earth, the way she fell on her knees in the principal's office and cried while apologizing to me. According to Kathleen, I was *her* student, *her* responsibility, so how could she let this happen? I don't blame her at all, but I know she blames herself.

"Yeah, I'm excited to see her, too …" I trail off and check my phone, tapping my thumb against the side. A whole year ago, Zack appeared from the back of that academy car, climbing out behind my dad. He helped him when he was drunk, and he told me … *"Your dad got some news last night."* An entire year later, and I still don't know what that news is, and Dad's acting weirder than ever. He's still trying to force a relationship with Jennifer, and he gave me Grandma's bracelet with his wedding band on it … I don't like it, not any of it.

I tap out a quick message to Zack: *Meet me in The Mess.*

He responds almost instantly: *Already there. Join me?*

"Hey," I say suddenly, lifting my gaze up to meet Miranda's blue one. "I'm going to go talk to Zack in The Mess for a while. Are you okay in here?"

"I'll hang out and wait for you," she says, leaning back into my pillows and making herself comfy. I grab a sweater and leave her there, knowing that the cameras will catch any suspicious activity. I want with all my heart to believe Miranda's innocent in everything that's gone on here at Burberry Prep, but I don't think I can know that for sure, not just yet. If she does nothing while I'm gone, that'll help go a long way towards easing my distrust.

I make my way through the halls as quick as I can. As much as I'm ready to stand up to the Bluebloods, I can't fight off a dozen people by myself. Fortunately, I manage to slip into the dining hall without anyone seeing me.

Zack's the only one there, sitting by himself at a table near the window. I make my way over and flop down in the seat across from him. His dark eyes lift up from his plate, but only briefly before he refocuses on his food. He's a huge guy, and he works out constantly, so that means he also eats like a horse. He's polite about it, but it's almost fascinating to see how quickly he can make food disappear.

"This is unusual," he says finally, after we've sat in silence for several minutes, and I've placed my order with the waiter. Tonight I'm having steak with chimichurri butter, asparagus, and garlic cheddar biscuits. Fancy.

"What is?" I ask, my heart beating as he sits up and slips out of his letterman jacket, revealing a tight white wifebeater underneath. It looks like it's about to rip in half it's so tight. Or maybe that's just wishful thinking? Why does Zack have to have such rock-hard biceps and broad shoulders? It's infuriating.

"You, coming to see me." He sets his fork down and then signals the waiter over with a dessert menu. Have I mentioned how amazing the desserts are here? They serve things like *crème brûlée* and *tiramisu* and *bread pudding*. All so very fancy. Back home in the Train Car with Dad, dessert is about as eclectic as dinner: pudding cups from the fridge, brownies from the bakery section of the supermarket, or if we're feeling adventurous then ice cream from the shop down the road. "What's up?"

I consider thanking him for helping me get on the team, but then I remember the cruel darkness in his eyes when he laid into Ileana, and I'm just not sure I have it in me. Leaning forward, I put my palms on the table and school my face into the most serious expression I can manage.

"Last year, when Dad got drunk during Parents' Week, what did he tell you?" Zack goes completely still, his dark eyes lifting up to mine. There's something strange about the way he's looking at me that makes my stomach flip over with nausea. It's bad. Whatever it is, it's so, so bad.

"He hasn't told you?" he asks carefully, and I almost choke on my water as I struggle to take a sip. I push the glass aside and lean even farther forward.

"Zack, what the hell is going on?" He lets out a string of frustrated curses, and then sits back suddenly in the chair, running his palm over his short, dark hair. He looks like he wants to throw something. His teeth are clenched tight, his right hand is gripping the table for dear life, and I swear there's a bead of sweat that forms on his temple and runs down the side of his face. "You're scaring me."

He looks at me for a long moment, and then sighs.

"I can't lie to you, but I can't tell you the whole truth either. For that, you'll have to talk to your dad." He leans back in his chair and just looks at me, this dark, broody asshole thing going on that I shouldn't like, but sort of do anyway. *He's as bad as the rest of them,* I remind myself, *worse maybe.* "You know your parents are having an affair, right?"

I just stare at him unblinking for several seconds.

"Come again?"

"Charlie and Jennifer are seeing each other behind Adam Carmichael's back." He smiles tightly, but there's no warmth there. Sympathy, maybe, but that's it. My mouth opens, closes, opens again. No words come out though. How the hell does Zack know that? Why would my dad confide something like that in him?

I decide to ask.

"Don't take this the wrong way, but ... how do you know that?" I lean forward, putting my forearms on the table. Zack watches me carefully, like he's trying to absorb my every movement. The attention makes me feel fidgety, and I wiggle in my seat, refusing to think about that time I wiggled in Creed's lap ... Ahem. "I mean, why would my dad tell something like that to a high school student?"

"He didn't." Zack shrugs his massive shoulders. That seems to be his go-to response to everything. "I came over once to help him fix a leak in the roof and walked in on them ..."

He trails off, and I add with a dry note to my voice, "kissing?"

Zack raises his dark brows at me, but then smiles a little.

"Something like that. Anyway, he said they were in love and they'd been seeing each other." Zack looks down at his empty plate as the waiter comes back to deliver my food and take his dessert order. Then, of course, he clams up and leans back in his seat, like that's all there is to say on the matter.

"So the news he received ...?" Because even *if* Zack is telling the truth—which I'm not sure of—then what drove my dad to drink during Parents' Week last year? Clearly, he would already be aware that he was having an affair with Jennifer, even though it's news that would drive *me* to drink. "Maybe … she was going back to that Carmichael guy?" Zack just stares at me, and I groan in frustration.

"That's all you're going to tell me, isn't it?"

He smiles, and it's a much prettier smile, so much so that I feel a bead of sweat run down my spine. Yikes. I'm not entirely sure he's ever smiled at me like that before.

"Are you excited for your first game?" he asks me, and I narrow my eyes. Coach Hannah has been working us *hard* for the last week, and I expect that even though this is Parents' Week, she's going to be working us just as hard, if not harder. Newbies weren't allowed to cheer at Friday's game, but Parents' Week culminates with the final game of the season for Burberry Prep's new all-star football team. Just adding Zack to varsity has shaken up the entire school; it's like we actually have some pride in sports now. Of course, the cheerleading team is so green there is no JV/varsity distinction at this point, but that's not why I joined. I don't actually care for sports at all.

"Mm." I make a non-committal noise and Zack chuckles, picking up his fork to poke at his tiramisu. What spoiled brats this school breeds. The only time I've ever had tiramisu was when Dad worked two weekend jobs to save up to take me out to a fancy Italian dinner to celebrate making the honor roll in middle school. So yeah, it's been years. I decide the next time the waiter pops over, I'll order some, too.

Because not only am I going to make honor roll again, I'm

going to steamroll right over Tristan to do it.

"I'll be playing extra hard, knowing you're there to cheer me on," Zack purrs—yeah, really, *purrs*—and I frown. If I didn't hold myself to higher standards, I'd break his knee cap so he'd be forced to sit out the game, and miss out on the scouts that are supposed to be showing up. Zack Brooks doesn't need scouts though, nobody at this school does. If any one of them actually decides to play for a university, it'll just be for fun. None of these guys is actually interested in a career in the NFL. NFL players are poor compared to the net worth of the average Burberry Prep players' family.

"Oh, trust me," I tell him as I pick up my fork and stab it dramatically into my slab of steak. I'm smiling when I cut into it. "I won't be cheering you on. I'm just there for intel. I hear the Idols have gone to every game this year." Lifting my eyes from my plate, I see Zack clenching his jaw. He's moved pieces of his tiramisu around his plate, but has yet to actually eat any of it. A chill travels down my spine. "They hate sports. Last year, they didn't go to a single sporting event, except once or twice to see Gena swim." I cock my head to one side. "And they really hate you, so … I'm guessing this has something to do with the Infinity Club?"

"Haven't you learned your lesson with the Infinity Club?" Zack whispers, and then he's standing up and pushing away from the table. He grabs his letterman jacket off the back of his chair and storms out of the room.

Bingo.

Looks like I hit a nerve.

Zack needs to win this game on Friday, I'll bet.

103

And I really need to have a conversation with Charlie.

The next morning, I'm up bright and early, using the iron in my room to smooth out the pleats in my white skirt and jacket. The second-year uniform is one of my favorites, all of that crisp white linen with just a touch of color in the red of the tie, the shiny black of the shoes, and the little stripes of black and red on the elbows of the jacket and the tops of the socks.

Just for fun, I put on the necklace Tristan gave me. I imagine it'll mess with his head, making him wonder how exactly I ended up getting it back. Knowing that Dad's likely to be late, I hold back and wait to head for the courtyard until I'm sure most of the other students will have cleared out. I'm out for blue blood this year, and I'm willing to take punches to get it, but I won't accept any attacks from those assholes that are directed at my father.

On my way down the hall, I notice that one of the office doors is open. It's of note to me because I come down this way all the time and never once have I seen it open. In fact, it's usually locked. The school staff has officially moved into the new outbuildings, and nobody uses the old chapel offices anymore.

"You've disappointed me, son." I hear a patronizing tone that sets me on edge. It's so frustratingly condescending that it makes my teeth hurt. Even though I know I shouldn't, I end up creeping forward to peep in the glass window on the door.

What I see in there makes me raise my brows.

Tristan's standing with his back straight, his face frozen into an expression of bored disinterest. Unlike Creed, however, he doesn't quite manage to pull it off. Actually, for the first time ever, he looks truly terrified beneath the mask. Even when he saw his dad's car floating in the pool, it wasn't this bad.

Tristan Vanderbilt is scared of something, huh?

Apparently, he's scared of ... his dad?

The man sitting on the edge of the old desk looks like a mature—and if possible *crueler*—version of his son. He's got that same raven-dark hair, those gray eyes, and a smile like a snake. The moment I lay eyes on him, I know he's bad news. Guess the apple doesn't fall far from the tree.

Tristan doesn't say anything, just stands there and stares his father down. There's the slightest quiver in his shoulders that doesn't seem right. Is he actually trembling? That's when I notice the slight glisten of red at the corner of his mouth. Is that ... blood?

"You're right," Tristan says, and that's it, just those two words. His uniform is as perfectly pressed as always, just sharp lines and creases that could cut. His tie is straight, his jacket buttoned, his hair smooth and shiny. But his eyes are disturbingly empty. Even his usual cruelty is missing. "I messed up."

Mr. Vanderbilt sighs and taps his fingers against the leg of his immaculately pressed suit. Just like his son, there's not a single thread, button, or hair out of place. And there's no doubt in my mind that his suit costs more than my father's yearly salary.

"I'm still struggling to understand how my car ended up in a swimming pool."

Tristan flinches, and my heart begins to race. If he hasn't ratted me out yet, he's not going to. But still …

"I told you: it was a senior prank." His voice is cold, empty, dark.

After a moment, Mr. Vanderbilt goes to reach for something in his pocket, and Tristan flinches like he's been struck. But all his dad does is produce a black box with a little crown on the top. He passes it over to his son, and Tristan takes it warily, cracking the top to reveal a black and red Rolex watch. He turns it over and I see a custom engraved infinity symbol on the back.

Well, damn.

"A senior prank?" Mr. Vanderbilt asks as he takes the box back, removes the watch, and gestures for his son to hold out his arm. "And how, exactly, did the seniors get my car out of our garage in Los Angeles?"

Tristan says nothing, just lets his dad put the watch on for him.

"I haven't seen the class rankings posted yet. Have you?" Mr. Vanderbilt's voice just drips with menace; the high cheekbones and straight, ridged nose that look so regal on his son become villainous when he reaches out and snatches Tristan by the tie, yanking him close.

Tristan simply licks the blood from the corner of his mouth and stares his father down.

"You are a Vanderbilt, son. This country was built on our dime and our whims. Do I need to reiterate the shame you bring on our entire family, on the company, when you let yourself lose to commoner trash?"

My mouth drops open, and my entire body goes ice-cold.

Based on Tristan's lack of empathy, I just sort of assumed his family was awful, but seeing it in person? I'm gobsmacked. Despite my dad's many faults, I love him and he loves me. I can't even imagine being treated like this by him. Hell, I can't even imagine Jennifer treating me like this.

"I understand, Father," Tristan whispers as his dad releases him abruptly, and he stumbles.

"Good. Then get out there and check the roster. If I don't like what I see, this isn't going to be a pleasant week for you, son." Tristan nods, and then turns abruptly, heading for the door so quickly that I don't have time to scramble out of the way.

All I manage to do is back away from the door, so that it's somewhat plausible that I was just walking by.

Tristan freezes in place, and a hundred emotions work their way across his face before he shuts them all down and just stares at me with a storm gray gaze.

"Hey." It's the only word that'll come out of my mouth.

After a moment, I hear Mr. Vanderbilt answer his phone, false laughter ringing out from the open door. Tristan pushes it closed with a palm, his chest rising and falling with heavy breaths that don't show on that stoic face of his.

"Are you okay?" I ask, even though I know I shouldn't bother. He was horrible to me, the worst of all the Idols. And yet ... I can't control that small surge of empathy. Tristan turns on me in an instant, storming across the hall. I end up backing up, even though I don't mean to.

He gets right up in my face, jaw clenched, anger surging through him in waves.

Without a word, he reaches up and snatches the necklace from my throat, breaking the chain in the process. My heart is racing so hard and fast that I can barely breathe. When he turns and storms over to the trash can, I'm left gaping as he yanks the Rolex off his wrist and shoves both pieces of jewelry as deep into the bin as he can get them, staining the sleeve of his perfect white jacket with something red that I think is ketchup. But then he sniffles and I realize that blood is actually running from his nose. It drips onto his chest and sleeve as he turns back to face me.

"Do not talk to me, Charity," he snaps, practically grinding his teeth. "Do not look at me. Don't even think about me. If you do, I'll break you worse than Zack did. And I won't be there to make you throw up the pills when I'm done." He spins on his heel and storms down the hallway, leaving me gaping behind him.

What the hell was that all about?!

I flip him off behind his back ... and then I dig through the garbage again.

BAD, BAD BLUE BLOODS

I know things are going to get bad for me this week when I step into the courtyard with the stag statue and the fountain, and find Harper du Pont deep in conversation with my father. Shit, I took too long.

Moving as fast as I can, I close the distance between us and step up beside Charlie with a huge smile on my face.

"Dad."

"Marnye-bear!" he says, giving me a huge hug. It feels so good to be in his arms that for a split-second, I forget that the queen bitch of Burberry Prep Academy is standing right next to us, her glorious brunette hair blowing in the wind. My jaw clenches, but I manage to maintain a grimace, if not an actual smile. "I was just talking to your friend, Harper."

"Well, friend wouldn't quite be the right word." It takes physical effort, but I resist the urge to tell Charlie that Harper is one of the ones who beat me, and that it was on her orders that it happened at all. I had that chance, last year, when I was questioned by the staff. They all saw what the boys did, how they threw the panties, but hardly anything came of it. Ratting the girls out would likely do little to nothing. No, I'll take my own revenge, thank you very much.

As things stand, the only punishment the boys received was a slap on the freaking wrist. They had their honors and letters from first year rescinded, and I'm pretty sure the academy squeezed some fat donations from their parents. Once again, their money saved them from facing any consequences for their actions.

"Oh?" Charlie asks, looking between Harper and me with a confused expression on his gently wrinkled face. Harper smirks at me, but I could give a shit less. Instead, I reach under my shirt and pull out the necklace. When Tristan ripped it from my neck, the clasp snapped, but I simply tied the chain into a knot. Crafty, right?

When her blue eyes land on the pair of roses dangling on the end, I see her face light up with fury.

"Dad, among other ventures, Harper's family runs Myler Medical Technologies," I begin as Harper glares at me. "Her sister took over as CEO about ten years ago, and slowly raised the price of the epinephrine injector pen from fifty dollars per injector to six hundred for a two-pack. It raised the company's profits to a record-level two billion dollars per year, and her own salary to nineteen million." I look from Harper to Charlie. "You know how our neighbor was allergic to bees? And how her insurance wouldn't cover the price difference, so they went without? And then Erica ended up dying from—"

Harper steps so close to me that I actually have to move back a space to keep her from touching me.

"Did your daddy tell you yet how he's got late-stage colon and lung cancer? My family has kindly offered up medical care, free of charge, to help see him through it. Good luck, sweetie." Harper leans in and kisses me on the cheek as my head spins, and I end up sitting on the bricks without even realizing that I've fallen.

My knees are bloody and Dad's trying to talk to me, but I can't hear anything but a ringing in my ears.

Zack is there suddenly, his mother by his side, and they're both trying to help Charlie get me to my feet. I sag in their arms as they lift me up, my head spinning, my stomach twisted with nausea.

"It's not true," I whisper, looking up and into my dad's brown eyes, so like mine that it's as if I'm staring into a mirror. His hair is tousled by the wind, his smile so sweet and genuine that it feels impossible. It's impossible. My dad is not dying. He's not. I refuse to believe it. "Please say it's not true." I'm sobbing now, and Zack's trying to put an arm around me. I jerk away from him and stumble.

"Honey, please sit down," Dad says softly, but I need a minute. I just need one minute. I turn and run across the courtyard, passing a smirking Harper as I go.

"*Please say it's not true,*" she chortles as I sprint past.

My feet skid on the bricks, and I whirl around, tears streaming down my face.

"What did you just say?" I grind out, and Harper tosses her hair.

"You heard me: your dad's dead without my family's charity. Try to be a little grateful, bitch." Red flashes across my vision, and before I can think better of it, I launch myself at Harper. My right fist flies forward and hits her in her pretty face. There's a satisfying crack of cartilage before blood begins to pour from her nose.

I've just broken *Rule #1: No Violence*.

But … my dad …

"Charity!" a familiar voice calls out seconds before Zayd's arms wrap around me from behind. I flail and struggle against him, throwing an elbow back that nails him right in the ribs. He grunts, but his tattooed arms stay tight around me. I hit him again and manage to break free before I'm launching myself at Harper and knocking her to the brick walkway.

"Marnye, stop!" Miranda and Kathleen Cabot appear with Creed close behind. He watches with that bored, lazy look of his as the two women yank me off and haul me back several feet. Harper pushes up to her feet, smirking, blood running over her lips. She looks *happy* about what's just happened.

And then I realize the mistake I've made, and a small, sad sound slips past my lips.

"You are so done, Working Girl," Harper crows, using the post near her to stay upright. I notice that nobody offers a hand out to her. My eyes dart around the gathered crowd, from Dad, Zack, and his mom, Robin, running up to us, and then over to Miranda, Kathleen, and Creed. Zayd is behind me, panting, his uniform as disheveled and wrinkled as always, his tie hanging loose and crooked. "I'm reporting you."

Harper reaches up to rub some blood from her face.

"No, you will not," Kathleen snaps, her voice so fierce that Harper's attention snaps over to her. "There may not be an official report, but I know what you and your little friends did to Marnye last year. She had broken ribs and a cracked tooth. I'm not usually a supporter of an eye-for-an-eye justice, but young lady, if you don't walk away and clean yourself up right now, you'll be expelled right alongside her."

Harper gapes, her attention going from Kathleen to Robin to Charlie, and then back to me.

"That's true, Kathleen: it was Harper. Harper and several of her friends. I wouldn't want to drag anyone else into this." *Pause, breathe, get control of yourself.* "If you talk about my dad again," I whisper, stepping forward so suddenly that Miranda doesn't get a chance to stop me before I spit the words in Harper's face, "you'll be so fucking sorry."

And then I throw Miranda's hands off, push past Zayd and Creed, and disappear into the gardens.

The first person to find me is Zack.

I sigh as he comes around the corner, and stay where I am, huddled on a stone bench and hugging my knees. All I can think about is Dad and how good of a heart he has, and how the world needs more men like him, not less. No, instead people like Mr. Vanderbilt get to thrive and prosper, and Dad works his whole life at jobs he hates, loves a woman who betrayed him, and gets struck down with the most horrible disease known to man.

"I hate cancer," I tell Zack as he sits down beside me, dressed in his uniform with his letterman jacket over the top. He looks too good in it; it's not fair. I want to hate him, but I feel so alone right now. If Dad ... without Dad ... it's just me. I should really go find Miranda and Andrew, talk to them instead. But I just sit there with Zack a few inches away from me, his brown eyes focused on the grass at his feet, his shoulders hunched. "This was the news you didn't want to tell me about, huh?"

He nods, but he doesn't say anything at first. Several minutes pass before he speaks.

"Now all the Idols know. They're going to use Dad against me." Zack purses his lips and sits up, looking over at me with a much softer gaze than usual. On Friday, I'm going to destroy him. I almost feel bad about it. Maybe I should? But I can't forgive him so easily.

"If you ever need dirt on anyone in the Infinity Club, I probably have it. You know my dirt now, and Lizzie's. But there's so much more. You'd be shocked at the things I could tell you."

I scoff at him.

"Maybe, but at what price? What do you want from me, Zack? If it's just guilt that's spurring you on, then you can stop. I don't need your sympathy or your pity."

"It's not pity, Marnye. You're beautiful, you're smart, you're driven. What's there to pity?" He says it all like it's a matter of fact, that of *course* I'm all of those things. I shift, uncomfortable with the praise. If I were a better person, I'd let all of this revenge crap go, transfer to a different prep school and just keep my head buried in my studies.

Something must be seriously wrong with me.

"And guilt? Of course I feel guilt," Zack spits, running his palm over his dark hair. He exhales, and his broad shoulders fold inward, like he's trying to sink into himself. "But that's not why I'm trying to help you."

"Then why are you?" I ask, looking up.

Zack turns to me then, and there's something burning in his gaze that scares the crap out of me.

"Remember when we had our first kiss?" he asks, and I almost choke. "Those feelings … they were terrifying to me. You can't feel like that when you're so young, and I—"

I make a choking sound, and Zack pauses. It's Monday morning, and I haven't turned my phone in yet. It's clutched in my left hand, and I make a sudden, split-second decision to start recording, just in case. Zack waits several beats before taking a deep breath, and forging on.

"When I made that bet, I didn't think about the name and face of the girl who would die. I'm sorry. A hundred times over, I'm sorry. But I did it: I made that bet to get you to kill yourself, and I came at you relentlessly. There is no such thing as forgiveness for me."

My heart clenches painfully, but I'm too twisted up with emotion right now to understand how I'm supposed to process that. Instead, I turn away and change the subject, shutting my phone off at the same time.

"I need to find my dad," I blurt, lunging to my feet. I

stumble slightly, and Zack is there to steady my elbow. His touch burns through my jacket; it's as if his bare skin is touching mine. I can practically feel the whorls of his fingertips.

"I'll take you to him," Zack says, his face shutting down into that impenetrable mask that I'm used to. He starts to lead the way, and I pull out his grip. Instead of getting upset, he just smiles at me. "By the way: have you seen the class rankings yet?"

I shake my head. Do I really care about class rankings when my dad is sick? Honestly, all I want to do in that moment is drop out and go home, so I can take care of him. I'm guessing that's why he's avoided telling me all this time. He's too freaking selfless. It's not *fair*. My eyes water and Zack reaches out to rub a tear from my cheek with his thumb, trailing strange sensations across my skin.

"You beat Tristan Vanderbilt again," he says with a low chuckle, and I almost laugh. Almost. But nothing in this world is more important to me than my father. *Nothing.* "You're number one again."

"Number one?" I echo, and my heart drops into my stomach. If I'm number one … then why do I feel like I'm coming in dead last?

I close my eyes, exhale, and then open them back up.

I've never needed to be stronger than in this moment.

Squaring my shoulders, I take the lead and head back to the chapel.

CHAPTER

7

Dad won't talk to me about his illness. If I bring it up, he changes the subject. If I cry, he holds me tight. He most definitely does not get drunk this year.

On Friday, just before the big game, he cups the side of my face with one of his rough palms and gazes lovingly into my eyes. My throat gets tight, and I choke on unshed tears.

"Marnye," he begins, his voice soft, "you've always known what you've wanted, even as a little kid. You went through a hard time in middle school, and yet you never stopped fighting. You got this scholarship on your own merit, and you do nothing but continue to exceed my expectations."

"Dad—" I start, but he cuts me off.

"As a boy, I dreamed of going to a school like this. There was an all-boys academy just outside the town I grew up in called Adamson. I fantasized about going there every day, but I never tried to change my circumstances; I just accepted them." I try to speak again, but he shushes me gently. "All week, you've been hinting that you want to come home and take care of me. I don't want that for you."

"Nothing is more important to me than you," I choke out, but Dad's already shaking his head. Everything makes sense now: his gifting me his mother's bracelet, trying to force a relationship with Jennifer, his getting drunk last year at Parents' Week. It's all coming together into this horrible conclusion that I just want to wake up from.

"And nothing is more important to me than you, Marnye-bear, but you've got your whole life ahead of you. I'll do whatever it takes to be there for as much of it as I can, but you *cannot* give up this opportunity. I won't let you." He sighs and drops his hand to his side. He's so different from all the other parents in their expensive suits, designer clothing, and fancy high heels. Charlie Reed wears raggedy old jeans, the watch I got him for Christmas last year, and scuffed work boots. It only makes me love him more that he wears it all with pride. "I see the way they look at you."

"Like they hate me and want me dead?" I ask, and Dad smiles softly.

"Like they're jealous, Marnye."

"Jealous of me?" I echo with disbelief. "With their Lamborghinis and their yachts and their mansions?" I sound so pathetic when I say that, it makes even me cringe. I know better than anyone that money isn't what makes a person happy. Dad makes me happy; learning makes me happy; friendship makes me happy.

"Money can't buy confidence or love or genuine sense of self. Marnye, you are better than their superficial shit." I raise my eyebrows because I've rarely, if ever, head my dad curse around me. "Honey, the best revenge is success. Remember that. Keep doing your thing, and make me proud. That's what I want for you. Make a better life for yourself than the one I gave you."

"You gave me a great life," I blurt, and Dad laughs, pulling me in for a hug. I'm wearing my new cheerleading uniform: a polyester shell with long sleeves, and red and white stripes under the word *Burberry* sewn into the front, paired with a short black skirt and sneakers. Underneath, I've got on shiny black shorts with the school logo on the right butt cheek. Seems a weird place to put it, but it is what it is. The uncomfortable material rubs me the wrong way as Dad gives me a squeeze for the ages.

He pulls back and puts his hands on my shoulders.

"My little girl, a cheerleader," he says, and then he chuckles as I narrow my eyes. "Never thought I'd see the day."

"I'm just doing it for college," I repeat, and then silently add in my head *and revenge.* "Besides, it's good exercise." Dad grins at me and hooks an arm around my shoulders, trying to head us in the wrong direction. I laugh and turn him around, guiding him to the back door and the waiting academy cars. The football field is so far from the chapel building that it takes a good half hour to walk down there. Some people left a while ago to head down, but Dad and I ate in The Mess together, and I refused to be rushed.

"Whatever the reason, I'm excited to see you perform," he says, leading us out to the vehicle. We slide in, and the driver moves to shut the door when I hear a voice call out to hold the car.

It's Zayd fucking Kaiser.

Great.

He climbs in, and then freezes when he sees my dad and me.

A frown pulls at the edges of my lips, but then the driver is shutting the door, and it's a bit late to back out. Dad must recognize Zayd as one of the panty-throwers because he does not smile at him or greet him.

Zayd slumps down on the opposite side of the limo, dressed in a white tank with his band's name—Afterglow—scrawled in black cursive across the front. His jeans are black, and far too tight, which I actually like. He's got on Doc Martens covered in roses, and I'm pretty sure he added a few new tattoos over the summer. My fingers remember tracing his ink as we made out in my dorm room. Of course, he was doing it all just to film it and humiliate, but … that's a whole other issue.

"Your dad cares so little about you he didn't bother to show up again?" I ask, and Charlie gapes at me.

"Marnye," he warns, but that's the only chastising I get.

Zayd just stares back at me, his lids ringed in liner, his lip piercings black and pointy, his brow piercing a black hoop. He nibbles at his lip rings for a moment before responding.

"He's got a job that people actually care about," Zayd snaps back, and I can tell I've hit a nerve. Good. Screw him. I *chose* him. I chose him and he betrayed me. It makes everything so much worse. His characteristic tobacco, clove, and sage scent fills the air in the limo, and my nostrils flare. "He's not, like, you know, some easily replaceable blue collar worker that could be substituted with a monkey or a machine."

"At least my dad has a heart and gives two craps about me," I snarl, and Charlie puts a hand on my knee. "Musicians are a dime a dozen. Your dad is nothing *but* a performing monkey dressed in tattoos and the words of some ghost writers who pen hits for the masses. Give me a break."

Zayd scowls at me, shoving up from his seat and pushing open the door while the car's still rolling to a stop. He takes off as Dad sighs and gives me a look. I cringe, but only because I'm frustrated that he had to listen to this bullshit. Zayd deserves whatever I throw at him.

The football stadium is huge, much fancier than you'd expect for a high school. Actually, it reminds me of that one time Dad took us to a U of O home game at Autzen Stadium in Eugene, Oregon. It's far too elaborate, especially considering that before this year, our team was ranked, like, dead last in their district.

Zack has changed all of that.

If they win tonight's game, they'll be going to the playoffs.

I'm going to make sure that doesn't happen.

Tonight, we're playing Grenadine Heights High—the number one team in our district for almost two straight decades. It's sort of a big deal.

Dad leaves me to go take his seat in the stands while I join Coach Hannah and the rest of the girls just outside the entrance to the stadium. The way they look at me as I saunter up to them ... priceless. Ileana curses under her breath, just loud enough for me to hear, but not enough that the coach notices.

Coach runs us through our warm up and stretches, my heart racing, sweat dripping down my spine. And it's from more than just the exercise—I'm about to wreck Zack Brooks' football career, and bring down the rest of the team with him.

I might move slow, but I'm a planner. It's what I do.

After we warm up, we head into the stadium and take up our positions at the edge of the field. As far as coach is concerned, games are practice. We're gearing up for competition. When the Burberry Prep football team is licking their wounds, I'll be helping their cheer team get their first ever trophies.

The timing was delicate on this one, so I shift from side to side, glancing briefly up at the scoreboard and the clock. The minutes tick past slow as hours as we gear up for our first ever cheer. I'm a bit of an academic and a bookworm, and this is so not my scene, but I force a smile. It's hard, though, with Tristan, Zayd, and Creed in the audience. I can see them, front and center, flanked by the Inner Circle. Pretty sure they're all staring at me.

As we start our routine, I notice that Coach Hannah's phone is buzzing.

My mouth twitches, half in grimace and half in grin.

If I'd wanted to, I could've done any number of things to Zack Brooks, something like spiking his food or drink with steroids and reporting him. But that's not my game here. I don't *want* to bring myself down to their level. Does it make things harder? Sure. When I sat down and made those rules though, I was serious.

Let them hang themselves with their own rope.

If they didn't fuck with me, if they *stopped* fucking with me, then nothing bad would happen to them.

Coach Hannah glances from her screen and up to me, my arms in the air, my tight polyester shell riding slightly up. She turns to her assistant coach, and I see them whisper briefly. In the stand, Principal Collins has her gray brows raised, her mouth slightly agape. And as we finish our cheer, I glance over my shoulder and see the varsity football coach—Buck Rolands—calling Zack off the field.

Zack jogs over, pulling off his shiny black helmet, his brows crinkled, his big, muscular body made to look even larger with all the pads he's wearing. He pauses next to his coach and glances down at the video on the phone screen.

His face goes shock-white before he glances over at me and meets my eyes. I smile, but it's not a pretty smile. No, it's one of those *fuck you* smiles that the Idols have given me countless times in the past year and a half.

What goes around comes around, I think as Principal Collins makes her way down the steps, and the crowd begins to buzz with gossip. I've sent the same video to every member of staff. It wasn't hard to get their numbers. Actually, because this is a boarding school, every student is given an emergency list of the staff's personal cell numbers in case of an accident or emergency during off-hours. Using it for a non-emergency is strict grounds for suspension, but I have that covered: I used a burner phone.

Remember those imperative items that I just *had* to shop for?

Yeah, well, that was on the list.

A hushed argument is carried out between Principal Collins, Vice Principal Castor, Coach Rolands, and, a few moments later, Zack's mother, Robin. All I've ever seen or heard about that woman is that she's nice to a fault. I used to wonder, back at LBMS, how she ever created such a monster as Zack Brooks. I hear his father and grandfather are real pieces of work, but Robin was never anything but nice to me, even when her son was bullying me to the point of suicide.

The look on Zack's face as she watches that video … it almost hurts me.

I toyed with this for a while, wondering if it broke rules two and three: *No friendly fire* and *No innocent bystanders.* But … all I did was reveal the truth.

Briefly, I close my eyes. I don't need to see the video to know that it says.

There's Zack, telling me to kill myself and filming it. He sent me the video, too, all those years ago, emailed it to me, so I could watch it over and over again. I never told anyone. Not once. But I still had it, buried under years of other emails.

It's followed by his voice, from just a few days ago. *When I made that bet, I didn't think about the name and face of the girl who would die. I'm sorry. A hundred times over, I'm sorry. But I did it: I made that bet to get you to kill yourself, and I came at you relentlessly. There is no such thing as forgiveness for me.*

Let's see how this zero tolerance bullying policy works.

Zack's face falls as his mother turns to him, looking at her son like she doesn't even recognize him. His helmet falls from his fingers, and within minutes—*minutes*—phones all across the stadium are pinging with the link to the video. Students share it with each other, leaning their heads together and whispering. Parents see it. It's out there, and it can't be taken back.

My heart is racing so fast that I feel dizzy, and *everyone* is looking at me now.

"May I use the restroom?" I ask Coach Hannah, and she blinks stupidly at me. There's pity and sympathy in her gaze now, but I don't care. She nods, and I push past the other girls, heading for the long, dark tunnel that leads from the locker rooms to the field.

As soon as I'm hidden in its shadowy depths, I lean my back against the wall, my breath coming in panting gasps.

When I hear footsteps, I don't expect to see Zack storming down the hall, his face dark and drawn in. He sees me and pauses close, too close, so close that I can see the pain in his eyes. I expect, like Zayd, for him to throw his hurt back in my face.

"I'm not playing in tonight's game," he whispers, and we both know that that means: Burberry Prep will lose. "And I'm off the team." I purse my lips, and he closes his eyes, his head sagging, chin falling to his chest. "In-school suspension, at a minimum. No off-campus privileges. My Mom's going to disown me." He groans and crouches down, putting his hands over his face. For a moment, I just watch him. "They're going to discuss the rest of my punishment on Monday."

"You deserve it, every single scrap of it," I tell him, pulling back a few inches, like I'm afraid he's going to strike out at me. Zack stands up suddenly and tears his jersey over his head, dumping his shoulder pads to the floor with a growl.

C.M. STUNICH

When he turns to me, he's shirtless and sweaty and glorious.

Too bad I hate him.

"You're right," he blurts suddenly, and my eyes go wide with shock.

"Ex-excuse me?"

Zack takes several steps towards me and pauses, swiping his palm down his face.

"You're right. Marnye, you're right." He drops his hands by his sides, and it's freaking impossible for me not to notice how muscular his arms are, how rounded his biceps, how flat his chest. My breath hitches as he takes a step forward, and I cross my arms over my chest to keep myself in check. Zack's eyes drop down to my waist, and his brows go up. When he reaches out to me, my heart stops in my chest. He takes the edge of my skirt and with a little tug, pulls me forward. His fingers dive under my waistband, searing me with wicked hot heat and dragging my waistband down just far enough that he can see my tattoo.

He lets out a long string of curses, his voice so dark it's almost scary.

"Marnye, what is this?"

"The Infinity Club," I start, sucking in a deep breath and puffing out my chest. I wish he'd take his fingers away. It feels good for him to touch me like that, and that's the last thing I want. I won't let myself get soft on these guys. There's nothing sexy or cool or endearing about being an asshole. If this were a bully romance, well, I'd probably end up marrying Miranda because I just don't abide by bullies. "They're going

126

to learn that they can't treat people like collateral damage."

Zack rubs his knuckles against my tattoo, and curses again before lifting his eyes to mine.

"You don't know what you're getting yourself into," he whispers, and I purse my lips. I *know* that, and yet … I can't seem to control myself. These rich a-holes need to learn that a person is a person, no matter the size of their bank account. There's no such thing as Social Darwinism or royalty or Idols, it's all a façade, a bunch of bullshit that lets certain people get a free pass for throwing away their humanity. "You don't have the resources or the insider knowledge to take down the club."

"I don't—" I start, and Zack leans in toward me, so close that I can see his pulse thundering in his throat, can trace the beads of sweat running down his muscular chest.

"But I do," he says, and his eyes fall to my lips. My body trembles as his huge form towers over me, his knuckles stroking my tattoo. Damn hormones. He leans in a little bit closer. "I can help you, Marnye."

"I'm never going to fall for you," I blurt, but my eyes can't seem to look anywhere but the thickness of his lower lip. "*Never.*"

"Good," he whispers, closing his eyes and putting his forehead against mine. He's sweaty, but I don't care. My palms somehow end up on the flat planes of his chest, my fingertips curling against his damp, hot skin. "Because I'm in love with you, even though I know I'm not good enough for you." My heart stops in my chest, and my eyes go wide. My gaze transfers from his lips to his eyes, and it stays there; I can't look away. Zack puts his left hand over one of mine, pressing my skin against his. His right hand continues to stroke my tattoo. "You want to know why I'm helping you? Now you know. But you'll never be with me, and that's okay. Because I'm not enough for you. I'm the kind of person who tries to make a girl kill herself to get into some stupid club. All I want to do is try to make up for it, even if takes me the rest of my life."

"Shut up," I whisper, but he just leans in even closer and puts his lips right up against mine. I can taste him now, right there on my mouth. I flick my tongue out and we both groan as I trace his lower lip. "I don't trust you, and I don't believe you. Whatever you have to say, it's all bullshit to me."

"Good," he repeats, his mouth moving against mine. "Maybe someday, you'll forgive me and we can be friends. Until then, let me help you."

I'm panting; he's panting.

We're sharing breaths.

After a moment, Zack turns his head slightly to one side, and I follow his gaze.

The Idols—all six of them—are standing there watching us.

Tristan's face is hard, dead, cold. Creed's hands are curled into fists at his sides, belying the bored, lazy expression in his half-lidded eyes. Zayd, he's just scowling openly, even as he's holding hands with Becky. It's so clear in their gazes how much they all hate Zack. Despise him, even. Looking back on that day at the lake, I can see things as they really are. Hindsight is twenty-twenty, and all that.

They didn't tell me about Zack and Lizzie because they

cared about me.

They told me about Zack and Lizzie to hurt me. And hurt me they did.

I turn back to Zack.

"Let me kiss you," he whispers, and I realize then that I'm trembling. I've just destroyed this guy's football career, lost the big game for the academy, maybe even sent Zack running back to Lower Banks High. And yet ... "Let me help you, and I'll only go as far as you'll let me. We can take down the Infinity Club together."

"Pretend to date you?" I ask, and he shrugs his big shoulders, his favored response to every question.

"Or just fucking kiss me."

My heartrate picks up speed, and a bead of sweat works its way between my breasts, tickling my skin. Zack moves his hand and tugs up the waistband of my skirt to hide my tattoo. He grabs hold of my hip then and pulls my body against him. Before I can think too hard about it, my hands are sliding up his chest and curling around his neck.

Our mouths clash together in a rush of heat and desperation and need.

It feels so good that it almost hurts.

Zack's mouth is warm and soft, and he tastes like cherry Gatorade. He wraps his left arm around me and lifts me up against him, his tongue teasing mine, taking control of the kiss without being domineering. I tell myself I'm only doing it because they're watching. That's what I *tell* myself, anyway. On the inside, I'm melting.

"Well, well, it's the Working Girl doing what she does best," Harper sneers, but I barely hear her. I'm so wrapped up in Zack's big, strong arms, in the taste of his hot mouth on mine. Even if I hate him, even if I've just gotten him expelled … this feels too good.

And if it hurts the Bluebloods, then that's just the cherry on top.

We stumble back into the wall, but I know I can't let this go any further.

Zack must know it, too, because he pulls back and rests his forehead against mine for a moment. Both of us just breathe, slow in and outs. We're both trembling, even as he moves away from me and picks up his discarded jersey and pads.

I don't look at the Bluebloods as I fix my uniform and brush my palm over my hair before exchanging a look with Zack. He gives me a grim smile before heading into the locker room, and I turn back for the field.

"Fucking whore," Becky snarls as I pass, but I just pause and smile at her.

"Takes one to know one," I say, and then I'm sweeping past and heading back for the cluster of cheerleaders in their black, red, and white uniforms. I know I'm going to have to talk to Dad after about Zack, but that can wait.

For now, I dance.

BAD, BAD BLUE BLOODS

Revenge On *The Bluebloods of Burberry Prep*
A list by ~~Miranda Cabot~~ *Marnye Reed*

*The Idols (guys): Tristan Vanderbilt (year ~~one~~ **two**), Zayd Kaiser (year ~~one~~ **two**), and Creed Cabot (year ~~one~~ **two**)*
*The Idols (girls): Harper du Pont (year ~~one~~ **two**), Becky Platter (year ~~one~~ **two**), ~~and Gena Whitley (year four)~~*
(graduated), Ileana Taittinger (year one)
The Inner Circle: **~~Andrew Payson~~**, *Anna Kirkpatrick, Myron Talbot, Ebony Peterson, Gregory Van Horn, Abigail Fanning, John Hannibal, Valentina Pitt, Sai Patel, Mayleen Zhang, Jalen Donner ...* ~~*and, I guess, me!*~~ **Kiara Xiao, Ben Thresher**
Plebs: everyone else~~*, sorry. XOXO*~~
~~Zack Brooks~~

CHAPTER

8

Halloween is on a Thursday this year which makes partying difficult, especially with all the Bluebloods—and Zack—restricted to the Burberry Prep campus. According to school gossip, there's going to be a party Friday night at the cemetery. Technically, that *is* on campus, so there's less risk of being discovering.

"I'm over the 'slutty' theme," Miranda says, flipping through a magazine as we sit in The Mess and binge on a colorful stack of macarons. "For Halloween, I mean. Not that there's anything wrong with that, I just … feel like I'd rather go as a giant bowl of popcorn than a sexy kitty, sexy firefighter, sexy nurse, or sexy warthog."

"Warthog?" I choke, pounding on my chest with a fist and raising a brow. Miranda throws her head back and laughs, the sound like the tinkling of bells. I notice Jessie Maker

watching her and biting her lower lip. Those two …
"Whoever dressed as a sexy warthog?"

"Academy legend says that in the nineties, when *The Lion King* first came out, that Ms. Felton came to school dressed as a sexy warthog, in furry panties, a furry bra, and tusks. The yearbook from that year is missing from the library which totally makes me think it's true." She stuffs a pink cookie in her mouth and presents me and Jessie with the glossy page of the magazine.

Ah, print is still alive and well on the Burberry Prep campus, particularly between Monday morning when we hand in our phones, and Friday evening when we get them back. Of course, I snuck a burner phone in here by hiding it in a box of tampons (of which I carefully used glue to reseal the flap so it looked unopened). I'm sure I'm not the only student to have thought of that.

I examine the costume—it's a giant bowl of popcorn made out of papier-mâché that's totally not going to work considering Halloween is *tomorrow*—but it's cute.

"We could dress up as macarons," I suggest, lifting one of the pretty cookies up to the light. "You know, put some of that temporary dye in our hair, wear matching dresses and heels."

Miranda squeals and rises up from her seat, nearly knocking the macaron tower over as she throws her arms around my neck and practically strangles me in the name of hugging.

"That's such a cute freaking idea!" she gushes, eyes sparkling. "And *we* all still have our off-campus privileges. We could go after school today, just run into town and grab a few things." Miranda snaps her fingers as Andrew walks in, carrying his bookbag over his shoulder. He raises his eyebrows at her. "But only if you go in full drag."

"Drag … for what?" Andrew asks suspiciously, and Miranda tosses him a yellow cookie which he just barely catches.

"Halloween. I'll do your makeup, and we can get you a wig when we go out today. We're dressing as macarons, like all colorful and cute. You'll love it. Besides," she waves her hand dismissively in his direction, totally lost in her own world, "you've been saying you wanted to try drag."

"Um, try drag in private in a place my dad would never —" Andrew stops abruptly as the door to The Mess opens and Zack walks in. My heart flip-flops in my chest, and my throat closes up to the point that it's hard to breathe. That kiss, that kiss, ah that fucking kiss … But I hate him. Piece of shit.

I focus on my cookie and stuff it into my mouth. Unfortunately, it tastes like cherries which just reminds me of the taste of Zack's mouth.

"Zack, will you do drag with Andrew?" Miranda asks as he pauses far too close to me. I can smell his cologne, this musky, sporty mix of citrus, mint, and cedar that drives me nuts. "Like, full on makeup, wig, dress, heels."

Zack shrugs his broad shoulders.

"Yeah, why not? What is Halloween for if not for girls in short skirts and dudes in drag? I was going to go as Russell Brand, a la Aldous Snow in *Forgetting Sarah Marshall,* but this sounds better." I glance up at him through the feather gold bangs that fall across my forehead. He looks back at me, and I have to hold back a sigh.

BAD, BAD BLUE BLOODS

I might've gotten him good, but that doesn't mean I forgive him. My revenge on Zack Brooks is satisfied for now, but that's not going to magically clear the air between us. Not by a long shot.

He was *this* close to being expelled. *This* freaking close. Because the video was from middle school, the academy didn't feel it had the grounds to take things quite so far, but Zack Brooks is on thin ice. Any grade less than a C or a scrap of proof that he's bullying this year, and he's out. As things stand, they took his letterman jacket away, kicked him off the varsity team, and gave him in-school suspension. He has no off-campus privileges, and Burberry Prep lost the game to Grenadine Heights. The entire football team hates Zack now, and my dad … Well, that was a tough one to deal with. I came too close to breaking those rules again. Scary close. I explained to my father that Zack and I had patched things up, but I'm not sure if they'll be friends again. The way he looked at Zack after, that was almost punishment enough. I could see the pain in Zack's eyes.

To distract myself from the hunky ex-football player beside me, I pull out my journal, unlock it, and start writing. The others have learned not to bother me when I'm penning my thoughts.

Zack and Andrew pull up chairs, and the others talk about their costumes as I write.

Less than fifteen minutes later, Creed shows up.

He's alone, but that doesn't matter.

As soon as he sees Miranda with us, his ice-blue eyes narrow to slits. He saunters over to us with that lazy, rolling gait of his, like at any moment he might just lie down on the floor and take an angry nap. Yeah, I know, that doesn't *really* make sense, but I swear, that's what Creed looks like: a pissed-off narcoleptic.

"Miranda," he says, and his sister stiffens up under his stare. "Can I speak with you for a moment?"

"No, you may not, *Creed*," she snaps back, lifting angry eyes to her twin's face. They're so similar in appearance, it's eerie. If I'd never seen them in the same room, I might believe that they were one person, a shapeshifter who could swap genders. I once read a book called *He & She* where a woman would change genders every time she had an orgasm. That could be Creed and Miranda, two sides of the same coin.

"I need you to get something off-campus for me tonight. It's for my costume."

"Maybe you should've thought of that before you displayed such barbaric and despicable behavior?" Miranda quips, turning back to her tea and sipping it slowly. The metaphor in her actions isn't lost on me. *Sip that tea, Miranda,* I think with a grin.

Creed notices my expression and turns to face me. I stare him down, curling my arm protectively around my journal, so he can't see the words written in it. Bet he'd love that, to read it aloud to the academy the way he did with my essay.

"What's so damn amusing to you?" he drawls, as insouciant and dismissive as always.

"You, waltzing around the school like you think you're the prince. Maybe you are, but you'll never be king." My grin rachets up a notch, as wide and maniacal as the Cheshire Cat's. "Tristan will always rule this school. At best, you're second in command. At *best*. Then again, your grades are trash, and you don't bother to apply yourself. At least Tristan can boast that much."

If only I could describe the way his body stiffens up, like he's suddenly carved of stone. Every wrinkle in his shirt, every crease in his slacks, it all looks chiseled from limestone. When he opens his mouth, Miranda lunges up from her chair and gets in his face.

"Don't. Just don't. Leave her alone, Creed. Mom's already disgusted with you. And now, after the incident with the Bentley, so is Dad. Don't dig yourself an even deeper hole." Creed's blue eyes go wide, but he manages to school his expression quickly, and his gaze narrows back to that heavy-lidded bedroom look that he enjoys so much.

He turns away from us and heads to the Idols' table, sitting down and snapping his fingers for the waiter. That motion alone drives me *nuts*. These people might work here, but they're not his personal freaking slaves.

"Fucking creep," Zack murmurs, but really, he doesn't have much room to talk, does he? And yet … when I look at him and he stares back, I can see in his eyes that he's sorry. And not just because I punished him. No, he was sorry long before that.

I refocus on my journal, fully aware that Creed is watching me the entire time.

Good.

Let him watch.

Because what I have planned for him requires his cooperation.

Bet he gives it freely and willingly.

"I look ridiculous," Zack says with a laugh, examining his sea green dress, heels, and wig in the mirror. He's such a big, bulky guy, I can't exactly disagree. I clamp a hand over my mouth to stifle a chuckle, and he glances over his shoulder at me, batting his falsies in my direction. Laughter explodes from me anyway, and he grins. Usually, he's as reserved as Tristan, all dark and brooding and probably evil underneath, but right now … he's actually kind of cute. "Andrew's the hot one. I'd bang him, if I were into, uh, what's it called?"

"When two drag queens have sex? Is it kiki or kaikai?" Miranda taps her frosty pink lips with the tip of one finger. We even managed to squeeze getting our nails done in last night, so we've got matching acrylics. Since Zack is banned from leaving campus, he got a sort of shitty paint job from Miranda this morning. It only helps add to the hilarity of his look.

"Oh my god, Miranda," Andrew says, fluffing his pale blue wig in the mirror. "Kiki is just a chat, a conversation. Kaikai is when two drag queens … you know …"

"Fuck?" Miranda replies, and we all groan. She's so crass

sometimes.

"You watch more *RuPaul's Drag Race* than anyone," Jessie says, speaking up for the first time, and twirling so that her frothy white tulle skirts spin around her. Miranda watches, her gaze softening as she takes in the brunette with an appreciative once-over. I hate to admit it, but Zack is looking at me in much the same way. "You know the terms better than Andrew does."

"It's true," I say, still chuckling as I check my own hair in the mirror. My rose-gold hair is perfect, since I've been designated the yellow, lemon-flavored macaron. We're all wearing necklaces made of real cookies, and our perfume is coordinated to our specific flavors. Actually, we make a pretty cute little group. "So … we do the whole school thing," I start, referencing the academy sponsored party in the gym, "and then how do we get to the cemetery? I doubt sneaking the cars on campus is going to work."

"We'll have to walk," Miranda says with a groan, sticking her tongue out at her heels which, by the way, cost almost a thousand bucks. I bought my own shoes this time at an outlet store for thirty-five big ones. These are by far the priciest shoes I've ever purchased for myself. Zack, Miranda, Andrew, *and* Jessie all offered to get me something else, but I refused.

Despite what Tristan, Zayd, and Creed think, I am *not* a charity case.

"I can always carry you, if your feet hurt too much from dancing," Zack says, and the way he's holding his face, the purr in his voice … it'd be sexy if he didn't look so ridiculous in an ill-fitting dress with his massive muscular shoulders showing. Andrew actually looks sexy as hell. If I were into girls, I think I'd be into him the way he's dressed now. Even Miranda whistled appreciatively when he came out of the bathroom for his big reveal.

"Thanks, but I think I can manage walking," I reply, forcing a smile and running my palms down the front of my glittery yellow gown. "Shall we?" I hold out my arm for Andrew, and he takes it. I notice Zack looking longingly at us, but technically, we've decided that Miranda and Jessie are a couple for the night, and I'm going with Andrew.

Zack is … going stag.

Good for him.

The Halloween party looks much the same as it did last year. Only the first-years seem actually excited to be here. Everyone else is simply making an appearance and waiting for the real event to start. Amongst the cheesy disco balls and streamers, it's easy to spot the Idols at their table near the stage. They all stand out like sore thumbs, sucking the life from the room.

Well, at least that's how it feels to me.

As soon as we walk in there, all eyes are on us. The Bluebloods continue to glare as we scout out a table, grab some snacks, and sit down to chat. *Their* gazes in particular feel like they're burning into the back of my head. Freaking Tristan, Creed, and Zayd. Ugh. The girls have come at me plenty since heading back to Burberry, but I have yet to see those assholes make a move.

That scares me.

"Harper's nose is still swollen," Miranda whispers, and I

grin, just before she drags me out on the dance floor and makes me work for it. Jessie joins us a while later and steals my dance partner. Andrew, meanwhile, is off dancing with some cute first year guy, and I'm left to grind it alone for a while.

That is, until Zack shows up. I pause in my movements, my heart pounding so loud that I can hear it over the thumping bass of the music.

"Hi," I say, and he smiles. It's a nice smile, too, one of the truest emotions I've ever seen on his face. When the administrators asked me into the principal's office after the game and asked if I knew who had sent the video, I played dumb. Outright lying isn't my thing, but they in no way suspected me, so it was easy to dodge their interrogation. What they *had* asked me was if I felt unsafe with Zack Brooks attending Burberry Prep.

I'd had to answer that direct question with a direct response.

No, I don't feel unsafe.

"Hi," he says back, and the music switches to a slow song, one that makes me feel like that swarm of butterflies is taking off inside of me again. I'm all aflutter. "May I have this dance?" I suck my lower lip under my teeth, and decide that even if he is a bit goofy in that green wig, he's still handsome. Closing my eyes, I remember dancing with Zayd at that party last year, how our bodies had seemed to meld together. Will I ever feel that way with a guy again?

I guess I could at least try to find out?

I let Zack take my hand in one of his while the other falls respectfully to my waist. The floor clears of dancers, leaving only a few couples left to sway with the music. I giggle at first, because Zack in makeup just isn't the sexiest combination, but as we begin to move, I start to forget. All I can see is the deep brown of his eyes, and the way he looks at me.

"Because I'm in love with you, even though I know I'm not good enough for you."

My cheeks flush. Did he really say that? Did he really *mean* that?

Our eyes are locked as we sway, spinning in slow circles with orange, black, and white spotlights tracing over our skin. As we turn, I can see Zayd in his stupidly tight Power Rangers uniform watching us. He's dressed as the red ranger, which suits him. His mask is off currently, and I meet his gaze briefly over Zack's shoulder before I turn back to that soft, brown gaze.

If I had to guess … I'd say Zayd looks jealous. But that can't possibly be true. If he cared at all about me, he wouldn't have done what he did. At any time, it would've only taken one of the guys to tell me the truth about what was happening, to step in and make things right. Just one of them. Even if it were an unbreakable Infinity Club bet, could they have looked anymore excited about what they were doing? And how about an apology?

No, there's no way Zayd is jealous. No way.

Zack and I continue to dance, and shortly after, we're joined by Tristan and Harper. Tristan's all done up like the Mad Hatter, complete with top hat and everything. He holds Harper possessively by the waist, and dances far too close to us. Every time we turn, I see them, her dressed up like Ariana Grande, and him with his blade gray gaze locked on her face.

There's a little pang in my chest that I can't identify. But what I do notice is that when Zack spins me, and the rose necklace flutters, Tristan sees it. For a microsecond, his eyes widen, but he's brilliant at hiding it. Just brilliant. The next time we make eye contact, he's scowling at me.

Creed has disappeared, dressed once again like a pirate (same as last year) with an unbuttoned red blouse, a plastic sword, and breeches so tight that there's little left to the imagination. I'm guessing that's why he was asking Miranda to buy him something yesterday: he didn't expect to lose his off-campus privileges and ended up without a costume. Sucker. He doesn't come back for the next several songs and by then, I've already forgotten about him. Him, and Tristan, and Zayd.

For whatever reason, Zack has that effect on me. I grin as he dips me, laugh as he lifts me back up, and squeal as he hoists me into his arms and spins us both around in circles.

When we leave for the cemetery portion of the party, I'm grinning ear to ear. I even let him hold my hand as we take off our heels and run barefoot through the grass and under the shadowy limbs of trees. It's the perfect, foggy Halloween night, too.

My heart is racing as we stumble onto the party with our hands still linked.

I expect trouble, but there's no resistance when we show up. For the most part, everyone ignores us.

For the most part.

"Careful if you're drinking, the tattling teetotaler's here," someone mumbles, but really, should those in glass houses throw stones? This all started because Creed and his cronies reported *me* for drinking last year. Bunch of bullshit.

Zack grabs a beer, so does Miranda. Andrew, Jessie, and I stick with sodas, heading onto the dock to dangle our feet in the icy water for a while before we realize that the majority of the students have disappeared into the actual graveyard.

"Should we check it out?" I ask, this little niggle of suspicion working its way up from my stomach and into my chest. My heart pounds as I check my phone, pulling up the footage from the security cameras. There's nothing there, but a quick rewind shows … My mouth drops open as both Zack and Miranda lean over to peer at the screen.

It's Creed, rifling through my stuff, looking for my journal, *finding* my journal.

"Oh my god," Miranda whimpers, slapping her hand over her mouth. "Creed, you fucking idiot."

I push up from the dock, leaving my heels behind, and take off for the graveyard with the others following along behind me. Déjà vu hits me hard and fast as I come around the corner and find Creed lounging on top of one of the mausoleums with a horde of ghouls and ghosts surrounding him. Devils and demons, Miranda calls the Idols and their Inner Circle. She is spot freaking on.

Just like last year, I stand there with my heart pounding as Creed clears his throat, lifts up a bobby pin and picks my look. Just like last year, he's the perfect picture of beauty and cruelty as he flips through the pages and stops on one at random. Just like last year, he opens his mouth to read my personal thoughts and feelings to an uncaring audience.

Unlike last year … I'm ready for it.

"Give me the word, and I'll kick his ass," Zack snarls, reaching up to take off his dangly earrings. It's pretty funny actually, but I don't want Creed Cabot to know that I've been onto him and his asshole friends all along. I put a hand against Zack's chest to hold him back.

Creed smiles, this easy, satisfied expression, like a cat who's just killed a mouse. What he doesn't know is that the mouse was already poisoned and now he's infected, too. Curiosity killed the cat, after all.

"*Dear Journal,*" Creed begins, his beautiful voice dripping ice. The crowd titters already, excited at the thought of bloodshed. Becky, Harper, and Ileana are lounging on tombstones in their short-shorts and miniskirts, grinning and laughing. Tristan and Zayd each sit on a different headstone nearby. "*Today was hard. Too hard. When I walked into math class and saw Jalen and Ebony sitting together, it all came back to me.*" Creed pauses for a minute, looking up to scan his audience. His gaze comes to rest on me, and I swear, I almost just throw my head back and laugh. When he returns his attention back to the page, I stifle my chuckle with my hand and Zack gives me the strangest look.

"Creed, don't," Miranda pleads, stepping forward and pulling off her pink wig. She moves between our little group and the gathered horde of Bluebloods and Plebs. Several of the boys step up to block her, but keep their hands well off of her person. There's not a person at Burberry Prep who doesn't know what Creed did to Craig Taittinger. "You're better than this: prove it to me."

Her twin pauses for a moment, looking up again. There's a war going on in his eyes, but the battle's over before it's even begun. Tristan turns around and levels him with a deadly stare.

"Keep reading."

"I don't take orders from you," Creed snaps, and this strange bird of hope takes flight inside of me. An Emily Dickinson poem comes to mind: *"Hope" is the thing with feathers.* If Creed actually defies Tristan, if he puts aside the journal, then …

"So you take orders from your sister then? Or is it Charity that's got your panties in a wad?" Tristan turns fully to face Creed, and they have a stare down that reminds me of two alley cats I once saw outside the Train Car, locked in a fierce battle of wills. Unfortunately, Creed scowls and breaks the stare, opening the journal back up.

"This should be good," Harper crows, and I feel this satisfied little twitch in my hand when I think about punching her. I shouldn't have resorted to violence, but my dad … My daddy … No. I can't think about that right now. Charlie is having a bunch of tests done this week, and I'll know more by the time fall break rolls around. This time, I am most definitely *not* staying at school to play poker with the Idols.

"*It all came back to me,*" Creed repeats, carrying on without a hitch in his voice, *"that night when Tristan triumphantly announced that he was going on a date with Ebony.*" Creed pauses for a moment, crinkling up his face. I can see Tristan's shoulders stiffening from here. Jalen Donner is no longer looking at me and laughing. Neither is Ebony.

Instead, she's gaping at Creed while Jalen turns his attention to Tristan.

"Keep going!" Becky shouts, and the crowd echoes their sentiment. The confusion on Creed's face quickly shifts to perverse joy.

"*I had wondered when he and Ebony had broken up. Unfortunately, it came out that she was still dating Jalen and had no intention of breaking up with him. I guess they're childhood friends or something? Anyway, it seems Tristan and Ebony had plans to meet up and ... have sex? I'm not sure, but since I've already caught him in the act with Kiara Xiao and some random fourth-year girl, I doubt he had plans to pick flowers and make daisy chains.*"

Creed pauses as Jalen lets out a roar of frustration and launches himself at Tristan. There's a split-second there where I think he's actually going to get him, but then Tristan steps nimbly out of the way and Jalen stumbles into the cement side of the mausoleum.

"Jalen, stop!" Ebony is screaming, her little red riding hood costume fluttering as she chases after her boyfriend. "It's not like that."

Tristan dances back from the cluster of headstones, putting himself in the center of the gravel path and crouching like he fully expects a fight. He gets one, too, when Jalen comes at him again, throwing a punch that Tristan just narrowly ducks. His top hat flutters off and lands on the ground, crushed in seconds by Jalen's boot. He's dressed up like Lara Croft—probably thought it was funny as hell—so when he launches himself forward again, his fake boobs bounce.

And ... I've got everything on film. It's shaky and blurry and probably not at all in focus, but my phone is running constantly, clutched at my side and carefully aimed in Creed's direction. In the foggy darkness, it's pretty hard to see, especially with the glowing jack o' lanterns everywhere.

"Jalen, don't," Ebony screams again, and he whirls to face her, panting, pointing a finger in Tristan's direction.

"Did you sleep with him?" he asks, and Ebony glances away sharply. Jalen lets out another roar of rage, and then he spins and goes for Tristan yet again. This time, they end up exchanging blows.

"I didn't!" she shouts, trying to yank her boyfriend back. "We never slept together." Jalen pushes Tristan, and the king of the school actually stumbles a bit, blood running down the side of his mouth as he sneers at one of the most loyal members of his Inner Circle. One of his most loyal members who's just been thoroughly betrayed.

"Marnye," Zack breathes, and he looks at me with a new level of respect, eyes wide. "Holy shit." I smile tightly, but this isn't over, not even close.

"We never slept together, but I wanted to," Ebony chokes out, tears running down her face. "You're so obsessed with football and working out. We never spend time together. Tristan is ..."

"He doesn't give a shit about you!" Jalen screams, panting, blood streaming from his nose. His brown eyes are wide and wild. Frankly, he looks like he's about to cry. "I do." He slams a fist against his chest and gets in Ebony's face. She just stands there, eyes wide, staring at him. "I love you,

Ebony. I fucking love you. I always have."

"Well, I don't love you," she says, and then starts to sob. A few of the other girls, like Abigail and Valentina, come close and put their arms around her. Jalen stares at her in shock for several seconds before *he* begins to cry, these big, soppy messy tears that actually make me like him more. Boys should be able to cry; it's disturbing that society tries to tell them otherwise.

But we've already learned that people like John Hannibal and Gregory Van Horn are walking nightmares.

"Are you fucking crying? Pussy bitch." John cackles, his laugh like that of a hyena on the prowl. It's disturbing. He's dressed like a serial killer tonight, too, with faux blood all over his shirt. How lovely.

Jalen turns again, so suddenly that Tristan's still in the process of wiping crimson from his lips. He tackles him, and it takes several of the other boys to pry them apart.

Creed ... is absolutely loving this moment.

"Tristan Vanderbilt is a walking STD. He will sleep with anything that moves, but he's so disrespectful I'm not sure how he even gets girls." Creed chuckles as Tristan grits his teeth so hard it looks like one or two might just crack. Or hell, maybe Jalen will crack them for him? The boys start scuffling again as Ebony sobs and wails like she's the victim here. *"The sad thing is, he's truly the king of Burberry Prep, and for good reason. I mean, who else would stand up to him, certainly not—"* Creed turns the page and pauses abruptly, the amusement vanishing from his face. His gaze lifts up to mine.

I'm damn sure this is the end, that that's all he's going to read, but good old Greg hops up and snatches the journal from him, thrusting it into John's hands.

"*Certainly not Creed Cabot. If ever there was a definition for wannabe, he's it. He tries so hard to be Tristan Vanderbilt, it's pathetic. He could never match up to him—and that's pretty sad, since the him in question is a womanizing lothario.*" John snickers as Zayd throws his head back and howls with laughter. Meanwhile, the fight between Jalen and Tristan escalates.

"*The only one worse and more pathetic than Creed,*" Greg continues as he reads over John's shoulder, dressed up like Geralt from *The Witcher* video games/novels. Cosplay like that might look hot on someone like Zack who has the shoulders and muscles to carry it. On Greg, it looks even worse than Zack's too tight green dress and pearl necklace (the plastic kind, not the pervy kind, obvs). "*Is Zayd Kaiser. I mean, seriously. Does he think his music is actually good? At least Creed's and Tristan's dads show up to the school to support their kids. Zayd's dad doesn't even bother.*"

Zayd's face is now tight and white, and he's looking at me like I'm a monster.

Here's the thing: if they hadn't stolen my journal and read it, none of this would be happening. None of it. The Bluebloods have brought this on themselves.

Miranda is standing there shaking with rage. I feel bad for what she's going through, but I didn't make her brother do any of this. No, he broke into my room all on his own. I bet the guys made copies of my room and locker keys before they handed that bundle over to Vice Principal Castor. How they got keys for my new dorm locks, I'm not sure. It's horrifying to see how far their treachery went.

"If I were you," I say, and as soon as I speak, the entire cemetery goes quiet. The only sound is the eerie whisper of the wind through the graves, the song of ghosts. "I would stop reading now. Keep going, and you *really* won't like what else I have to say in there."

Harper snatches the journal from John's hand and tucks it under her arm, standing up and lifting her chin in defiance. The way she looks at me, I can tell I've struck a nerve. Tristan is supposed to be this piece of American royalty, his family's fortune built on shipping and railroads in the country's infancy. The Vanderbilt name will give her a prestige that the du Pont name will never have. She's got all the money in the world, so there's not much left to strive for but this.

Only, she'll never have it.

I'll make certain of that.

"This party is officially *over*," Harper snaps, and the crowd groans and grumbles in displeasure. It's disturbing though, to see how quickly they all scramble to comply with her orders. Where Tristan is the king of the academy, she is most certainly the queen. She'll be a hard one to take down. "Tristan, let's go." He sneers at her, spitting blood and glaring at Jalen before he turns and storms along the path after her. When he passes me, he spits more blood at my feet, but I don't move, just stand there and stare him down.

He tears away from me with a string of curses and disappears into the fog. Jalen just collapses to the gravel and sobs while Ebony drifts away with Valentina and Abigail. The way she looks at me as she passes says all I need to know.

151

She's a lightweight, and I've already shoved her out of the ring.

Creed doesn't move from his place on top of the mausoleum. Zayd, too, is frozen in place.

"Be careful, boys," I warn them, this strange little purr in my voice that I hardly recognize. "I'm coming for you."

I turn away and grab Zack's hand, dragging him with me.

On Sunday evening, I make a video compilation of Creed going through my stuff, stealing my journal, and reading it aloud, and then I email it to Kathleen Cabot with the following message: *I really liked your son once, and he hurt me so bad I couldn't breathe. He seems determined to destroy me, but I don't want to report him to the administration. Mrs. Cabot, I trust your judgment implicitly.*

And all of that, is pure unadulterated truth.

Revenge On *The Bluebloods of Burberry Prep*
A list by ~~Miranda Cabot~~ *Marnye Reed*

*The Idols (guys): Tristan Vanderbilt (year ~~one~~ **two**), Zayd Kaiser (year ~~one~~ **two**),* **~~and Creed Cabot (year one two)~~**

Bad, Bad Blue Bloods

*The Idols (girls): Harper du Pont (year ~~one~~ **two**), Becky Platter (year ~~one~~ **two**), ~~and Gena Whitley (year four)~~* **(graduated), Ileana Taittinger (year one)**

The Inner Circle: ~~***Andrew Payson***~~*, Anna Kirkpatrick, Myron Talbot,* ~~*Ebony Peterson*~~*, Gregory Van Horn, Abigail Fanning, John Hannibal, Valentina Pitt, Sai Patel, Mayleen Zhang,* ~~*Jalen Donner ... and, I guess, me!*~~ **Kiara Xiao, Ben Thresher**

Plebs: everyone else~~, sorry. XOXO~~

~~Zack Brooks~~

CHAPTER

9

I only have to survive one more week until fall break. Then I can go home and see Dad. Then I can take a break from all of this. To be quite honest, it's *exhausting*. Not only am I studying my ass off, working out for the cheer team, and playing the harp in every spare second of my time, but I'm always on high-alert at. One wrong move, and I'm dead.

On the plus side, these last few weeks have been almost … fun? Miranda has stopped talking to her twin completely. I mean, like complete and utter silence. Even I can see that it's killing him. He looks almost pale and sad when he thinks nobody's looking. If he's even remotely aware that there are eyes on him, he puts up his arrogant, haughty front like a shield.

Kathleen Cabot appeared the Monday after the Halloween party in her white stretch limo, marched down the stone halls in her Louboutins and grabbed her son by the ear. According to Miranda, she's *this* close to pulling him out of Burberry Prep and enrolling him in an all-boys military academy. She's beyond disappointed him in, beyond fawning over me (in front of Creed), and basically begged me to keep tutoring him.

It's a chore, but I do it. We sit side by side in the library every Monday, Wednesday, and Friday for two hours, and speak in low, clipped, studious tones. I get credits for it, at least, and I don't try to sabotage his work. It's enough for me to do my job.

After we finish up on that last Monday, I start to pack up my things and Creed leans back in his chair. With his angelic white-blond hair and ice-blue eyes, the white of the second-year uniform looks like it was made for him. The way he lounges, too, is quite incredible, like he's boneless and deserves to be carried about on a golden litter.

"Do you like tormenting me?" he asks, and I turn to gape at him.

"Are you serious?" It's now my turn to lean back in my chair, and give him a once-over. "That's a joke, right? You know who started this, don't you? I'll give you a hint: it wasn't *me*."

Creed doesn't react. Actually, he looks like he's about to fall asleep. Or have sex. Maybe the latter and then the former? I have no idea.

When he reaches out and tucks some loose strands of rose-gold hair behind my ear, I'm too startled to react.

"The girls want to kill you," he says, and I'm actually quite sure he's *not* speaking metaphorically. "Watch out for them."

"And you?" I retort, crossing my arms over my chest. Creed's eyes drop to the bare bit of skin above my blouse. It was a bit hot in here, so I took my red tie off and unbuttoned a few buttons. It feels like he can see everything, the way he's staring at me. "What do you want?"

"I want you to *leave*," he says, stressing that last word and then falling back into the usual nonchalant gaiety of the idle rich. "Get out of Burberry Prep, and make yourself at home somewhere else. Why not go buddy up to your friend Lizzie at Coventry Prep?"

"Lizzie and I are *not* friends," I bark, and Creed laughs, the sound just as merry as Miranda's. However, where she reminds me of the school bell, happily reminding us all it's time for learning, Creed's bell-laugh is like the death knell of a church tower during a funeral.

"You seem to be *friends* with Zack Brooks. How is it he gets a free pass and she doesn't?"

"He did not get a free pass," I say, forcing myself to stay calm. Creed *wants* me to get pissed off and react. We just stare at each other, and it doesn't escape my notice that his shirt is also unbuttoned. I can see a bit of his chest, and my fingers twitch on the edge of my chair. Also, our knees are far too close, just a scant two inches apart. If I moved, I'd bump against his long, long legs. I stay perfectly still. "You saw what I did to him. Be glad all I've done is destroy your relationship with your mother and sister."

Creed's jaw clenches, the only sign that I've struck a nerve.

"If I wanted you to fall to your knees and weep for my mercy, I could have that." He leans suddenly toward me until our faces are inches apart. "I could *destroy* you, Charity."

"Really? Because everything you've thrown at me thus far has been weak as hell. I'm not afraid of you, Creed Cabot." We maintain this stare down, even though it kills me. His lips are so close, I can remember what they tasted like the night of the winter formal, that glorious night that I sat on his lap and kissed him in the crisp cold winter air. *Crap.* He smells good, too, like fresh linens and soap. *Don't think about his scent, Marnye, that's ridiculous.* "You can *say* all these horrible things if you want, but you're not going to act. Because if you do, you'll dig your own grave. Your sister already hates you, just keep pushing her and see how evil you can get before she abandons you completely. It must hurt a lot, to lose a twin." I cross my arms over my chest as Creed exhales and closes his eyes.

Yep.

He's like a neutered dog.

I was right to cross him off my list.

"You were bullied, too," I whisper finally, and he sits back, looking away sharply. His pretty blond hair falls forward and covers his face. He taps at his lips with a long finger, and I just can't help but admire how long all of his limbs are. He's tall and trim, but still muscular. The way his shirt pulls at his shoulders gives away a developing physique. "How could you do that to me?"

"How could you choose *Zayd?*" he hisses, turning back to me suddenly. I remember the way his face looked when I walked down the steps into the graduation gala in that red dress. My heart hurts a little, but I push the feeling aside. "Zayd." Creed laughs, the sound dry and reedy, and then he stands up. Well, more like he *unfolds* his long limbs from the chair, towering over me as he reaches up and pops open one more button. "If you'll excuse me."

He takes off around the table, pausing to meet up with Ileana Taittinger.

I watch him flirt with her as my insides twist into a dangerous knot. She's got an old name, a very well established family legacy. Hmm.

Maybe I crossed his name off just a *little* too soon?

I'll have to keep an eye on them.

For now, I gather my books, rise to my feet, and leave the sanctity of the library.

Dad isn't able to get off work to come and get me for fall break, so Zack gives me a ride home in his orange McLaren. We sit in silence for a good portion of the drive which I actually like. When I'm around Zack Brooks, I don't feel like I have to force anything. The quiet between us is companionable and easygoing, not strained or awkward.

BAD, BAD BLUE BLOODS

"I can't believe you're still hanging around me," I tell him, glancing up from my phone screen to look at his face. All I'm doing is trolling gossip sites anyway. Every single freaking article is about this prince guy, this Windsor York. He sounds like a total a-hole to me. He'd be right at home at Burberry Prep. According to the online gab rags, he sleeps with every celebrity, model, or billionaire heiress he can get his hands on. Reminds me of a certain someone, but at least his smile in all the pictures is nice.

Still … another manwhore, gross. No thank you.

I shut my phone off.

"Why is that so hard to believe?" Zack asks, his voice unbelievably soft. I notice he does that around me now, softens all of his hard edges. It almost … makes him likable. Almost. But not quite. He's taken up track now, and he's stupid good at it. I imagine he'll be earning himself another letterman jacket next year. Really, I should take him down another peg. But am I going to? We'll see. I don't trust him as far as I could throw him which, considering how muscular and tall he is, would not be all that far. "I told you how I feel about you."

My nostrils flare, and my throat closes up. Oh god. Now the silence really does feel awkward.

I stare out at the road and focus on the yellow lines.

Zack doesn't love me. That's weird. He's a freaking psycho bully. Remember how he treated Ileana during tryouts? He's a monster inside; he can't be trusted.

And yet, I'm so relaxed around him that I fall asleep and drool all over his expensive sports car. The next thing I know, he's carrying me into my bedroom at the Train Car, and tucking me in. Pretty sure I imagine it, but I think he kisses my forehead before I pass out again.

In the morning, I'm woken up by the scent of dad's famous vanilla waffles and I've forgotten all about the almost-possible-maybe-didn't-happen kiss.

"Good morning," I say, giving him a huge hug. He looks good, actually, much better than I'd feared. "How are you feeling?"

"Wonderful, actually," he says, handing me a plate. I smear peanut butter all over my waffles and douse them in real maple syrup. Don't ask: it's a Reed thing. As I sit down on the couch in the living room, I'm overwhelmed by emotion and have to choke back tears. I will *not* think negatively about my father or his prospects. What good would that do him? "The Du Pont Medical Center is incredible."

My mouth purses into a thin line, and I have to resist the urge to voice my fears. Why, exactly, Harper is helping my father out, I don't know. To hold it over my head? I can only imagine the whole situation is going to end poorly. If she messes with my father's heath however … god help her.

"Also, I wanted to talk to you about your mother …"

"Please don't make me see her," I blurt. I'm not ready for that. Jennifer and I have a strained relationship at best. Being home means taking care of dad and getting a break from the rat race that is Burberry Preparatory Academy. If I have to spend any forced afternoons with her, I'll collapse.

"I won't," Dad says, surprising me. I put my fork down and lean back into the cushions, playing with Grandma

Reed's charm bracelet. I don't dare take it to school with me. Can you imagine what those Blueblood psychos would do if they got a hold of it? "It was wrong of me to try to force a relationship." He swallows hard and glances away, like he's ashamed about something. I narrow my eyes.

"You didn't buy a chicken instead of a turkey again this year?" I ask, already thinking ahead to Thanksgiving dinner. Charlie chuckles and glances back at me, the skin around his eyes crinkling as he smiles.

"Wow, you know me too well," he says, laughing. But it feels so … forced. That was *not* what he was going to say. I narrow my eyes, but Dad's already standing up and moving into the kitchen to fry up some eggs. I'm already stuffed, but I don't have the heart to tell him no. Besides, I just like watching him cook, smelling the smells, sinking into the ratty old couch.

If the Idols think money buys happiness, I feel sorry for them.

This, this right here is what life is all about.

Dad isn't exactly thrilled to receive an invitation from Zack's family to have Thanksgiving dinner at the Brooks' place. He hasn't said much since the video came out at the football game, but I know he's upset. More for me than for him, but still, even though I told him I forgave Zack, it isn't enough. Nor should it be, considering what Zack did to me.

Still, when the invitation comes, it's tempting to go.

"I did not know he was the one that drove you home from school," Dad says, crossing his arms over his chest and looking at me like he's severely disappointed. I tuck my bottom lip under my teeth and grimace. I never lie to my dad; I try to make it a habit not to lie at all. The thing is, I didn't exactly tell him either.

"Dad," I start, glancing over at the brown paper bags full of groceries on the counter. I went shopping for everything we would need to have a huge Thanksgiving feast, but I'm just … tired, and Dad's tired, and quite frankly it sounds kind of fun to hang out with Zack. Does that make me a crazy person? "Look, I'm not trying to minimize what Zack did to me. But I know you like to hang out with him, and I know he kept you company last year when I was gone. Going over to his house for dinner doesn't mean that he's been forgiven or that has sins have been forgotten." I exhale and slide my palms down the front of my red skirt. "But don't you think he deserves a second chance? You gave one to Jennifer."

Charlie purses his thin lips and tucks his hands into the pockets of his paint-covered overalls. He must believe in second chances, or he really wouldn't be having an affair with Jennifer. We haven't talked about that yet; it seems so unimportant right now. Dad's health is the only thing that matters.

"I guess they'll probably have a full spread over there …" He starts, and I grin. I don't need to keep pressing: I've already won him over. Dad says I forgive too easily, but he also believes in the power of forgiveness. It's a fine line to walk.

So on Thursday, we had over to the Brooks' family home in Dad's rusted-out Ford. It rattles down the pristine white limestone driveway, coming to a stop near an impressive set of steps. The porch on this house is as big as the entire Train Car.

Zack is waiting outside, leaning casually against the wall near the front door with his big hands tucked into the pockets of his black slacks. I surprised to see him dressed up in a white button-down and jacket. He seems so uncomfortable in it, like he'd rather be in sweats and a tank, working out in the gym. Even though he seems nonchalant, I can tell he's nervous about our visit. Probably nervous about confronting my father. As he should be, anyway.

Charlie gets out of the car in his unflattering yellow and red plaid button-down (I tried to convince him not to wear it) and brown slacks. Pretty sure this is the same outfit he wore to his friend's wedding two or three decades ago. He's also wearing an extreme frown that looks carved into the slightly wrinkled planes of his face. As he makes his way around the front of the truck and heads up the stairs, Zack lifts his head and meets my eyes.

There's no doubt about it: my heart stumbles, trips, falls. I have a hard time breathing, and my palms are suddenly sweaty. I curse those damn teenage hormones out again, and roll my eyes as Charlie approaches Zack with a no-nonsense expression on his face.

"Zack."

"Mr. Reed."

The two men stare each other down, and I wait at the bottom of the steps to see who will break the tension first. Even though I can tell it pains him, Zack is the one to do it, glancing away from my father and toward the rocking chair covered pumpkins, bits of hay, and a smiling scarecrow. The entire porch is decorated in fall themes: orange, red, and yellow leaves, turkey silhouettes, horns of plenty. I wonder who did the decorating? Probably someone that was paid to do it. The Brooks don't exactly strike me as a family who does their own decorating.

Zack looks back to my father again, and meets his stare dead-on.

"Sir, I apologized to your daughter once, but I'll do it again. I'd like to apologize to you, too." Zack lifts his chin proudly. "For the things I've done, there are no words to make up for it. But I really am sorry. From now on, I'll try to be a better man. It wasn't Marnye's job to teach me how to be one, but she already has anyway." Zack turns his brown gaze over to me, and I feel a little thrill shoot through me. It takes everything I have in me not to fidget. "Thank you, Marnye."

Before I can think of what to say, the front door opens, and Zack's mom, Robin, steps out. She's dressed in a tasteful cream suit with low heels, her chocolate hair frothing around her face. When she sees me, she smiles.

"To be honest," she says, as she tucks her hands in her

pockets and steps onto the deck, "I didn't think you were going to accept our invitation. But I'm glad you did." Robin glances over at Charlie, and they shake hands in a very businesslike manner. I know they had a long, long conversation at the football game, but I'm not entirely sure how it went down. "Come on in."

Robin gestures for us to head inside, and we do, moving down a long, marble hallway and into a formal dining room that's laid out like a magazine spread.

"My parents love to put on a show," Zack whispers, leaning over my shoulder and putting his lips near my ear. My entire body goes white-hot in an instant and goose bumps spring up along my arms. Luckily, Dad is too busy being introduced to Zack's sister, Kelsey, and some family friends of theirs. Zack's dad is nowhere to be seen. "Just ... don't praise my mom for her home cooking," he adds with a slight quirk of his mouth. "It's all catered."

Zack pulls out a chair for me, and I tuck my fluffy red skirt under my thighs before sitting. He rests his hands briefly on my shoulders before pushing me in and sitting beside me. Charlie's definitely watching us now, and I flush.

"I have to admit, I didn't want to come over here," Dad says as he sits across from me, and Robin takes up her spot at the head of the table. Zack's sister sits across from him, and the couple—I didn't catch either of their names—is at the end of the table. "But my daughter is a very forgiving soul. It's a trait I can't bear to discourage."

I smile tightly, and Zack raises both of his dark brows. If Charlie only knew ... Would he be proud of me? Or disappointed? I try not to think too hard about it.

"Well, my son is quite the opposite, unfortunately," Robin says, and Zack narrows his eyes. He looks at his mother, and they exchange one of those quiet, personal conversations that requires no words. "He seems to take after his father, sadly enough."

"Why do you say things like that?" Zack whispers, his voice low and dark, menacing. "You know that's a bunch of bullshit. I'm *nothing* like him."

"What you did to this girl," Robin says, as she stands up with a pair of carving knives in hand. She's a bit scary like that. "That was something your father would've done at your age. If you're ashamed, then good: you should be."

Zack scowls, but I smile. Robin reminds me of Kathleen a little, just a bit … softer? After a moment, she sighs and forces a smile of her own.

"I love you, son. Don't mess this up. Pulling a girl's pigtails because you like her isn't cute."

"Like her?" Dad echoes, looking between me and Zack like he's just now figured something out.

Oh god.

Robin chuckles as Charlie narrows his eyes on her son. Meanwhile, Zack just sits there like he always does, a chiseled bunch of muscles and a narrowed dark gaze. When he glances over at me, I suddenly decide we're sitting too close. But would scooting my chair away a few inches be too obvious? Probably.

"The boy has a crush," Robin says, and her friends both laugh while Dad sits there with his brow all scrunched up. Zack's sister, Kelsey, isn't shy about voicing her opinions either. She doesn't look like Zack or her mother, so I figure her pale orange hair and light green eyes are a product of their father's genetics.

"He pined after her all last year. It was absolutely intoxicating."

Zack growls at his sister, but Robin just tsk-tsks at them and starts to carve the turkey, passing out slices to me and Dad first, then her friends, her daughter, and lastly, her son. She winks at him when she finally passes over the plate.

"I'm just glad they're both going to the academy," Kelsey says, smiling prettily at me. She seems nice enough, but I'm so wary of beautiful girls now. I shouldn't be—that's some stupid internalized misogyny right there—but it's true. I'm scared of beautiful boys, too, so at least nobody could call me sexist. "Zack's basically obsessed."

"Okay, Kelsey, you can shut the fuck up now," Zack says, but I'm holding back laughter, and Dad is terrified out of his mind.

"The f-word at the dinner table? Come on, Zack Marcus Brooks, have some class." Robin takes her seat, and we all serve ourselves from the side dishes. Everything looks so pretty, like it's from a cooking show or something. It's prettier than last year, when Zack and I sat at a big, lonely table all by ourselves. This is much better.

I'm overwhelmed briefly by déjà vu, like I'm playing out the same story out, just with a different outcome. Creed with the notebook, Zack at Thanksgiving. But this time, when the bet is won, and hearts are being shattered like fragile glass baubles, it won't be mine that's on the ground in bloodied pieces.

No, this time, it's the Idols who are going to get a taste of their own medicine.

I smile as I scoop up a bit of sweet potato and catch Zack watching me.

Underneath the table, his long leg bumps into mine, and I feel my throat get suddenly tight. Butterflies take over, and it takes all I've got to focus on the conversation at hand. Apparently Robin's friends own a vineyard and they're looking for someone to create some custom ironwork arches, benches, and beds for their B&B. Dad ends up with a job and a glass of scotch that costs more than his car, while Zack and I retreat to the backyard and dip our legs in the heated pool.

We're sitting close enough that our thighs line up. It's funny, looking at them like that. Mine is so much smaller than his.

"You pined for me all last year, huh?" I ask, and Zack's mouth purses tight. He has such a full lower lip. As I stare at it, I can't help but remember that kiss at the football stadium, and it's just … like, *all of the feels.* All of them.

"Maybe." He turns to look at me, moonlight catching on his masculine features, that straight Greek nose of his, that full mouth. Goodness. I exhale sharply and turn away, looking out across the water. "Would it make any difference?"

"Not really." *But maybe.* I keep that thought to myself, knocking my heels against the side of the pool. "How did you and Lizzie come to make that bet anyway?"

Zack goes still beside me, but after a moment, he exhales, like he's given up.

"Lizzie was a senior member of the Infinity Club; she was

sponsoring me. A sponsor always has to challenge their new recruit to a game with high stakes. She was goaded by the other girls. Don't let Harper or Becky or anyone else pretend to be innocent in all of that."

"And you? Who were you goaded by? Are you going to blame Tristan, Creed, and Zayd for what you did?" Zack shakes his head, reaching up to run his palm over his hair. His shirt is unbuttoned now, and he's rolled his slacks up to his knees. Seeing his interactions with his mother, it's clear he wore the outfit to please her. It's kind of cute actually, to get this little snippet of his life that shows he cares. It makes this very clear distinction in my mind between Zack and Creed.

Creed doesn't care if he upsets his family or not. Well, I mean he *cares*, but yet he does it anyway. It's so frustrating to watch.

"No. I take full responsibility for my actions." Zack sighs again, like he's suddenly so tired. "But you've seen them: they're monsters. All three of them. Honestly, Marnye, take your revenge and then run. You won't see any remorse from them."

"I'm not expecting any," I admit, looking at the curving maze of gardens that makes up Zack's backyard. Well, *one* of his backyards I guess, considering I've already seen three of his family's houses: this one, the lake house from last year, and the place he used to live when he attended LBMS. I wonder why his grandfather chose to cut his family off in the first place … and what spurred him to give it all back? "That's not the point of all of this. Their whole lives, they've gotten away with whatever they wanted. The rest of their lives, they probably will, too. For this one, tiny blip on their timeline, I want them to know what it feels like. If it stops them from victimizing one person, then it's worth it."

"And that's it?" Zack asks, voice gently probing, but not pushing. "It has nothing to do with the fact that they broke your heart?"

I purse my lips tight and dig my nails into the cement edge of the pool.

"If it does, it's none of your business," I tell him, my voice rough. He turns away sharply, and we sit there in silence for several minutes, the water lapping at our bare legs.

"We don't deserve you," Zack growls finally, pushing away from the edge of the pool. "Not a single one of us. Remember that, Marnye." He turns and pads away with wet feet.

I sit there staring at my reflection until Charlie comes to get me, wondering about my own motivations.

Wondering if my broken glass heart isn't still making me bleed.

CHAPTER

10

After break, school starts off at a run and doesn't slow down. I have so little downtime that my revenge plans come to a brief halt while I catch up on my studies, cheer team practices, and orchestra rehearsals. Zack has started training for track and field in February, and Miranda is off in la-la land with Jessie. They are now officially dating. I'm excited for them, but sometimes I catch Miranda gazing off into the distance like she's daydreaming about someone else.

Uh-oh.

My tutoring activities with Creed continue, and the school's so impressed with my 'resilience' (as they've called it), that I've been drafted into being a student mentor. Basically, I'm there to help students who are having issues with bullying, or help guide first-years who are struggling. Of course, nobody ever signs up to work with me. I still get credit for it though, so that's fine.

During the end of our first week back, I strike gold by pure accident.

I'm on my way from my dorm—somebody's scratched the

word *Brothel* into the door yet again—to the mixed media room to practice some songs for the winter concert. When I get there, however, the room is occupied by Zayd and his cronies.

His howling laughter echoes out into the hall as I pause and glance in. Becky is all over him, making my stomach turn as she nuzzles up against him. She's changed out of her uniform into a pink tank with no bra, and she's pressing her chest against his. I wonder if they've had sex? I figure they probably have, and my stomach twists in disgusts.

I end up clutching a fist against my chest, feeling the frantic rhythm of my heart.

Did I … get my heart broken by Zayd?

It certainly feels that way, watching him laugh and joke with his friends. When he presses a flat kiss to Becky's mouth, a sour taste rises in the back of my throat. His hair is now dyed a pale blue with dark roots, and his makeup is stage-dark, like he's getting ready for a concert. All that eyeliner highlights how beautiful his green eyes are, how long his lashes.

"Like, my new album sucks, but it's going to sell, you know that I mean?" Zayd asks, his husky rockstar voice giving me the chills. Without a second's hesitation, I pull out my phone and start recording. There's nothing like letting these Idol idiots hang themselves.

"You mean because Plebs are so fucking stupid, they'll buy it regardless?" Becky asks, her laugh this grating sound that makes my skin crawl. She enjoys torture and pain like nobody but Harper du Pont.

"Yeah, like," Zayd starts, and then he gets out a cigarette and lights up. Smoking inside the chapel building is a strict taboo, but he doesn't seem to care, blowing gray smoke out from between his sexy lips. Watching his tattooed fingers clutch the cigarette shouldn't turn me on—I *hate* smoking, as a rule—but some random rebellious part of me is turned one. "I write this profound shit, and it does well, but not good enough. The record label is breathing down my neck for another hit. So they have some ghost writers drum up this drivel, and tell me it's going to make me famous. Maybe there's a reason some people are poor? They're stupid enough to spend what little money they have on this crap album."

The whole crowd laughs, and my gut turns to ice. Wow. How fucking dare he insult his fans like that? Raking in their hard-earned money and mocking them for it.

"Anyway, you guys want to hear the new single? The peons are going to absolutely lap it up." Becky climbs Zayd like a koala, and I swear, there's this flash of annoyance on his face as he gets out his phone and presses play on a pop-rock song that's a bit catchier than I'd like to admit.

Guess there's a reason I'm a peon, right? *Dick.*

"Once this is over, let's go back to my room and I'll suck you off," Becky purrs, rubbing herself all over Zayd and licking along the length of his ear. He pushes her back a step and she stumbles.

"Can we, like listen to this damn song?" he snaps, and her blue eyes go wide. She reaches out and pinches Zayd's tattooed arm with her long nails, and he sneers at her.

"You were all down for fucking until you started playing around with the Working Girl. Guess I can't compete with a prostitute's skillset, huh?"

"Becky, shut the hell up," Zayd groans, letting his head fall back, ink crawling up from underneath his wrinkled academy shirt.

"No, I will not shut up," she continues, and Sai Patel, Mayleen Zhang, Greg, and John all exchange looks with each other. "You have been so freaking weird. All summer you were weird. What is it about that low-class bitch that you're so obsessed with?"

Zayd drops his head and narrows his green eyes. I sense vitriol in the air.

"Low-class? Marnye might be trailer trash"—ouch, Zayd —"but she's a hundred times classier than you. I'm so done with your shit, Becky. You want me to be your boyfriend or something? Newsflash: I'm not interested anymore. Fuck, I was *never* interested. It was a game to see if I could get you, and guess what? You were a hundred times easier to dupe than Charity ever was."

Becky reaches out and slaps Zayd as hard as she can before turning and storming up the steps toward me. I scramble out of the way and duck into The Mess before she gets out the door. There's no one inside, fortunately, and once I think she's had enough time to leave, I creep back out.

Zayd's just started another song, so I wait there and record the entire thing.

"Pretty sure I'm as fucked-up as they come, the only one who knows the loneliness of my throne. Through the darkest nights there's only one bright star, but when I reach up, it's just way up there, off in the void, the black too far."

Mm.

I'm not sure I believe the ghostwriter bit.

Those lyrics *scream* Zayd Kaiser to me.

After it's over, there's a bit of silence before Sai Patel's laughter snaps out like a whip. He has a pretty strong New York accent, so it's easy to tell who's speaking. Other than the usual bits and barbs, he hasn't stood out to me much.

"That's the dumbest shit. Holy crap, man, that's garbage." The other boys laugh, Mayleen's feminine giggles interspersed throughout. When I peep around the corner, I wonder if I'm the only person who sees how tight Zayd's jaw is.

On Monday, I head out into the hall and a storm of chaos ensues.

"Marnye, oh my god," Miranda gushes, grabbing my hands, her face flushed pink. Her eyes are sparkling as she yanks me down the hall, our white skirts billowing, as we head to the courtyard and push through the throng of people to the front. There's a fancy black sports car down there, no driver in sight.

"Um, what?" I ask, as Miranda spins to me, smacking me in the face with her shiny blond hair. She almost smells like Creed, too. Is it weird that I notice that?

"That's Zayd's agent's car," she chokes out, pointing at it. "Before Ms. Felton collects our phones, *look it up*." I pull my phone from my bookbag and do as she's asking. Not that I need to, since I know exactly what's going on. "This has your signature all over it," she whispers, leaning in toward me as several staff members try to herd the students away from the courtyard. I glance up and our eyes meet. Miranda squeals, and I smile sheepishly.

All I did was upload Zayd's conversation, and part of his song. That's it.

His own words, however, are like a hole in the side of a ship, slowly filling with water. Zayd Kaiser is going to sink.

Son of Famous Rocker Billy Kaiser Rips on his Fans

That's the first article that pops up. They didn't even identify him by name in the headline, just by his dad's accomplishments. Good. My brows go up as I keep scrolling.

Easy-to-Love Zayd Kaiser is Actually Full of Shit

Oh, I like that headline.

"Marnye," Zack says, coming to stand beside us. His hair is still wet from his morning shower—he always makes time to shower after his morning run—but his uniform is in order, even if his tie is slightly crooked. "This is brilliant."

The crowd parts and a hush falls over the gathered students as a man in a suit storms forward, a shaggy-haired guy in jeans close on his heels. Zayd is right there, trailing along behind him, his face crestfallen, his eyes wet with angry tears.

He follows the other two men down the steps to stand by the car, and they speak in hushed tones for several minutes before Zayd steps back and the others climb in and speed off.

"That was Billy Kaiser," Miranda whispers in my ear. It's pretty easy to tell, even without her confirming it. The way Zayd watches him, with this mix of hatred and yearning, he couldn't be anyone else. After a moment, Zayd turns and heads back up the steps. At first, I think he's going to walk on by, but then he stops and turns.

Our gazes met, and the crowd takes in a collective inhale as Zayd makes his way over to stand in front of me. His chest is heaving, and he's soaked in sweat, his pale blue hair stuck to his forehead. There's no gel in it this morning, no liner around his eyes. He looks like he wants to kill me.

"What have you done?" he snaps, but all I do is stand there and stare. I make myself remember my panties in his hand, that video of us kissing on the screen. The trophy, his face, the way he just stood there with his arm around freaking Becky Platter instead of me.

"Challenge accepted, met, and executed," I say, and Zayd lets out this scream that's strangely melodic. He was born to sing. Also born to be a dick, apparently. He reaches up and grabs his hair in two fists like he might be *this* close to having a nervous breakdown.

Zack steps up next to me, crossing his arms over his massive chest, like he's a bodyguard or something.

"You do *not* fucking intimidate me," Zayd hisses, sneering. "You're no angel, Zack Brooks. Eventually, Marnye will see it, and she'll dump you for someone like *me*." This last part snaps off his tongue like an insult before he spins away and storms through the crowd, elbowing people out of the way as he goes.

My list is in the front pocket of my bag, so I pull it out, unfold it, and enjoy the squeak of the red Sharpie in the silence of the courtyard.

It feels so good to cross Zayd's name off my list.

Tristan is a tricky little Idol to pin down. I almost feel like he's actively avoiding me which makes zero sense, considering all the threats he's leveled my way.

So my next step is sitting down with Miranda and going over exactly what happened in the Hamptons during the summer. According to her—and she *is* the gossip queen— Lizzie Walton declared war on the Burberry Prep Idols. Tristan, in particular, was on the receiving end of her wrath.

"She did it all for you, I think," Miranda hazards, but even though I've sort of forgiven Zack, how can I deal with Lizzie? What can I do to get back at her that will even the odds? But contacting her is probably the best chance I have at finding some way to get under Tristan's skin. I mean, I'm still kicking his ass in the academics department, but I did that last year, too. It's not enough, not even close.

Besides, I won't admit it aloud, but … I miss Lizzie. Every Friday, I looked forward to our conversations. Burberry Prep life feels much emptier without her.

"She's still in love with him, too," Miranda adds with a wistful, sad sounding sigh. "She's going to marry that douche guy, what's-his-face, the one that always adjusts his junk and licks his lips while he does it? Anyway, she's going to marry him, but it's going to be Tristan she's dreaming about on her wedding night."

"Do you think he still loves her?" I ask, an idea taking place in the back of my mind. Even though I know it's ridiculous, I wait with bated breath for Miranda to answer my question.

"Definitely," she says, and it's like an arrow's just gone through my heart. Doesn't make any sense. As soon as I saw Tristan look at Lizzie Walton last year, I knew it, too. Everyone knows it. He never loved me. How could he? It was a game all along. *Although Zack* … Nope. I shut that part of my brain down and refuse to go there. Dating Zack won't work, not with the plans I already have in mind. "Why? You want to share a room with him on the ski trip or something?" Miranda chuckles, and I wrinkle my nose. "Are you *jealous*?"

"Gross," I laugh, pushing at her as she pushes back at me. "I'm not going on the ski trip." Miranda blinks stupidly at me. Instead of the winter formal, second-years are given the option to attend an academy-sponsored ski trip. The cars leave the last Friday before winter break, and drop students at their houses (or the airport) on Tuesday which is Christmas

Eve.

"You *have* to go on the ski trip," she groans, putting her forehead down on the picnic table. We're sitting outside, enjoying the icy morning and the bright rays of sunshine that make the frost evaporate like fog. "It's a rite of passage."

"The last time you used that phrase on me, you dragged me to that beach party."

"And you had fun, despite the assholes in residence, right?" she asks, lifting her head up from the table. I sigh, and Miranda smiles softly. "I know you want to get back home to your dad, but it's just a few days." I give her a skeptical look, tapping my fingers on the table. "Oh, at least think about, Ms. Revenge. But factor this in, at least: there's so much cheating and fooling around on the ski trip that it's now academy legend to call the lodge *Hookup Point*." She grins at me as I raise my eyebrows. "Do you see how messed-up Jalen and Ebony still are from the journal? Come on the ski trip, and I guarantee you'll find some dirt worth digging up."

"After some careful consideration …" I begin, and Miranda squeals with laughter, giving me a huge hug. From the corner of my eye, I see Creed watching us and flip him off.

His sister would rather be with me than with him.

He smirks at me as he rounds the corner, and I see then that he's got Anna Kirkpatrick on his arm.

Hmm.

Fine. Challenge accepted is right.

"I'll go," I tell Miranda, watching Anna carefully.

If she's not messing around with one of the other

Bad, Bad Blue Bloods

Bluebloods, I'll be shocked.

Loyalty isn't exactly in their DNA.

The door to the music room opens, and Zayd walks in, surprising me. He's got his fingers tucked into the pockets of his wrinkled white academy slacks. His jacket is nowhere to be seen, and his tie is loose and flipped over his right shoulder. With the sleeves rolled up, I can see two muscular arms wrapped in ink.

My fingers pause in their dance across the harp strings, putting an end to the harp solo from Donizetti's opera *Lucia di Lammermoor.* I sit back in my chair and watch him warily as he approaches. Mr. Carter is in his attached office with the door closed, so nothing truly bad can happen here. I cross my arms over my chest and wait.

Oddly enough, one of the things I miss most from last year is having Tristan attend my orchestra practices. Having him sit in one of the back rows, fingers steepled, eyes locked on me ... There was an intensity in him that transferred to my music. I feel like I played better when he was around.

Zayd comes all the way down the steps of the auditorium and pauses next to the raised platform in the front. I'd call it a stage, but it's only ever used for teachers giving lectures. No performances actually happen here.

"Is this how you got me?" he asks, reaching up to rake his fingers through his pale blue hair. He looks around the room like he's never seen it before. But I know he's in here all the time. That look of sweet, mussy confusion is bullshit, just like all his other expressions. Zayd plays charming very, very well. "Eavesdropped outside this door and fucked me?"

"All I did was upload your own words to one website." I hold up a single finger. "One." His green eyes meet my brown ones, and I can't deny that there's chemistry between us. There's always chemistry between us, whether I want to admit it or not. His being a jerk doesn't change that. "If you hadn't said those things, then they wouldn't be around to haunt you."

I lift my hands back to the strings of the harp, and get ready to play again, dismissing him. He doesn't go anywhere though, just sits down to watch and listen. I play through three songs before I realize he's not going away, dropping my hands to my lap and glaring.

"What do you want?" I ask, and Zayd smiles tightly. He uses his tongue and plays with his lip rings for a moment before responding.

"I have to admit," he says, tapping inked fingers on the arm of the chair, "you've got bigger balls than I thought."

I frown at him.

"Bigger ovaries, maybe?" I almost smile, but Zayd just

shrugs and stands up. He's like a dream in the white second-year uniform. It's as if the total lack of color on his outfit emphasizes how much color he's got all over his skin. He moves over to stand beside me, and my breath catches in my throat. I know I'm not the only one that notices. Zayd reaches out to tuck a loose strand of hair behind my ear, and I let him, even though I know I shouldn't.

"Whatever you want to call it, you've got it. Big balls, ironclad uterus, deep dark mojo … Anyway," he points two fingers at me, like he's miming a gun, "you shot me right in the crotch with that one. Bull's-eye, bingo, win for you. The record label's just pulled my new album." He frowns down at me, and there's a well of sadness in his emerald green eyes that surprises me. It mirrors the face of the girl whose expression I saw in my reflection that day last year. So good. He's hurting. It's what I wanted, isn't it?

"There will be a new album," I say with a sigh, putting my hands in my lap. I have special permission to wear white academy slacks when playing the harp. It's a pedal harp, so I need to use my foot, and if I wore the standard second-year skirt there would be more on display than just my music. "That's the problem with all of you; you'll never know what it's truly like to hurt. There's always more money, new opportunities, underhanded favors …"

Zayd shakes his head, and reaches into his pocket to pull out a small packet of papers. He hands them over to me, and I hesitate a moment before taking them.

"Nah, not this time. My dad is so pissed, he thinks this might affect his career too, so he's asked the label to drop me completely." Zayd waits a moment as I unfold the papers, frowning as I find a copy of the test I took on Friday. Well, the test is the same, but the answers are not the ones I gave. My name might be on top of the paper, but this is not my test. "You are now looking at an unsigned, penniless musician." Zayd laughs and reaches up to twist his gelled hair into little spikes.

I'm so distracted by the test, and the essay underneath it which also has my name but not my words, that it takes me a moment to register what he's just said. I look up.

"They don't want you to, like, give a statement or something?" I ask. Zayd gives me this wry little smirk, like he could care less. It's quite obvious he cares a whole hell of a lot.

He ignores my question, brushing it aside with a wave of his hand.

"Look, you're not going to catch Tristan with his hands in the cookie jar." Zayd reaches out to tap the papers in my hand, and our fingers brush together. Heat leaps from his skin to mine, and we both shiver. It's not fair. It's not fair that I have chemistry with an asshole like Zayd Kaiser. "That's a test with a score of about …" Zayd pauses to think for a minute. "Sixty-five percent? In the essay, that's a copy of Gena Whitley's essay from last year. Plagiarism and all that."

"Why do these things have my name on them?" I ask, feeling my heart thunder wrapped rapidly in my chest. It should've occurred to me that the idols would try to strike me where it would hurt most (other than my dad, of course): academics. I look up at Zayd. "And why are you showing me these?"

Bad, Bad Blue Bloods

"Becky left her jacket with me the other day," Zayd starts, rolling his eyes like he just can't with her. The funny thing is, they are two peas in a pod; they deserve each other. "These fell out of it. I have to take them to her now, and I figure when she does her third period office work tomorrow, organizing Miss Peregrine's papers, she'll swap these out for your real test and essay."

Zayd reaches out to take the papers, and I let him, thoroughly confused.

"Why are you telling me this?" I repeat, as Zayd tucks the papers away into his bookbag. "I don't understand."

The guys have been much easier on me this year than last year, but that doesn't make any sense. They must be gearing up for something big.

"For what it's worth," Zayd says, turning away and glancing over his shoulder at me, "as soon as I found out that Becky had hit you, I haven't touched her. I just couldn't." Zayd wrinkles his nose, and shakes his head. "I don't want you to get hurt, so please, for the love of all that's holy, Charity, just go."

Zayd turns back around and heads up the stairs. I watch him go, and then I do my best to come up with a plan.

CHAPTER
11

After cheerleading practice the next day, I head to the office of our English teacher, Miss Peregrine. The room is locked and dark, the lights off, and the shade over the small window pulled down. To get in, I'm either going to need a key... or a lockpick.

Cursing under my breath, I head back to the chapel building, down the hall and out the stained glass doors on the other side. Once I get to Tower Three, I take the elevator to the fifth floor and head over to Zack's room. I barely raise my fist to knock when he's opening it, dressed in low-slung sweats, no shirt, and a fine layer of fresh sweat.

"Marnye?" he asks, stepping aside to let me in. There is some seriously sexy jazz music on, and all the shades are pulled down. For a moment there, I wonder if I'm interrupting something that I don't want to see.

BAD, BAD BLUE BLOODS

I spin around, and find Zack is suddenly standing far too close to me. He smells good too, which is really weird considering he's all sweaty. But seriously, there's something so different between fresh sweat and old sweat. The latter is disgusting, but the former ... it's almost like a cologne. I find myself attracted to it even though I don't want to be.

"Is there a girl in here?" I ask, and Zack narrows his eyes on me. He takes a step forward, and I take one back. The movement surprises him, and he ends up raising one of his dark brows.

"That bother you?" he replies, his voice dark and smooth and cold as bittersweet chocolate ice cream. He takes a step toward me again, but I have nowhere to go. My butt bumps up against the table, and Zack puts one hand on either side of me.

"No," I lie, ducking out from underneath his arm and stepping aside. When I turn back to face him again, he's smirking. My first instinct is to wipe that look off of his face, but instead I just sigh. "When we went to Lower Banks, didn't you get in trouble for stealing a car?"

Zack is still smirking as he leans back against the table and crosses his muscular arms over his bare, sweaty chest. We always seem to be together when he's shirtless, Zack and me. Like the universe is trying to throw us together.

"Yeah, so?" He looks me up and down appreciatively, and I shiver. I'm wearing the short black practice shorts with the rhinestones on the butt cheeks that I hate, a pair of red bike shorts underneath, and a black razorback tank top with the Burberry crest logo on the front. Even cheerleading *practice* comes with required uniforms.

"I need your help," I say, hating the phrase even as it leaves my mouth. "Could you pick a lock on a teacher's door?"

Zack thinks for a moment, letting his chin fall down and his eyes close. After a moment, he looks back up at me and gives me a sexy sideways smirk.

"I could. It's risky though, with the bodyguard guy patrolling the halls, and all those new cameras. But if we had a cover story, some reason to be over there that didn't involve … whatever it is that you're up to, it might work." His smirk turns into a grin, and I shift uncomfortably. "I'm assuming this has to do with the revenge plot?"

"Maybe …" I hedge, and Zack's grin gets a little wider.

"Let me put a shirt on then." He pauses and takes a few steps closer to me, his chocolate brown eyes staring at me through his thick lashes. "Unless … you'd rather I wasn't wearing one?"

"Shirt is fine," I blurt, holding my ground. "But if you have an extra sweater, I'll take it. It's freezing outside." Zack laughs at me, and snatches his hoodie from the back of the couch, tossing it over to me. I slip it on and quickly realize that drowning in a big, soft, Zack-scented hoodie is both a blessing and a curse. *If I were his girlfriend, I'd wear his hoodie all the time.*

"Right," Zack says, taking in my much smaller form as I burrow in his hoodie, and running his tongue over his lower lip. "Sure, and lock picking kit."

"You brought a lock picking kit to the academy?"

Zack glances over his shoulder and grins, this dark sensual

expression that gives me goose bumps.

"I guess you can take the boy out of the bad school, but you can't take the bad out of the boy." He winks theatrically at me, and I can't decide if what he's just said is sexy or hilarious.

I choose the safer option and laugh, but that doesn't mean that my heart doesn't race or that I don't bundle the hoodie close around me.

Zack and I head outside together, moving through the winter-dead gardens toward a cluster of admin buildings. There are a few students here and there, but because of the cold front we got last week, most people are still inside. It really is chilly out here.

Campus security patrols the area regularly, and I know there are cameras, too. I also know that the footage isn't regularly checked, not unless there's a problem.

Besides, Zack says he has a plan.

As we approach the door to Miss Peregrine's office, Zack grabs me by the shoulders and turns me around, looking straight into my face with a very serious expression.

"Will you trust me with this?" he asks, voice sober. "I'm

not asking you to trust me all the time, just right now."

I nod my head, and before I know it, Zack is backing me up against the door. He wraps his right arm around my waist, pressing our bodies together. His mouth drops to mine, warm breath fluttering across my lips.

"Can I kiss you again?" he whispers, and then he smiles softly. We're so close, I can feel the emotion against my own mouth. "It's all part of the plan, of course. Although, I can't deny that seeing you in my hoodie isn't exciting as fuck."

With his left hand, Zack pulls a small metal tool from inside his pocket, and inserts it into the lock on the door. There's not much in these offices but papers, framed certificates, and desks, so the locks aren't exactly high-tech. I imagine Zack will have us in in no time.

I also suddenly understand what he meant by having a plan. If we're caught, all the security guard will see are two students making out. They won't see the lockpick, and they won't need to ask what we're doing out here. Even if we get in trouble, we can claim we were trying to get into the office to … have some private time together.

The logical part of me wants to admit that this is a brilliant plan; the nonlogical part of me has a racing heart, sweating palms, and a sudden heat flaring between her thighs.

"Kiss me," I choke out, before I can lose my nerve and take off running. Not only is what I'm about to do important for my revenge against Tristan, but it's also important so that I don't lose what I've worked so hard for. If that plagiarized essay comes out, I could very well be expelled.

Honestly, some part of me, buried in the deep dark

shadows of my chest, has her feelings hurt. I knew Tristan wasn't a good guy, but I always thought that at least when it came to academics, we are willing to fight clean. Looks like I was wrong. And that kills me. "Do it—" I start, and Zack cuts me off with a punishing kiss that's all heat and passion and desire.

His right arm flexes, and it's a joy to feel those rock-hard muscles pulling me against him, tucking my body against his. His smell, that grapefruit and nutmeg musk of his, surrounds me like a cloud. Not only does *he* smell glorious, but his hoodie's not half-bad either.

His tongue slides across my lower lip, dives into my mouth, and draws an embarrassing groan from me. My hands fist in the front of the hoodie that he's wearing, and within seconds, there's the clicking sound of a lock, and the pair of us are stumbling into the empty office.

Zack heels the door shut behind him, but he doesn't stop kissing me. In fact, I somehow end up sitting on the edge of Miss Peregrine's desk with his huge body between my thighs. He pushes up against me, and I can feel a hardness in his sweats that wasn't there before.

This is such a bad idea, I think to myself, but that doesn't stop me from wrapping my legs around him and kissing harder. Zack is moaning now, too, and after he slips the little metal lockpick back into his pocket, he uses both hands to cup my ass. His fingers knead my flesh as I arch into him. Heat blossoms so wild and hot between us, that I almost forget what I'm doing and why I'm there … that I almost forget what he did to me.

Then the realization of where we are and how dangerous

this is hits me.

My palms come up to push against Zack's chest, and he pauses, lifting his mouth just slightly away from mine. I can still feel the hardness between his legs, and the answering heat between mine.

"Will you keep watch at the door?" I whisper, and Zack closes his eyes like he's in pain. He exhales sharply, closes his eyes and nods before stepping away. When he turns around, and thinks I'm not looking, he reaches into his sweats and … adjusts himself.

Even with my body flushed and hot, and a warm liquid feeling between my thighs, I manage to get up and find a stack of papers next to a scanner and a shredder. There are instructions on the wall, laminated, and impossible to miss.

1. *Scan both sides of the assignment.*
2. *Check to make sure the images are readable.*
3. *Shred the pages.*
4. *Make sure each assignment file is labeled with the student's name and ID number.*

Shit.

Frantically, I search the stack of papers in the wire basket next to the scanner, and breathe a huge sigh of relief when I find the ones with my name on them. Next, I search out Tristan's assignments.

For a moment, I get lost in the words of this essay. He's a brilliant writer, maybe better than me even. I tell myself I'm reading the assignment to make sure this plan will actually work, if there's anything in Tristan's essay that will give the fake one I wrote away. But no, even though he's a good writer, he's like me: he only writes academically, not with his heart or soul.

The only time I wrote that way... No. I refuse to think about Creed reading my essay aloud. I got him back, and I got him back good.

I take Tristan's essay, fold it up, and slip it into the front pocket of the hoodie. Then I take out two more essays from inside that giant pocket, one that's a reprint of the essay I originally turned in, and one that's a plausible but pretty terrible essay. I thought about writing Tristan an F-worthy paper, but I thought that might be too obvious. I even considered putting his name on Gena Whitley's plagiarized essay, but that's not my style either.

I slip the two new essays back into the pile, making sure I put them in the same spots that the others were before. The plagiarized essay with my name on it also goes in my pocket, and then I do the same for the tests. Only this time, since the names can be easily erased, all I do is put my name on Tristan's paper, and his on the one that was planted by Becky.

"One of the campus security guards just walked by," Zack whispers. "This might be a good time to slip out."

I double and triple check to make sure that we have everything we came with, and that everything is left exactly as is.

When I move to stand beside Zack, he glances over at me, his gaze still lust-darkened, his lips still swollen from our kisses.

He opens the door and we step outside, making sure it's locked before we close it. We head back to the chapel building; I disappear into my dorm and close the door quickly behind me while Zack pads off down the hallway.

We don't talk about what happened in Miss Peregrine's office for a long, long time.

Next week, just before winter break, when grades are posted again, Tristan's drops substantially and I am now clearly in the lead again.

Take that, asshole.

CHAPTER

12

"Tristan is furious," Creed says, as he drapes himself over the chair next to mine in preparation for our tutoring session. I glance over at him, but I have this rule about having personal or private conversations with the Idol guys. It's just a no-go at this point.

Still, I can't help myself from teasing him.

"Whatever for?" I ask innocently, using my academy-issued iPad to pull up the assignment that we're supposed to be working on.

Creed laughs, and his laugh is just as lazy as everything else about him. Insouciant. Cavalier. Disregardful.

"Oh, don't act like such an innocent little lamb," he purrs, leaning in toward me, his eyes half-lidded, a wry smile on his lips. We haven't talked about what happened on Halloween. I imagine we're never going to. "We all knew what Tristan, Harper and Becky had planned. So who told you?" I ignore him and focus on the assignment. Not only am I helping him with his, but I also have to complete mine. "Was it Zayd?"

"Why don't you focus more on your work and less on what everybody else is doing? Maybe then you could stop being second-best to Tristan." I make myself smile as Creed frowns. In the back of my mind, I'm still dreaming up ways to mess with Tristan Vanderbilt. All I did this time was avert disaster for myself. Knocking him back to the second place spot he would've been in anyway if he'd left my essay and test alone, is not enough.

I think my only option at this point is Lizzie. I'm going to have to give her a call after this.

Creed reaches over suddenly, grabbing the arms of my chair and turning me to face him. One of his knees goes between my legs, and his hands keep my wrists pinned to the armrests. He leans in so close that our cheeks almost touch.

"If we wanted to," he starts, putting his mouth to my ear and giving it a little lick, "we could destroy you and have you begging for more within the span of a week. We could make your entire life a living hell, not just the one you have at the school."

Since Creed's knee is between my thighs, that puts my own knee up close and personal with his crotch. I knee him hard in the junk, and he releases me, rearing back like I've … well, just kicked him in the balls. His eyes narrow to slits.

"If that's the case, then why haven't you done it already?" He stares back at me and says nothing, does nothing. "I know your personal reasons, but what about Tristan? What about Zayd?" I stand up from the table, shoving my supplies into my bookbag and turning a full-force glare on Creed. "Here's some dirt to deliver back to the King." Creed's face twists in disgust at the word. "Tell him that I'm nowhere near done with him. If he wants to mess with the bull, he's going to get the horns." I lift my chin up, spinning in a swirl of skirts, and take off through the quiet darkness of the library.

Creed doesn't bother to follow or call after me. But that place where he licked my ear … it still burns.

There's a party the Thursday before winter formal, and the day before the second year's leave for their ski trip. The only reason I know about it is because the Idols paid one of the Plebs to use their off-campus privileges to go and buy them new dresses. The girl, that very same Clarissa that badmouthed me and was banned from the swim team by Zayd last year, is the one talking about it in the hall as I walk by.

After classes let out for the day, I dress up, head over to Zack's room, and pray that he is not shirtless and wearing shorts again before I knock.

When he answers, he's still dressed in his academy uniform, and he raises his brows at the pink jumpsuit and heels I've got on.

"You look nice," he says, and the way the word nice

comes out of his mouth … I know he means a whole hell of a lot more than just that. My cheeks flush, but I manage to hold his gaze without stuttering.

"Thanks. I'm on a mission tonight. Would you mind accompanying me?" Zack looks pretty shocked, but I know I can't go to an Infinity Club party without an Infinity Club member. I thought about asking Andrew, but despite Creed's warnings, Greg and John are stalking him in the hallways, trying to find him alone in a dark corner, if you know what I mean. Last time it happened, it was a Saturday night, and Andrew videoed the entire encounter. He just barely managed to make it back to his dorm in time. So I don't want to put Andrew in danger, and the only Infinity Club member I know that I don't have an ongoing feud with is Zack.

"Where are we going?"

I smile, and with my left hand, I play with the necklace hanging around my throat.

"To the Infinity Club party."

Zack's smile falls away, but mine stays right where it is.

BAD, BAD BLUE BLOODS

This time, the Idols have commandeered the use of the amphitheater, the same one that I was beat up in, doused with paint, and humiliated beyond belief.

Does not feel like a coincidence to me.

Zack leads the way, dressed casually in jeans, sneakers, and an old football hoodie from his last school. He peels down his waistband and shows his infinity tattoo to the guy at the door before we head inside. The last few Club parties I've been to didn't seem this official. They must be amping up security.

"You could've taken him," I whisper, smiling, "even though he is a fourth year, and I'm pretty sure he's on the varsity team based on the way he glared at you."

Zack gives me a little grin and shrugs his massive shoulders.

"Yeah, he's on the team, so by default he hates my guts." His mouth twitches a little. "But yeah, you're right: I could've taken him. Thing is, I'm guessing you have some special shit to stir up tonight. I didn't want to steal all of your thunder." Zack keeps my arm tucked in his as we weave through rows of seats filled with students making out, drinking, or playing cards. On the stage at the front of the room, that very same stage I sat on with my harp, the Bluebloods are situated around tables covered in what look like … knuckle bones? Gross.

"You remember the plan right?" I ask Zack, as I feel all of those judging eyes swing over to me. He nods briefly, and we make our way up the steps towards the table where Tristan, Zayd, and Creed are sitting with Becky, Harper, and Ileana.

Tristan sneers at me, and tosses the bones on the table. I

mean, he can't exactly complain about what I did to him considering it was a lot less bad than what he wanted to do to me. I didn't give him the plagiarized essay, even though I could have.

"You must be stupid, if you came here willingly," he snaps, losing that practiced self-control that I both hated and admired from last year. I can see the faintest outline of a bruise on his face, and my hand clenches into a small fist at my side. As much as I dislike the guy, I think his dad might be beating him. That's never okay.

"Are those bones?" I ask, looking skeptically at the little white and cream-colored bits on the table. Harper flips her brunette waves over her shoulder and smirks at me. Her right hand comes to rest on Tristan's, and she weaves their fingers together before giving his a squeeze. Much as I hate to admit it, the sight makes me feel sick to my stomach.

"My dad has a private museum in his New York penthouse. He's a bit of the Civil War nut." The way Harper's smiling at me reminds me of the Grinch, like the expression is crawling across her face like a disease. "He has a whole storage room full of useless artifacts he's forgotten about. These bones were never going to see the light of day anyway, so I borrowed them." She shrugs her shoulders, her shimmery black dress catching the light. "And they only cost him, what, four or five hundred K?"

"You're playing jacks with real human knuckle bones?" Zack snarls, stepping up so close to the table that it rattles. "What the fuck is wrong with you? Do you have any respect? These aren't just game pieces, these are parts of actual human beings."

I speak up before anyone else can, letting my history buff side show.

"In France, in the 1800s, when the church moved bones from a crowded cemetery to the now famous catacombs, there were big holes left in the ground filled with human fat. Merchants gathered the stuff and made candles and soap. They then labeled them as the Innocents, and sold them to the wealthy who knowingly used them despite being aware of where they came from. They actually liked that, thinking of human beings as worth so little they could burn them simply to light a room." I turn to look at Zack, even as Becky sneers and starts bitching.

"Like we give a crap about some stupid history lesson. They're long dead, and nobody gives a shit but you what happens to the bones of some dumb ass soldiers. If they mattered, they'd have been generals or presidents or politicians, and their bones wouldn't have been rotting in some storage unit." Becky reaches up to touch her hair, which is twisted, coiffed, and covered with so much hairspray that it's hard to see the chunk that I cut off. Knowing it's there is enough for me though.

I ignore her and focus on that, fully aware that Creed and Zayd are watching me.

"Certain individuals see other humans as lesser than them, like they think they're gods or something. But tell me: how does a god get an ugly, bald patch shaved off the side of their head?"

Becky stands up, like she's going to launch yourself at me. I just stand there and stare at her as Harper grabs her arm and digs her fingernails into her best friend's skin. The two of them exchange a look that I can't quite read.

"We're here because I want to make a bet," Zack says, looking from Creed to Zayd to Tristan. He pauses with his dark brown gaze hooked on Tristan's cold gray one. "The three of you. Let's hit up a table and talk." He gestures with his chin and walks away, but according to him, and the rules of the Infinity Club, when someone challenges you to a bet, you're required to at least hear them out.

"This shit is so fucked-up," Zayd murmurs as he rises to his feet, raking his fingers through his hair. Creed says nothing as he, too, stands up. Tristan is the last one to get up, but as he moves away, he brushes his shoulder against mine, and I swear I see stars. He stops suddenly, like he didn't expect that. Low, almost inaudibly, I hear his voice near my ear.

"You are unfrigging believable," he murmurs, and I can't quite decide if that's an insult or a compliment. I watch the four boys move away before taking Tristan's seat at the table.

"You are not a part of the Infinity Club," Ileana snaps at me, curling her gold painted lips up over her teeth. She's right: that tattoo on my hip burns as if it's being freshly etched into my skin. I am not a part of the Infinity Club and I never will be. Thank God.

"No, but I'm here as a sponsored guest. I can make a bet, too." I fold my arms on the table, careful not to touch any of the knuckle bones. If there was some way for me to take them, and donate them to a museum or give them a proper burial or something, I would. As things stand, all I can do is throw out a silent apology to the souls that used to belong to these bits of ivory. "And trust me: you're gonna want to make this bet."

"Really?" Harper drawls, leaning her elbow on the table and resting her chin in her hand. Her blue eyes sparkle with hate as she takes me in. "And why exactly would I want to do that? I could simply ... call my family's medical center and tell them to stop treating your father. Basically, bitch, you're mine."

My heart stops, and I feel this cold fear creep over me. But I suspected this; I knew this was coming. Hell would freeze over before Harper would help me willingly.

I sit still, keep smiling, and refuse to show my cards.

"How about this," I start, meeting her eyes and refusing to acknowledge the other two girls. She'll love that, the self-professed queen of the school. "I'll make you a bet: if I win, you give my dad the same medical care that you'd give to your own father." I pause for a minute. "No, you give my father *better* medical care than you'd give your own father. The best of the best, spare no expense. If *you* win, I will get on my knees before you in front of the entire school and tell everyone that you were right, that I'm worse than a Pleb, or that I'm a whore, whatever. I'll kiss your feet, and I'll pack up and leave the academy and you'll never have to see again."

Harper's leaning forward now, her eyes shining, her sociopathic tendencies showing all over her face. I'm not sure that I've ever really known what the word *hate* means until now. I don't think I hated the Idol guys, not even after what they did to me. Pretty sure I hate Harper du Pont right now.

"I'm listening …" She purrs, her voice like needles as it digs into my eardrums. She reeks of peaches too, and I decide the scent is now entirely ruined for me. Every time I smell it, I'll think of her and that disgusting smile.

"If I lose, you can pull my father's medical care completely. But for now, you keep treating him." Harper narrows her eyes, but at least she's still listening. "Here's the bet: by the end of the year, I make Tristan, Creed, and Zayd fall in love with me." Her eyes widen in disbelief, and the look of glee that flashes over her face tells me that she already thinks that she's won, that what I'm proposing is an impossibility. I keep talking. "But you are *all* forbidden from telling them about this bet. If I get them to come with me to the second-year graduation getaway, that counts, and I win."

"You could just trick them into driving with you or something," Becky sneers, her voice like nails on a chalkboard. "No, they have to show up, with you or not, but they all have to think that you're going to be their date to the party that night. They have to *want* you to be their date." She smirks at me, and I purse my lips, but I nod anyway.

"They come with me to the graduation getaway at the lake, and I win. If they don't, at the party that night, I'll do what I said. I'll give in, I'll give up, and I'll leave. You'll win." Harper considers this for a moment, rolling one of the knuckle bones around on her palm.

"Fine. But that doesn't mean I'm going to stop tormenting you." She smirks at me again, and I just know she's already got something planned. "There is no truce between us, but I'll let your pathetic father beg scraps from my medical clinic.

When I win," she continues, and her use of the word *when* does not escape me, "I want your humiliation filmed, and *you* are going to be the one who posts it on YouTube from your own account."

My nostrils flare, but I nod anyway, and reach out to take her hand. We shake on it, while Becky and Ileana exchange looks.

"Don't think you're getting out of this bet," Ileana sneers, and I'm surprised to see how well she fits into this pit of snakes. She might be a first year, but she's just as vicious as the other two Idols. "My father has a team of secret police, and I'm not afraid to use them."

Her threat does not go unnoticed, but I ignore her as I rise to my feet, head off in search of Zack, and hope that the Idol guys turned down whatever ridiculous bet that he came up with. If they realize it's a ruse, too bad. If the girls tell, Harper automatically loses.

"Oh by the way," Harper calls out, and I turn around. She lifts her left hand and flashes me a massive rock on her ring finger. The ring that she's wearing, I bet its worth is in the millions. The necklace I wore tonight to piss Tristan off feels like a cheap trinket from Claire's in comparison. I manage to keep my expression calm, my face schooled, even though on the inside I feel like I might puke. "Tristan and I are engaged now. Thought you might want to know that."

She, of course, waits until after I make the bet to throw out that bit of information. That sneaky, psycho bitch. But you know what? The best revenge of all is that I'm still not worried. If I want Tristan, I can fucking get him.

Without saying a word, I turn and walk away, a new plan

hatching in my mind.

Not only is my bet with Harper part of my revenge plot, but for my father, I'd do anything. There's more riding on all of this than just my damn pride.

CHAPTER
13

The ski lodge is a mess of duffel bags, backpacks, and milling students. Everyone is dressed to suit the weather in beanies, scarves, ski pants, and boots. Miranda looks absolutely gorgeous in a head to toe lavender look, while I rock a pink outfit that she purchased for me as a surprise. I couldn't even begin to tell her how thankful I was; if she hadn't gotten this for me, I would be wearing jeans and a hoodie.

Jessie and Andrew sip hot chocolate on the large couch while the staff check us in, and start handing out room assignments. Me, I'm too busy watching the double doors with the deer carved into them. Zack seems to realize that I'm waiting for someone, but he doesn't say anything, pulling his beanie low over his ears and watching me. The way his eyes follow me across the room makes my body ache and throb with the memory of our kiss and the hardness between his thighs.

I wonder what it would've felt like to reach down and cup it …

My cheeks flame, and I adjust my own pale pink beanie as Zayd's howling laughter fills up the entire room with its soaring ceilings and wood beams. There's a fire crackling in the fireplace, the one that's so big that five students could stand inside of it comfortably. It should be homey in here, but it's difficult to enjoy it with the Bluebloods around.

I sit down on an armchair while Miranda tells a story to Jessie and Andrew, gesturing so wildly with her hands that within a few minutes, she's got a good dozen people listening and chuckling. Creed watches his twin like a man starved, desperate for her affection and still denied it. That's my continuing revenge on him. As long as he continues to be a dick, his mom and sister are on my side.

Tristan, on the other hand, is about to get a huge slap to the face.

I'm so busy watching that door and waiting, that I don't notice Zack is gone until he comes back, offering me up a cup of hot chocolate and a smile.

"Here," he says as he hands it over to me, a dollop of whipped cream and chocolate sprinkles on the top. I cover it with my hands, grateful for the warmth after being outside. It was a long walk from the parking lot to the lodge's front door. "Revenge requires sustenance after all."

I grin at him as I take a sip, his huge body perched on the arm of the chair I'm sitting in. I'm tempted to lay my hand on his knee, but why? What would that even mean? So instead I keep my hands cupped around the hot chocolate, and sip slowly.

Mrs. Amberton hands me a key to room 301 and tells me

BAD, BAD BLUE BLOODS

that Miranda and I will be sharing. The whole school knows by now that Miranda and Jessie are dating, so Jessie is put in a room with a random Pleb girl I've never seen before. Andrew and Zack are paired up, and my palms start to sweat as I notice Tristan heading up the stairs toward his room. I'm not ready for him to leave yet. Not just yet …

As if she's taken classes on how to make a grand entrance (as far as I know, maybe she has), the double doors fly open with a swirl of snow and in walks Lizzie, dressed head to the toe in designer athletic wear, her red and black plaid jacket slightly unbuttoned, just a hint of cleavage showing.

She sees me right away and I stand up, handing my empty hot chocolate to Zack before she throws her arms around my neck and gives me a huge hug. Last night, I messaged her to make peace. In reality, I've added her name to my list and crossed it off in the same go around.

Based on the conversation I had with Lizzie last night—most of which consisted of her profusely apologizing to me and begging for my forgiveness—she doesn't know Tristan is engaged. I can tell by the way she talks about him, that she's still in love with him. When I glance over my shoulder and see him frozen on the stairs, one hand white-knuckled on the banister, his eyes all for her, I know he's in love with her, too.

A few of Lizzie's friends are with her, all of them wearing matching Coventry Prep beanies, the school crest sewn into the side. It's a little cliquish for my taste, but it's nice to see a swarm of queen bees sweep into the room that are actually on my side. It has not escaped my notice that the Bluebloods are bristling.

Lizzie's guardian approaches the counter and starts up a

209

conversation with some of the Burberry Prep staff, wrapping her arms around Ms. Felton. A smile works its way onto my lips before I turn back to Lizzie herself.

"Our school doesn't do second-year trips, so it was a nice surprise to get your invite," she says, her own engagement ring sparkling as she reaches up to tuck her black curls behind one ear. She turns her amber gaze over to Zack, and they both smile sheepishly before turning their attentions back to me.

The last time I was in the same room with the two of them, I was having my heart broken in two. This is so much better because this time, it's Tristan and Lizzie who are going to feel that pain. Part of me aches at the idea of Lizzie getting hurt; she's so sweet and genuine. It's impossible to imagine her making that bet with Zack way back when. Either the two of them have changed immensely since then, or else they're as full of shit as the rest of the Bluebloods.

"I'm glad you're here," I tell her, and I mean that, even if it is all a part of my plot. Ugh. It shouldn't be this hard for me to extract vengeance. I'd rather just be a naïve, happy chick with no vendettas. I decide that once I graduate from Burberry Prep, I'm done with revenge plots forever. "I don't ski, and I hear learning isn't exactly easy. I need you guys to take turns babysitting me in the lodge."

Lizzie chuckles, and it's such a gentle, cultured laugh. She's pretty, too, and nice. I'm damn near positive she's as close to perfect as any human being ever gets. That is, if you ignore the bet she made with Zack,

Like a viper, Harper slithers over to us, flashing her own ring in Lizzie's face.

"*What* … are you doing here?" Harper grinds out between her perfect, white teeth. She flashes me a look of pure venom that I pretend not to notice. Lizzie's face shuts down as soon as she sees that ring, and a tension creeps into the air that has nothing to do with me. I'm not even involved in their resulting stare down.

"I was *invited*," Lizzie says, managing to maintain a fairly neutral expression. Impressive considering Harper's devolved into an ugly monster in the same span of time. Right on time, Tristan appears on Harper's left, his gray gaze focused on Lizzie. But only for a second … He then moves his attention over to me, and I'm almost startled by it.

"Oh, *honey*," Harper purrs, latching onto Tristan's arm. The way his mouth wrinkles into a sneer when she touches him tells me all I need to know. He doesn't like her, never will. Not that it matters. He'll marry her anyway if it's what'll give him the most money and power. My stomach twists into an infinity-shaped knot. "The Working Girl invited your old girlfriend to ski with us. I'm not impressed."

"What do you want me to do about it?" he snaps at her, his face impassive. "I can't exactly kick Lizzie and Charity out into the snow, now can I?" Harper gapes at him, flicking her tongue against the side of her mouth and leveling her glare on Lizzie. I may as well be invisible. After all, it's not me that her fiancé's in love with.

Not yet, anyway.

In my heart though, I wonder if I'll ever be able to wedge Lizzie out of that special place in Tristan's chest. She could very well lose the bet for me. I exhale sharply, and Zack reaches down to take my hand, giving it a squeeze.

"You're engaged?" Lizzie whispers after a second, looking at Tristan from hurt baby doe eyes. I feel like I might cry for her. Damn it. Damn, damn, damn. Well, I'm glad I already crossed her name off the list. This is too much. "You … could've told me."

"Publicly? At a party? Like how you told me?" Tristan snaps, his nostrils flaring. He's trying to maintain his composure and failing miserably. Harper looks gleeful right about now. I want to beat her up for them both. "Why should I? What are we to each other? Clearly, not friends."

Lizzie's eyes blur with tears, and I grimace, squeezing Zack's hand back for comfort.

"You're right," she whispers, "we're not friends. But that's okay: I didn't come here for you." She reaches down to take my hand, notices Zack's curled around it, and raises her brows. I quickly shake him off and grab onto her, pulling her away from the crowd and up the stairs.

I think that's enough revenge for us both.

This time, however, it doesn't taste quite so sweet.

Lizzie falls asleep on my bed, so I take hers, and Miranda

ends up staying with Jessie. I wonder if they're um, *sleeping* together, but I'm too nervous to ask, so I don't say anything. We spend the next morning sitting in the lodge and eating from the buffet, sipping hot cocoa, and talking about the summer.

Most all the Bluebloods have houses in the Hamptons and spend a good portion of their summer there. Lizzie and her friends cut them out of most of the important social engagements, and refused them entry into any of their parties. Even as she's describing her shadiness, she's trying to be nice about it.

"I mean, we didn't hurt anybody …" she adds, but I'm already smiling as I imagine Creed's, Zayd's, and Tristan's faces as they show up at the place of a supposed party with their entourage, and find nothing and nobody. Amazing.

Tristan comes in the door covered in snow and sweating. When he sees Lizzie and me in the lodge, he scowls, storms up the stairs, and slams his door. While Lizzie's discomfort brings me zero joy, I quite like seeing Tristan throw tantrums like a child.

It gets a little weird though on Sunday when his father shows up.

I come to find out that Mr. Vanderbilt owns the place. Fantastic.

Now, when *he* sees Lizzie, me, Andrew, Miranda, and Zack eating lunch in the restaurant the next day, there's this look that crosses his face that scares the crap out of me. William Vanderbilt could have me *assassinated,* and then cover it all up. That's how freaking rich he is. And clearly, he doesn't like me. Pretty sure he doesn't like Lizzie either, based on the way his eyes travel over our group, dismissing everyone but the two of us.

For dinner that night, outdoor heaters are set up, and food is served on the patio. Surrounded by snow and glistening with twinkling white lights, it's magical. It's no accident that I slip into the shimmery black dress that Tristan sent me for the graduation gala last year. Or … the jewelry I so carefully select.

Adjusting the watch on my right wrist, I step confidently outside and pass right by William's table. His eyes immediately catch on the red and black Rolex that he gave to Tristan. If I could only use one word to describe his expression, it would be annihilation. I've blown his mind.

Tristan sees me a moment later, and this lick of fear takes over his face as he glances from me to his dad. Either William will think Tristan gave me the watch or else he'll have to come clean about throwing it in the trash.

He grabs my wrist as I pass by, and heat shoots up my arm and spears me in the chest with flames. I meet his gray eyes without fear.

"What the hell are you playing at?" he asks, looking from the necklace to the watch, and then back to my face. "What is it that you want?"

"I want you to realize that what you did to me was wrong. I want you to treat people better in general. I want you to know that your money doesn't mean you can get away with murder." I shake his grip off and shoulder past him, heading over to Lizzie's table. She watches me as I sit down, her brow scrunching slightly. "You okay?" I ask, and she nods, spinning her engagement ring around on her finger.

Andrew is watching her, too, and there's a dark melancholy to his expression that I wish I could wipe away. He doesn't want to be engaged at all, let alone to a girl. I feel sick with sadness for him.

"I'm okay," Lizzie replies with a long exhale. We both watch as William summons his son to his side. Harsh, low words are spoken before Mr. Vanderbilt reaches out and grabs Tristan by the wrist so hard that his son cringes. My heart thunders, and I almost stand up. Lizzie puts her hand over mine. "If you go over there, you'll make things worse." Her voice comes out in a near whisper as William drags his son into the lodge.

I can't help it.

I force myself out of my chair and weave through the crowd to the door, slipping inside and catching a glimpse of the two men moving in the direction of the VIP room on the opposite side of the lodge from the bar.

I'm not sure what I'm doing exactly, but I sneak over anyway. The door is closed, but I can hear voices coming from inside.

"... the commoner wearing *your* watch."

Tristan is dead silent.

"And Lizzie Walton? I've forbidden you from seeing her. Do you think these secret trysts of yours are going to amount to anything but a bastard heir and a teen whore I'll have to pay off? What the hell is wrong with you?"

"A bastard like me, you mean? Am I such a goddamn disappointment?" My mouth drops open at the vitriol in Tristan's voice. There's the sharp crack of flesh on flesh, and I cringe, trying the door knob. It's locked.

There's a long silence, like maybe they're waiting to see if whoever's on my side of the door will try it again. Finally, Tristan speaks up, his words mollified.

"It won't happen again," Tristan says, his voice low and hoarse. "Marnye must've … thought it was okay to wear the watch after we slept together." *Slept together?!* Gross. But I guess it's as plausible a lie as anything else.

"You are engaged, son, to a du Pont. Do I need to remind you how important that is? The company is going under. Without their money, we lose everything. If you'd like to live in the trailer next door to your whore, then by all means, keep defying me." William pauses and sighs. "And don't let me see you around Lizzie Walton again. This time, I'm giving you a warning. You won't like what I do next time."

I scramble out of the way before the two of them come back out.

I do not miss the blood on Tristan's mouth this time.

When I get back to the room that night, I cross his name off my list, and feel fucking sick about it. I will never use William Vanderbilt against his son again. Never.

But in my phone, there's a recording with his voice on it.

Try me, asshole. Try me and see what happens.

BAD, BAD BLUE BLOODS

The rest of winter break is uneventful. Dad doesn't invite Jennifer over again although he does bring her up a few times. Zack stops by on Christmas day with gifts for me and dad. Charlie gets a pair of new boots, a Carhart jacket, and a shiny new tie. Me, I get keys in an envelope, and give Zack a look. There's the address for a storage unit on the other side.

"What is this?" I ask, but he just shrugs, wishes us happy holidays, and leaves.

The next day, Dad and I drive to the storage place, find the unit that Zack's written down, and unlock it with the keys. Inside, there's a golden pedal harp.

My phone drops to the ground, and I clap my hand over my mouth.

The instrument that's sitting in that unit is worth over thirty-thousand dollars.

"How are we going to get this home?" I choke out, once I've finally fought back tears and found my breath. Sitting down in the wooden chair next to it, I strum my fingers across the strings and sigh at the beautiful notes. "Where are we going to put it?"

"We'll figure it out, Marnye-bear," Charlie says with a soft smile. And the next day, he shows me the cute little two bedroom house in Grenadine Heights that he's rented for us.

Pretty sure that's the best Christmas I've ever had.

CHAPTER

14

The wind teases my skirt, making it billow around my thighs just enough that my garters show. I ignore it, leaning against the wall of Tower Two with my shoulder. My pulse is racing with nerves, but I'm excited to do this, to be the new student's guide. And I guarantee I'll do a hell of a lot better at my job than Tristan Vanderbilt did for me. I hadn't expected to get called into Principal Collins' office so bright and early, but that's the life of a student mentor. Guess they're going to actually make me earn those credits. And hey, maybe the new kid won't be as big of a dick as all the others?

First day back at Burberry Prep Academy, and I've already had a note shoved in my locker telling me to kill myself (so original, been there, done that, asshole). There was a dildo on the floor in my room, but I've now got footage from my cameras showing Sai Patel and some of his own personal cronies putting it in there, and then taking turns snapping photos with my panties.

It's fine though. I don't even need those pictures to destroy him. Miranda was right: I've got pictures of Sai and

Abigail making out at the lodge. All I have to do is show those to Greg, and it's game over.

I watch the horizon, waiting for the shiny black academy car to crest the hill. Standing up straight, I approach the front steps and wait as it rolls around the circular drive, and comes to a slow stop, wheels crunching over the gravel. It feels like forever before the driver finally gets out and moves around to open the back door.

My breath stops in my chest.

One long leg extends from the back, cloaked in perfectly creased white slacks. A long, lithe form follows, tall and handsome and wearing a bright, white grin.

I'd almost forgotten all those news articles Miranda shoved in my face. If she hadn't sent me the link to yet another exposé on the guy, I would've forgotten about him completely. The world's youngest billionaire. Tenth in line to the throne. Great-grandson to the *Queen* of freaking England.

Windsor York.

A freaking prince.

"Well, hello there," he says, tilting his head to one side, his hazel eyes glimmering with color. There are specks of gold, green, and brown swimming in a blue-gray gaze. I'm immediately mesmerized by the color. His red hair is short, but playfully mussy, tousled and dark, almost crimson. And that smile … it's impossible to look away from. "Windsor York, at your service. You must be Marnye Reed?"

I nod, but my throat is suddenly dry, and there are no words.

The prince adjusts the lapels of his second-year jacket and

looks around, taking in the courtyard and the fountain with mild interest. He then adjusts his gaze to me, and mild interest turns to piqued curiosity. Windsor's eyes take me in, inch by inch, absorbing my appearance from head to toe. He seems to like what he sees, too, which makes my cheeks flush pink, and sends my heart racing.

The new student I've been asked to mentor is ... a prince. A prince. A freaking prince?!

"You're quite the pretty little thing, aren't you?" he asks, his voice crisp with an English accent. If I said I wasn't into it, I'd be lying. His grin sharpens up and he extends an elbow for me to take. "I assumed they'd be sending some crusty old school marm to give me a tour. This is much, *much* better." He holds out his arm for me to take, and I just stand there like an idiot, staring. After a moment, he cocks his head to one side and makes this cute little moue with his mouth that sends my hormones into a frenzy. "You don't want to escort me, milady?" he asks, milking his accent for everything it's work. Swallowing hard, I take the prince's arm, and shivers crawl up and down my spine—good ones, too. *Oh no.* I feel like I crush far too easily on hot guys. It's a habit I really need to break. Who's to say this guy isn't as snooty, self-absorbed, and cruel as the rest of them?

Bet he's worse.

"Do I ..." I start and then my throat gets so dry that I have to pause and swallow before continuing. "I mean, should I call you prince?" I ask, and Windsor pauses for a moment before chuckling, this happy little sound that's pretty much the antithesis of all the other guys at this school—even Zayd. It's pretty refreshing actually.

"You know who I am? That's bloody fantastic. But prince? God no. Call me Windsor. Or Wind. Or even Windy, but preferably not if you're interested in dating me as that's what my grandmother calls me." He pauses and flashes another grin, whistling as we make our way through the courtyard. I'm not quite sure how to respond to that, so I say nothing. After a minute, Windsor glances down at me with a slight frown and a single cocked brow. "You don't then, I take it?"

"Don't what?" I ask and he laughs at me again, but not like he's teasing, more like he finds me amusing.

"Don't want to date me?" he clarifies, and my flush intensifies. I look straight ahead, down the corridor toward the stained glass doors.

"I'm not about dating anyone at this moment," I say, and the words come out so cryptic and full of meaning that both of Windsor's brows go up this time. Crap. He looks intrigued now, and I don't particularly want to be intriguing to anyone, not even to a gloriously handsome prince.

"Shame," Windsor says, but at least he says it with a smile.

We push through the doors to the chapel building … and come to a grinding halt.

The Bluebloods are standing just inside the door, with Tristan and Harper at the front, Zayd, Becky, Creed, and the new girl, Ileana, just behind them. The rest of the Inner Circle is fanned out behind them. When Tristan sees me with Windsor, something dark lights up his eyes, and his frown pulls down the edges of his mouth.

BAD, BAD BLUE BLOODS

"Are you Windsor York?" Ileana Taittinger asks, twisting her dark hair around a finger. The way she looks at the prince is terrifying, like she very well might eat him for breakfast. Her uniform top is unbuttoned, all the way to the scalloped black edges of her lacy bra. I glance at Windsor, expecting his eyes to drop right to her cleavage. Instead, he focuses on Tristan and smiles brightly.

"Windsor York, at your service. Please, call me Wind. And you are?" He tugs me forward with his hold on my arm, bringing me in close proximity to the Bluebloods. The way Becky glares at me, I can almost feel her hatred burning holes in my skin. Her hair is pulled up into a bun, and hair-sprayed to high hell, but there's no missing the giant chunk I cut off, not today. A smirk teases the edges of my mouth, and she notices.

"Have you introduced yourself to the prince properly yet," she schmoozes, miming a blow job with her hand, her tongue poking at the inside of her cheek.

"Well, I haven't asked him yet if he wants a blow job, but he already seems more interested in me than Zayd was in you. *Once this is over, let's go back to my room and I'll suck you off,*" I coo, imitating her nasally voice. "I can say with all honesty: I've never been brushed off quite so thoroughly as you."

"I'm going to fucking kill you!" Becky screams, launching herself forward. Zayd grabs her around the waist and hauls her back. I hate that watching him touch her upsets me so much. His green eyes meet mine, and he grits his teeth as he yanks her back in line. *"As soon as I found out that Becky had hit you, I haven't touched her. I just couldn't."*

Zayd's words sound loudly inside my head, and I smile. It's not a nice smile either.

"Bloody hell, you Americans are crazy. We've just met and you want to kill me?" Windsor asks, cocking his head to one side. He reaches up and adjusts his tie with his left hand, one single brow raised in question. Becky is panting now, and she shakes Zayd off to turn and glare at me again.

"Not you, the little whore next to you. That's our resident Working Girl. If you want a cheap fuck, you can visit her in the Brothel. Otherwise, you're better off sticking with us." Becky sneers at me, the expression twisting her pretty face into something horrible. I raise my chin and then flip her off. There's just something wrong with the chemistry between us; it doesn't work. "You bitch." She sneers and tries to come at me again, but Tristan holds out a hand and the Bluebloods freeze. Well, everyone but Creed. He leans back and rolls his eyes before yawning.

Tristan, though, is most definitely their king.

His blade gray gaze burns with fury as he looks at me standing there with the prince. His mouth is downturned, his expression as dark as his hair. He looks like he wants to kill someone. Maybe me, maybe Windsor, I'm not sure.

"Welcome to Burberry Prep," Tristan says, his voice cold and threaded with steel. "You have a choice to make: come with us or fall with her." He gestures in my direction with his chin, and I hold my breath, eyes sliding over to Windsor York. He's been to schools like this before, elite boarding facilities all over Europe. Surely, he'll know how the hierarchy works. I don't stand a chance.

I move to take my arm from his when he tightens his grip on me, throwing a blinding smile in the direction of the Idols and their Inner Circle. Creed's eyes meet mine, half-lidded and lazy as usual. But there's a tightness to his chest and shoulders that I can't possibly miss.

The tension stretches out between us and them, this thread that's pulled so taut I can hardly breathe.

And then Windsor laughs. The sound is light and airy and fluffy. It almost makes me smile. Almost. But then I catch Zayd's look, this muddied, confused sort of expression that tears at me. I could feel bad for getting his off-campus privileges revoked and ruining his music career, but then I think about the way he curled his arm around Becky's waist while I stood there dripping red paint and holding back tears.

"For you all to have such a vendetta against this girl, she must be pretty damn special." Windsor shrugs his shoulders, the stark white of the jacket highlighting how colorful his eyes are, how red his hair. *He's freaking gorgeous,* I think, but then maybe it's just because he's defending me against them? I have no idea. "Thanks, but no thanks. I'll take my chances with the most beautiful girl in the room." He grins as Tristan frowns, and Harper steps forward, tossing her glossy brunette waves over one shoulder. Since I cut that hunk off of Becky's hair, she's been extremely careful to stay away from me. I'm going to have to come up with another plan. "Besides, when I set my sights out to destroy someone, I like challenging targets. You all will do quite nicely, I believe."

"You're making a huge mistake," Harper purrs, sauntering forward with her hips swaying. She's supposed to be with Tristan, but it looks like she's making the moves on Windsor

York. Guess she's spotted an upgrade? I noticed that after Lizzie showed up at the lodge, she spent the rest of the trip avoiding her fiancé like the plague. "We own this school, Wind." She smiles coquettishly and takes another step closer as Windsor raises his eyebrows. They've only just met two seconds ago, and she's already calling him by his nickname. How cute. "Choosing the Working Girl over the school's elite is a mistake that'll haunt you way past your days at this academy." She reaches up to touch his lapels, and his smile curves up in an inviting way. I see him lean toward her, like a flower straining for the light of the sun, and my heart sinks.

On the plus side, I see Tristan's frown turn into an outright scowl.

Harper is going to get it for this stunt later on, and I didn't have to lift a finger.

Windsor puts his mouth right up close to Harper's and breathes on her lips. She sighs and practically falls into him.

"Darling," he purrs, his voice like silk on the skin. I shiver as the syllables fall over me like a caress. "I'm the Duke of Westminster, the great-grandson of the Queen of England, and in possession of a fortune worth over nine billion British pounds. Whatever you have to say, whoever you are, it means quite literally nothing to me." He pushes Harper back with a single finger on her chest and she stumbles, mouth gaping open.

Windsor smiles; it's not pretty anymore.

Uh-oh.

He lifts his eyes up and rakes them over the group of Bluebloods, like he's searching for something. Clearly he doesn't find it because a huge grin appears on his face, and then he's turning to me, eyes sparkling. I'm going to have to be careful with this guy; he is not as nice as he seems.

Hmm.

Somehow, that makes it easier for me to smile back.

"Bunch of self-important arseholes," Windsor says with a shrug of his shoulders. "I can trace my bloodline back for centuries; I don't need to prove myself. And you," he looks me over carefully while the collective whole of the group bristles, "are clearly quite easy on the eyes, and quite right in the head to avoid these assholes. Shall we go then?"

"I'd love to," I say, a new idea blooming in my chest.

The Bluebloods now hate Windsor; Windsor hates the Bluebloods.

This could work.

"This is a mistake you're going to regret," Tristan warns as we move past, but his voice is hot with anger and his dark gaze is quite clearly focused on Harper. Good. My plan all along was to let their own weaknesses, mistakes, and sins burn them from the inside out. The way Tristan treated Harper in the limo was my first clue that their relationship isn't as peachy as Harper wants it to be.

"I think it's a bold career move that's going to bring me hours of entertainment." Windsor produces his schedule with a flourish and passes it over to me, and we move on down the hall, leaving the Idols and their Inner Circle safely behind us.

"I love you so much! If I were attracted to boys, I'd be all over you," Miranda whispers, her voice harsh, eyes brimming with happy tears. Windsor smirks, and pushes some loose hair from his forehead with his palm. It sticks straight up in the front, like a little cowlick or something. "Seriously, I've been following you on the news since forever. And when I heard you were coming to America, I knew. I just *knew* you would come to Burberry Prep."

"I've received quite a mixed bag of welcomes today," he says with a grin, reaching out to ruffle up my hair. I'm so stunned by the action that I just stand there. Zack narrows his eyes and crosses his arms over his broad chest, taking in the prince like he's not particularly impressed. "Those blokes near the front door," he continues, gesturing with his thumb in the direction of the courtyard. "They your ex-boyfriends or something?"

"Huh?" I choke, and both Jessie and Miranda crack up. "What? No. No. Ew. No." *But also, maybe, kind of, sort of …* Windsor cocks his head to one side and studies me before giving this loose, easy shrug of his shoulders that says he could give two fucks less, and was mostly just curious.

"Why?"

"They all look at you with a certain … shall we say, *je ne sais quoi.*" He laughs and shakes his head. "Usually, I have an uncanny ability to guess when two people have slept together. I was getting mixed messages between you and those guys." He pauses again and then raises his palms up while he clarifies. "Not all of them though, just the three ring leaders: the gray-eyed one, the lazy one, and the musician."

"I never slept with them," I squeak as Zack and Andrew both look at me like they're trying to figure out if that's the truth or not. "I'm a virgin." The words tumble out before I can stop them, and then I groan, clamping a hand over my eyes just before Zack's brows go up in shock. "Why did I just say that?"

"I have a habit of digging the honesty out of people," Windsor explains, clearly so full of himself that I expect peacock feathers to pop out of his butt at any moment. He thinks very highly of himself, certainly. "It's a gift."

Windsor looks around the student lounge—a place I *never* hang out but which is essential to any student tour—and reaches up to straighten his tie. He's got epaulettes on his jacket shoulders which I've never seen on anyone else's academy uniform, but okay.

"You've met the Bluebloods then?" Zack asks, and Windsor turns his hazel gaze on my new football player friend. He studies him with total disinterest, but not a complete lack of warmth like Creed or Tristan might.

"Bluebloods?" Windsor asks, and then he laughs. It's such a bright, airy sound that it startles me. "How quaint. Yes, I've met them. Instantly disliked them. Can't wait to knock their worlds upside down. Wankers." He wrinkles his nose up. "At least I know which girls not to shag. What's wrong with that psycho one, with the missing chunk of hair?"

I laugh and clamp a hand over my mouth as a group of fourth year girls waltz by and then stop to gape. Windsor checks them all out, winks coquettishly, and then turns back to me, curiosity brimming in his eyes.

"She cut all my hair off last year, and dyed it bright red," I explain. "Well, her and Harper—the brunette one that tried to hit on you." Windsor nods, crossing one arm over his chest and resting his chin in the palm of his other hand. He smells like daffodils and shoe polish, and I'm sort of digging it.

"I see, I see. So why does the one still have all of her hair?"

"I haven't been able to get close enough to her to cut it off," I blurt, and then I kick myself because I met this guy all of two seconds ago, and I'm spilling all my secrets. Jesus. He's dangerous as hell; I need to be careful with the prince.

"Makes sense," he replies, and then Miranda starts to gush again. I let her while we continue the tour, making our way from the lounge to The Mess. The rest of our little group bails when the first class of the day starts, but Windsor and I have free passes to explore the academy's campus. It's extensive, and we end up finishing just about the time that The Mess starts serving their dinner menu.

Windsor is charming, handsome, personable … but it's very clear to me that while some of the others, like Creed, pretend not to give a shit, Windsor York really, really doesn't.

He smiles at me across the dinner table, and I smile back.

But that's as far as our relationship will ever go.

Unfortunately, right after that smile, he needles me until I start spilling the truth about what happened last year. Not that it matters: he was bound to find out anyway, so at least he's getting the story from me first.

"On the bright side," he starts, playing with his fork in fine, delicate fingers, "when I wreck them later, I won't have to feel an ounce of remorse." Windsor smiles at me, winks, and then digs into his dessert.

The next day, I turn the corner in the chapel building, finding Harper and her cronies on one side. Windsor York is on the other, flirting with some third-year girls. As soon as he sees me, he lifts two fingers in a wave, bids goodbye to his giggling fan club, and starts walking my direction. As he passes Harper du Pont, he pulls something from his pocket, walks right up to her, and chops her ponytail off at the base.

Her friends shriek as she reaches up with her hands to touch the back of her head. Her pterodactyl screech echoes through the halls as Windsor saunters up to me and tosses the ponytail my way.

"Token of my friendship," he says, winking at me as I gape and look between him and the cluster of Inner Circle girls fluttering over their now-weeping Idol. "We have the same homeroom, don't we? Walk with me?" Windsor offers me his arm, and I decide then that he's good people. Really fucking good people.

When Friday of that week rolls around, I spend every spare second I have—which isn't a lot—searching for news stories about him online. The reason he's here in America and at Burberry isn't pleasant: Miranda was right when she mentioned him crashing a boat into a harbor and severely injuring several partygoers.

Also, no surprise: he's a major lothario. He's slept with dozens of famous people already, and he's only sixteen. Apparently, he's a major scandal to the crown. So while he technically has a fortune of his own, his mother is still legally in charge of his person until he turns eighteen. Fascinating.

CHAPTER

15

That weekend, gossip about a party in the woods has spread like wildfire. It's not a club party, but it is being sponsored by the Idols. Surprisingly, I open my door to a knock on Saturday morning and find Windsor York waiting for me. He's dressed in a loose blue shirt with a V-neck, jeans, and what look like brown riding boots.

"Good morning, *ma chère*," he says, but I'm not impressed. I've heard him call, like, six other girls *ma chère*. Although I have to say, his French is impeccable. "Did you get my texts last night?" I nod, and do my best not to smile. Windsor's been sending me all sorts of amazing articles with prank ideas that I could use on the Idols. They're a bit extreme for my tastes—remember: let them hang themselves with their own rope—but I appreciate the effort. The prince seems to have taken this whole revenge thing on with a gusto. "And did you get my voice message this morning? It's rude to ask a lady out via text, so I've improvised and simply texted a recording of my voice."

"How … debonair of you," I choke, but I'm smiling anyway. "No, I haven't checked my texts. Where, exactly, are you inviting me?" His eyes sparkle as he stands up straight and raises an eyebrow at my cracked bedroom door. With a sigh, I step back and let him in. He takes in the room with a single sweep of his eyes before spinning back to me. His red hair is nice and clean, and sticking straight up in the front. I'm not sure how though because I don't see any gel. Guess it's just a random quirk of his.

"Whenever I transfer schools—and I transfer schools a lot —I always make sure to hit the first party of the year running. I hear there's one in the woods? Not quite my usual scene, but I'll take it." I smile as I head into the kitchenette area to make some tea. Windsor watches me plop a Lipton tea bag into a cup of lukewarm water and toss it into the microwave.

He looks like he might puke.

"Most of the Bluebloods are banned from going off campus for the remainder of the year," I explain as I press the buttons on the microwave. Without skipping a beat, Windsor reaches over my shoulder and grabs my hand, gently pulling me back. He then goes about pulling out a kettle from one of the cabinets, filling it with water, and putting it on the single burner stove. "What are you doing?"

"Making you a proper cup of tea." He crosses his arms over his chest and shakes his head. "I wouldn't be a proper English bloke if I allowed that"—he points at the microwave and sneers—"to be consumed in my presence. Don't you stupid Americans know how to make tea the right way?"

"There's a right way?" I ask, and he groans, putting his

face into his hands. He's like a caricature of a prince, all over-the-top, sweeping bows, speaking in French. It's almost too much. And yet, I kinda like it anyway. "Well, excuse me. I grew up in an abandoned Train Car on instant ramen noodles and pb&j sandwiches. My mom abandoned me and my dad when I was a kid, and we did the best we could." Windsor slowly parts his hands to peer out at me, and I realize I've just done it again: showed him all my damn cards.

Crap.

"Welllllll," he drawls, dragging out the *L* in that word far past it's usual point, "even if you've committed an atrocity against crown and kingdom with your god-awful tea, you seem to have turned out alright. Most people suck on the dick of money like it'll come cash in their mouths and make them rich. You seem ... beyond despondent, more disgusted. I quite enjoy that."

"The dick of money?" I ask as the kettle starts to steam and Windsor pulls it off the stove with a pot holder I never use. He looks through my cabinets and finds the loose leaf English breakfast tea that Dad gave me for Christmas. It even came with a metal strainer and a special mug that I haven't used yet. I watch as Windsor prepares a cup for me. "That's ... a very creative metaphor."

"Simile: I used the word *like*." He grins and waves his hand dismissively. He's not quite as tall as Zack, but he's well-built, and he's got an air of confidence that's infectious. His hair is almost crimson, but I'm pretty sure it's natural, and there's a curve to his upper lip that draws my attention. "Marnye Reed, will you please do me the honor of escorting me to tonight's party?" He holds up his palms toward me.

"Not as a date: you were very clear about your ideas on dating. Besides, I've already found three or four girls that I fancy. I was just hoping we could go as friends." He hands me the mug and our fingers tangle together. My breath catches, but Windsor doesn't seem to notice, not the way Zayd or Creed or Zack would. Tristan just ... screw Tristan.

"Yeah, sure, why not?" I reply, taking a sip of the tea. My brows go up and Windsor chuckles, pressing a kiss to my cheek. I tell myself it's just a European thing, but the place his lips touched tingles like crazy.

"See you at five, love." And then he disappears, letting my door swing shut behind him.

Zack is not pleased to see Windsor in my room when he shows up later, a cluster of wild winter flowers in his hand. When he gives them to me, I flush a dark red color and stumble three times trying to say the word *thanks*.

"Are you two an item?" Windsor asks, now dressed in a loose, silky cream shirt that's unbuttoned nearly to his navel. He tucks his fingers in the front pockets of his black slacks and looks between me and Zack with narrowed eyes. "You sure you're a virgin? I could swear the two of you have shagged."

"Yeah, well, maybe your intuition isn't as amazing as you claim," I retort, but now that Windsor's brought up sex and Zack in the same conversation I can't stop thinking about our make-out session. Gah. I was not supposed to fall for my tormentor. There's nothing cool or feminist or progressive about that. If I think too hard about it, it makes me feel sick.

And yet … Zack's been nothing but nice to me. People can make mistakes, as long as they acknowledge them and learn from their experiences, right? Right? I so want Zack Brooks to be redeemable.

We head out the east door of the chapel, meet up with Miranda, Jessie, and Andrew then start off toward the lake. About halfway there, we find the bonfire, the beer, and the fighting.

Oh, that's right.

I'd almost forgotten about that email I sent last night. Or all the changes I made to my list.

Revenge On *The Bluebloods of Burberry Prep*
A list by ~~*Miranda Cabot*~~ *Marnye Reed*

~~**The Idols (guys): Tristan Vanderbilt (year one two),**~~
~~**Zayd Kaiser (year one two), and Creed Cabot (year one two)**~~

*The Idols (girls): Harper du Pont (year ~~one~~ **two**), Becky Platter (year ~~one~~ **two**),* ~~*and Gena Whitley (year four)*~~ **(graduated),** *Ileana Taittinger (year one)*

237

C.M. STUNICH

*The Inner Circle: ~~Andrew Payson~~, Anna Kirkpatrick, Myron Talbot, ~~Ebony Peterson, Gregory Van Horn, Abigail Fanning, John Hannibal,~~ Valentina Pitt, **~~Sai Patel,~~** Mayleen Zhang, ~~Jalen Donner ... and, I guess, me!~~ **Kiara Xiao, Ben Thresher***

Plebs: everyone else~~, sorry. XOXO~~
~~Zack Brooks~~
~~Lizzie Walton~~

Sai Patel is doing it with Abigail Fanning, who's supposed to be dating Gregory Van Horn; I emailed proof to the entire Blueblood court. And because I hate Greg so much, I've doubled up and sent Andrew's bullying video to Creed. I've already crossed his and John's names off because, well, they're not going to last the night.

They've almost made it too easy for me.

"And here I was expecting tonight to be boring," Windsor declares, his grin so bright that he stands out like a white splotch in the darkness. The bonfire is roaring, and there are people drinking and dancing, but the majority of the attention falls on Greg, Sai, and Abigail. There's a lot of crying, begging, pleading, and so on and so forth. It's actually pretty boring, after what happened with Jalen, Ebony, and Tristan. Been there, seen this. Besides, once a cheater, always a cheater. Frankly, I'm shocked that Greg took Abigail back after Tristan outed her for sleeping with him last year.

"What is this?" Creed asks as he moves up beside us, holding out his phone. His half-lidded gaze falls on Windsor as the prince's grin slides away and something much more predatory takes its place. "Payson?"

"I don't answer to you anymore," Andrew says wearily, exhaling heavily. But he knows I sent the video. I made sure to ask because, you know, *No Friendly Fire.* "But what's it look like, man?"

"Are they bothering you, too?" Creed asks, turning to his sister. I hate to admit it, but he looks hot as hell in a black button-down and jeans. His outfit's wrinkled just enough to give off that devil-may-care attitude of his.

Miranda turns up her nose at her brother, hooks her arm with Jessie's, and drags her through the crowd toward the keg. When Creed turns to me, Zack steps forward and pushes me slightly behind him. The move is protective, and sort of adorable, but also … I can take care of myself. I step up beside him as Windsor whistles under his breath.

"Back off, Brooks," Creed says, his voice so sharp it gives me whiplash. He is *not* in the mood to take shit tonight. He looks back at me, his ice-blue eyes catching the orange light from the fire. When he flips some of that white-blonde hair off his forehead, my heart does somersaults and I tell it quite firmly to sit still and forget about Creed Cabot. "Are they picking on my sister?" he demands, but I simply cross my arms over my chest.

"Does it matter? You told them to knock their homophobic bullshit off, and they keep doing it. Doesn't that undermine your authority as an Idol?" I shrug my shoulders loosely, but then I remind myself: the most important part of your plan starts here. Taking a step forward, I put my hand on Creed's shoulder and his entire body goes stiff.

Our eyes meet, and I have to swallow three times before I remember how to speak. For a split-second there, I wish I could close my eyes and transport back in time to the winter formal.

"Is that a yes or a no?" he says, his voice this debonair blasé that actually makes my heart flutter. Even though his eyes are barely open, and his body looks boneless and exhausted with boredom, he also looks like he's about to kill someone. It's there in the way his long fingers tighten around his phone. Since the people he's about to kill are John and Greg, I'm all for it.

"It's an *I can't betray your sister's trust ever again*, Creed," I say, but that's pretty much a copout answer because when Andrew first showed us the video, Miranda's face got tight and she looked at Jessie like she'd give anything to protect her. It's not Miranda that's being picked on: it's her girlfriend.

He nods his chin briskly, like he respects my answer at least a little bit.

When he turns and heads over to the fight, Sai is bleeding, Abigail has disappeared into the woods with Ebony—guess cheaters of a feather flock together—and I take up position on a fallen log to watch the show.

"This is massively entertaining," Windsor whispers as he passes by me, his daffodil and polish scent drifting in the air as he pauses next to the drink table and starts mixing cocktails like a damn bartender. When he offers one to me, I refuse.

"My father's a recovering alcoholic," I explain, and

Windsor shrugs.

"Same with mine, only he's dead now so I guess he can't be recovering. Have one drink, it won't kill you." Zack growls at him, almost quite literally, and the two men get into an odd little standoff. They've only just met, and I don't like their tension. "Suit yourself then," Wind replies, tossing one drink back, and then the next.

"He likes you," Zack says as Windsor moves away to make another drink. I'm desperately trying to watch the situation with Creed, Greg, and John, but the strong thread of jealousy in Zack's voice draws my attention. I give him a questioning look as he stares back at me with that dark, unreadable expression of his.

"He just met me," I reply, but Zack's already shaking his head.

"I'm a guy, Marnye. The way he's looking at you … he's interested." I shrug my shoulders, but there's a warm little fire in my stomach that I try desperately to put out. I don't *want* Windsor to be interested in me. I have enough guy troubles as it is.

"He's interested in pretty much every girl at the school," I reply, and that's the truth. Even if Zack is right, and Windsor is interested, it's in a shallow, casual way. He's a player, not partner material. If I wanted a quick, um, *shag* then he'd be the guy I'd seek out. If I wanted a boyfriend … my attention slides away from Creed and over to Zack.

"He'll probably murder them right here," Zayd says, making me jump as he appears out of the shadows. "You've just signed their death warrants." He's smoking a clove cigarette that smells too good for words, but that I wish desperately I could tear from his inked fingers. Those things are ten times worse than normal cigarettes. Ugh, come on Zayd Kaiser …

"They deserve it," I reply, and he howls with laughter, tipping back a red Solo cup filled with beer.

"Yeah, sure, maybe. Still, Creed is gonna fucking kill them." He sits down on the log beside me as Zack glares, and Windsor flirts with some random chick at the drink table. I ignore it all and turn back to the fight.

"I am fucking done with the two of you," Creed says as Greg and John exchange looks. They don't look particularly scared of him. They should be though. They really should be. "I told you to lay off of Andrew and Miranda."

"We never touched Miranda," John says, swaggering forward.

Uh-oh.

His brown eyes glimmer with defiance as he tucks his fingers in his front pockets and lifts his chin.

"Although maybe if we had, she wouldn't be a fucking dyke anymore." There's this moment where everything is still, save the crackle of the fire and the wind in the trees. When Creed moves, that insouciant imperviousness of his falls away, and he becomes a machine. He nails John in the throat with a punch that sends the other man falling back into his friend's arms.

That's when the cracks start to show, and all of my planning comes together in a glorious moment.

"What the fuck, man?" Greg snarls, blood from his fight with Sai flecking his lips. "You think we didn't all read about that shitty bet you pulled on our own sister in that whore's journal? You're a hypocritical asshole. Lay off."

Creed grabs John by the shirt, yanks him forward, and throws him to the dirt before he goes for Greg. I don't even have to film it this time because everybody else already is. Besides, I don't need anymore damning footage of Creed. As it is, this is not on his list of things I want him to pay for. I don't condone violence, but it's almost admirable.

"What the hell is going on?" As soon as I hear that pterodactyl screech, I know who it is. Harper du Pont appears out of the trees dressed in Louboutins and some fancy designer dress that rides up so far on her thighs that I can see the lacy white panties underneath. She storms across the clearing and gets up in Creed's face, just after he knocks Greg to his knees with a punch to the stomach. "Leave them *alone*," she hisses, and there's a collective intake of breath from the crowd.

Idol versus Idol.

I'd sort of hoped this might happen.

Harper has always had per people; Tristan has always had his.

What was it he said in the limo that day?

"If you keep talking, I'll toss you right out of this limo, and we'll find out if the Plebs enjoy their queen better ... or their king. Don't test me, Harper."

There were cracks in the skin of this court, and they were bleeding blue blood long before I ever set my sights on them.

Tristan appears a moment later, swiping his hand down his face. For a second, I imagine that he and Harper were having sex in the woods, and I feel nauseous. But then I realize they were probably fighting. She's too worked up; he's too pissed off.

"Creed gave these assholes an order, and they fucked it up," Tristan snaps, circling the small group like a caged lion shaking out his mane. "Leave him alone to mete out his own justice."

"Since when do you care so much about Cabot?" Harper growls back at him, her brunette hair short and fluffy with frizz. It's a pretty amazing sight to behold; I won't lie. She hasn't noticed that me or Windsor is here yet; I imagine when she does, she'll have another fit. "What? Are you two gay for each other now, too?"

Tristan's storm gray gaze snaps to life with refined cruelty, a hint of malice balancing on the blade-thin edge of his stare. He looks beautiful in his blue shirt, gray wool coat, and black slacks, like a model on his way to a shoot. His raven-dark hair shines in the bonfire's light, picking up all the subtle blue highlights.

He circles around and ends up standing near me. Unlike Harper, he doesn't miss me or the prince standing there in the shadows. His jaw tightens, and he turns away, back toward his fiancée.

"If you undermine Creed's authority, you undermine mine. You know the rules: you control the girls, and I control the guys. Don't fuck this all up because you're pissed about your hair." Tristan's words are cold, cruel, and precise, like a blade to the gut.

Harper's eyes widen, and she looks past him to me and Windsor for the first time before snapping her gaze back to

BAD, BAD BLUE BLOODS

Tristan.

"At least John and Greg are always on my side," she says as the two boys help each other up, bleeding and groaning. Creed looks unfazed, almost bored.

"Are they?" Tristan asks, moving up to stand in front of Harper. "Are they always on your side? Because last time we hung out, all they did was talk shit about your mom, and lament the fact that we were together so they couldn't sleep with you anymore."

Someone gasps theatrically, and I glance over to see Becky with a solo cup in one hand, the other lifted to her throat as if in shock. Ever the drama queen. Like Creed to Tristan, it must kill her that she's not the queen of the school. Since I haven't quite started on my revenge with the girls, I make a mental note to exploit that weakness.

"Really?" Harper snaps, tugging her dress down in the front and closing her eyes for a moment. When she opens them, they are blazing with fury. "Because all I hear about from the girls is how you stopped fucking them long before second year started. You stopped fucking them soon after you made that stupid bet with Creed and Zayd. If I didn't know any better, I'd say you had a thing for the Working Girl. Should I call your dad and tell him about it?" She turns away with a huff, and half the Bluebloods go with her, including Greg and John.

Once they've gone, there's a moment of quiet. Nobody moves; nobody speaks. I can't see Tristan's face, but his shoulders are drawn so tight it looks like he's in pain.

Finally, Creed makes the first move by heading over to the drink table and pouring himself straight vodka. He tips it back, scoffs, and swipes his arm over his mouth. The music starts up again, and Windsor moves over to stand beside me. He doesn't seem to care that Zayd is sitting right next to me.

"I have to say, I've only just arrived at Burberry prep, but it's quite obvious …" Windsor reaches up and brushes some hair from my forehead, making me shiver as our eyes meet in the firelight. "That the ones who think they're in charge are actually following someone else's unspoken orders." He winks at me, before holding out a hand and inviting me to dance.

I exchange a look with Zack, and find his face an impenetrable wall of stone. My hand seems to reach out of its own accord. Windsor's fingers curl around mine, and he pulls me to my feet. Zayd mumbles something under his breath that I can't quite hear, and as Windsor yanks me into the crowd, I catch his green gaze watching us with envy.

Nobody will dance with you like I did, his expression says. *Nobody can mold your body to theirs the way I can.*

I turn away, and focus on Windsor's hazel eyes as he sweeps me off my feet into a princely waltz. No, he doesn't dance like Zayd, but he has some impressive skills nonetheless. After a few songs, Miranda takes over, then Zack.

He may not be as graceful as Windsor, as agile as Miranda, or as sensual as Zayd, but he's big, warm, and he holds me so tight I feel like I could never fall with him holding me.

We don't stop dancing until dawn peaks its bright, little fingers over the edge of the horizon.

CHAPTER

16

"There's more to the story than you're letting on," Windsor says, sitting on the edge of one of the school's many planter boxes.

Part of my biology grade this year includes helping out in the academy gardens. I'm supposed to be showing Windsor what to do, but instead he somehow winds up sitting and chatting will I do work. I sit back, wipe my hands on the knees of my overalls, and glare up at him. We're in the greenhouse, so it's hot enough to make me sweat. I swipe an arm across my forehead.

"Of course there's more to the story," I say, pulling out a carrot and swinging the orange length of it at him for emphasis. "We just met. I'm not about to spill all my secrets to you, despite what you might think."

Windsor smirks at me until I drop the carrot in his lap, smearing his pristine overalls with dirt. He wrinkles his nose, but tosses the vegetable into the basket before pulling out a few more. I'm guessing this is the most extensive gardening work the prince has ever done.

"I've pieced together quite a lot about your escapades from academy gossip, and I've seen your efforts reflected back in the party." Windsor tosses his fourth carrot into the basket before standing up and swiping his palms down the front of his overalls. "I want to help." I glance skeptically up at him, and he smiles bemusedly down at me. "After all, they threatened me the moment I walked in the door. I can't exactly let that go, now can I?"

I snort, pulling the last of the carrots out of the dirt, and putting them into the basket before standing up and turning to face Windsor.

"Don't pretend this is all for my benefit," I tell him, picking up the basket and moving over to the large, industrial sink in the corner. Carefully, I tip the basket of carrots out into the stainless steel basin and turn on the removable faucet, so I can rinse them off. After this, we'll deliver them to the kitchen, and we'll have the rest of the afternoon off. "I researched you: Miranda is practically an expert on your life." Dirt swirls down the drain as I glance over to the prince's handsome face. He really does look like royalty, almost too perfect to be real, as if he should exist in a painting or a sculpture and not necessarily in real life. "You have a reputation for being … How should I put this, a bully who enjoys bullying bullies." I exhale. It's a mouthful, but it's true.

Windsor doesn't pretend to deny that, but he does reach into to the sink, snatch a carrot, and bite off the tip. When he extends his hand and rubs his muddy thumb against my lower lip, my knees get seriously weak, and I have to clutch the edge of the sink to keep from wobbling.

BAD, BAD BLUE BLOODS

The guy is an incorrigible flirt, and even though I know that, it doesn't stop me from liking it.

"I like to take down big prey," he says with a grin, "it's true. I like a challenge, Marnye. Let me help you the way your friends can't." Windsor steps towards me, and cups my face between his dirty palms. "They were all here last year. Whether they were complicit or not, they're all tied together. But not me. I'm new, no strings attached, no ulterior motives. I just find it amusing to bring down those who think they're too high to fall." He releases me suddenly and steps back, leaning against the wall beneath the window. Cold, winter sunshine streams in and makes his hair look like blood. The way his hazel eyes take me in, it feels like he's stripping me bare. "There's no harm in that, is there? Besides, what's it hurt to have an extra pair of eyes to watch your back?"

I sigh, but I don't answer him. We met a week ago. What can I say, I don't trust the guy.

By the end of this week however … something happens that makes me start to.

There's nothing I hate so much as swimming; not because of the activity itself, but because it leaves me alone and vulnerable with every girl at that school who hates me.

Now that I'm on the cheerleading team, I don't have to do it much, but Burberry prep is an old-fashioned school that still requires students to learn how to swim before they're allowed to graduate. Miranda's been complaining about it all week, loudly proclaiming that the public schools don't do this anymore, and that it's unfair and impractical.

"What does swimming have to do with surviving in today's society?" she asks anyone that will listen, but it doesn't matter. On Friday, students dress down in batches and take turns swimming laps in the pool for Coach Hannah.

I'm in the last group of the day to go, clustered up with people like Harper, Becky, and Ilean. Talk about a raw deal.

We dress down, and I'm subject to an inordinate amount of strap-snapping from the other girls. By the time we actually get out the locker room and over to the pool, my back is pink and sore from having my bathing suit yanked and snapped against me. It's infuriating, but I've already broken my no violence rule once, and I won't stoop that low again. Let them pick on me: I have much better things planned.

We all climb in the pool for warm-ups, stretching, and following Coach Hannah as she runs through the routine on dry land. About halfway through, she gets a phone call from her daughter who's just days away from having a baby. She briefly excuses herself, and I sigh as I bob in the water, wishing this day would just end. I know I can swim, not only because of last year's PE classes, but also because I spent the summer practicing.

What I don't realize until it's too late, is that the girls are slowly forming a circle around me. Harper smirks at me as I finally take notice of the fact that I'm surrounded by Bluebloods and Plebs alike.

Warily, I sigh, and run my palm over my wet hair. "What do you want, Harper?"

"What do I want?" she asks, eyes widening in shock, like I've just personally offended her or something. "I want my fucking hair back."

"Yeah, we all do," I retort snootily, tired and overworked and ready for bed. "So what?"

Harper sneers at me, an expression I am well-used to. I don't mind when she does it, because what she doesn't know is that she's no longer pretty when she's scowling like that.

"I don't know what you did to get the prince on your side so fast, probably spread your legs or whatever, but I don't like it. You've turned him against us when he should be on our side; frankly, we should kick Zayd or Creed out and Windsor should be an Idol." Harper swims closer to me, and I back up, but there's nowhere to go. "I'm going to teach you a little lesson about stirring shit up during my parties. Ladies." She gestures with her chin, and the girls all swim closer, grabbing onto my shoulders, arms, even snatching clumps of my hair.

Before I can even register what's happening, they're pushing me under.

I'm so shocked, but accidentally take a breath, chlorinated water rushing into my lungs, stealing my breath away. I begin to choke, but that only makes things worse as I'm now

251

inhaling huge mouthfuls of water. My arms and legs thrash, and my nails rake across the skin of the girls nearest me, but it doesn't do any good. There are so many of them that they keep me under with little effort.

Time seems to slow to a crawl, so that I'm seeing each second as a whole minute. I see their legs, dancing beneath the water, the curves of their dark blue academy-issued swimsuits across their thighs. My eyes seem to catch on the black number four on the pool wall, indicating the depth of the water.

Is this really happening? I think, the strength and speed of my struggle slowing dramatically. *Am I really going to drown in four fucking feet of water?*

My vision starts to darken at the edges, while the center flickers with little white stars. Once that starts happening, all I can think about is my dad and how much I'm going to miss him. My next thoughts … don't make a lot of sense.

I think about Zack, about Tristan, Creed and Zayd. Will any of them miss me? Will any of them care that I'm gone? I know Miranda will, and Andrew, too, probably.

But soon, those thoughts fade away, too, and I start to feel sleepy.

The next thing I know, there's a huge splash that rocks me and jostles the grips of the girls holding onto me. Strong arms wrap around my waist and pull me up and out of the water before hoisting me onto the edge and laying me flat on the cement.

Someone is leaning over me, but I can't see who it is. My vision is too unsure, and I feel like my consciousness is coming in and out. My mystery savior covers my mouth with his own and breathes life into me.

That's the last thing I remember before waking up in the nurse's office.

The official story is that I got out of the pool to use the restroom, tripped, fell, and hit my head before tumbling into the pool.

It's tempting to rat the girls out, but there are fifteen conflicting stories to compete against mine, so I say nothing. Charlie is called, but the nurse insists there's no reason for him to drive all the way out here, and he's got work anyway … but I sure wish I could see him.

That was scary as hell. I almost *died*. Never did I believe the girls would actually push me that hard.

It turns out that Windsor York is the one who saved me.

Zack looks sick with guilt, and stays by my side the entire day until the nurse discharges me. Miranda, Jessie, and Andrew also come to visit, but it isn't until I get back to my dorm that I find Windsor waiting for me. Zack stiffens up slightly, but the two men are at least polite to each other as we approach and Windsor pushes up from the wall.

"Ah, milady," he says, taking my hand and putting my knuckles to his lips. "She lives."

"Thanks to you," I say, feeling this cold, scared sickness roll over me. Revenge was sweet … until it wasn't. Now I'm terrified. I had no idea this was turning into a life or death situation. Creed's words echo in my head: *"The girls want to kill you. Watch out for them."*

"Mm." Windsor drops my hand and studies me with a very serious expression. Behind me, my friends fan out like a cadre of bodyguards. I wonder if maybe I should call Kathleen Cabot and ask for that Kyle guy back? I haven't seen him around campus in weeks, so I'm guessing he's left. I know she wouldn't hesitate to send him or someone else to watch over me though. "To be quite honest with you, I was only heading out to the pool to perv on you in your swimsuit. My actions were not entirely honorable." He steps back from me and sighs, and if he were anyone *but* a brand-new transfer to the school, I'd think he was in on it, like he'd set the drowning up just to save me.

"Well, thank you anyway," I say, and we stand there staring at each other for several moments more until Zack clears his throat. All I can think as I fumble my key out of the pocket of my robe is that Windsor's mouth was on mine, and I was too out of it to remember. Somehow, focusing on the not-quite-a-kiss thing keeps me from realizing how deep this shit goes.

The Infinity Club is out for my blood.

Literally.

I head inside … and everyone follows.

Instead of fighting it, I embrace the fact that I'm not alone, letting Zack tuck me into bed before Miranda crawls up on top of the covers and cuddles me. Jessie glares which is hilarious because, unfortunately, I'm as straight as an arrow. If sexuality were a choice, I would one hundred percent choose to be a lesbian. Not only would life be easier, but I'm pretty damn sure Miranda is much safer dating choice than anybody else at Burberry Prep.

Windsor leaves to grab his—get ready for this—personal tea pot, cups, saucers, and a random assortment of his prized loose leaf teas, so he can make us a proper afternoon tea, complete with finger sandwiches he swiped from the kitchen.

The guy's been at Burberry for all of two weeks, and he's managed to charm his way into the librarians' hearts, the kitchen staff, and the campus maintenance shed. Just yesterday, I walked outside and saw him leading a girl into the building where they keep all the lawn mowers and things.

Perv is right.

After we eat, Miranda puts on *Not Another Teen Movie* which makes everyone in the room groan.

"This is my *mom's* favorite movie," Zack says, but we all end up relaxing and watching it anyway. It's still funny, even if it's old.

"Next year, I'm going as Janey Briggs for Halloween," Miranda declares, sweeping her blonde hair up into a ponytail to imitate the main character's infamous 'glasses, ponytail, and paint-covered overalls' look. I give her a look because we all know she absolutely will not go like that. She won't wear anything on Halloween that isn't cute and at least a tad revealing. She says she doesn't subscribe to the short and slutty rule, but she does, and she likes. Nothing wrong with that though.

"You Americans and your Halloween," Windsor drawls, sitting in the chair in the corner. He's the only person not on the bed which is fine by me. I'm having enough trouble remembering how to breathe with Zack sitting so close to me, his huge body practically engulfing mine.

"Do you realize that even as little as I'm around you, you start off at least half your sentences with 'you Americans'," I quip, making small quotes with my fingers. I drop my hands back into my lap before I realize that they're still shaking. Pretty sure I'm exhausted, but I'm also scared to go to sleep. Once I do, I'll have to remember that blackness closing in on me, the water choking me, the burning pain in my lungs …

"You're just so adorably fun to make fun of," he says, shrugging his shoulders as he slips back into his jacket. I'm guessing he got special permission to add those damn epaulettes. They look freaking ridiculous, but I suppose if a rockstar can get special permission to have tattoos and piercings, a prince could get permission to get gold eighties-esque shoulder pad things.

"I happen to think British people are ridiculous," Miranda quips right back, and Windsor grins, lifting his tea cup up and then taking a long, slow sip. "Are you seriously over there, sippin' tea?" she asks, throwing a pillow at him. Just to clarify: Miranda learned the phrase *sipping tea* from watching RuPaul's Drag Race. It means, like, to tell the truth in a sort of shady way or to listen to other people gossip.

BAD, BAD BLUE BLOODS

Andrew is grinning, enjoying the exchange, but I see the way his eyes take in Windsor. He totally has a crush on the prince. Hell, so does Miranda, and she's gay. Pretty sure the whole of Burberry Prep Academy is in love with the prince.

"Why don't you have bodyguards?" I ask him as he stands up and starts to clean up the empty tea cups. "I feel like there are probably a lot of people that would want to kill you: foreign governments, criminals looking for someone to ransom, dads of girls you've slept with."

Windsor shrugs and washes the dishes, stacking them neatly in the box he used to carry them over. It's kind of cool to see a billionaire prince doing domestic work. I shift and accidentally end up pressing against Zack. More specifically, pressing between his legs. My back is to his front, and when I wiggle again, I hear him exhale sharply.

"Don't like to be followed around all the time. Bloody annoying. I figure if I get shot, I probably deserve it." He uses his wet palm to push red hair from his forehead, and it stays right where it is: sticking straight up.

Zack's arms slide around me, and I shiver, putting my hands over his as he clasps them over my stomach. I'm totally aware that Jessie, Miranda, and Andrew are all staring at us, but I can barely hear anything over the pounding of my heart.

"I should've been there to help," he whispers, sounding pained. I close my eyes, but I have no idea what to say. This whole day's just been … fucked. I don't curse much, but there's not many other words in the English language that could encompass what I just went through. "I'm sorry, Marnye."

There's a brief moment of silence before Windsor starts

rinsing out the teapot.

My friends start making their way off my bed, stretching and yawning. Soon, I'll be in here all alone, staring at the wall and reimagining that scenario over and over again. Oh god. No, thank you. I wet my lips, desperate to ask someone to stay with me.

The obvious choice is Zack, but … I lean back into him, and I like the way he feels so much that it's scary. If he stayed in here tonight, then I—

A knock sounds at the door, and we all jump.

Miranda and I exchange a look, but Windsor's already swept over to answer it, flinging the door wide and giving us yet another taste of his eccentric personality. I think that's a real world metaphor right there: he isn't afraid, isn't tentative, and so unashamed that he's willing to open the door on everything without a second thought.

My mouth drops open when I see who's waiting outside.

The Idol boys are on my doorstep.

Tristan Vanderbilt. Zayd Kaiser. Creed Cabot.

The three of them are standing there, dressed in their

matching but oh-so-differently-worn uniforms. Tristan's is spic and span, creased to the heavens; Zayd's is wrinkled, mussy, and unbuttoned from neck to navel; Creed's is clean and fresh, but gently tousled like he's just woken from a nap.

My throat goes dry as Tristan crosses his arms over his chest.

"What happened today? We can't get a straight answer from the girls. I want it from the horse's mouth."

"This *horse* was almost killed by your fiancée and her besties today," I snap, starting to shake. Something about seeing all three of them together like that ... I feel both rage and melancholy. Rage because I feel like no amount of revenge will ever be enough. I want more. I want to tear them down and break them until they come to me on their hands and knees, begging for release. And yet ... I miss them, too. Terribly.

Life is confusing, and it sucks.

Tristan strides forward, but Windsor puts out his boot, blocking him. That's another thing I've noticed: Windsor York is the only guy at this school who wears boots instead of loafers with his uniform.

"You can't come in without the lady's permission," Windsor says, his voice coloring with a threat. "This is her space, not yours."

The King of the School bristles, and sneers, but there's something else going on with him that I can't place. He's practically shaking.

"We want to talk to Marnye—*alone*." Tristan stares Windsor down, but instead of buckling like most people do, the prince just smiles.

"That's up to her. Ask nicely and maybe she'll say yes."

"Like, bro, who the fuck are you?" Zayd snaps, pushing Tristan out of the way and pausing in the door. He glances over at me, and to be honest, he looks like shit. He actually looks like he might puke all over the expensive rugs Kathleen Cabot bought for my dorm room floor. I'm walking on more money in here than my dad has in my college fund. "You just moved in here, and you think you know shit about what goes on?"

"I know the Infinity Club owns this school," Windsor begins, ticking things off on his hand. "I know they're desperate to have me as a member, but I've refused over a dozen times. I know that you're all part of the Club, and that you used poor Marnye here as a pawn in one of your asinine bets." He shrugs his shoulders as pretty much every person in the room gapes at him.

I mean … of *course* a rich, handsome prince knows about the Infinity Club. But also, wow. Wow.

"Marnye, can we come in?" Creed deadpans, leaning his shoulder against the doorjamb, his blue eyes focused on me. With Miranda here, he'll be on his best behavior, so at least there's that.

I sigh and rake my fingers through my hair.

"Yeah, why not?" I say, and Zack bristles behind me. The three sets of matching glares the Idols throw him when they walk in don't help. Swear to god, he even *growls* at them.

"Should we go?" Andrew asks, glancing over at Miranda and Jessie. He turns back to me and lifts his chin, like he's determined to be here if I need him to, but also willing to leave if that's what I want.

"Everyone can stay," I say loudly, as Windsor shuts the door and locks it. Smart man.

Jessie, however, looks intimidated as hell and politely excuses herself. Nobody else makes any move to leave, and Windsor re-locks it behind her.

The Idols fan out near the end of my bed. Zayd looks ashamed to even be standing in here, his eyes wandering the room. I wonder if he's remembering how he hid a camera in here to film us making out, and then shared it in front of the entire freaking school? I hope so.

We all just stare at each other, and it's awkward as hell. If I have to watch these videos later, I'm going to get secondhand embarrassment. At least I know my cameras are still running. If the Idols say or do anything incriminating, I'll have it on film.

"I told you to watch out for the girls," Creed says with a sigh, like he's so tired he might just flop onto my bed and cuddle up with me and Zack. There's something about that thought that excites me, but it's an impossibility from a distant galaxy that *will never happen*, so I push it aside. "I *told* you they were out to get you."

Tristan glances irritably in his direction before turning his silver eyes on me. His attention makes me want to shift uncomfortably which just makes me rub against Zack, and then it makes Zack … Well, he's hard again. Pressed right up against my back. *Help me, RuPaul*, I pray, because I'm really not all that religious, and I'm not sure who to ask for advice.

"What happened today?" Tristan says, his voice cold and authoritative. Everyone in that room perks up to listen …

except Windsor. He yawns and flops down in the chair again, swinging one leg over the arm to watch.

Sucking in a deep breath—air never tasted so good—I quickly relive the story. Only Zack's warm, muscular arms keep me grounded as I talk about those horrific few moments. They felt like freaking hours, though I know based on my level of consciousness at the end there that it was probably only two or three minutes max.

The Idols listen and then exchange glances.

Zayd's the first one to speak up.

"Jesus fucking Christ, Marnye." He sits down on the edge of my bed, refusing to acknowledge any sort of social grace or any boundary between us. He looks at me with those emerald green eyes of his. "Why the hell did you come back here?"

"You guys keep asking me that damn question!" I shout, and the words come out much stronger and harsher than I intend them to. I'm panting as I close my eyes and force myself to breathe. "Why do you think I came back here? I earned a scholarship to the best prep school in the country. Why *wouldn't* I come back?" I open my eyes to glare at them. "Despite what your rich idiot asses might think, poor people *do not want to be poor.* Everyone dreams of being able to feed and clothe their family, to live without having to worry that the electricity is going to be shut off, or that their debit card won't work when they're trying to buy groceries. Why did I come back here? Because I want to graduate, go to college, and get a good job. I want to take care of my father, and I want to have a life where I can have kids and take care of them, too." I pause in my rant and notice that the entire room has gone silent. Even Miranda is staring at me with a new sense of understanding.

It's shocking, the level of privilege these people have, and they don't even know it.

"I came back here, so I could get back at you for what you did to me," I add, and then I just give in and relax against Zack. Even if his dick is digging into my back, I don't care. He's clearly not doing it on purpose. "So please stop asking me that question. It's ignorant and asinine, and it's not going to get you anywhere."

"Marnye," Zayd says, ruffling up his pale blue hair with inked fingers. He glances up at Creed and Tristan before turning back to me. "There's so … fucking much. I don't even know where to start or how to tell you without breaking all sorts of Club rules, but …"

"The girls have a bet," Tristan says, very matter-of-factly. He tucks his fingers into the pockets of his slacks, and gives a tight, unhappy little smile. "They want to see if they can do what Zack and Lizzie couldn't." My heart stops beating for a whole minute there, I swear. It's like it's been replaced with a cube of ice.

"They didn't act like they were trying to get me to kill myself: they acted like *they* wanted to kill me with their bare hands." Tristan exhales, but it's Creed who answers, his eyes sliding from me to Miranda and back to me again.

"Well, that's definitely the bet. The Infinity Club is all about those with power changing the world with the flick of a single finger. If the girls can't get you—an average commoner—to kill yourself or leave the school, then clearly they aren't ready to step into the shoes of their respective family businesses." Creed sounds like he's discussing the weather, not a disgustingly corrupt and secret billionaire Club with no morals, and an even dumber name. "That's the gist of it, anyway."

"Fantastic," I say, feeling exhausted all of a sudden. But then suspicion starts to creep in. "Why are you telling me this?"

"Despite what you might think," Tristan snaps at me, "we never wanted you to *die*." He turns on his heel and heads for the door, slamming it behind him.

"You should just leave before you get hurt," Zayd says, pauses, and then adds, "again."

"I'm not going anywhere," I snap, glancing over and catching Windsor's gaze. He winks at me with his pretty hazel eyes.

"There's not a single club member who doesn't have the resources to bury you, Marnye," Creed drawls, leaning back against my wardrobe. "Face it: you're outnumbered, outranked, and can be out bought at any moment."

"Not necessarily," Windsor purrs, standing up and heading for the door. He opens it wide and holds out a hand, indicating to the two remaining Idol boys that it's time to leave. Reluctantly, they both do. I watch them go, feeling my heart pound like crazy in my chest. *This is nuts; this is absolute insanity,* I think. I'd heard high school was hell … but I didn't expect this. "With me by her side, Marnye won't have to worry about silly things like money."

Zayd and Creed both glance back in surprise, but

BAD, BAD BLUE BLOODS

Windsor's already slamming the door in their faces.
    Guess they're surprised I bagged a prince as a friend.
    Guess I'm lucky he's a revenge-crazed bully of bullies.
    Lucky freaking me.

CHAPTER
17

There's a definite shift in dynamics after the drowning. Creed has stopped flirting with Ileana, and I rarely see Tristan and Harper in the same room. She is, however, still wearing her ring, and I can't stop myself from thinking about William Vanderbilt and the crack of his palm against his son's face. No matter what, Tristan won't dump Harper. Not unless ... I get Lizzie involved.

I put that plan aside for now. I can't pair Tristan up with Lizzie until after I win my end of the year bet with Harper. There's no way I can compete with Lizzie Walton for Tristan's affections, so I'm not even going to try. Instead, I focus on casually working myself into situations where I know the boys will be present. They're as standoffish and weird as they've been all year ... at first.

But the more I try, the easier things get.

BAD, BAD BLUE BLOODS

We're nowhere near the level of ease and companionship that we had before, but I'm making progress. Of course, from my end, we'll never have that sort of connection again. Zack, on the other hand, is truly remorseful. Or at least, he's convinced me that he is. I'm pretty sure the Idol boys are still *not* sorry about what they did to me.

"I still don't get why they told me," I tell Miranda as she flips through a *yaoi* manga—a boy on boy Japanese comic book. The drawings are, um, very explicit, and the funny thing is, she's even more into it than Andrew is. When she showed it to him, he wrinkled his nose, shrugged and said, *"I think those are more ... aimed at women?"* And then disappeared into the depths of the library.

"Because they're manipulative sociopaths," she says, closing the cover of the book and glancing up at me. She's lounging on bean bags in the 'Quiet Nook' which is actually where everyone used to go to make out before the librarians moved the shelf with the new release hardcovers and exposed the corner to the side door. It's not quite so private anymore. "I'm sorry, I know Creed is my twin, but I don't trust him for shit. I told him as much last night." She pushes up from her position on her stomach and nestles into a glittery white bean bag. "He swore up and down and all over hell that they're telling the truth, the whole truth, and nothing but the truth. The thing is, Marnye," she continues, tucking some of that shimmering blonde hair behind her ear, "they're all a part of that damn Club. It's so strict that people get hurt when they don't follow the rules. So maybe Creed's lying to you or me or both of us to protect himself. It wouldn't be the first time things had gone down like that."

She crosses her legs at the knee, leaning back so far that I can see her garters. Last year, I just assumed she was wearing them to impress a crush. Now, I'm pretty sure she just wears them because they're hot. They're even *in* the school dress code: *Academy-issued thigh-high socks can be worn with garters.* Of course, it also says: *Garters may not be visible at any time, not even when the arms are raised*, but that doesn't stop us all from rolling the waistbands of our skirts.

"I have my reasons for trying to get close to them again," I murmur, but clearly I'm being cryptic as hell, and Miranda sighs.

"So I figured. Just … be careful, okay? Your revenge thing is fine, but don't let it take away your natural sweetness." She leans over to brush loose hair from my forehead, and smiles.

"I am not naturally sweet," I reply with a roll of my eyes, and she laughs.

"Are you kidding? You're so sweet you're practically syrup." Miranda pauses suddenly and glances away, biting her lower lip. I raise my brows because I can tell something important is about to come up. "Hey Marnye …"

"Yes?" I start, grabbing her abandoned *yaoi* manga and opening it to a random page. There's a full page drawing of two guys on a bed, and I think … Oh. Based on the next panel, I don't have to *think* about what they're doing: I know. My cheeks turn pink as I keep flipping through.

"Jessie and I broke up." She blurts this out in a rush and then peers up at me from under blonde brows. I've stacked two bean bags on top of each other to make a chair, raising myself up several inches above her. Better to be here than back in my room, all alone. For the last week and a half, I've begged Miranda to stay with me because I can't bear the silence. As soon as I lay down and the light on my bedside table clicks off, I start remembering the water filling my lungs.

"Wait, this isn't because of me, is it?" I ask, and Miranda flushes even brighter than I am after looking at the *yaoi* drawings. Damn. Now I feel like complete crap. I knew I shouldn't have asked her so many times to sleep over.

"You needed me: you suffered a trauma," she starts, and then she glances away sharply and exhales, her gaze fixated so purposefully on a copy of a book about sea turtles that I know her mind is a million miles away. When she glances back, I see she's about to say something important, but gets interrupted by Creed.

"Boys' love?" he asks, appearing out of nowhere and sweeping the manga from my hands before I can stop him. "How gauche. I've told Miranda not to waste her time reading these things: it's basically porn in the shape of a comic book."

"How about you get fucked?" Miranda snaps at her twin, and I raise my eyebrows. "If Marnye cared what you thought, she'd ask." Creed narrows his ice-blue eyes at her, and they have an epic stare down that only a pair of twins could accomplish. Flames practically crackle in the air between them.

It doesn't bother me though because Creed's one and only admirable trait is the protective brother thing. He'd kill for his sister; I know he would.

"I'm going to excuse myself," I murmur, standing up and slipping away.

I end up bumping—quite literally—into Zack in the next aisle. He actually looks surprised to see me, a book of poems open in one hand, his academy-issued tablet on the table next to him. Aww, he's actually studying. Zack is by no means the top of the class, but since the school year started he's worked his way up from the bottom twenty percent to the top fifty. Huge improvement.

"Do you need any help?" I ask, peeping at the cover to see what he's looking at. "Ah, Emily Dickinson. Did you know many of her poems are still under copyright? She's a classic, a legend, and she's long-dead. Do you want to know how messed up copyright law has actually become? It used to be a tool of the people, and now it's used against the people by corpor—"

Zack puts a finger on my lips to shush my rambling, and then leans down suddenly, replacing his hand with his mouth.

The book of poems falls to the ground between us, and I'm soon standing with my back against a wall of literature while Zack explores my mouth with his tongue. His big arms sweep around me, filling me with this sense of protection and safety. When did that happen? When did I go from hating Zack to … *liking* him?

We break apart with a small gasp, his dark eyes locked on mine, burning with need.

"You can tell me about Emily Dickinson, or copyright law, or random historical facts whenever you want, Marnye. I think it's hot."

"Hot for me to tell you the library wing was an addition added to Burberry in the early nineteen hundreds by a grant from the Vanderbilt family?" I choke out and Zack grins. He kisses me again, and I swoon so badly that if his arms weren't there, I would fall over.

"So fucking hot. Except for the name Vanderbilt. Let's just leave that part out." He moves to kiss me again when a dramatic throat clearing breaks us up, a sudden foot of space appearing between our bodies as we turn to find Windsor York ... lounging on top of a book case?

"How did you get up there?" I choke out, and he shrugs. He's all stretched out on the wood like it's a hammock or something. "You're going to get suspended," I warn as he looks down at us with his hazel eyes sparkling.

"Don't stop on my account. Occasionally I get tired of fucking and like to watch." My nose wrinkles, and Zack scowls, gathering his book from the floor. Windsor doesn't seem to care, sitting up and swinging his legs over the side. He hops down to the ground next to us. "So." He props his forearm on the shelf above me and leans in dramatically. "I was thinking: you've got a few names on your list that aren't crossed off. Small fries, though. We should knock those out, and then focus on the girls."

"I showed you that list, so you could offer suggestions, not take over," I say with a roll of my eyes. Windsor raises his eyebrows and gives this self-satisfied little smirk that I couldn't force my mouth to make if I tried. Once, I stood in front of the mirror to see if I could get my expression to look as haughty and arrogant as the Idols, and I failed miserably. "I'm working my way up to the girls. They're the most difficult."

"You've also gone too soft on the Idol boys, in my not-so-humble opinion," he continues, and I duck under his arm to head back over to Zack. Heat is still coursing through me, rampant and white-hot, infectious. Now that I've had a taste of him, I just want more. So much more. I could easily see dating him one day …

One day.

But the Idols already think I'm dating him, and I need the boys to think I'm accessible enough that they could get me as a date to the graduation getaway. Unfortunately, I might have to put a bit of space between me and Zack for now.

"Windsor, I told you my story, yes, but that doesn't mean you know everything." *Told you my story, hah, please. Basically you sit across from me in The Mess everyday and work your princely magic until I spill all my secrets.* "Forget about the guys for now. The girls are trying to *kill* me, remember? Can we focus?"

He sighs and shrugs, rolling his shoulders as he taps his fingers along the spines of several poetry volumes and then selects one at random. He flips it open, glances at the poems inside and sighs.

"I've memorized all of these," he says as he flicks through the pages. "There's nothing quite so charming as a man that can recite poetry from the heart. Wouldn't you say so, mate?" He glances up and smiles at Zack, but Zack is not impressed. The only thing he likes about the prince is that the prince hates the Bluebloods as much as we do. What was it he said? *"They're only playing at being royals."* Pretty sure he finds

272

them as amusing as hamsters on a wheel.

"You know, all I have is at your disposal as well ..." Zack begins, running his palm over his chocolate brown hair. It's grown out quite a bit since he got kicked off the football team, but it's still short. I resist the urge to touch it, too. "We don't have to put up with him." Windsor chuckles and snaps the book closed, shoving it back onto the shelf.

"Your money, *Monsieur Brooks,* is all tied up in your grandfather's spindly old hands. Isn't that why you joined the Infinity Club? To get it back?" Zack's face pales as I glance over at him. Holy ... shit.

"You joined to get your money back?" I ask, and all the pieces start to click together. At least I have a *why* that explains why Zack made that bet with Lizzie. Does it make things easier? Not exactly. But it's nice to know. Speaking of Lizzie, I'm starting to look forward to Fridays again, so I can text her. She knows all about what the Burberry Idol girls did to me, and she is out for blood. Pretty sure I have her help and resources, too.

"I'm sorry, Marnye," Zack whispers, and we end up staring at each other for so long that when I blink and come to, Windsor has disappeared. "I'm so sorry." There's nothing for me to say, so I just smile tightly and we drop the subject altogether. Zack gathers up his stuff, and we head toward the exit where Creed and Miranda are, still wrapped up in a very twin-like argument. They look like blonde, blue-eyed clones.

They pause, and in near perfect unison, turn to look at me.

My cheeks flush under their scrutiny, but Creed pretends not to notice, turning and sauntering off toward the hall. Miranda takes up my right side and starts to loudly complain about her brother's idiocy. On the way out, we pass right by Ileana, Becky, and Harper. Creed's already paused there, and I can hear him murmuring in low, tight tones.

Miranda does not hesitate to get involved.

"You stay the fuck away from my brother," she hisses, shoving Ileana in the shoulder. The first year girl stumbles and whirls on her with narrowed eyes. Harper and Becky just stand there, smirking. Seeing them all together like this brings those memories roaring back to the surface, and I feel sick. I think I sway on my feet, but Zack puts a hand on my elbow and steadies me. "He might want a good name to go with our fortune, but you won't see a damn dime of the Cabot money. You're not good enough to be his hairdresser let alone his girlfriend or future bride."

Creed doesn't argue. Actually, I think I see the corner of his mouth twitch in a barely suppressed smile.

"This conversation doesn't involve you, dyke," Ileana snarls, and Creed's face turns to stone. Ileana whips back around toward him, but it's too late: whatever they might've been talking about is over. Hopefully they weren't doing much more than breaking up or exchanging quips. I mean, the girl tried to freaking drown me.

I glance over at Creed, but his ice-cold stare is focused on the Idols.

"She said you should be kicked out," I blurt suddenly, nodding in Harper's direction with my chin. "Harper did. She thinks Windsor should be an Idol and not you."

"Yeah, well, that was before I realized he was a Brothel client, too, just like all the rest of them." Harper grabs Ileana by the arm and pulls her back. "Forget about Cabot. There are other, better guys to choose from."

"None as rich though," Creed drawls, tucking his hands into his pockets, and letting this lazy smirk take over his face. "Enjoy your dwindling fortune. Being old money is nice, but only when you actually *have* money."

"Screw you, Cabot," Ileana snaps, tossing her long hair over her shoulder. Maybe eventually, I'll cut hers off, too. "You're making a huge mistake here. Fucking huge. You'll never be respected in the Club. You'll always be the new guy whose mommy bought his way in."

"And you'll always be the girl with the chip on her shoulder because I'd willingly fuck the Working Girl before I'd ever lay hands on you." Creed turns on his heel and saunters off as my eyes widen, and Ileana's mouth drops to the floor. The glare she turns on me is pure hate.

"Next time," she snaps as Harper and Becky flank her, "there isn't going to be a prince to save you."

CHAPTER

18

I've been secretly dreading Valentine's Day since … well, the school year started. Last year was eventful enough. This year … I'm not sure what I should do. I decide that, as much as it pains me, I have to send the Idol boys roses. If I want to draw them in the way they did me, why not use the same techniques?

So, I order a rose each for Tristan, Zayd, and Creed as well as for Zack, Miranda, Andrew … and Windsor. Why not? At the last minute, I even order one for Jessie. She might not be dating Miranda anymore, but she's still getting picked on by the Inner Circle, and I feel like it's at least partially my fault.

"What a quaint little tradition," Windsor says, pausing next to the seller's booth to sniff the bouquet that's on display. That's his personality right there: he's very much a stop and sniff the roses type. "But I have too many girlfriends to send out roses. If I tried, I'd probably forget a good half dozen, and that wouldn't be pleasant, now would it?"

I give him a disgusted look, and he smiles at me, bending down to sign the form as I frown.

"You just said you're not sending flowers? What are you doing?"

Windsor reaches into his pocket and pulls out a five dollar bill, tossing it on the table and stepping back.

"You don't want a flower? Really, it's the least I could do for my new friend. You're truly the only person who talks to me who doesn't want money, sex, or gossip." Wind shrugs his shoulders and then pauses as Tristan approaches the table, pausing next to me, his peppermint and cinnamon scent overwhelming as I suck in a sharp breath.

I'd sort of forgotten how awe-inspiring it was to stand so close to him. That moment on the boat when he grabbed my arms and kissed me hard and fast. *"Just remember that Creed isn't the only one that's interested."* My heart melted when he said that. Even knowing it's all a lie now doesn't make that feeling go away.

"Fuck these stupid roses," he says, his voice like the fine edge of a knife. I'm okay where I'm standing now, but one wrong move and I'm going to get cut. I'm going to bleed. "I've put myself on the *Do Not Send List.*"

Tristan ... is talking to me? I blink stupidly at him.

"There's a *Do Not Send List*?" I ask, and he nods.

Windsor makes a noise behind us.

"That's a fabulous idea ... sign me up. Or rather *unsign* me up."

Tristan and I both ignore him.

"Did you hear about the spring break trip for the honor students?" His voice is so hard to read; it's impossible for me to figure out what he's thinking.

"To Paris?" I ask, and he nods briefly. Of course I've heard of the trip. It's been featured like a prize in every school newsletter since that first week in September, a special treat to dangle in front of the student body to get everyone to work harder. The thing is, I've heard the Plebs talking: *it's just Paris, who cares?* Pretty sure the only person here who hasn't been to France is me. "I haven't let myself think about it. I've been so busy that my grades have slipped …"

"You're still number one in the class," he says, gray eyes so dark they're more of a charcoal than a silver right now. I wonder if he's thinking about that test and essay, how he'd probably be the highest ranked student in the school if I hadn't sabotaged him. Or rather, if I hadn't turned his sabotage back on him. "It'll be me and you on that trip. Nobody else comes close."

"I …" *Have no idea.* Tristan looks up, meets Windsor's eyes, and sneers before he heads off down the hallway without so much as a goodbye. Interesting.

"Sunny, cheerful bloke, isn't he?" Windsor asks, coming to stand beside me with his hands in his pockets. "And, by the way, I asked them to make an exception: you're the only person allowed to send me a rose." He bends down and gives me another of those quick, European cheek kisses. My silly American heart takes it far too personally, and I have to hold back a small sigh. My fingers touch my cheek, and I turn away to head down the hall, being careful to avoid the boys for the rest of the day.

With Tristan and Windsor both on the *Do Not Send List,* most of the attention on Valentine's Day goes to the girls. All the Idol women are showered with roses, same goes for Valentina and Abigail. I guess the Plebs used to call them the fucked-up foursome. Must be the fucked-up fivesome now with that horrid bitch Ileana in their ranks.

Me, I get roses from Miranda, Andrew, Windsor, and Zack.

They've all written super sweet little cards, and I even get a tiny present from Zack, wrapped in shimmery opalescent paper. He grins sheepishly when he delivers it to my dorm later.

"It goes with the one I gave you for your birthday," he tells me, and I realize with a start that I've never opened it. I excuse myself on the pretense of needing to pee, and grab the unwrapped package from my wardrobe drawer, popping into the restroom for some privacy.

There's so much tape on the package, that I have to use

my nail clippers to cut into it.

Inside, there's a pair of season tickets to the San Francisco Symphony clipped to a small rectangle of cardboard. My mouth drops open, and I feel terrible for leaving the gift for so long. To be quite honest, I forgot all about it. My loss, I suppose, since I could've used these during winter break to go with my dad.

When I step out of the bathroom, Zack's waiting on the edge of my bed with the other gift. I hold the tickets up and he smiles, not like he's upset or anything, but more like he's not surprised either.

"I figured you hadn't opened it," he says, and I cringe. "That's okay. At least you've got them now." I sit down next to him and carefully unwrap the new package, finding another ticket to match the first two. "You know, in case you wanted to take Miranda or something ..." he adds, but I know we're both thinking about if he and I were to go together. We're sitting so close that I can feel his body heat, and I have to close my eyes against the curiosity about what would happen if I were to give in and go to him.

"Thank you for these. You always give such thoughtful gifts." My hands are trembling, and my heart is racing. Pretty sure those are the only words I'm going to be able to get out. I like Zack now, I really do. Part of me wishes he really was my boyfriend. Maybe, later, he can be. Just not right now.

"Are you going to the garden party?" Zack asks softly, but I'm already shaking my head. I have a few deliveries to make: small care packages for each of the Idol boys with an attached, handwritten note. *I miss you.* It's the best I can do.

I'll deliver them while *they* are all at the party, so I don't have to see their faces when they read it. If one of them were to reject me outright … I can't think about that: my dad's wellbeing is on the fucking line.

This Valentine's Day is so different than the last one. All I can think about is Zack and how much I want to go and dance with him. Yet, I've got my bet with Harper, and I need to keep the Idol boys from seeing too much of me with him.

Like I told Windsor: I'm not about dating anyone just now.

It's all so confusing.

I exhale and Zack stands up, turning around to look at me with a small smile.

"Hey, it's okay. I get it." He knows about the bet—he's the only one—so I look up with an apologetic expression that I hope he understands. "Get some rest and I'll see you tomorrow."

"Thank you," I repeat again, blushing furiously when he leans down and kisses me hotly on the mouth. Zack turns and leaves, and I curl up on my bed with my roses, my tickets, and some chocolates that Miranda gave me.

It's best if I leave the boys alone on such a romantic day.

I'm already confused enough as it is.

C.M. STUNICH

The following week, the staff acknowledges Tristan and me in the morning announcements as the honor students selected for the spring Paris trip. Part of me wants to refuse, so I can go home and be with my dad, but he assures me that he's feeling much better and that I should go. I feel selfish as hell, but I know the trip will give me a good opportunity to bond with Tristan. He's the most difficult of the Idols to find any time alone with. He's always surrounded by fans … or Harper. Although I haven't seen them touch each other since the drowning incident.

"Don't you wonder when the girls made that bet?" Windsor asks me as he escorts me to cheerleading practice. I shrug. The thought had crossed my mind, but what does it matter? I'm not going to hurt myself like that ever again. The Idols can do their damned best. By the end of this year, I'll have secured treatment for my dad, the boys will have learned a valuable lesson, and then next year … I might have to use next year to focus my revenge-attention on the girls.

"I suppose. Why?" he shrugs like it doesn't matter, but he's got this mischievous smile on his face that scares me. "Don't go getting any ideas. Plans as delicate as mine can't be rushed."

"Sure they can," he says as he opens the door to the gym for me. "You're just too … high-class about it. Don't wait around for them to give you ammo. Make your own."

"No." I look him dead in the face. "If it takes me the rest of my Burberry career to finish that list, fine. I'm not going to stir shit up where there isn't any. Every single one of the Bluebloods has dirt that will rise to the surface eventually."

Windsor looks skeptical, but since we're at the gym already, the conversation is over. He's not allowed in anymore after the girls got so distracted by him during the last practice that they dropped a first year girl during our stunt routine. She's okay, but her twisted ankle is the size of an eggplant. Same color, too.

"Whatever you say, milady," he says, sweeping a dramatic bow just before the door closes.

With a sigh, I head inside and try to focus on keeping my own ankle un-twisted. Having a head too full of boy thoughts is distracting.

At least by the time Friday rolls around, Tristan has started showing up at my orchestra rehearsals again. The first time he does, our eyes meet from across the room, and it's like this connection between us that was pinched and shriveled opens up, and blood begins to flow all over again.

He smiles at me from the back row, and even though it's far away and hard to see, I almost think it might be genuine.

Maybe.

Of course, the rest of the time, he's still very much an asshole.

"Windsor York has no business on this trip," he snaps as Ms. Felton raises an eyebrow and hands us both our passports back. I wouldn't even *have* a passport at all if Burberry Prep didn't require one for admission. I got it last year, tucked it away in a drawer, and assumed I wouldn't be using until I was thirty.

Looks like I was wrong about that one.

"No business on this trip?" Windsor pouts with a little moue. "Why, Mr. Vanderbilt, I'm bloody hurt. Don't you know I lived in Paris for years?" Tristan looks irritated, but he says nothing, instead keeping his attention on our teacher. She's seated behind the desk in her office on the top floor of Tower One, looking between the two boys and sighing.

"You know there's a student guide every year, Mr. Vanderbilt, and this year, it is Burberry Prep's turn to provide that student. There's no one here besides yourself who has his level of experience. I'm sorry you two seem to be having a problem with each other, but as your actions at the end of last year were less than savory, I think you should just count your lucky stars you're even a student at the academy at all."

Tristan's jaw clenches in frustration, and he flicks a glance my way before leveling his glare back on Windsor. The prince is just smiling away, happy as a clam. He's loving this moment way too much.

"Now, Miss Reed, I've asked you this in private, and I'm going to ask you again: are you *sure* you're comfortable attending this trip with Mr. Vanderbilt. If not, he will be replaced with the third-ranked student in your grade, and given alternate trip arrangements." There's a long, tense moment where Tristan, Windsor, and Ms. Felton are all staring at me.

If I were on my regular revenge track, I'd probably take that opportunity to boot Tristan out of the travel group. The thing is, he's been to Paris before, and he can afford to go whenever he wants. It wouldn't be such a big hit to him. But seeing his face at the graduation gala when I reveal my bet with Harper? That sounds so much better.

My heart aches and throbs, but I ignore it. My emotions for the Idol boys are confusing as hell, but I can't let them derail me. Last year, I paid too much attention to my heart and hormones, and it didn't end well.

"I'm fine," I tell her, and she nods, rising from her desk and showing us out the door.

Windsor quickly makes himself scarce, but Tristan surprises me by following me to The Mess. He even sits down at my usual table, taking Miranda's spot and staring at me.

"Do you still have the watch?" he asks, and I nod. "The necklace?"

"Why?" I whisper, and he sighs, looking tired all of a sudden.

"Can I have them back? I'll pay you for them. I just … don't think it's a good idea if either Harper or my dad sees them again." He looks right at me, and there's this stark truthfulness in his gray eyes that I've never seen before. My mind immediately goes back to that moment in the library where he could've gone further, done more, touched me in more intimate places … and didn't. Did he know we were being filmed? It's hard to say, but I imagine yes. "Actually, I shouldn't be sitting here with you at all."

"Because the Plebs might put your head in a guillotine if they see you with the Working Girl?" I query. It's supposed to be a joke, but Tristan doesn't seem to find it funny. He just sits there and stares at me, his raven-dark hair falling across his forehead, his tongue tracing his lower lip as he glances away.

"Could you bring the watch and the necklace on Monday? I've got cash."

"I don't want your cash, Tristan," I whisper, but I've still got that debit card he set up for me, so I suppose that's not entirely true. "But yes, you can have them back."

He's quiet for a moment, and we both pause as the waiter approaches and we put in our order. Neither of us says anything as we sit and wait for our food, but when his foot bumps mine under the table, our gazes snap up and lock. It's like there's a thread between us, pulling us together when every rational part of me says I should be keeping us apart.

It's all for the bet, I tell myself, but even that's a lie. I wonder if the guys ever felt like that when they were with me last year. Did they ever struggle with any real emotions?

"Why did you pick him?" Tristan asks suddenly, but I notice he doesn't move his foot. We stay touching. "Why did you pick Zayd?"

I tuck my lower lip under my teeth and glance away, but I don't have an answer to that question. *I didn't want to choose; I hated it. But this is the real world, and I couldn't have all three of you. There was no right choice, and somehow, I knew that no matter whose dress I wore, it would be the wrong one.*

"It's complicated," I whisper, but Tristan scowls at me. "What? I cared about you guys. Wasn't that the point of the bet? To make me ... think I might be in love with you? You all succeeded, so there. If you need more trophies, I'll order them for you." He snaps his attention back to mine, and his hands tighten into fists on the table.

"You think you have it hard?" he asks, and there's this thread of helplessness paired with the steel in his voice that I don't understand, that I can't interpret. His gray eyes are stormy and clouded with frustration. "I don't *get* to love. I'll never know if someone truly cares about me, or if they're after my name or my money. And my dad ... you saw my dad when he gave me the watch. Besides, I'm not stupid: I know it was you outside the VIP room at the ski lodge. He doesn't love me: he owns me. I'm just a pawn for his bullshit."

I swallow hard, my heart pounding. My first response is to drawl: *ahh, poor little rich boy.* I should. I should say that and watch the hurt flicker across his face. But then there's the bet ... and also, there's my humanity. I can't make myself say it.

"If you really want it, one day you could find it," I whisper, and Tristan stares at me across the surface of the table.

"Find what?" he growls, reaching up to mess with his dark hair.

"Love. It's possible for someone to love you for you, Tristan. Trust me, I know: I was there."

He drops his hand and stares at me like he's seen a ghost.

In the next instant, he's standing up and shoving the plates, cups, and silverware to the floor. They crash and break as he leans over and grabs me by my tie, yanking me forward as he covers the surface of the table with his body. His mouth crashes into mine, and I break and burn in a million different ways.

Tristan's tongue sweeps my lower lip, pulls it between his teeth, and then claims me completely and wholly, in a way I've always dreamed of. My hands come up to grab onto his shirt, but he grabs both wrists in one of his own and holds them in place between us, making it look like I'm begging for more of him. Maybe I am, I can't tell.

He kisses me until the door to the kitchen opens and our waiter appears.

When he releases me, the sudden break between us leaves me ice-cold, and I slump back in my seat.

Tristan storms out of The Mess, slams the door, and abandons me with a salad, a thumping heart, and a whole tornado of emotions that wreck me from the inside out.

Crap.

Revenge is best served cold, right? This feels steaming hot, and I'm not sure if I hate it … or love it.

CHAPTER

19

During my tutoring sessions with Creed, I make sure that we talk about things other than work. I even accept a few invites from Miranda to hang out in their apartment. Slowly, Creed starts to come around, and even though he ignores me in the halls, he's very close to the same guy I remember from last year when we're in private.

We're back to watching movies on his couch, and it's not a rare occurrence for me to come over and find him in nothing but sweats, a towel around his neck, a glass of water in his hand as he takes me in with a sweep of those cold, blue eyes.

Oddly enough, I'm having the most trouble getting Zayd to talk me.

A week out from spring break, I get tired of it and track him down in the music room while he's playing guitar. He doesn't notice me until I'm standing right next to him, humming some song under his breath that I'm surprised to find I actually like. I've never been much for contemporary music, so that's a huge thing for me.

"Whoa, Charity, what are you doing here?" he asks, blinking his green eyes at me and looking almost sheepish about being caught with his hands on an instrument. I cross my arms over my chest and watch him as he sets it aside and turns to stare me down. He looks too tired to pull the full rockstar asshole routine.

"I'm here because you're avoiding me." Zayd's nostrils flares, but he has nowhere to hide, so he's forced to sit there and deal with me. "Why? You told me about Tristan's plan with the essay and the test, and then you came to my room to tell me about the bet the girls made. You must care a little, or you wouldn't have bothered. Besides, for guys who claim they hate my guts, Creed and Tristan seem willing to hang out."

Zayd's shoulders stiffen, and he grits his teeth. He rubs one inked hand up his other equally tattooed arm. His sleeves are rolled up, his red tie completely undone and hanging over his mostly unbuttoned shirt.

"Fuck off, Charity," he says, but there's no heat left. I wonder what else is going on behind the scenes with the boys that I don't know about. "You shouldn't have come back here, you know? Like, didn't we make it obvious that you don't belong here?"

"Why?" I challenge, stepping forward and getting into his space. My pulse is racing so fast that I'm starting to feel dizzy. "Because I'm poor? Or because you don't want me to get hurt?"

"Both? Neither? I don't fucking know." He stands up, and I'm forced to take a small step back to keep us from brushing together. I'd forgotten how tall he was, how beautiful, his hair freshly dyed with that same sea green from last year. It's hard to look away from his lip rings when he starts to tease them with his tongue. "Look, you took my music career away from me. What more do you want?"

"I want us to be friends again," I blurt without meaning to. I'm actually starting to wonder if I'm straying from my chosen path here, if there's more going on between us than just revenge and hormones.

"Yeah, well, we were never friends," he says, but when he tries to walk away, I grab his hand and squeeze it. Our eyes meet, and I refuse to look away first.

"You shouldn't be so hard on your ghostwriter," I say, and he blinks confusedly at me. "That song, the one you hate so much, the one your friends laughed at … I liked it. A lot. So don't knock whoever the record company paid to write it, okay?'

Zayd stares at me for longer than should be appropriate before tearing his hand from my grip and bailing up the music room steps and out the door. For several moments after, I feel too heavy to move, so I slump down on the table where Zayd was sitting, and just try to remember how to breathe.

"Bravo," Windsor says, surprising me as he appears from the darkness of Mr. Carter's office. "You're really sticking it to them."

"Leave me alone, Wind," I groan, but he ignores me and sits down in a chair with a black instrument case in his hand. When he pulls out the flute, I raise an eyebrow. "Like I said, you don't know everything. Just … help me with the girls, okay? I could really use a friend right now." I push some hair away from my forehead.

Windsor watches me for a moment, and then holds up his instrument.

"Play a duet with me?" he asks, and I blink in surprise. I had no idea he could play the flute. Of course, he *is* a prince, so I'm sure he plays a dozen instruments I don't know about. He hands me some sheet music. "You can follow this, can't you?"

I nod, and he grins, gesturing with his chin in the direction of the pedal harp.

Even though I'm exhausted and could really use the sleep, I sit down, set up my music, and wait for him to start playing.

Windsor is good, almost too good. The way he plays makes my heart flutter with each note, this cheerful but introspective collection of sounds that seem to draw my fingers along the strings as if by magic. Once that song is done, we play another. And another. We play for so long that my hands begin to cramp, and one of the security guards finally comes and kicks us out.

The prince walks me back to my room with an unhurried ease, and when he gets me to my door, he leans in for another of his cheek kisses. I mess it all up by turning my head, and our mouths brush for the briefest of moments. It's a short, sweet, accidental kiss, but it makes my toes curl, and a small, strange sound rises from my throat.

The way Wind looks at me … I feel all sorts of flutters inside. Guess I'm crushing on the damn prince as much as everyone else. He smiles, like he knows what I'm thinking.

"Like I said, prettiest girl in the school. If you want to try dating, lovely, just let me know. I can't promise it'll last long, but I bet we could have some fun together." He stands up straight, pushing his red hair off his forehead to make it stand up. His hazel eyes watch mine for a long moment, before he nods, bids me adieu, and disappears down the hall towards the courtyard and the towers.

Me, I flee into my dorm room, lock it behind me, and sit on the floor for almost an hour, lost in thought.

Life at Burberry Prep is never boring, now is it?

The trip to the airport is tense. Windsor and Tristan are like oil and water, with me stuck in the middle. I do my best to ignore it and stay neutral between the two, but they don't make it easy.

Fortunately, we're flying business class. I guess this means that I get an entire miniature palace to myself. My seat turns into a bed, I've got a huge screen to watch movies, and the flight attendant even stops off to give me a warm towel to clean my hands. It's pretty … luxe.

"Never sat in business class before?" Windsor guesses, leaning over the back of my seat. "Me neither. Of course, that's because when I fly, I usually go in my family's private jet. But I suppose this will do."

"You're an arrogant asshole," I grumble, still enchanted by the set up. He laughs at me, but I'm just thrilled to be going on a trip at all, private jet or no. I'd happily sit on the toilet for the entire duration, just for the honor of being able to travel. I've only been on a plane once, and that was just to fly down to see my grandfather before he passed away. It was nothing like this.

After we take off, Windsor undoes his seat belt and spends half the flight picking out movies with me and providing his unusual commentary. When I head to the bathroom, I catch a glimpse of Tristan's face, drawn taut with irritation. His eyes find mine, but we haven't talked since he kissed me, so I'm not really sure what to say.

Instead, I use the bathroom as fast as I can and flee back to my seat, putting on my headphones to shut the prince out for the rest of the ride.

Once we land, clear customs, and finally get to our hotel, I'm *exhausted*. Ms. Felton gives us each the keys to our own rooms—spoiled rich kid privileges, I suppose—and I flop down on the bed only to pass out right after. In the morning, we all have breakfast in the upstairs lounge with sweeping views of the city and the Eiffel Tower.

Both boys watch me like they've never seen me before, as fascinated with my reactions to landmarks as I am with the landmarks themselves.

"It's like seeing it for the first time all over again, isn't it?" Windsor whispers at one point, but then we're being swept up into a larger group, slapped with name tags, and taken out to the see the city. The one rule we have is that we cannot for any reason, leave our partner's side.

And by partner, of course, our guide is referring to Tristan. Each prep school has sent their top two students to dress in uniform and represent their academy as we tour the city. As the student guide, Windsor is all over the place, and I don't see much of him.

Several years back, the Notre Dame cathedral caught fire, but it's been restored to—from what I read online—much of its former glory.

That's where we start our tour of the city in the early morning.

As we're weaving our way through the crowd inside Notre Dame, the priests chanting their ghostly hymns, I feel this wild excitement burst open in my chest. Not only am I in Paris, freaking *Paris*, but I'm in a building that dates back almost a thousand years. The history buff in me takes over and before I realize what I'm doing, I'm wrapping my arm around Tristan's and squeezing.

He stiffens up for a second, but it doesn't last, and then he's relaxing and letting me cling to the crisp white sleeve of his academy jacket.

"Are you seeing what I'm seeing?" I whisper, trying to be respectful of the service taking place. I'm in no way religious, but I'd rather not be rude. I look up at Tristan, and he raises his eyebrows. A little flutter starts up in my belly, but I tamp down on it. The last thing I need to be feeling for this guy is … flutters. But we're paired up together for the remainder of the trip, and I'm determined to have a good time. Besides, if I don't hold onto his arm, I'll get swept away in the crowd. It's happened a few times already.

"I've seen it before," he says, like he's bored out of his mind. His gray gaze sweeps over me and then flicks away, toward a wall of carvings with a sign explaining their origin. Apparently, the entire church used to be covered in them, but this is the only surviving segment. I'm practically salivating. "But you look like you're about to have an orgasm."

He says that last word so loudly that several people turn to look at us, and I flush.

"Don't say orgasm so loudly in a church," I choke out, and Tristan laughs. It may very well be the most genuine sound I've ever heard pass by his full, sensuous lips. *Oh no. No. No. You're doing it again, Marnye, you're forgetting what he did to you.* My mind conjures up the image of Tristan's face from last year, the cruel sound of his words. *"And you know what? The only prize ... was that trophy. We did it for fun."* My tummy butterflies land and refuse to take flight again.

"You know," Tristan continues, his voice much more pleasant than the echoes in my head, "that orgasm isn't a bad word." He turns to me, our arms still linked. Somehow it's more intimate like that, to be face to face with him with our arms woven together.

"I never said it was," I whisper as the priests stop singing, and the sermon begins. It's in French, so I can't understand a word of it. It sounds pretty enough though.

Tristan leans down and puts his thumb against my lower lip. Half of me considers biting it off while the other half ...

doesn't want to admit how damn good it feels.

"The passionate joining of man and woman, it's not a sin, it's God's blessing in the bedroom." He leans in closer, like he's going to kiss me, but I pull back, yanking my arm from his. He smiles seductively, this practiced motion that I bet he's used on dozens of girls. *Don't think about Kiara Xiao*, I tell myself, but my mind goes there anyway, and I shiver. She's been nothing but a nightmare to me, and she's only just become a Blueblood.

"You don't strike me as a religious person," I say, and Tristan shrugs, digging his hands into the pockets of his white slacks. A huge group of tourists pushes past, and I get jostled and shoved. Tristan's there in a split-second, putting himself between them and me, and putting his hands on my shoulders to steady me. He levels a glare on the crowd that instantly puts a space bubble around us, and then he stands over me with this possessive tightening of his fingers that I don't understand. For someone that hates me as much as he claims to, he sure does like to touch me.

"I'm not religious," Tristan replies, finally letting go of me. He turns back to the long row of carvings, kings and bishops and Jesus himself done up in fine detail. "None of this interests me."

"But this is history," I say, holding a hand out to indicate the church, my heart pounding wildly. This is seriously the longest conversation we've had the entire year. It's making my pulse race like crazy. "We can learn so much from the past." I step closer to the velvet rope and curl my fingers around it, wishing I could get just a little bit closer. "People make mistakes, Tristan, and if they don't learn from them,

C.M. STUNICH

nothing changes." I level a look on him that he returns with unflinching ease. After a moment, he steps closer and holds out his elbow. I take it, noticing that his body tenses when I dig my fingers into his jacket.

"My dad hates you, you know. He thinks you're the devil incarnate." He says this casually, but with a hardness to his voice that says he wants me to know this for some reason, like it's super important. I take note and file that away, but I refuse to let thoughts of William Vanderbilt interrupt my afternoon.

We spend the rest of the day in the Latin Quarter, walking past bars where Ernest Hemingway drank, and pausing at street vendors selling oil paintings of the city. The coffee in Paris is atrocious, the pastries fantastic, and the company … not so bad as I'd thought.

Spring break might be two weeks long, but we only have five days in Paris, so we pack them as tight as we can with activities, using our second day to tackle Disneyland.

Tristan lets me cling to his arm and gush as we make our way from one ride to another. Despite his uptight personality and generally bad attitude, he's not a bad park buddy. He doesn't shy away from any ride, not even something as silly as the tea cups. He takes a selfie with me in front of the pink Disney castle, and even has lunch with me at the Pirates of the Caribbean restaurant. By the end of the day, I'm sort of enjoying parading around the park in our matching white uniforms, watching girls' eyes track our movements with unbridled jealousy.

On the train ride back to the hotel, I fall asleep with my

head on Tristan's shoulder, and some strange, quiet part of me imagines him stroking his fingers through my hair.

On our last day in Paris, we hit the Eiffel Tower, but it's a little too crowded to be enjoyable, so we excuse ourselves to the park across the street to take pictures. Everything seems normal until Tristan stops walking abruptly.

"You okay?" I ask, blinking up at him.

"Marnye," Tristan starts, turning to face me. The way he's gazing down at my face, with his gray gaze softened, his mouth parted slightly, I expect something big. My heart races, and I feel my throat getting tight. No words will come. Instead, I wait for his. "There are so many things … You can't stay at Burberry Prep. The Infinity Club is—"

"Don't blame your actions on the Club," I tell him, finally finding my voice again. My breath comes in short, sharp, little pants. "Don't do it. If you have something to say to me, then say it. But don't stand there and hide behind the club."

Tristan scowls, but then shakes his head, his raven-dark hair fluttering in the breeze. If I tilt my head just slightly, I can see the Eiffel Tower, standing proud in the pale blue afternoon sky. He takes another step closer to me and then raises his hands to my shoulders, laying his palms gently on them. My body tingles at the touch.

"Marnye," he starts, sounding so different than usual, almost eager, almost … sorry. "I'm—"

"Well, well, didn't realize you two were so close," Windsor's voice calls out, and I swear, there's a sudden flash of rage in Tristan's gaze before a wall smashes down his emotions. I watch in desperate sadness as he locks away whatever he was going to say, and drops his arms to his sides before turning to glare at the prince. "Oh, don't mind me. I'm content to stand here and watch." Windsor smiles, but it isn't pleasant. He's clearly plotting right now. As much as I like him, I always have to remember that I'm walking on a razor's edge. He's as dangerous as the rest of them.

"What are you even doing here?" Tristan growls, that practiced self-control of his slipping for a moment. "And I don't mean at the Eiffel Tower: I mean on this trip, period."

Windsor shrugs his shoulders, palms up and out, in a helpless little *who me?* sort of a pose. He tucks his hands in his pockets, kicks at a stray pebble, and saunters over to us, his posture screaming nonchalance. The thing is, I've known him for months now, and I can see a tightness around his mouth that isn't normally there.

"Well, I live purely for the conquest of leisure and enjoyment. And what is Paris, if not the city of excess?" Windsor's smile slips as the wind rustles his red hair. His hazel eyes are all for Tristan; he barely looks at me. A moment later, his mood snaps, and he's smiling again. "Besides, I'm the student guide, remember? I lived in Paris for three years. That, and I've spent every summer here since I was three."

The boys are on either side of me, both substantially taller, both handsome but in different ways. My gaze flicks between the two of them, and my pulse picks up speed. I feel almost lightheaded, trapped between two worlds. American royalty and British royalty. It's a stand-off for the ages, that's for sure.

Suddenly and without warning, both boys launch their

hands at my wrists, gripping me almost too hard. Windsor is on my right and Tristan on my left. I'm left blinking stupidly and wondering why they're gripping me for dear life.

Tristan's gray eyes narrow to slits and Windsor smiles nice and wide, but scary. The former says something in French, words that roll off the tongue as easily in the language of love as they do in English. Windsor listens, flicks his attention my way, and then looks back at Tristan. His response is just as lovely, flowing with ease off his tongue. I catch a few words and phrases: *la petite amie, belle,* and *elle est à moi.* Or … I think that's what I catch. But that's about it. I don't even know what any of it means.

"Marnye, choose," Tristan declares, his chin held high, his dark hair obscuring his brows as its tousled in the breeze. "Pick one of us to go with. Right now."

I gape, and my mouth parts in surprise. Choose? Between my enemy-turned-bet and my new friend? Surely Tristan isn't egotistical enough to think I'd pick him. Besides, I already made a 'choice' once, and it didn't exactly go over well for me. Before I can even process the thought, Tristan's grip tightens, but Windsor's loosens, and he lets go of me suddenly, leaving a cool space where his hand had rested seconds earlier.

He says something else in French, and Tristan's eyes flash with triumph, but then Windsor tucks his hands in his pockets and leans down to put his lips near my ear. When he speaks, his mouth brushes my earlobe and I shiver.

"I won't make you choose, love, not today." He chuckles and I shiver. "But if you really want your vengeance, slip this in his pocket when you get the chance." I feel a slight weight in my right jacket pocket, and I blink in surprise as Windsor backs up, nods at Tristan, and winks at me. He turns on his heel and takes off in the direction of the Eiffel Tower.

What ... is all this crap about? My right hand surreptitiously dives into my pocket, and I feel a small plastic wrapped item. Glancing down, I see white powder and my face blanches. Is this ... what I think it is?! Windsor's just put cocaine in my pocket.

Oh my god.

Tristan relaxes slightly, and looks askance at me. Whatever he was going to say earlier, it's gone, wiped clean from his face. He looks as cold and immovable as ever. His hand drops from my wrist and he takes a small step back. We exchange a long look, and my stomach flips over with nervousness.

He made me think I cared about him.

I won't be lied to again.

But ... I need him to go to the graduation gala with me. Since he's engaged to Harper, he's a much harder target than Zayd and Creed.

"Where to now?" I ask, and he glances away, toward the park on our left, tucking his hands into the pockets of his slacks. As soon as I've got a moment, I dump the baggy into a trash can. Hang them with their own rope. So far as I know, Tristan doesn't use cocaine. I'm not going to do this to him. I broke my rules once to punch Harper; I won't do it again.

"Back to the hotel. We have to leave for the airport early in the morning." He glances briefly in my direction again. "You know, my father owns a vineyard in Reims, and my family makes champagne. One day, I'll take you there." And then he turns and walks off, leaving me feeling both confused and elated.

This bet may very well be the death of me.

CHAPTER

20

The rest of my spring break is spent decorating my new room, luxuriating in the bath (we never had a bath at the Train Car), and exploring the fancy Grenadine Heights neighborhood that our new rental just *barely* borders. But, technically, we *are* in the boundaries of Grenadine Heights; it's pretty freaking cool.

Dad can only afford this though because he got those welding jobs from Robin's friends at Christmas. They liked his work so much that their friends have hired him, and their friend's friends. I just hope the jobs don't run out one day and we end up back at the Train Car. Technically, we own that free and clear, and rent the plot for some nominal amount. For now, it still belongs to the Reed family.

I'm so irritated with Windsor that I ignore his texts for three days before I respond.

BAD, BAD BLUE BLOODS

The cocaine thing was over the top, I tell him, and he sends back an emoji shrugging its shoulders. When I don't find that particularly funny, he writes to me again.

You're right. This is your game, not mine. I'm not used to that.

He waits a few minutes as I sit naked in the bath and stare at my phone, and then he starts typing again. I'll probably end up dropping my phone in the water at one point, and then we'll truly find out if it's waterproof or not. My skin is all wrinkly, and prune-y but I'm not ready to get out yet.

What I'm trying to say, milady, is that I'm sorry.

I read Wind's next text with a sigh and then message him back: *You're forgiven. Just don't do it again.*

I'm about to set my phone aside when another text comes in, but this time, it's not from Windsor. No, this time it's from Zayd.

Spring break on tour with Dad blows. XXX

Butterflies take over my stomach, and I have to resist the urge to squeal. No way. I'm not actually that excited, it's just … the bet and everything. Now that the last days of March are wasting away, I've realized that I only really have April and May to get the guys to fall in love with me.

Two months is not a lot of time, and June hardly counts since our last day—and the day of the graduation gala—is the fourteenth.

Nothing happening here either. Any cute groupies at the concerts?

I have no idea why I asked that, and I cringe right after hitting send. Zayd starts typing and I get back several laughing emojis that remind me of his howling laughter.

305

C.M. STUNICH

They're all like in their fifties, he replies, and then, *It's torture. Dad's music sucks, too.*

I laugh, and sink a little lower in the bubbles. We keep texting, and by the time I realize how long I've been in the bath, the water's cold and Dad's home from work. I send Zayd one last message and climb out, toweling off and slipping into jeans and a t-shirt.

Anyway, with Zack gone to visit his grandfather, I'm all alone in Cruz Bay with no one to hang out with. I'm not sure if that's a blessing or a curse. I'm enjoying my time relaxing and hanging out with Dad, but I'm pretty sure he's been sneaking out at night to see Jennifer. We haven't talked about it, but I'm just so glad his tests have been coming back with optimistic results, I don't press the matter.

Not until dinner that evening.

"Jennifer would like to extend an invitation for you to spend the summer with her," Dad says over the drawl of country music. We're sitting at a steakhouse that I paid for with that bet money of mine. I told Dad the truth: I won money playing poker. He didn't ask how much which is good because I refuse to lie, but I'm also reticent to let him know. If he finds out I'm mixed up in the weirdness of the Infinity Club, he'd probably pull me from Burberry Prep kicking and screaming.

"You're still seeing her?" I ask, picking at my baked potato with my fork. Dad sighs and sips his beer, taking his time before answering me.

"Not that it's your business," he eyes me with a critical gaze, "but yes."

306

"But she's not going to leave her husband for you?" Dad says nothing. "And it doesn't bother you that you're complicit in her cheating?" This time, he gets mad and puts down his fork. He looks at me with this deep-set frown in his face that I don't like. Charlie never frowns at me like that; I blame Jennifer. "She abandoned us, and she left me at a rest stop because I was *inconvenient*. Dad, this sucks."

"Marnye, that's enough."

My lips purse and I set my fork down, leaning back in my chair with my arms crossed over my chest.

"I'd like to never see her again, to be honest with you. I'll be declining her summer invitation. *Unless* her invitation means I'd get to meet my sister, then I'll consider it." The way Dad's looking at me, I'm guessing not. "Then the answer is no. The woman's a coward who's denied me a relationship with the only sibling I'll ever have."

Charlie grimaces.

"Fine then, Marnye, don't go. But I'm a grown man, and if I want to have a relationship with your mother—"

"Jennifer," I correct, and he sighs.

"—*Jennifer*, then I will. And you don't have to like it, but you can at least be respectful of it."

Neither of us talks for the rest of the meal, and when I get home, I lock myself in my room and play my harp until the sun comes up.

Screw Jennifer.

She didn't want to be my mom when I needed her, so I'm not interested in having her around now.

There's so much tension in the house after that, I'm almost relieved when Andrew picks me up in his limo, and we head back to Burberry Prep.

I hit the ground running when I get back, diving into my studies and making sure my grades stay sharp. I also put extra effort into spending every spare moment with one of the Idol guys. Tristan … is complicated. We had a great time in Paris, and I felt like we were actually making progress, but now that we're back on campus, he's being standoffish and weird.

Creed and Zayd are much easier to come by, and even though I think they're a tad shocked to see me open and forgiving, they start to grudgingly seek my company out, too. At the end of the week when I text Lizzie and tell her about Tristan, she's strangely quiet. She gives me a few short, clipped replies, but that's about it. Her feelings for him seem to be as strong as ever, and for some reason, that bothers me. I don't know why, but it does, and I don't like it.

Miranda, too, is acting a bit strange, asking me all sorts of questions about what I'm doing with the guys. She's not dumb enough to think I've actually forgiven them, but to her credit, I think she may be a tad worried about what I might do to her twin. I give her the best answers I can, and hope she can forgive me when the time comes.

The following weekend, Miranda tells me that Creed's stolen the key to the athletics center, so he can use the hot tub. Technically, it's just for student athletes who need the heat to soak sore muscles, and its use has to be approved by the school nurse.

When I find him in there, he's just lounging in the bubbles with his eyes closed. I say nothing, tossing my towel onto the steps, and climbing in. He hears the splash of my foot hitting the water, and groans.

"Miranda, I said you could use it later. What part of—" He stops talking as he opens his eyes and sees me there, submerged to my knees and standing on the circular bench seat. I lower myself into the heat as Creed's lids droop to their usual half-mast status. "Well, hello there." The guy sounds so relaxed and cavalier, like he hasn't a care in the world. I wish my life were like that. Pretty sure his isn't either, but at least he puts up a good front.

"You don't mind if I join you, right?" Creed shrugs his pale shoulders, and I can't quite keep my gaze from tracing down to the fine planes of his chest. He really has a beautiful body. "You're not dating anyone right now, are you?"

"What would you care?" he replies smoothly, but not in a cruel way. This is just how he is, insouciant and lazy and haughty.

"Just curious if there might be some angry Blueblood girl after me for being half-naked in a hot tub with her boyfriend," I say, and one of Creed's brows goes up.

"Half-naked?" he says, narrowing his eyes to slits. "If you think I'm only half-naked under all of these bubbles, you're more naïve than I thought."

My mouth gapes as Creed smirks at me, and my eyes immediately drop down to try and catch a glimpse … Guess he decides that vague references aren't enough, and stands up, flashing me his full, um, glory. *Holy freaking crap,* I think as Creed moves around the bench to sit close to me. We're not quite touching, but it feels like it, especially knowing he's not wearing anything at all.

"And if you get caught in here by a staff member?" I choke, trying to avoid thinking about the nice, hard length of his dick … No. No, no, no. Forcefully, I yank my mind from the gutter.

"Then I'll stand up, flash them, and they'll be so uncomfortable at seeing a student's cock, they'll let me off with a mark or two." He's so full of himself, it makes me want to pick. But that's not what I'm here for. I'm trying to rebuild the relationship we had last year. "What I want to know is why you're here, and your boyfriend isn't."

"Boyfriend?" I ask, and I think of Windsor a split-second before Zack. Why or how that happens, I'm not sure, but it pisses me off. "No, I don't have a boyfriend."

"You just kiss Zack Brooks for fun?"

"I kissed you for fun last year," I say, and it's the wrong subject to bring up because Creed goes immediately silent. We sit there together in the heat and the bubbles, both staring in different directions. When he looks back at me, he tucks his fingers under his chin and stares me down like he's interrogating me.

"Why are you talking to me anyway? You said you missed

me. Fine. But don't pretend you're over what happened."

"I punished you," I tell him, and he cringes. He knows I'm talking about the journal, and about the email to his mother. "We're even now. I want to move on, Creed. Your sister is my best friend, and your mom is my sponsor, and … we had a lot of fun together, didn't we?" He says nothing, just stares at me. "What I'm trying to figure out is when it changed for the three of you. At first, I could tell you truly hated me for who I was and what I stood for. But I think that after you made that bet and started spending time with me, things changed. Now I'm wondering if you three are pushing me away this year to protect me."

Creed snorts, but he doesn't respond, and I'm feeling suddenly worked up, like I'm onto something.

"That's why you're being standoffish and weird and mean, but it's also why you haven't come at me with everything you've got. Some part of you, even if it's buried deep down … maybe doesn't hate me quite so much as you want to?"

He ignores me, but I'm suddenly shaking and sweating all at once. It's true, isn't it? As hard of a time as I'm having feigning interest without feeling true feelings, they had the same problem last year. This fucking sucks. If my dad's health weren't on the line, if my career at Burberry wasn't … would I stop the bet with Harper now? It suddenly feels like overkill. I'm almost glad there's no way to back out of it. These boys need their lesson to come full circle.

"The girls aren't going to stop until you're irreparably damaged," Creed says, sighing. He glances over at me and his lids open more than usual, exposing those gorgeous blue eyes of his. He takes me in appreciatively. "You've caught the attention of the Infinity Club, Marnye." *Oh god, he just called me Marnye.* "Leave, and stop torturing us."

Us.

He just said us.

"Torturing you, how?" I ask, and then Creed's moving with lightning speed, dropping that lazy prince act for the unstoppable nightmare he is when he's defending Miranda. He yanks me onto his lap, and I'm suddenly just straddling his hardness with my arms around his neck, his hands on my hips.

Our kiss is sudden and fierce, and it makes me forget that any time has passed since the last moment his lips were on mine. I forget the pranks and the bets and the torture, and I'm just grinding on him and kissing, small moans escaping us both.

Creed is the one who pushes me back, blue eyes sparkling. This time, his heavy-lidded gaze is anything but lazy. All it says to me is *sex*.

"How far do you want this to go?" he says, voice sharp with need. I swallow hard, and exhale, curling my fingers around his muscular shoulders. We press our foreheads together, and I feel like I might die. Despite everything, I missed this piece of shit. All I want is an … an *I'm sorry.*

"Are you filming it this time?" I whisper, and Creed goes stiff beneath me. I mean, stiff in other ways, less good ones.

"No."

"Are you …" I lift my eyes up to his, and I can't help but think about Zack. This feels somewhat like a betrayal. I told him we weren't dating, that I could never be with him, but …

"Do you take pleasure in what you did to me?"

Creed wraps his arms around me and pulls me close.

Please say it, I think. *Please.*

"If you think I'm going to tell anyone about this, I won't." He exhales, and there's the first genuine bit of emotion I've seen from him in a long time. "You need to leave the school before it's too late."

"I'm not afraid of Harper and her bitch friends," I snap, and Creed grits his teeth.

"Maybe you should be." I sit down harder on his crotch and he groans. "Jesus, Marnye."

"You destroyed me," I choke out. I don't mean to, but the words just fall from my lips. My body is still pulsing hot, my nipples hard, my lips aching from our kisses. "Why? Why, Creed? Was it fun?"

"I'm fucking sorry!" he roars, and it's so outside his usual scope of self-expression that I'm beyond shocked. "I'm sorry I did it. But why did you have to pick him and not me? What the fuck, Marnye?" Creed grabs the back of my head and kisses me with so much heat and want that my head spins. *This could all be a trap. For all I know, Valentina or Ileana is hiding around the corner and filming us.*

My body moves of its own accord, rocking against Creed's lap while our kissing reaches a crescendo. He shudders underneath me, groaning, his muscles going taut, hips bucking up towards mine. It takes me a moment to realize what just happened, and then I'm rearing back, cheeks flushed, mouth tingling.

"Did you just …"

"You were grinding on my bare crotch," Creed whispers

back, eyes closed, breath coming in heavy pants. His right hand sweeps down my back to cup my ass, and I'm pretty sure he's looking to see what's under my swimsuit …

I jerk back, scrambling to the opposite side of the hot tub.

That's about when Miranda, Andrew … Zack and Windsor all appear.

"Oh." Windsor says, sounding far too perky for the amount of tension in the room. I have no idea what I look like, but I catch Zack's dark gaze, and I see the fury there. He looks like he might kill Creed. "Have we interrupted something? You've most definitely had sex now, haven't you?"

"No," I blurt, but I suppose it was as close to sex as I've ever gotten … "No, we … no."

Miranda looks like she wants to puke. I'm a little surprised considering I thought she wanted me and Creed to be friends again.

"I'm gonna go," Zack says, turning and striding off, his towel thrown over his muscular shoulders, his shorts riding low on his hips. I can't look at Creed, and Windsor's satisfied smirk is infuriating, so I stand up and climb out of the hot tub, snatching my towel as I pass Andrew. He just looks embarrassed, and confused. Guess I would be, too, if I thought my friend was out for revenge and ended up making her tormenter orgasm in a hot tub.

"Zack, wait," I call out, padding after him, cheeks red, body flushed. He makes it outside before I grab hold of his arm and get him to whirl on me.

"Did you just screw him?" he shouts, but I'm shaking my

head and then covering my face with my hands. "I thought you didn't believe in these stupid Infinity Club bets? I get what you're trying to do, but to go so far? To fuck a guy you hate? How could you, Marnye?"

"He ... we were just kissing, and he ..." I have no idea what to say, and I end up dropping my arms by my sides. Zack just stares at me and swallows hard. When he kisses me, I let him. I let him sweep my wet body up against his, and I love being in his arms so much that I'm ... confused.

Did I cheat on Zack with Creed? Or am I cheating on Creed with Zack? Did I cheat on either of them when I kissed Tristan? Oh god. I'm not a cheater. I *hate* cheaters. Jennifer is a cheater. I can't be.

"How are you going to choose?"

Miranda asked me that question last year. I hated it then. I hate it even more now.

I push Zack away from me, wrap my towel around my shoulders, and run all the way back to my dorm.

CHAPTER
21

"Whatever you did," Miranda says, as I eat my food as fast as I can. I just want to finish my meal and get out of The Mess before Tristan, Zayd, Creed, Zack, or Windsor shows up. Is that too much to ask? "Creed is now obsessed with you." I choke on a cherry tomato, but I can't ignore the slight accusation in her words.

"Are you okay?" I ask, and she sighs, putting her elbows on the table and resting her chin in her palms.

"You must be up to something. There's no way you'd forgive my brother quite so easily." I stab another piece of lettuce and bring it to my lips. "I believe you when you say you didn't sleep with him, but whatever happened … I don't think you even understood it. Are you sure you know what you're doing?"

316

BAD, BAD BLUE BLOODS

"I told you," I whisper, keeping my voice low. There are other students eating in the restaurant with us, but they're all Plebs. We're relatively safe, but I don't doubt any overheard conversation will make it back to Harper. "He just ... *came*." Miranda wrinkles her nose and looks at me in horror.

"Please stop saying that. It's so freaking gross. That's my *brother*. My *twin*. I don't want to hear about his ... eww. Just no." She sighs and sits up straight, pausing as the door opens and ... Zack walks in. Oh fantastic. He spots me right away and makes a beeline straight for this table. Would it be wrong if I just got up and ran?

He sits down next to me, and awkward silence descends.

"Can we have a moment alone?" Zack asks, and Miranda rolls her eyes.

"Yeah, sure. Babe, come find me later and we'll all watch *RuPaul* in Andrew's room, okay?" I nod, and she takes off. I stare at my salad while I wait for Zack to talk.

"Are you mad at me?" he asks, and my head jerks up and around. My brows are crinkled, and I'm so beyond confused I don't quite know what to say.

"Aren't you mad at me?" I ask, and he sighs, jaw clenching as he looks away. "I ... did that with Creed, and ..."

"I already told you, we can't be together. I don't fucking deserve you, Marnye. It was wrong of me to react like that. I know there's no future for us." My heart drops, and I want to scream. *There could be a future for us, you idiot! Fight for me.* But at the same time, I feel like a cheater who doesn't deserve Zack. I feel like my mom.

"I cheated on you," I choke, and he spins to face me with

his eyes wide.

"Cheated? You can't cheat on someone you're not with." He stares at me with so much longing that my heart begins to pound, and I feel like I might pass out. Things only get worse when the Idol boys stroll into the room and spot us there in the corner.

Tristan's nostrils flare at the sight of Zack, Creed immediately makes his way over to me, and Zayd gives a cute, little wave.

Crap. Crap, crap, crap.

I shoot up from my chair, heart pounding, as Creed puts an arm on either side of me and pins me to the wall.

"Avoiding me won't do you any good," he says, and I think I forget my own name for a minute there.

"I wasn't avoiding you," I whisper, wondering how much he's told Tristan and Zayd. The other two look a bit confused, to be honest. "I just … I have a lot going on, okay?" Creed narrows his eyes on me and then glances at Zack like he's garbage.

"Why don't you get lost, so Marnye and I can talk?"

"Marnye, and I *were* talking, so how about you fuck all the way off?" Zack snarls. Tristan pretends like he doesn't give a shit and heads straight for the Idols' table. He is engaged, after all, and I make a mental note to push harder with him. April is already coming to a close, and what have I accomplished this month besides … spending time in a hot tub with Creed.

Putting my palm on Creed's chest, I push him back a step and move away from the two guys. Zayd watches me carefully, tucking his inked fingers in his front pockets. He's clearly interested in whatever's happening between us.

"What the hell is going on?" he asks as Creed and Zack look at each other like they might come to blows. As if my day isn't shitty enough, Windsor chooses that moment to walk in. He makes his way right over, grabs me by the arm, and levels one of those fantastic grins of his at the other boys.

"Do you mind if I borrow Marnye here for a moment? Mentoring duties and all that." He drags me away, and I breathe a sigh of relief as soon as I get out of the room, bending over and putting my palms on my knees for support. Windsor rubs my back in gentle swirling motions. "There, there. I know what it's like to juggle several girlfriends at once. I recognize the panic on your face."

"Do not compare me to you," I whisper, forcing myself to stand up. "I do not have multiple boyfriends. I'm just … juggling my own interests against … other things." Windsor stares at me for a long moment, hazel eyes mischievous.

"Other things?" he asks coyly, and I can just feel the truth resting on the back of my tongue. What it is about him that makes me want to spill the beans, I'm not sure. It's infuriating, to be quite honest. "You mean like this mysterious bit of revenge you won't talk about?"

"Look, I …" I look at Windsor, and I just feel so full of emotion, I want to choke. "I need to get the Idols to go to the graduation getaway with me." That's all I have to say, and then it clicks in his mind. I can see the second that it happens. "They bet they could make me fall in love, so …" It sounds pretty freaking lame coming out of my mouth right then.

"I see," Windsor drawls, tapping at his chin, like all the

pieces are falling together. "You're throwing yourself at those idiots to win a bet?" I nod, and I feel ashamed. I don't feel like a badass, revenge seeking missile anymore. I feel like Marnye Reed, a girl who's gotten herself in over her head. I actually *like* Zack. And I like Creed. I like Zayd, too. And Tristan. They've been trying to protect me from the girls all year; I can see it now. It doesn't make their behavior right, but it does make me want to know more. More about them, their feelings, more about what could happen if I spent more time with them.

"I need to make them fall in love …" I start, and the task feels so monumental that I don't even know where to begin. I'm running out of time, and my dad's future is on the line.

"Oh, love," Windsor says with a chuckle. He pushes his red hair up and off of his forehead. "You know how I'd first guessed you'd fucked?" I nod, warily, but I acknowledge him. "I thought that's what I was sensing, but I was wrong."

"Right, because I've never … slept with any of them." *I've only made Creed come in a hot tub,* I think, and I want to choke and then disappear into a hole in the ground. "So what?"

"You've already won, you shagging wanker," Windsor says, shaking his head at me. "If you ask, they'll go to your party with you. It's so bloody obvious it's practically written on the wall." I gape at him, but he seems so damn sure of himself, it's hard not to … freak out and feel satisfied at the same time.

"They don't love me," I say, and Windsor shrugs, the epaulettes on his jacket wrinkling with the motion.

BAD, BAD BLUE BLOODS

"They like you enough that they'll go. Just ask, Marnye. Take them, crush them, win your bet, and then figure out if forgiveness is something you're interested in." He frowns briefly. "Although I *was* looking forward to eating them alive. You will let me help with the rest of your blue-blooded friends however, won't you?"

I nod, but I'm so speechless, I don't know what to say.

Windsor grins, puts his arm around my shoulders, and leads me away from The Mess.

"Let's go get you a drink: you could clearly use one." I follow along after him, even though I have no intention of consuming any alcohol. Guess I needn't have worried: as soon as we get to his dorm room, Windsor makes me a cup of tea with milk and two sugars. And he's right: after I drink it, everything seems just that much clearer to me.

It's a fine balancing act, keeping up with all of my relationships. And I don't just mean the ones with the guys, Miranda and Andrew and Lizzie, too. The end of the year academic load is heavy, and I find that I spend most of my time just trying to keep up with my activities, let alone my friendships and my … other entanglements.

Creed is the first one I ask, marching right into his apartment after Miranda opens the door, and pausing next to him while he lounges on the couch. My face is bright red, but I've got some of my conviction back. Whatever happens with the boys later, they need to learn a lesson *now*. I'll take them to the getaway, and I'll see how they react. After all, I survived it. They can, too.

"Go to the graduation getaway as my date?" I ask, and Creed glances lazily up at me. He's so beyond gorgeous it's hard to believe what actually happened between us. "To the party I mean, at the Royal Pointe Lodge. Go with me, officially."

"Harper won't like that," Creed says, and I end up scowling. His eyebrows go up in surprise.

"I don't care what Harper likes. She doesn't own me. Does she own you?" This time, it's Creed that's sneering. He runs his tongue across his lower lip, and then nods, once, sharply.

"Fine then." He pauses. "Wear my dress?"

I consider that a moment, and then shrug.

I chose once, and it didn't feel good. This is sort of the opposite scenario, but I still won't choose. Either all three Idol guys go with me, or none at all.

The next day, I make sure to seek Tristan out while he's separated from Harper, leaning against his locker with one shoulder, eyes closed. He seems surprised to see me when he finally opens them up.

"What do you want?" he asks, like we didn't hang out for

a week in Paris, or share a kiss in The Mess. I've given him back his jewelry, just like he asked. He barely said thank you. I'm starting to wonder if taking Windsor's advice is a mistake. I feel like Tristan is nowhere near ready to say yes to this. He looks so unapproachably gorgeous that I don't know what to do.

"You ... you're engaged to Harper?" I ask, and his brow crinkles, mouth twisting into a scowl. "Even after she tried to drown me?"

"I explained this to you," he says, but there's this quaver in his voice that reminds me of a trapped animal, looking desperately for escape. "My dad won't allow anything else."

"Do you even like her?" I ask, and he just stares me down with his cold, silver gaze.

"I stopped liking her when I found out she beat you." That's all he says, and the words are cold enough, but the meaning behind them makes my heart flutter.

"So, can you do me a favor?" My heart is racing so fast now, I can feel it in my palms.

"What?" Just that one word. Tristan seems like he's on edge now, too.

"Be my date to the party at the lake house." He sighs and swipes his palm down his face, like he's suddenly tired. I move forward and grab the front of his academy jacket, and he freezes like he's been slapped. "Do you like me, Tristan?" I ask, and I realize I'm asking so many questions with that one single sentence. I'm asking him if he's sorry, if he's willing to cause a rift in the Bluebloods, if he can prove to me that he knows what the girls did was wrong. In the pool, backstage at the concert, they took things too far. Way, way,

way too far.

He reaches down and takes my hands in his, the warmth of his skin overwhelming me. His peppermint and cinnamon scent surrounds us and he leans in, breathing against my hair. He doesn't kiss me though, not like I want him to. His hands squeeze mine just a bit harder before he's pushing them gently away. A slight scowl takes over his lips, but I'm pretty sure it's not intended for me.

"I'll take you to party," he says, his voice so smooth it's like silk, "but after that … no more. Marnye, you can't stay here, and you can't have me." Tristan pushes me away and turns quickly, moving down the hallway so fast that by the time I decide I want to go after him, he's disappeared. Even when I peek around the corner, there's no sign of him.

My stomach drops, and I can't decide if that was a victory … or a defeat.

Zayd is the last one of the Idols that I seek out. Maybe because I feel like there really was something between us, so his betrayal stings the worst? I don't know. For whatever reason, he's pulled away from me even more so than Tristan.

The texting's been helping, but whenever I approach him in person, he seems to find a reason to run.

We're in the middle of a long text conversation when I find him sunning himself outside on a picnic table. *Boo* is the last thing I send before I poke him in the shoulder and make him jump.

"You're running away from me," I say aloud, and he sits up, crossing his legs and raising his pierced brow at me.

"Um, no? I'm just sitting here," he says, giving me a cocky, stupid little smile that's one hundred percent fake. "If I were running, Charity, you'd know, because you'd see my tight ass booking it across the field." He grins as I climb up on the table to sit beside him.

"Do you still have the trophy?" I ask, and I swear he chokes on his own spit. He tries to cover up the motion by getting out a cigarette and a lighter, and peering around to check for any staff members before he starts smoking it.

"Maybe, why?" he says softly, and I can feel it, that gap between us widening again.

"Could you bring it to Royal Pointe?" I ask, and he looks at me like I'm a crazy person. "It'd be cathartic for me to have it." I glance up at him from under a fall of rose-gold hair. "Be my date to the party."

Zayd scoffs.

"Why would you want to go with me? Charity, really, are you a glutton for punishment?" I glance over at him, put my hand on his knee, and then lean forward like I'm going to kiss him. Surprisingly, he pushes me back. "No. No, I'm not doing this."

"Why not?" I ask, and I feel all those horrible emotions

bubbling up inside of me. Zayd sighs and looks away, smoking his cigarette, his sea green hair tousled by the wind. After a moment, he ashes his cig against the side of the table and burning embers crumble to the bench seat below.

"Because, I don't understand you. We … treated you like shit. And then you came back all dolled up and ready to kill. Then the girls …" Zayd just stops talking and sighs, closing his eyes for a moment. When he opens them, he looks at me. "This whole *year* is for fucking nothing if you go to this party with me."

"It's not. It's your chance to say sorry, if you're sorry at all."

Zayd freezes and reaches up to run his fingers through his hair. My skirt rides up my thighs as I adjust myself, and he notices right away, taking in my garters and thigh-high socks with interest. My finger reaches out and teases around the edge of the Burberry Preparatory Academy crest that's sewn into the pocket of his jacket.

"The girls have been after your blood since before winter formal last year, you know that right?" Zayd looks over at me, and the stark truth is written all over his face. My hand moves from his pocket to the bit of tattoo I can see on his chest. When I dive my fingers underneath his shirt to touch his skin, he doesn't stop me. Instead, he reaches up and presses my hand against him. "I can't just undo everything that's happened. That's what going to this party with you would mean."

"It would mean the world to me, is what it would do," I tell him, and our eyes lock. Tentatively, he hooks an arm around my waist and pulls me into his lap. It feels so good to be sitting with him again that for a moment, I just close my eyes and relax into it.

"You don't have any business hanging around with an idiot like me," he says, and I can hear it in his voice now, guilt, thick and heavy and weighing him down. "This is a den of wolves, Marnye, and you shouldn't be here."

"And yet I am," I say, thinking of the tattoo on my hip. "Go to the party with me, Zayd."

After a moment, he sighs and puts his chin on the top of my head.

"Fine, but shit, this is stupid," he grumbles, growling a little under his breath. "You're going to get yourself fucking killed, Marnye."

The scary part about his statement is that … he's almost right.

CHAPTER

22

The academic battle royale at the end of the year almost kills me. I'm so tired I can barely keep my eyes open, and my test scores are so alarmingly close to Tristan's that it comes down to just a few assignments. Namely, that poor essay score and test grade he earned himself by messing with me. If he hadn't done that, he might've won.

"Congratulations, Marnye!" Miranda cheers, throwing her arms around my neck and giving me a squeeze. Andrew is holding balloons and chocolate, while Zack's got a case of beer and a congrats card, and Windsor spins a freshly delivered pizza on his palm that he snatched from the end of the year pizza party in The Mess. Nobody actually hangs out at the pizza parties: students just jack food and run. The staff doesn't even mind. Why should they? Today's the last day of exams, and tomorrow is the official last day of school and the graduation gala.

None of us will be there however because we'll all be on a four hour drive to Lake Tahoe, and the Royal Pointe Lakeside Lodge and Guesthouse. It used to belong to the founder of the academy, Lucas Burberry, but was gifted to the school's foundation after his death. It's worth over *seventy-five million* dollars, and houses a massive dock that's become a hangout for the super-rich. Most of the students at Burberry have parents who keep boats there.

My friends pile into my dorm, and we pass around the pizza, beer, and sodas while a movie that nobody's watching plays in the background. Vaguely, I wonder where the Idols are right now. The girls have backed off quite a bit since the drowning, but I don't think that's out of charity or because they feel bad. Oh no, I imagine things are about to get way worse for me.

Windsor lays on the bed with his head in my lap, and I get these strange tingles all over my body. I know he's just naturally flirty and touchy-feely, and the last thing I need is another guy to worry about, but there's something about the prince that makes me feel strange inside. Good strange, too.

Zack watches us, but he hasn't said anything since that day in The Mess. Part of me hopes that he's just biding his time and waiting until after the graduation getaway to make a move. The other part of me is unsure if she wants him to. Because … what about Creed or Zayd? Tristan … is a separate source of anxiety all on his own. I'm interested in him, and I have been for a while, but I didn't want to admit it because one, he's a total fucking asshole. And two, I can't decide if he's going to marry Harper to please his family or run off into the sunset with Lizzie Walton.

Either way, that doesn't leave a lot of room for me.

I push those thoughts aside and try to enjoy myself—and my victory over Tristan because, come on, how great is that? Eventually, we all fall asleep, and I wake up a few hours later tangled up with Andrew, Miranda, and Zack. Windsor is nowhere to be seen, but when I get up to go the bathroom, I notice the door to my room is cracked, and decide to see if he's outside.

He is, watching the sun come up. I sit beside him, and we just hang out there for a while in silence.

"You know," he says, glancing over at me. I'm shivering a bit in the cold morning air, so he scoots closer and pulls me into his lap. The movement makes my tummy feel like I'm on a rollercoaster. "I think I might actually like it here. Usually, I stay at a school for however long it takes me to meet and date all of the girls, and then I do whatever I have to do to get kicked out."

"Sounds pretty lonely to me," I tell him, and he shrugs. I can smell him now, like daffodils, with undertones of ebony wood and blue cedar. I'm not sure if it's a cologne, or just his natural scent. Either way, it gives me butterflies.

"I'll come back here next year," he repeats, and I smile. "I mean, at least for a short while."

"I'd like that," I say, and we continue to admire the sunrise.

Later, I'll find out if the Idols are going to actually show up at the party … or stand me up. My entire future is on the line here, my dad's *health* is on the line, and it's just too much to put my faith into boys who've already betrayed me.

"Windsor," I start, and he nods in acquiescence. "I don't want to assume things are going to go badly tonight ..."

"But if they do, jump in the pool and give you mouth to mouth?" he asks, and I grin.

"Yes, please."

"Now that," he declares, before standing me up and lifting me along with him, "was a metaphor."

There are academy cars arranged to take students to the lake, but now that the year is over, the gig is up and everyone just wants their cars back. Andrew is so freaking sweet, and lets me drive his Lambo again, even though I'm pretty sure I've gotten more than my fair share of justice out of that favor.

He rides in the back with Windsor while Miranda sits in the passenger seat; Zack takes his own car, and the Idols— who are still car-less—ride with one of the other Bluebloods.

"Why aren't you driving some fancy ass sports car?" Miranda asks, turning around to look at the prince. "You're practically famous for buying and then wrecking the best of the best." Windsor grins, but when I look up at the rearview mirror to see his reflection, a strange shadow crosses his face.

"Just too lazy to drive, I guess," he drawls, but I have a feeling that's not the whole truth. Today, however, is not the day to press. I have enough crap to deal with already.

The drive is pleasant, easy, and sort of funny because there's just this long string of luxury cars working their way through the woods, millions and millions of dollars' worth of steel and leather and rubber.

We all park in the gravel lot outside the lodge, and carry our bags to the main house. There's a beach house, too, but second years are not allowed to stay in it. That's a third year privilege. Oddly enough, there's also this glass box that looks like an elevator called a funicular that goes from the main house all the way down to the beach. It's sort of like a slow-moving roller coaster with an enclosed car, all on its own miniature railway. Frankly, it blows my mind to see people piling into it, and taking a quick ride down to the shore. But nobody else seems impressed, so I try to keep my cool. Peasant problems, am I right?

For the first half of the day, the staff hovers, and Zack, Windsor, Andrew, Miranda, and I entertain ourselves with games—no stakes involved, sorry—and snacks. Once night rolls around, the Infinity Club takes over, and the staff becomes mysteriously absent.

Clearly, the damn Club has fingers in the Burberry Prep admin office, too.

Harper and her friends disappear to get changed, and I start to sweat when the Idol boys are nowhere to be seen. They got in a car, that much is for sure, but I haven't seen them since.

"Relax," Zack whispers as Windsor studies my face. Miranda and Andrew have gone to their rooms to change, too, so we have a moment to talk freely. "They'll be here."

"They better be," I mumble, and Windsor and I exchange a look. While I'm distracted cleaning up the card game, he disappears like he always does, but I tell myself not to worry. He was there at the pool when I needed him, and he promised he'd be here tonight. Whatever needs doing, Windsor York will get it done.

When Harper and her entourage come down the stairs in glittering gowns with full hair and makeup, I take that opportunity to switch into my own outfit: a rose-gold corset and short, voluminous skirt to match my hair. Paired with some black heels, it's a pretty damn cute outfit. I spent far more on it than I should have, but I wanted to look the part.

I wanted to look like a winner.

Heading back into the huge open lodge room near the balcony, I find Harper du Pont waiting for me. The main house is over sixteen thousand square feet, so it's pretty easy to get lost. Maybe she thinks I'll run off and try to duck out on our bet?

"So?" she asks as my heels click across the floor, and I come to stand in front of her, holding my clutch like a shield in front of my body. "Where are they?" My eyes scan the room and find Zack in the corner, arms crossed over his chest, leaning against the wall to watch and wait. Miranda and Andrew are on the back patio, sitting around one of the fire pits with drinks in their hands. They don't know about the bet, so they're completely unaware of the tension building just inside the sliding glass doors.

The rest of the Bluebloods lounge on sofas and chairs in the room, watching me. They remind me of a vampire clan or something, pretty but dangerous. Elegant on the outside, blood-sucking demons underneath. My eyes narrow as Harper starts to pace around me.

Music begins to pour from the speakers, and the room fills with a huge crowd. There are second years, third years, and fourth years all mixed together. Doesn't matter: they all know where the drama and action will be, and that's wherever the Idols and their Inner Circle are.

Minutes tick past, and I sit down to wait. Almost an hour in, I start to get worried. I'm texting the guys, but getting no responses, and Harper is beginning to get impatient.

"You have until fifteen after," she snaps at me, putting her hands on either one of the chair's armrests and leaning in so close that I can smell her signature peach and vanilla scent. My stomach turns over with nausea, and Zack comes to stand beside me. "Fuck off, Brooks. This is Club business; you can't do shit." He growls at her, but he doesn't move from his spot, flanking me like a bodyguard.

By this point, Miranda and Andrew have figured out that something's up.

"You did what?!" Miranda snaps at me when I tell her, and I cringe. "I mean, it's half brilliant and half completely and utterly insane." She digs her own phone out, and starts to blow up Creed's. "There's no reason he shouldn't be here," she mutters, exhaling sharply. "He wouldn't do something like that."

By this point, news of the bet is spreading like wildfire. Everyone knows. And they're all laughing at me.

It takes the Idols until an hour and a half *after* the party's supposed to have started to show up.

I shoot up from my chair as the three of them walk in, still dressed in their school uniforms.

Zayd is the first to spot me, and he makes his way right over.

"Car trouble," he says, and then he's scowling as Greg Van Horn walks in behind him. He's whistling and spinning his keys around on his finger, and that's when I start to wonder if the guys were supposed to get here at all. Harper looks pissed. "Let me clarify: car trouble *and* phone trouble. Somebody stole our fucking phones."

"Must've been a senior prank again, don't you think, Harper?" Tristan asks, coming to stand right in front of her. "What the fuck is this all about? Clearly, you didn't want us to show up tonight." She shrugs her shoulders like she doesn't know what he's talking about.

I glance back at Creed as he comes to stand beside me, his eyes taking in the crowded room and the eagerly glinting eyes of the Bluebloods and Plebs alike.

"Marnye?" he drawls, his devil-may-care voice sending chills down my spine.

Harper decides to take over, coming to stand so close to me that the fabric of our dresses mingles together.

"So, Marnye, which one of these men is your date for tonight?" I glance between the three guys, and then I look her dead in the eye.

"All three of them," I say, as Tristan turns to look at us,

narrowing his eyes before he glances at Creed, and then Zayd. That's when I notice Zayd's bag sitting near the door … and the stupid trophy from last year resting against it. Moving over to pick it up, I turn to face a suddenly silent room.

"Well?" Harper asks, looking at Tristan quite pointedly. She reaches up with her engagement ring and wiggles her hand around for everyone to see. "Tristan? Is that true? Are you this girl's date? I mean, she bet you would be. All three of you. She bet she could make you fall in love with her. So tell me: did she succeed?"

Clutching the trophy, I feel my heart race as the Idol boys exchange looks. There are no fancy videos or cans of paint or panties to throw, but at least I got them here. At least I did it. That is, if they choose to tell the truth. One lie from one boy could sink me right now.

"It's true," Zayd says, nostrils flaring. He stands up from his spot on the chair and addresses the room. "I'm here as her date."

"So am I," Creed drawls, watching me clutch that trophy with a certain sort of acceptance in his blue eyes. Miranda makes a squeaking sound, drawing her brother's attention. They share one of those silent twin looks, and I exhale sharply.

I figured … the Idols would be pissed off.

Zayd and Creed, at least, don't seem to be at all.

"I'm done hurting her," Zayd says, his voice so loud it echoes through the cavernous room. Becky is gaping at him, but he doesn't seem to give a shit. "Sorry, but I quit the game. I won't do it anymore. Let Marnye have the trophy and leave her the fuck alone."

Harper's jaw clenches as she turns to Tristan.

"I'm your fiancée," she says carefully, stepping close to him and taking hold of the lapels of his wool coat. "And I've got William on speed dial. So tell me, Tristan, are you here with me tonight … or with her?" The leader of the Bluebloods looks from Harper to me, his gray eyes burning.

"You know I've never been a faithful boyfriend," Tristan muses absently, tucking his hands into his pockets. "Not to anyone but Lizzie." He looks past Harper and straight at me. "I'm here with Marnye, too. So whatever stupid shit you bet her, give it up. You've lost."

A slow easy smile works its way across Creed's face as he steps up beside me and Andrew scrambles desperately to get out of his way. Miranda is still gaping, and Zack is still frowning. Me, I'm just hugging the trophy and trying to figure out if this is a dream. It's working out well, almost too well. The only thing is … the Idol boys don't seem to care that I'm trying to exact revenge on them. It's like it doesn't even matter to them at all. Or … maybe it does matter, but in a different way than I'd expected?

"You're joking?" Harper scoffs as she glances back at Becky and Ileana before turning to me. "What the fuck did you do? Do you have a magic freaking vagina or something?" The crowd murmurs, and I frown.

"If I had sex with them or not is irrelevant," I snap, clinging to the trophy and feeling like I've just aged ten years in five minutes. "They're here, with me, and that's that. You have to take care of my dad at your family's medical center. And sorry, I won't be groveling at your feet, so you can film it and post in on YouTube." A ripple works its way through the crowd, and I see Creed's blue eyes widen.

"You … made a bet for your father's cancer treatments?" he asks mildly, and I nod.

"So, you started treating the man, threatened to stop doing it, and then somehow cornered Marnye into a bet you thought you couldn't lose?" Zayd clarifies, and he sounds pissed, his rockstar voice rumbling with a slight growl. "Jesus, Harper, you're even more fucked up than the rest of us."

"I didn't corner her: she came to me," Harper chokes, turning to Tristan. "All I was trying to do was get rid of her. It's what we've been trying to do all along."

"I think I'll have a drink," Tristan says mildly, ignoring his fiancée completely. "Soda for you, Marnye?"

"Please," I whisper, and the crowd parts as Tristan turns and heads over to the drink table. They leave a clear path for him to walk back and hand the cup with its clinking ice cubes over to me.

"This is …" Harper starts, but the crowd's already moved on. Infinity Club bets happen all the time. They saw a winner chosen, and now they're over it. The only person who's still obsessing is Harper du Pont. "She invited all three of you. She thinks you're in love with her."

"Maybe we are? Who the fuck are you to judge?" Zayd snaps, rising to his feet. He towers over Harper, and I get a small surge of pleasure as she backs up. "Marnye won, Infinity Club rules. *Now move on and get over it.*" He pushes her back with a finger to her shoulder, and she lets out one of her trademark screeches before turning and stomping away.

BAD, BAD BLUE BLOODS

For a moment, I just stand there, shaking. And then I take my drink, my trophy, and my emotions, and I race up to my room and slam the door.

Miranda, Zack, and Andrew check on me, but I just need some time to process. I can't decide if I'm upset that the guys aren't emotionally wrecked the way I was ... or relieved. And then ... I feel so lost, like I have no idea what to do now.

After I've had some time to process, I dig around in my bags for some sweats, suddenly desperate to change out of this itchy dress, and realize that I've left my other bag in the car. Careful to avoid the crowd, I slip out the back door and past the gazebo where Harper and her cronies are drinking and complaining loudly about me.

Screw them.

I head over to the Lamborghini, unlock it, and grab my bag.

When I turn around, John Hannibal, Gregory Van Horn, and Harper du Pont are waiting for me with most of the other Bluebloods in tow.

"Get her," Harper says, and I don't even have time to

scream before Greg is clamping a hand over my mouth and yanking me against his chest.

No fucking way, I think as they drag me across the lot, flailing and kicking and clawing at Greg's hand. When John and that new guy, Ben, step in and each grab onto my legs, I know I'm in serious, serious trouble.

They take me around the back of the house and over to the funicular, shuffling us all inside, and pressing the button that'll take us down to the beach. Under any other circumstances, I'd be excited to ride in this thing. As of right now, I'm terrified.

We hit the beach and immediately go for the dock, loading up on one of the boats and heading out to the lake. Dozens of other students are already out there, partying on different boats. Harper chooses a spot right in the middle of Lake Tahoe, and has Sai throw the anchor over.

We're on the top deck now with nothing but a few lanterns and some white twinkle lights to brighten up the darkness.

Harper stares down at me, and then smiles.

"I think … we should start off the night seeing what a Working Girl can really do," she begins, nodding her chin in Greg's direction. His laughter is disturbing and dark as he and the other boys push me down to the deck and pin me with my legs spread wide.

That's when it really hits me that this is happening.

They're going to try and rape me.

I try to scream, but I can barely breathe past Greg's hand. Immediately, my flight or fight instincts kick in, and I begin to flail. But when the boys have trouble holding me down, they just pile on a few more Bluebloods until there are six people holding me hostage.

John gives over the holding of my leg to Mayleen, and then moves over like he's planning on kneeling down between my legs.

That's when I hear the sputter of a small engine, and the creak of a ladder before Zack Brooks appears over the edge. He doesn't hesitate before he throws himself at John, taking the other boy by complete surprise. A fight breaks out, and even with John, Greg, and Ben all attacking him at once, Zack stands his ground.

Now that there are less people holding me down, I fight even harder, dislodging Mayleen and kicking one of the kerosene lanterns. It breaks and then plunges over the edge, fire trailing along the spilled oil. Flames begin to lick at the side of the boat, and in quick succession, the other lanterns go up, too.

The Bluebloods holding me down drag me over to the ladder and basically toss me down to the lower deck. I hit with a grunt, just before Ileana grabs me by the hair, and some of the other girls get hold of my arms and legs. Even though I'm kicking and screaming, and flames are licking at the side of the boat, nobody notices or cares. The lake is vast, and there are plenty of bonfires on the beach, stereo systems blasting music, and screaming teenagers. I'm just a drop in a bucket.

Another small yacht has pulled up alongside the one we're on, and the girls drag me over.

I'm once again manhandled up to the top deck and shoved into a chair, ropes wrapped around my wrists and ankles.

Harper is panting and looking from me to the other boat where Zack is still fighting with his fists.

"Keep her here until everyone else shows up," Harper snaps at Becky, and I'm guessing she must have Pleb friends on the way, seeing as almost every Blueblood save Myron Talbot is here. "I'm done with this girl; this shit ends tonight."

Harper storms over to me, and I spit at her. Her palm quickly comes up and cracks me across the face.

"What is wrong with you?!" I scream back, but like I said, I'm pretty sure she's a sociopath or a psychopath or what the hell ever. Tonight, I beat her at her own game. She doesn't like that. Not one bit.

"Break her fingers." Harper snaps this order at her cronies, and then leans down to get in my face. "You will *never*, and I mean *never* play the harp again. How do you feel about that, you little bitch?"

"How do you feel about my boot up your ass?" Zayd says, appearing at the top of the ladder. He's bleeding from the edge of his mouth, but he looks okay otherwise. He's followed by Tristan, Creed, and Miranda.

Harper sneers at them as Zayd unties me and pulls me up, dragging us to the opposite side of the boat, so Tristan and Creed can help create a human shield around me. The rest of the Bluebloods come up the ladder, creating a divide in the center of the yacht. Zack is the last one up, and he ends up trapped behind them on the opposite side.

There are flames dancing across the water.

How that happened, I have no idea. One minute, we were

struggling on Harper's boat, and the next, the lantern was being knocked over and kerosene was spilling everywhere. How it got on the actual surface of the lake, I don't know.

My heart pounds as I clutch my hands to my chest like they're precious gems. *I almost lost my ability to make music with the harp ... forever.* That, and they ... I can't think about the almost rape. Not right now. The Idol girls crossed a line not once, not twice, but now three times. The boys are right: they really do want to kill me. The Infinity Club might very well be the death of me for real.

Tristan's jaw is clenched tight, his hands white knuckled and curled into fists. He looks at Harper with a glare that would scare the shit out of me if I were on the other end. She seems unfazed as she turns her blue gaze on me, pausing briefly to make sure she's still got a sizable entourage before she comes at me again.

"Whatever you're thinking about doing right now," Tristan says, his voice as smooth as pure cognac, "don't." He snaps that word off the end of his tongue, anger palpable in the chiseled lines of his handsome face. *They saved me,* I think, glancing from Tristan to Zayd's bloody lip to Creed with his arm around Miranda. Poor Zack is still stuck on the opposite side of the boat, behind a wall of enemy Bluebloods.

"If you do this," Harper begins, moving forward with her short brown hair—courtesy of Windsor York—billowing in the wind. *Don't dish it if you can't take it.* Moving back a step, I end up bumping into Zayd. One of his arms goes around me, and I'm suddenly overwhelmed with emotion. It's like with every breath, I waffle between being excited and being terrified. *Please don't touch me; touch me more; get away from me; kiss me until I see stars.* "Then you're giving up control of the school. You're Plebs, all of you."

Abigail Fanning and Valentina Pitt flank Harper as she moves toward us, the chair with the ropes still attached sitting between their group and ours. When I glance past Harper toward Zack, I can see that he's bleeding from his fight.

"If you think we'll fold that easy," Creed drawls, glancing at me and making my entire body light up with feeling. He's quivering, too, but he tries to keep it hidden as he tosses some of his angelic hair back from his face. Would this be an inappropriate moment to think about the hot tub? Yeah, probably. "Then you clearly haven't been paying attention. We'll destroy you."

Harper's mouth is as sharp as a blade, and her eyes glimmer with rage and hate. She does not like losing— especially not to someone like me. To her credit, she's managed to pull in most of the Bluebloods to her side. The rest, we won't know about until we get to shore. What she does have is a trio of boys—Greg, John, and Ben—who will likely become her side's version of the Idols.

"So you'll break up the greatest collection of Bluebloods in the history of Burberry Prep for some commoner? We're the future rulers of the *world*. People live and die based on the decisions our families make. Tristan, I'm your *fiancée*." Harper starts to move forward, and then pauses as the ladder creaks, announcing the newest attendee to our little soiree.

Windsor York, my secret weapon and amazing new friend, appears with a smirk.

"Well, bloody hell." He hauls himself over the edge and

then stands up before brushing his palms down the front of his uniform. His hazel eyes take in the scene in one, fell swoop. "Looks like I'm a bit late to the party."

Without hesitation, he moves over to stand in front of Zayd and offers me his hand. It's impressive how the flames from the burning boat turn his red hair, crimson. Zayd pulls me back when I reach out for Windsor, and the prince cocks an eyebrow before sighing.

"Yeah, way late, asshole." Zayd is pissed, but not at me and not even at Windsor, but at the whole situation. Even though I appreciate the sentiment, I elbow myself from his grip and take up a strong stance of my own. Even though my friends are here, and I appreciate them, I can't fully trust anyone but myself. "If we hadn't gotten here when we did …" Zayd's voice trails off, but he has to know that Windsor is most definitely on our side. He was just helping in other ways. That much I do know.

The prince gives Harper and friends a skeptical look.

"I disabled the motor on your friends' boat. I don't imagine they'll be showing up tonight." Harper turns almost the same red shade as Windsor's hair. She's furious. "And I'm not late." He gives a dramatic eye roll and a wink, that I'd return if I wasn't so shaken up. "I saw Zack on his way up here, with these idiots trailing behind." He gestures at the Idol boys, and Tristan snarls at him. "My time was better spent elsewhere. Oh." As if it's just occurred to him, Windsor snaps his fingers and lifts up the front of his shirt.

There's a tattoo there, an infinity tattoo.

The entire boat falls silent.

"I've been resisting the Club for a long, long time, but

Marnye needs someone on the inside to watch her back, so …
here I am!" Windsor lifts his arms for emphasis, ever the
showman. "Oh, and I'm an awful, dirty fucking wanker. I
don't have a trust fund, or parents breathing down my neck
that control my purse strings: I have *nine billion* in personal
assets to play with." Windsor pauses, resting his head in his
hand. "Well, *twelve* billion in US dollars, I suppose."

"Do you think I'm threatened by you?" Harper snorts a
laugh. "Some tenth-string prince from a country nobody even
knows about?"

"England?" Windsor asks, his voice tinted with wry
humor. "You do understand where the pilgrims came from,
right?"

Harper spins to Tristan, desperate to make headway with
someone. Clearly, Windsor isn't interested in her games. The
boy dances to the beat of his own drum, that's for sure.

"Last chance, Tristan." Harper is dead serious, but Tristan
simply smirks at her.

"You're going to wish you'd never met me," he says, his
voice like steel. Zack moves around behind the pack of
Bluebloods to stand beside me. I feel sick when I see the
blood running down the side of his face; he needs some
stitches, pronto. His dark eyes catch on mine, and I shiver. I
owe him for taking on Greg, John, and Ben. Three on one,
very impressive.

"Consider that goal accomplished," Harper snarls,
chucking the expensive ring at her ex-fiancé. Tristan catches
it no problem, and then turns to me.

"Let's go. I've got one of Dad's yachts." Tristan comes

346

over to stand beside me, cupping the side of my face as the other boys stiffen up. Well, except for Windsor: he just laughs and the sound echoes across the lake. The King of Burberry Prep then runs his thumb along my lower lip before he sneers at the prince. I use that moment to separate myself from him, giving my heart some distance so my brain can think clearly.

Miranda looks at me, and I'm having a hard time figuring out why she looks half afraid, and half jealous. Jealous of who? Not of me, right? She comes over to stand next to me, pulling away from Creed, and then whispers in my ear.

"Which one?" She takes in the boys with a reserved, sweeping gaze, while Harper and her cronies slowly file off the boat. Nothing more can be accomplished here. Next year … there's going to be a war.

I don't say anything because I'm distracted by Tristan getting up in Windsor's face.

"You, go home to England and fuck off; we don't need you here."

"And who, precisely, is *we*?" the prince asks, glancing at me with glittering hazel eyes. He cocks a brow as Tristan looks between the two of us and scowls. He straightens up his wool coat and turns his glare back on Windsor. "As far as I can see it, Marnye very much needs me."

"How so?" Tristan demands, lifting his chin in challenge. I'm not sure that I can ever really trust him, or that he'll ever really be mine, but … at least he's a powerful ally to have against Harper du Pont.

"Because, we're dating," Windsor says innocently. I'm not sure if he's trying to buy me time, give me an out, or … if he really would like to date me. I'll have to worry about that later. None of the boys seems particularly happy about it though.

Tristan just glances at me with his storm-gray eyes, and then turns to head for the boat's ladder. But Harper's still standing there, waiting. She meets his eyes with a challenge burning in hers, and then turns to me.

"Enjoy the summer, Marnye. It's going to be your last." Harpers turns, and disappears down the ladder, just before we hear a boat's engine start up with a grumble.

"Did she just threaten my life?" I choke out, but why should I be surprised? It wouldn't be the first time.

Well shit … School is out, summer has started, and in the morning, we're all supposed to head home. I'll go back to Cruz Bay and Charlie while the boys go … wherever it is that they go.

For now, it's all on hold.

Come September, all gloves are off. At least, that's what I think in that moment.

"Come on, Marnye, I've got a boat, too," Miranda says, grabbing my hand and pulling me away from the boys. I ignore them all as I walk past and climb down the ladder, but they follow after me anyway.

Second year at Burberry Preparatory Academy was hard as hell.

Third year's going to be a fucking nightmare.

EPILOGUE

When I first get home from the graduation getaway, I collapse on the bed in my new room, the harp Zack gifted me sitting against the opposite wall. I close my eyes and I'm out for a good twelve hours. When I wake up later, dry mouthed and in desperate need of water, I decide that I really am going to miss the Train Car. I'm proud of Dad for finding this house for us, and even in its modesty, it's four times bigger and ten times nicer than the trailer park.

Still … change is hard sometimes, even when that change is good. It takes adjustment. And anyway, I can only live in one place: I have to choose.

Padding into the kitchen, I squint through the bright sunshine as I dig through the cabinets in search of a water glass. They're all empty, so I move onto the boxes, tossing wads of brown packing paper on the floor. Once I find a cup, I fill it up, drink it all, fill it up again. And then I finally check my phone, scrolling past a text message from Dad letting me

349

know that he'll be home later tonight.

Last night was freaking insane, not to mention dangerous. Terrifying. I shake my head because I'm not ready to think about what might've happened. Instead, I focus on the positive. Later, I'm sure I'll have a complete breakdown as the emotions roll over me.

I did it. I duped the boys. I won the bet.

And yet … they stood by me anyway.

Thank god I have the summer to figure this all out, I think, just before the doorbell rings.

In bare feet and a wrinkled party dress, I pad over to open it, expecting a boy-free summer.

When I open it, there's not one guy standing on my porch: there are five of them.

Tristan, Zayd, Creed, Zack, and Windsor.

"We couldn't agree on who should come over and talk to you," Tristan begins, glancing back at the other four. "So, unfortunately, we all fucking showed up."

"Talk to me about what?" I ask, stepping back into the barren cavern of our new living room. Okay, so I say cavern, but really, it's a pretty small room. It's just way bigger than the Train Car. Seeing it filled with five gorgeous men—one of whom is a prince, one of whom is a rockstar, all of whom are rich as sin—it's a little overwhelming.

The boys definitely do not move as a unit. Actually, there's a palpable tension between them that makes me shift uncomfortably, sloshing water across the floor.

"We wanted to invite you," Zack says, narrowing his eyes as Windsor immediately notices an old family photo that includes my mom, picking it up and examining it in that way of his.

"Where?" I echo, feeling like I'm the last one to get the joke.

"Pack your bags," Zayd says with a grin, and I feel this strange pang inside my chest.

I did it; I completed my task and got revenge on the guys. What happens now?

"Pack my bags ... for what?" There I go, echoing questions as I sip my water and try to orient myself to the fact that there are five of the sexiest dudes alive in my living room.

"We're taking you to the Hamptons," Creed drawls, draping himself over our ratty old couch. I blink several times to make that statement register, and then glance at my phone as it buzzes. Miranda is texting me in a frenzy, half in excitement and half in rage that her twin's come over here without her.

"The Hamptons," I say slowly, and this time, it's not a question.

The Hamptons is *the* summer social hot spot for the Bluebloods of Burberry Prep. No, for any blue blood living in America. Lizzie will be there with her Coventry Prep friends. Windsor will be there, too, apparently, bringing a bit of English charm to the beach.

"The Hamptons," he repeats, slapping one of my dad's straw summer hats over my head. "Get packed, milady, and get ready. Harper is out for blood—and not just yours. That shore is going to be bathed in crimson, either way. Let's just make sure it's not ours, shall we?"

I gape at him as he takes off after Zayd, the two of them exploring my house like they own the place.

Me, I'm still standing there in a short, rose-gold dress with a red plastic cup full of water and clinking ice cubes, pondering my fate.

Revenge is wicked sweet, but forgiveness is a virtue.

Too bad I've never been holy.

To Be Continued ...

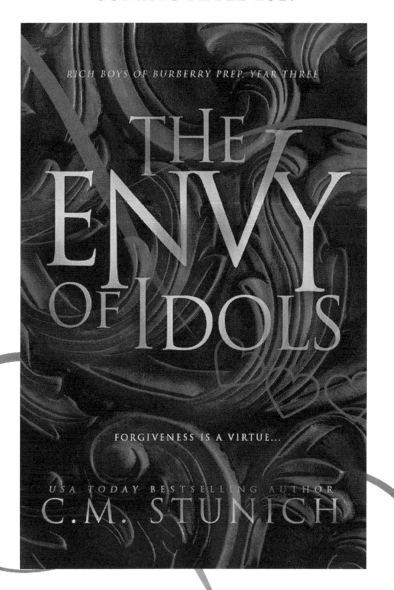

RICH BOYS OF BURBERRY PREP, YEAR THREE

THE ENVY OF IDOLS

FORGIVENESS IS A VIRTUE...

USA TODAY BESTSELLING AUTHOR

C.M. STUNICH

THE ENVY OF IDOLS
Rich Boys of Burberry Prep # 3

STALKING
LINKS

JOIN THE C.M. STUNICH NEWSLETTER – Get three free books just for signing up
http://eepurl.com/DEsEf

TWEET ME ON TWITTER, BABE – Come sing the social media song with me
https://twitter.com/CMStunich

SNAPCHAT WITH ME – Get exclusive behind the scenes looks at covers, blurbs, book
signings and more http://www.snapchat.com/add/cmstunich

LISTEN TO MY BOOK PLAYLISTS – Share your fave music with me and I'll give you my
playlists (I'm super active on here!) https://open.spotify.com/user/12101321503

FRIEND ME ON FACEBOOK – Okay, I'm actually at the 5,000 friend limit, but if you click
the "follow" button on my profile page, you'll see way more of my killer posts
https://facebook.com/cmstunich

LIKE ME ON FACEBOOK – Pretty please? I'll love you forever if you do! ;)
https://facebook.com/cmstunichauthor & https://facebook.com/violetblazeauthor

CHECK OUT THE NEW SITE – (under construction) but it looks kick-a$$ so far, right?
You can order signed books here! http://www.cmstunich.com

READ VIOLET BLAZE – Read the books from my hot as hellfire pen name, Violet Blaze
http://www.violetblazebooks.com

SUBSCRIBE TO MY RSS FEED – Press that little orange button in the corner and copy that
RSS feed so you can get all the latest updates http://www.cmstunich.com/blog

AMAZON, BABY – If you click the follow button here, you'll get an email each time I put
out a new book. Pretty sweet, huh? http://amazon.com/author/cmstunich
http://amazon.com/author/violetblaze

PINTEREST – Lots of hot half-naked men. Oh, and half-naked men. Plus, tattooed guys
holding babies (who are half-naked) http://pinterest.com/cmstunich

INSTAGRAM – Cute cat pictures. And half-naked guys. Yep, that again.
http://instagram.com/cmstunich

ABOUT THE AUTHOR

C.M. Stunich is a self-admitted bibliophile with a love for exotic teas and a whole host of characters who live full time inside the strange, swirling vortex of her thoughts. Some folks might call this crazy, but Caitlin Morgan doesn't mind – especially considering she has to write biographies in the third person. Oh, and half the host of characters in her head are searing hot bad boys with dirty mouths and skillful hands (among other things). If being crazy means hanging out with them everyday, C.M. has decided to have herself committed.

She hates tapioca pudding, loves to binge on cheesy horror movies, and is a slave to many cats. When she's not vacuuming fur off of her couch, C.M. can be found with her nose buried in a book or her eyes glued to a computer screen. She's the author of over thirty novels – romance, new adult, fantasy, and young adult included. Please, come and join her inside her crazy. There's a heck of a lot to do there.

Oh, and Caitlin loves to chat (incessantly), so feel free to e-mail her, send her a Facebook message, or put up smoke signals. She's already looking forward to it.